The War... ...p... ...p...s of brave heroes, and the rise and fall of powerful enemies. Now for the first time the tales of these mythical events has been brought to life in a new series of books. Divided into a series of trilogies, each brings you hitherto untold details of the lives and times of the most legendary of all Warhammer heroes and villains. Combined together, they will reveal some of the hidden connections that underpin the history of the Warhammer world.

## —◀ THE BLACK PLAGUE ▶—

The tale of an Empire divided, its heroic defenders and the enemies who endeavour to destroy it with the deadliest plague ever loosed upon the world of man. This series begins with *Dead Winter*.

## —◀ THE WAR OF VENGEANCE ▶—

The ancient races of elf and dwarf clash in a devastating war that will decide not only their fates, but that of the entire Old World. The first novel in this series is *The Great Betrayal*.

## —◀ BLOOD OF NAGASH ▶—

The first vampires, tainted children of Nagash, spread across the world and plot to gain power over the kingdoms of men. This series starts in *Neferata*.

Keep up to date with the latest information from the **Time of Legends** at *www.blacklibrary.com*

*More Time of Legends from the Black Library*

## · THE LEGEND OF SIGMAR ·
*Graham McNeill*

Book 1 – HELDENHAMMER
Book 2 – EMPIRE
Book 3 – GOD KING

## · THE RISE OF NAGASH ·
*Mike Lee*

Book 1 – NAGASH THE SORCERER
Book 2 – NAGASH THE UNBROKEN
Book 3 – NAGASH IMMORTAL

## · THE SUNDERING ·
*Gav Thorpe*

Book 1 – MALEKITH
Book 2 – SHADOW KING
Book 3 – CALEDOR

## · THE BLACK PLAGUE ·
*C. L. Werner*

Book 1 – DEAD WINTER

## · THE WAR OF VENGEANCE ·
*Nick Kyme and Chris Wraight*

Book 1 – THE GREAT BETRAYAL
August 2012

AGE OF LEGEND
*Edited by Christian Dunn*

**TIME OF LEGENDS**

*Book One of the Black Plague*

# DEAD WINTER

*The Black Plague*

### C. L. Werner

**BLACK LIBRARY**

*For Nathan and Mike, my fellow Colonials.*

**A BLACK LIBRARY PUBLICATION**

First published in Great Britain in 2012 by
The Black Library,
Games Workshop Ltd.,
Willow Road, Nottingham,
NG7 2WS, UK

10 9 8 7 6 5 4 3 2 1

Cover illustration by Jon Sullivan.
Map by Nuala Kennedy.

A CIP record for this book is available from the British Library.

UK ISBN: 978 1 84970 150 1
US ISBN: 978 1 84970 151 8

See the Black Library on the internet at

**www.blacklibrary.com**

Find out more about Games Workshop
and the world of Warhammer at

**www.games-workshop.com**

Printed and bound by CPI Group (UK) Ltd, Croydon, CR0 4YY

It is an age of legend.

It is a dark age, a bloody age, an age of unspeakable pacts and powerful magic. It is an age of war and of death, and of apocalyptic terror. But amidst all of the flames and fury it is a time, too, of mighty heroes, of bold deeds and great courage...

At the heart of the Old World lies Sigmar's Empire. Over a thousand years after the god-king's passing, it is a land in turmoil. The corrupt and incompetent Emperor, Boris Goldgather, has bled the common folk of the Empire to keep himself in comfort, leaving his people to starve. The border forts, the Empire's first line of defence against the many foes that threaten Sigmar's lands, lie unmanned and the Imperial armies struggle to repel the barbarous northmen, savage greenskins and monstrous beastmen that rampage through the provinces.

None know that the gravest threat to the realm lies not in the darkness of the forests or the mountain passes, but beneath the feet of men. The sinister, ratlike skaven, long believed to be a myth, plot to destroy the Empire. Untold armies lurk in dank caverns deep below the earth, unnumbered skaven from the warrior clans ready to spread across the lands of men and wipe them out. And in the deepest vaults, the demented plague priests of Clan Pestilens brew a noxious contagion that will bring the men of the Empire to their knees.

The Black Plague.

# GEOGRAPHICAL MAP OF THE EMPIRE

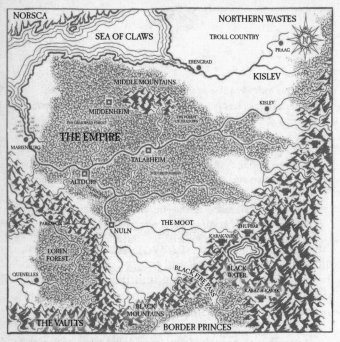

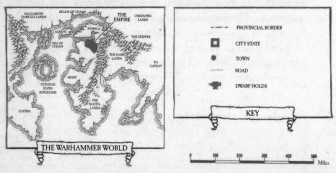

THE WARHAMMER WORLD

| | |
|---|---|
| – – – – – | PROVINCIAL BORDER |
| ⬚ | CITY STATE |
| ● | TOWN |
| ·········· | ROAD |
| ⛰ | DWARF HOLDS |

KEY

0   100   200   300   400   500
Miles

# ─< PROLOGUE >─

*Skavenblight*
*Geheimnisnacht, 1111*

THE PUNGENT SMELL of smouldering warpstone wafted through the blackened chamber, the corrupt fume slithering into every nook and cranny, oozing between the crumbling bricks, burning into beams of oak and ash, discolouring glass and tarnishing bronze. It was the stench of darkest sorcery and this was its night.

The noise of creeping rats inside the walls died out as the fumes incinerated their tiny lungs and liquefied their little brains. Beetles and roaches fell from the rafters, their bodies shrivelled into desiccated husks. Bats took wing, shrieking their fright as they desperately tried to flee the deathly miasma, smashing against walls and ceiling, raining down to the floor in battered, bloodied strips of quivering flesh.

Seerlord Skrittar's whiskers twitched as the smell of blood flickered amidst the searing scent of warpstone. It was an unconscious, instinctive association. Skrittar's mind was far too disciplined to be distracted in this, his hour of terror and triumph.

The Seerlord stood at the head of a ring of creatures dressed in grey robes. Like him, they were ghastly, inhuman things, abominable monstrosities that seemed to blend the most hideous qualities of man and rat. Great horns protruded from their elongated heads, terrible symbols were painted or branded into their furry foreheads; the eyes in their verminous faces blazed with malefic energies, glowing green in the omnipresent darkness. Their paws were folded before them, clawed fingers entwined, their fangs clashing together in a low chant of hisses and squeaks.

Seerlord Skrittar felt panic drumming inside his chest, as though any moment his heart might burst from sheer terror. The audacity of what he had thought to achieve! The arrogance! The impudence!

No! The Seerlord forced his nerves to quieten. There was danger, there was always danger when invoking the forces of darkness, when engaging in a conjuration beyond the blackest of the black arts. No other skaven would have dared what he had dared! Yes, the risk was great, but the reward was still greater!

His eyes narrowed as he gazed across the vast chamber. Eleven horned ratmen in grey robes, all of them the most potent of the Order of Grey Seers, with himself, the mighty Seerlord, and the Horned Rat himself symbolically assuming the sacred role of thirteenth intimate of the cabal. Each of the skaven sorcerers had imbibed in a potent mixture of wormroot and warpstone before the ritual, magnifying their own abilities yet further by devouring the still-living brains of their most gifted acolytes. The malign influence of Geheimnisnacht itself increased their powers still further, and whatever extra magic they needed they could draw from the warpstone fumes rising from six caskets arrayed about the edge of their circle.

Protection? Of course: a series of concentric circles composed of sigils and runes drawn in the blood of elf-things mixed with crushed warpstone and the powdered bones of dragons. The greatest protection, though, lay in numbers, playing the chance that if anything went wrong then the aethyric retaliation would claim a different ratman.

Skrittar gazed past his chanting minions, staring above them at the great window of stained glass. It was a relic left behind by the original builders of Skavenblight, the foolish man-things who had reared the Shattered Tower and engineered their vast city, only to have it taken from them by the Horned Rat and bestowed upon his favoured children – the skaven.

There was something of magic about that portal of stained glass set into a spider-web of iron. Only magic could have allowed it alone to survive the tolling of the thirteenth hour, when the Horned Rat's divine malignance had struck down the humans like a mighty earthquake and left their great tower broken and crumbling. Only the most potent of sorcery could have allowed it to endure a million generations of ratkin, staring like a great unclean eye upon the teeming hordes of Skavenblight as they birthed, grew and perished.

Through the window, Skrittar could see the gibbous moon of sorcery, the ghoulish Morrslieb with its erratic orbit and eerie allure. This night, the Chaos Moon was ascendant, perched exactly at the centre of the thirteen constellations. Glancing away from the moon's unsettling glow, Skrittar could see the fangs of the Big Rat and the long tail of the Little Rat, he could see the snarling muzzle of the Cornered Rat and the bloated carcass of the Drowned Rat, there were the feeble nubs of the Pink Rat and the murderous eyes of the Black Rat, and, whining off in the stellar shadows, was that cosmic buffoon, King Mouse, the meat that thought it was skaven.

Rare was such a conjunction. Maybe once in a thousand generations of skaven did moon and stars align in such a way. When such an alignment came to pass, there were certain spells and rituals, handed down from Seerlord to Seerlord, that could be performed. Magic of such awful potency that no other skaven was allowed to even suspect their existence. Yet there was only so much magic a single sorcerer could conjure, and Skrittar wanted far greater things.

The heathen vermin of Clan Pestilens were brewing some new contagion, a great plague they thought might finally bring the surface-dwelling man-things to their knees. Spies from every clan in Skavenblight had reported this to their warlords and now the whole Under-Empire was a seething hotbed of rumour and ambition. Outwardly, Skrittar dismissed the plans of the plague monks as diseased fantasies, delusions brought on by the maggots of madness burrowing through their brains. Inwardly, however, he feared that Arch-Plaguelord Nurglitch really did have such a weapon. If he did, the balance of power in Skavenblight would shift, the other Lords of Decay would scurry to curry favour with the plague priests and forget their true allegiance towards the grey seers and the Horned Rat.

It was something to make the Seerlord's glands clench, the thought that the plague monks would gain ascendancy over skavendom. It was a possibility that had led him at last to build this cabal and initiate the greatest feat of magic ever executed by skaven sorcery.

Skrittar raised his paws, invoking the thirteen secret names of the Horned Rat, scratching his god's mark upon the great ritual. At once, there came a shift in the chamber's atmosphere. It was not necessary to feel the power rising from the circle, he could smell it, almost see it, draining out from the grey seers like a tremendous shadow. Through the stained glass window, he could see the face of Morrslieb begin to darken, its ghoulish glow muffled behind the magnitude of dark magic assaulting it.

A squeak of anguish echoed through the chamber. Skrittar could smell black skaven blood on the air. He heard a body crash to the floor. A few instants later, there was a second shriek, a second crash. Then there came a third.

Fear coursed through the Seerlord's heart. Had he misjudged the potential? Was this too much power for even an entire cabal of grey seers to command? Around him he could feel the air becoming charged with an ever-increasing pulse of eldritch energy. He could see the moon growing dim as its very essence was overwhelmed by skaven sorcery.

A fourth shriek! Now there came anxious squeaks and whines from the other grey seers. One more death and the survivors would panic and break the circle, fleeing like fool-meat despite the havoc such an abrupt break in the ritual would cause. Skrittar ground his fangs together at the cowardice of his treasonous underlings. They deserved a bloody and unnatural death for their lack of fortitude. By their sacrifice, the Order of Grey Seers would ensure its place as masters of skavendom! It was their duty to stand and die for the glory of the Horned Rat and his true prophets!

Skrittar nervously nuzzled his chin against the elven talisman he wore, hoping its magic would be enough to protect him if his craven hench-rats broke the circle.

Before that could happen, the air lost the charge that had been building up inside it. The moon's glow was restored. The smell of aethyric malignity drained away.

The Seerlord ground his fangs, glaring at his nervous underlings. If he found out one of them had ended the spell prematurely, if he learned one of them was responsible for causing the ritual to fail…

Then there was a tremendous flash of light. The sky beyond the window was aglow with a spectral radiance, a great aura that surrounded Morrslieb. Skrittar hissed in triumph. The ritual had worked! By means of his sorcery, he had reached out and ripped chunks from the moon itself! Great shards of celestial rock that would now circle above the earth, waiting for that moment when Skrittar would call them down and claim them for his own! Because there was a secret about Morrslieb, one that even elven wizards treated as impossibility and which other skaven thought of as a wonderful myth with no basis in reality.

The Chaos Moon, dark Morrslieb, was composed of pure warpstone! The chunks Skrittar had torn from its face would be enough to drive the Under-Empire into a new era of might and power. It would be enough to make the skaven the uncontested rulers of the world. It would be enough to make Skrittar the wealthiest rat-man in skavendom, able to buy and sell the other Lords of Decay as though they were sacks of goblin-meat!

Seerlord Skrittar smoothed his whiskers, savouring the excited squeaks of the surviving grey seers. They knew what they had done. The ritual had exhausted them, left them drained and weary, but still their hearts burned with avarice as they imagined all the warpstone waiting to be called down from the sky.

Skrittar bared his fangs in a savage grin. The parasitic whelps would never share in that wealth. It belonged to the Order of Grey Seers and the Seerlord, not to a rabble of overly ambitious schemers and traitors! It was really too bad they knew too much. A little knowledge was a dangerous thing. A lot of knowledge was a death warrant.

Fingering his lucky cat's foot, Skrittar's gleaming eyes drifted to the darkness beyond the circle of power. He could just see the shape there, and only because he knew where to look for it and had saved enough magic to allow him to see it. A wiry figure, stealing unseen and unknown upon the exhausted grey seers, its body draped in a cloak of black, a mantle woven from the scalps of changelings and daemons. He could see the dripping daggers clenched in the killer's black-furred paws, the enchanted metal of the blades themselves saturated with poison so that the knives exuded a constant sweat of venom.

Deathmaster Silke, the supreme assassin of Clan Eshin, the finest murderer in the Under-Empire. His hapless minions should feel honoured. Skrittar had spared no expense to ensure that they wouldn't tell anyone else what they had done this night. He wondered if they would appreciate just how costly the services of the Deathmaster were. It was the finest compliment one skaven could pay another – spending a small fortune to murder them.

Skrittar watched as the first of his underlings went down, both of the grey seer's lungs pierced from behind by Silke's blades. Before the first victim had even hit the floor, the Deathmaster's invisible form was springing across the circle to open the throat of a second witless sorcerer. It was exciting to watch the slaughter, thrilling to watch an accomplished killer at work.

Just the same, Skrittar kept a good grip on his cat's foot and made sure he had an escape spell ready.

There was no knowing if the Nightlord of Clan Eshin hadn't made a mistake and 'accidentally' added an extra name to Deathmaster Silke's contract.

# ⤙ CHAPTER I ⤚

*Altdorf*
*Nachgeheim, 1111*

STEWARDS DRESSED IN rich doublets of crimson, their black boots polished to a reflective shine, hurried about the grand hall. Some circled the richly carved table of dark Drakwald oak which dominated the room, filling goblets and replacing victuals as the need arose. Others laboured to tend the three blazing hearths which opened upon the room, stuffing logs into the extravagantly sculpted maws of the fireplaces. Still other stewards, heavy black cloaks thrown about their shoulders, stood beside the mammoth picture window which stretched the length of the hall's western approach. The cloaked servants each held a long pole tipped with ostrich plumes, employing the curious tools to fan smoke from the fires through small vents set just above the frosted panes of glass.

The men situated about the great table paid no notice to the stewards, taking it for granted that an empty plate would soon have a sliver of cold venison upon it and an empty goblet would be refilled with dusky Solland wine.

Upon the dais situated at the far end of the hall, however, sat one who gave more than passing notice to the stewards, particularly those standing about the *Kaiseraugen*, that vast window which offered such a magnificent view of the River Reik and the ancient city nestled against its banks. The window was a masterpiece, crafted by the finest glaziers gold could buy. Dwarfcraft, for only the doughty folk from under the mountains could create such astounding artistry. Glass itself was an expensive luxury only the temples and the wealthiest nobility could afford. Something of the scale of the picture window would have bankrupted any single province. Only the Emperor could afford such indulgence. Gazing upon the window, Boris could almost feel the magic of the dwarfs rushing through his bones. It was sometimes an effort to remove his attention from the window and look past it upon the stunning vista beyond.

The mighty span of the Reik, greatest river in the world, and the opulence of Altdorf, the greatest city in the world. It sent another thrill coursing through his bones when he considered the river and the city. More than the opulence of the hall, the finery worn by servants and courtiers, the husky aromas of Tilean perfumes and Arabyan spices, the sweet melodies of silver-stringed lyres, the cool feel of velvet cushions – more than any of these, the sight of the Reik and Altdorf spoke to him of wealth and power.

His wealth.

His power.

If those churls allowed so much as a single smudge of soot to defile the *Kaiseraugen* he would have each of them discharged and then lashed to a ducking stool and hounded through the streets of Altdorf. The swine could try their hand at farming or starving!

The Emperor's brow knotted in puzzlement at that last thought. He raised a bejewelled hand to his chin and scratched at his thick black beard. Why should he care if discharged servants should starve? They were no concern of his. Still puzzled, he turned his eyes away from the distracting vista and returned his attention to the irritating babble rising from around the oak table.

The men seated about the table wore accoutrements to match the richness of their surroundings. There was a king's ransom on display, a riot of blackwork and brocade, exotic calico and fustian, silver-threaded gipons and folly-bells crafted from the most lustrous gold. Count van Sauckelhof, envoy of the Westerland Court, sported a lavish cloak trimmed in sealfur and embroidered with fish and ships in cloth of gold. Baron von Klauswitz of Stirland wore a stylish tunic of russet, its sleeves broken by scalloped slashes to expose the fine material of the shirt beneath.

There were, of course, exceptions. No amount of finery, for instance, could make Chief Elder Aldo Broadfellow look anything but ridiculous. The halfling's efforts to ape the styles of the Imperial court only made him look even more the buffoon, though at least the portly rodent had the good sense to keep his mouth shut and not draw further attention to his foolishness.

The same could not be said for Baron Thornig of Middenheim. Even in the Imperial court, the fellow affected the barbarous appearance of a half-civilised Teutogen, his shoulders draped with the snarling pelt of a white wolf, his hair and beard long and worn in the wildest state. The affectation of the backwoods savage was one designed to deliberately provoke the rest of the court, an effort to remind the rest of the Empire that the City of the White Wolf was full to brimming with wild warriors chomping at the bit to rush into battle once more.

It might do to remind Middenheim of her less than sterling record upon the battlefield in the most recent violence to disrupt the Empire. For all their vaunted prowess, for all their supposed woodcraft, the soldiers of Middenheim and Middenland had proven incapable of crushing the latest uprising of beastmen in the Drakwald. Perhaps old Ulric, god of wolves and war, had been caught napping.

A scowl flickered across the Emperor's lean features. His eyes turned towards the foot of the long table where sat a bald-headed man dressed in a black robe trimmed in crimson, a golden hammer embroidered upon the breast. Arch-Lector Wolfgang Hartwich, representing Grand Theogonist Thorgrad and the Temple of Sigmar. Since the Sigmarites had relocated the headquarters of their faith to Altdorf after the fire that had destroyed the Great Cathedral at Nuln and claimed the life of the old Grand Theogonist, their presence in the capital had become increasingly prominent… and intrusive. The arch-lector was an insufferable annoyance, fairly exuding disapproval with his every glance and gesture. If Ulric could be caught asleep, it seemed Sigmar was infuriatingly vigilant, his clergy only too ready to insinuate themselves into matters which were none of their concern.

Emperor Boris tapped the gilded arms of his throne, pondering the question of Sigmar and his temple. He knew the Sigmarite faith was stronger in the south than in his native Drakwald, fairly eclipsing the worship of other gods when it came to Altdorf and the Reikland. The Grand Theogonist was the most powerful priest in the Empire, the pretensions of Ar-Ulric notwithstanding. Worse, the Temple of Sigmar had a structure and organisation beyond any other faith. They could use that organisation to disrupt production and trade as effectively as any goblin invasion or beastman uprising. Even an emperor had to treat them with deference and care, lest he offend the Temple and the thousands of zealots who placed devotion to Sigmar above their duty to their sovereign.

'...but it remains to be determined how serious the menace is.'

Emperor Boris shifted in his throne, focusing on the gaunt, cadaverous figure of Palatine Mihail Kretzulescu. The envoy from the court of Count Malbork von Drak, Voivode of Sylvania, had risen from his seat in order to address the assembled dignitaries. Count Malbork was, ostensibly, the vassal of Grand Count von Boeselager of Stirland. Von Drak had purchased his title for a hefty contribution to the Imperial treasury and made little secret of his ambitions to make Sylvania an independent province in its own right. With tacit encouragement from Altdorf, von Drak had become too powerful for the grand count to simply remove. Stirland had to endure the voivode's talk of an independent Sylvania while trying to counter von Drak's bribes in order to ensure the Emperor didn't grant the territory its freedom.

The palatine's presence among the council was a vivid reminder to Baron von Klauswitz that Stirland had much to lose should its beneficence to the Imperial Treasury falter. A sycophant renowned for his oratory, Kretzulescu's resonant voice would wax elegant for hours unless stifled by higher authority.

'Sylvania will pay its portion,' Emperor Boris said, his deep, caustic tones smothering Kretzulescu's words. 'Every province in the land has a responsibility to protect her neighbours. Sylvania is no different. Von Drak will have to pay his share.'

Kretzulescu turned and bowed before the Imperial throne. 'But your Imperial Majesty, you have issued a diktat disbanding the Army of the Drakwald. Surely there is no further...'

'The beastmen continue to raid and maraud throughout the province,' snarled Duke Konrad Aldrech. The young nobleman's face trembled with emotion, his eyes glistening with the simmering fires of hate. 'It will take many soldiers to run the creatures to ground and wipe out their blot forever!'

'More soldiers than is practical, I fear,' stated Count van Sauckelhof. 'You cannot expect the rest of the Empire to beggar itself trying to rebuild a backwoods frontier no sane man would try to settle in the first place! I should think removing the Norscans from Westerland would be of greater importance to the Empire!' Van Sauckelhof's face went pale even as the outburst left his lips. Timidly, he turned towards the enthroned Emperor Boris, belatedly remembering that His Imperial Majesty was originally from the Drakwald and that Duke Konrad was also of the Hohenbachs.

Fortunately for the Westerlander, the Emperor was of too practical a mindset to allow loyalty to his family and homeland to interrupt the prosperity of the Empire. 'We all appreciate the suffering of Drakwald. The loss of Count Vilner is a pain that has touched us deeply. But this is not a time when we can allow emotion to rule above sense. We must look after the Empire as a whole, not allow the plight of any single province to weaken the others.'

Duke Konrad kept his face impassive, but his fist tightened about the stem of the goblet he held. 'Your Imperial Majesty, the Drakwald is in ruins. The foul beastmen have burned and pillaged a third of the province...'

'Then that leaves them damn little to destroy,' laughed the porcine Count Artur of Nuln. He wiped his greasy fingers on the embroidered tablecloth and fixed his piggish eyes on the fuming duke. 'Of course, if you'd like to arrange a loan, I'm sure we can come to terms.'

Before Duke Konrad could hurl his goblet into the chuckling Artur's face, the man seated to his right rose from his chair. He was a short, stocky man, somehow maintaining a wiry build, his jaw firm, his blue eyes possessed of a piercing clarity. His vestments were subdued beside the flamboyance of the other noblemen, consisting of a tan-hued tunic and dark breeches. About his neck, however, he wore the heavy gold pectoral of and Reiksmarshal.

Baron Everhardt Johannes Boeckenfoerde, the Reikland's most famous soldier and commander of the Empire's armies. His promotion to Reiksmarshal had been something of a scandal – never before had so young a soldier been elevated to such a position of authority. Yet even the worst critics of Emperor Boris admitted that the controversial decision had been one of the few moments of genius displayed by His Imperial Majesty. Boeckenfoerde had led the Empire's armies to victory against orc invasions in Averland and Solland, crushed a horde of goblins in Talabecland and defended the shores of Nordland against the longships of High King Ormgaard of Norsca. In the latest war, he had taken personal command of the campaign against the warherds of Khaagor Deathhoof. It had been the Reiksmarshal who conceived the elaborate trap which had lured Khaagor from the protection of the forest and into the pastureland around the ruined village of Kriegfels. He had ridden with the knights who charged the warherd and avenged Count Vilner by taking Khaagor's head.

There was no man in the great hall who commanded more respect than the Reiksmarshal. When he laid a restraining hand upon Duke Konrad's shoulder, the young nobleman's face flushed with shame at his lack of control.

The Reiksmarshal turned his gaze towards the throne, locking eyes with his Emperor before speaking. The soldier's jaw tightened. There was no need for Emperor Boris to remind him of what was expected of him. One look into the cold gaze of the seated sovereign made it clear.

'The warherds have been broken,' Boeckenfoerde said. 'What are left are small packs of scavengers that pose no threat to any sizable settlement. The towns of southern Drakwald have nothing to fear from them. It is the logging camps and cattle ranches in the north that are imperilled.'

'So you are saying the Drakwald still needs protecting?' the bearded Baron Thornig asked.

'Was it not by your suggestion that the Army of Drakwald was disbanded?' Count Artur quickly pointed out. The Army of Drakwald had been hastily assembled from contingents drawn from across the Empire. Crossbowmen from Wissenland, spearmen from Ostland, horsemen from Averland, swordsmen from Reikland, knights from the Ostermark and Middenheim. Now those contingents were already marching back to their homelands.

'Smashing the great warherds was work for an army,' Boeckenfoerde stated. 'What is left is a different kind of thing altogether. It will require...'

'Time for Drakwald to heal her wounds,' Emperor Boris declared. He motioned for Boeckenfoerde to be seated. 'We have spent enough blood and treasure crushing the monsters. We will spend no more. The beastmen are ruinous things. Without their leader they will break apart now, scatter back into the forest.' He turned his gaze again to the *Kaiseraugen*, watching the autumn leaves drifting down onto the slanted rooftops of his city. 'The brutes will seek their lairs once winter is upon us. Ulric's Howl,' he grinned at the use of the old euphemism for the winter wind, 'will thin out their numbers and come the spring there won't be enough of them left to threaten a Mootland bawdyhouse.'

The jest brought the expected laughter from the assembled dignitaries. Chief Elder Aldo Broadfellow cackled like a hyena, though his amusement didn't seem to reach his eyes.

'Then why do we not redirect our armies northwards to Westerland?' asked Baron Dettleb von Schomberg. The knight was an older man, his long moustaches faded to almost pure white, his head nearly as barren as the shell of an egg. But the physique beneath his black doublet remained a powerful one and there was a sharpness in his gaze that bespoke the keenness of his mind. As Grand Master of the Reiksknecht, he owed his loyalty to the Emperor but he owed his position to Sigdan Holswig, Prince of Altdorf.

The suggestion was quickly caught up by Baron Salzwedel. 'That makes sense, your Imperial Majesty,' the Nordlander exclaimed. 'If the beastmen pose no serious threat, then the army could be sent to deal with the barbarians and avenge the outrages of Ormgaard upon our people.'

'Ormgaard is dead,' snarled Duke Konrad. 'Or were you too drunk to see his head spitted on a pike on your way in here?'

Count van Sauckelhof glared at the Drakwalder. 'Ormgaard and his fleet may be gone, but he left a son and hundreds of blood-crazed marauders behind. Do you know that Norscan animal is calling himself Jarl of Vestland? They've occupied almost the whole of Marienburg!'

'Better to lose a single city than lose an entire province!' Duke Konrad shouted back. 'The beastkin have scattered my peasantry to the four corners of the Empire and slaughtered every steer and sheep they can find!'

'Truly spoken!' rose the thunderous voice of Baron Thornig. 'The beastkin are a blight that we've ignored far too long! They've despoiled not just Drakwald but Middenland as well.' The bearded baron waved his goblet at the fuming van Sauckelhof. 'As for this Snagr Half-nose and his sea-wolves, they'll lose interest in your fishing village soon enough and head back to their homes.'

'You said that last year,' van Sauckelhof hissed, 'and the Norscans are still occupying my city! They've burned down the Tempelwijk and built a fort from the ruins of the Winkelmarkt!' He turned his ire back upon Duke Konrad, wagging his finger at the nobleman. 'And don't think we aren't aware of how you Drakwalders have been thriving off our suffering! With Marienburg in the hands of barbarians, the river trade has been stopping at Carroburg and filling your coffers with taxes and tariffs! I shouldn't be surprised if you paid Snagr Half-nose to sack our city!'

'Maybe he should pay the Norscans to get rid of the beastmen,' quipped Count Artur, making no effort to hide his enjoyment of watching the argument.

'Enough!' The shout came from a hitherto silent man positioned at the end of the table. He was a lean, sturdily built man with piercing blue eyes and close-cropped blond hair. His vestments were of fashionable cut, but of simple material, the rings on his fingers boasting fine craftsmanship but unadorned by the jewels displayed on the hands of the assembled nobility.

The attention of the dignitaries turned towards the blue-eyed man. Count van Sauckelhof and several of the others made no effort to keep the scorn off their faces. Tradition allowed for members of the clergy to be treated as belonging to an equal station and the capricious decree of Emperor Ludwig the Fat had forced them to accept the Elder of Mootland as their contemporary, but there was no precedent forcing them to treat Adolf Kreyssig as anything but beneath their station.

Kreyssig was a peasant, a low-born ruffian who had managed to work his way into the graces of Emperor Boris and become Commander of the Kaiserjaeger. The Kaiserjaeger had originally been nothing more than woodsmen who organised hunts for the sovereign and his guests. Under Kreyssig's leadership, however, their powers and responsibilities had been expanded. The Kaiserjaeger had become the private constabulary of Emperor Boris, the secret police of Altdorf.

Whatever his position, Kreyssig was still a mere peasant, and that was enough for some in the room to dismiss him entirely. To suffer his presence at the table, even if custom dictated he remain standing while his betters sat, was a vexation many of the nobles found difficult to ignore. For Kreyssig to have the impertinence to shout down two scions of the Empire was beyond an outrage.

'You forget your tongue, churl!' growled Baron Thornig, his hand dropping to where he would have worn his sword had such a weapon been allowed in the Imperial Presence.

'I mean no disrespect, my lord,' Kreyssig said, bowing to the Middenheimer. 'However it ill becomes the decorum of this assembly for two noble peers of the Empire to make such hurtful and foundless accusations against one another.' Kreyssig turned to regard Duke Konrad and Count van Sauckelhof in turn. 'Your grace, I beg your indulgence if I have spoken out of turn. However

I am thinking only of the unity and fellowship of our nation…'

'Arguing over the Army of the Drakwald is useless at any event,' Reiksmarshal Boeckenfoerde said. 'The soldiers have been disbanded and are returning to their homes.' Again, he shot a glance towards Emperor Boris.

'The soldiers have been mustered out,' Boris declared. 'Even those who must return to Ostland and Averland should be home in time for the harvest.' He waved a bejewelled hand, motioning for the stoop-shouldered man seated near the head of the table to speak.

Lord Ratimir stood, adjusting the spectacles perched upon his hawkish nose, and started to read from a vellum scroll. A sickly pallor spread among the assembled dignitaries. In forty years, none of them had ever looked forward to anything the Imperial Minister of Finance had to say.

'Be it here decreed, on this day, the twelfth of Nachgeheim…' Lord Ratimir began.

'Just cut the pleasantries and tell us how much it will cost us,' growled Count Artur, all joviality absent now from his rotund face.

Lord Ratimir grumbled, folding the scroll in his hands. 'There will be a new war tax levied upon each able-bodied peasant. One schilling for all those aged between ten and fifty. One half-schilling for all those beyond the age of fifty or under the age of ten.'

The declaration brought protests from every quarter, the room descending into a bedlam of commotion.

'You can't expect us to pay this!' shouted Baron von Klauswitz. 'The Imperial levies on commerce are already straining the resources of our fields and farms! For every chilling that comes out of the ground, Altdorf is already taking five pfennigs!'

Emperor Boris rose from his throne, smashing his

goblet to the floor. 'Then you will have to manage your resources better!' He smacked his hand against his chest. 'We are responsible for defending the sacred empire bestowed upon mankind by Holy Sigmar himself! That is not a responsibility we will suffer lightly! And we will not allow any of our subjects to ignore their responsibility either!' Boris turned his head, motioning to Lord Ratimir. 'To guide you in your obligations, I have made an additional decree.'

Lord Ratimir unrolled the scroll and cleared his throat. 'Let it be herewith noted that there shall no longer be granted an exclusion for that class of peasantry known as *Dienstleute*.'

The statement provoked an even louder expression of outrage from the noblemen. 'You cannot be serious!' roared Baron Thornig. 'Middenheim alone keeps two thousand *Dienstleute* to defend the Ulricsberg and the forest around her!'

'And why do you need so many soldiers to defend your city?' Emperor Boris challenged. 'The beastkin have left your forest to ravage the Drakwald! What of Nuln, where there hasn't been violence in a hundred years? Count Artur has nearly four thousand *Dienstleute*, many of whom have probably never even held a sword! No! I shall not suffer the Imperial Treasury to be impoverished by greedy nobles trying to aggrandise their personal fortunes by declaring half their peasantry a dienstmann!'

'We can't possibly afford to pay for our soldiers as well as our serfs!' protested Grand Duke Bela, Count of Talabecland.

'Then don't retain them as soldiers,' Lord Ratimir suggested. 'Put them to work in the fields. Increase the harvest and your yield. Every man who takes up the sword and doesn't take up the plough is a drain upon resources rather than a creator of wealth.'

'Many of these men know no trade but that of the sword,' objected Boeckenfoerde. The Emperor gave his general a warning look, but the warning went unheeded this time. 'The fathers of many of these men were soldiers, as were their fathers before them. These men wouldn't know one end of a plough from the other.'

'It should be an easy choice, then, for the masters of such wastrels to discharge them from service,' Lord Ratimir said.

Several of the assembled nobles looked appalled at the suggestion. 'Where would these discharged *Dienstleute* go? What would they do?' demanded Baron von Schomberg.

'Work or starve,' was the Emperor's cold answer.

*Bylorhof*
*Nachgeheim, 1111*

TEMPLE BELLS RANG through the town's muddy streets, a doleful peal that echoed over the thatched roofs and far out across the fields and marshes beyond Bylorhof. In this time of calamity, it did not matter if the bells rested within a temple of Shallya or Morr, all the town's religions were united by common purpose and the edicts of Baron von Rittendahl, the prefect of Bylorhof. The bells were to sound from dawn until noon, warning the peasants that the corpse collectors were making their rounds. It was a time for healthy people to shun the streets and keep behind locked doors, praying to the gods for deliverance from the evil stalking Sylvania. It was a time for those whose household had been reduced by the plague to leave the remains out upon the doorstep for the collectors to bear away.

Few people dared venture upon the streets of Bylorhof while the bells tolled. Even the baron's soldiers kept inside their towers at such times. Abhorrence of the dead was instinctual in all men, but the fear was magnified if death was brought by some strange and unknown cause. The plague was something new to Sylvania, something unknown in that land of green hills and dense forests. The people cowered before the malignant disease, seeing it as a horror inflicted upon them by supernatural powers.

As he strode the empty streets, the priest felt the weight of his office like a great stone tied about his neck. His heart cracked a little more each time he passed a body lying strewn across someone's threshold. His eyes misted with pity when he saw the ugly red crosses daubed upon mud-brick walls, marking another home where the plague had struck. He shared in the frustration of the peasants when he saw crude corn-doll effigies lying half-burnt in the mud or the carcass of a shaved cat nailed above a threshold. In their terror, the people turned to every superstition recalled by their Fennone ancestry, evoking any kind of magic to combat the forces of Old Night. Many of the dead lying in the street had ropes tied about their necks, marking them as offerings to Bylorak, the ancient marsh god whose worship persisted even in the face of kinder, more enlightened gods. These bodies would be taken not to the gardens of Morr, but to the quagmire of Bylorhof Marsh, consigned to the muddy deep and the keeping of the god who dwelled there.

The priest smiled sadly as he watched a hay cart come trundling down the lane, bodies piled in its bed like cordwood. He watched it stop outside a mud-brick hut and observed as the men pulling the cart set the yoke down and started lifting corpses from the street. They took no especial precautions, these collectors of the dead, and their wasted frames wore the same woollen breeches and jackets as any peasant. Only the black caps crunched down about their ears denoted their occupation, that and the hollow, sunken faces that stared out from beneath their hats. There was no need for precaution, not for these men. In the minds of friends and family, the corpse collectors were already dead. They were another reason why the streets were empty when the bells tolled. The men who dragged the cart through Bylorhof were already infected by the plague.

The men loaded their grisly burden into the cart. The plague left little of its victims, withering them into desiccated husks. Even for the sickly collectors, it took no great effort to carry their macabre cargo. There were twenty or thirty bodies in the cart this morning, but the collectors were still equal to the task of dragging it down the street in search of more bodies. After a bad night, they might make ten trips between town and the marsh. The priest hoped it hadn't been a bad night.

Making the sign of Morr as he passed the cart, invoking the protection of his god for the souls of the dead, the priest proceeded through the deserted town, his black robes whipping about him in the crisp autumn breeze. The breeze brought the stink of the marsh slithering through Bylorhof, a smell which was ordinarily as unwelcome as a goblin but which was now considered far more wholesome than the reek of the unburied dead.

The priest, a servant of the god of death, was accustomed to the smell of corpses, but he shared the sentiments of the townsfolk. There was nothing wholesome about this plague and anything that would oppose it should be welcomed.

The priest rounded a corner, noting with some

misgiving the gnarled old oak standing in the square ahead. A horrible crime had employed that tree as its centrepiece. In their terror of the plague, the townsfolk were ready to embrace any rumour or superstition. An old-wives tale about dwarfs being able to curse men with hairs from their beards had provoked a mob into lynching the three dwarf smiths residing at Bylorhof Castle. The crime had outraged Baron von Rittendahl and in his anger he had appealed to Count Malbork von Drak for aid. A second tragedy had resulted from that unwise decision. Too disinterested to uncover the perpetrators, von Drak ordered twenty peasants chosen at random and flayed alive, their skins sent to one of the dwarfholds high in the mountains.

It had fallen to the priests of Morr to attend and bury what von Drak's men left behind. One of the dead had been a little girl not more than twelve winters old. The von Draks were infamous for their cruelty and the thought that Sylvania might break away entirely from Stirland with Count Malbork as its voivode was one that kept many people awake at night.

The priest hurried past the hanging tree, turning his thoughts away from lynchings and tyrants, even from plague and bells. It was Angestag and that meant he would break his fast with family. It was a ritual as old as his own childhood, the son of a sea captain in the great city of Marienburg. With so many of the family scattered all over the city or away on ships, it had been a strictly obeyed tradition among them that on Angestag, as many of the family as could would gather together for breakfast.

The priest stopped as he reached a narrow lane bordered on one side by the workyard of a cartwright and on the other by the stone walls of a granary. Further down the street rose a huddle of tall timber houses, the homes of Bylorhof's more prosperous tradesmen and burghers. It was to one of these homes the priest's path led. He smiled as he looked up at the threshold of his brother's home. No shaved cat nailed above the door or appeal to ancient gods chalked up on the wall, only a simple iron fish tacked to the door itself, an old Marienburger custom meant to promote good fortune.

After his first knock, the door was tugged open and an exuberant boy with blond hair and deep blue eyes grinned up at the priest. 'Uncle Frederick!' the boy hailed him, then turned around to shout his news to the rest of the household. 'Pappa! Mamma! Uncle Frederick is here!'

The priest stepped inside, setting his staff in a vase just within the entranceway. He turned and made the sign of Morr, a gesture meant to keep any wayward spirits from slipping into the house alongside him. It was always a good thing to be careful where restless ghosts were concerned. Especially in such unsettled times as these.

'The prodigal brother returns!' A tall, clean-cut man came striding towards the door, his face split in a broad smile. He bowed his head in respectful recognition of the priest's rank before taking a brotherly jab at Frederick's shoulder.

'It is wrong to scold him, Rutger,' a soft voice admonished the tall man. The speaker was a young woman, her golden tresses bound by a headscarf in the Sylvanian fashion, her slender figure pressed into a fashionable cotehardie gown after the Marienburg manner. Her pretty features formed a welcoming smile as she extended her hand to the priest. 'With what is happening in Bylorhof, a priest of Morr must have much to do.'

Frederick bowed, kissing the woman's hand. 'I am sorry I brought you here, Aysha,' he apologised. 'This is a poor place...'

Rutger scowled at his brother. 'If we'd stayed in Marienburg, we'd have been carved up by Snagr Half-nose by now. I'm only sorry more of the family didn't leave when they had the chance.' He smiled and reached to his neck, drawing out a brass pomander fitted to a chain. As he did so, his wife and son followed suit, displaying their own pomanders. 'See, we are all protected against the plague. A lot easier than to dodge a Norscan's axe!'

The priest couldn't share in his brother's jest. He'd buried too many people with posies in their pockets and pomanders about their necks to believe 'bad air' was the source of the plague and that a strong fragrance could protect against the disease. 'I still feel responsible. If you'd gone to Altdorf or Wurtbad…'

'There would have been no one there to welcome us and help us make a home,' stated Aysha.

'And from what I hear, the plague is there too,' Rutger said. He frowned a little as he looked down at his son. He reached over and tousled the boy's hair. 'I think we should save this discussion for another time. As my wife points out, you are a busy man.' The smile returned to Rutger's face as he led the priest into his home.

'Who knows when the brothers van Hal will have another chance to break their fast together?'

*Nuln*
*Nachgeheim, 1111*

DEAD LEAVES CRINKLED beneath Walther Schill's boots as he picked his way through the dark streets. The flickering glow of the rushlight he carried was just enough to reveal the half-timbered buildings squatting to either side of the narrow lane. This was an old part of Nuln, dating from the city's infancy, when it was just a little trading town nestled in the marshland where the River Reik joined the River Aver. The plaster walls rose from thick stone foundation walls, relics of the roundhouses of ancient Merogen fishermen. The combination gave the structures a peculiar appearance, with curving ground floors of heavy limestone and clay supporting timber upper storeys which were sharply angular. In more prosperous sections of the city, the buildings had a more harmonious appearance, but no one in the Freiberg district had the resources to rebuild. Those few who did had already removed themselves to the wealthy Altestadt across the river or the growing sprawl of the Handelbezirk south of the Universität.

A warm breeze whistled through the deserted streets. Except for a pair of dung gatherers, Walther was alone. Any decent folk, common wisdom claimed, should be abed at such an unseemly hour. The powers of Old Night, the wise said, were at their most malignant just before the dawn and the rising sun forced them back into their netherworld lairs.

Walther scoffed at such old superstitions. He'd never seen any evidence of Old Night and the Ruinous Powers, any proof of vampires and werewolves prowling the countryside seeking whom they might devour or malevolent warlocks biding their time until they could use their magic to change the unwary into snakes and toads. He relegated such talk to nursery nonsense like the Black Boar and the Underfolk, fairy tales meant to frighten small children into behaving.

Walther shifted the heavy linen sack slung across his shoulders, smiling at the weight of his burden. All his life he had laboured in the dark, making his living during those cursed hours when other men slept. A hunter had to bide by the nature of his prey. If that creature was one of darkness, then he had to become a creature of darkness himself. It was as simple as that. Even Verena would concede the logic of such a conclusion.

As he strode past the dung gatherers in their grubby woollen hoods, one of them looked up at Walther, wrinkling his nose and making an expression of distaste. Walther glowered at the grimy man, shifting his step so that he could kick a loose stone at the muckraker. 'I'll make more tonight than you'll see all month,' he grumbled at the dung gatherer.

'At least it's clean work,' the hooded man snarled, wiping refuse from the back of his hand on a strip of soiled felt.

Walther scowled at the dung gatherer and marched on. What did the scum know? In a few more weeks, the fellow would be begging pennies and picking eggshells from the gutter! The harvest was in, no one would want manure for their fields until spring. The muck-raker would be reduced to surviving on the pittance Count Artur paid to keep the streets clean. In the best of times, that would be just enough to allow a man to starve his way through the winter, allowing he didn't have a family to support. And these were anything but the best of times.

By contrast, there was always a demand for Walther and his profession. The very repugnance with which even a dung gatherer regarded his trade ensured there would always be work for a rat-catcher. It had always puzzled Walther why most people looked upon rats with such fear and loathing. Certainly they were noxious little pests, but hardly things to evoke horror. Still, if people wanted to be stupid and afraid, Walther was quite happy to exploit them. Five rat-tails would bring a bounty of two pennies from the city coffers, as much as a dung gatherer would be paid for an entire week of shovelling the streets.

The rat-catcher cast a backwards glance at the hooded men and their little cart filled with dung. They'd be hard-pressed selling the night soil this time of year. No farmer would need manure now. It was possible they might be able to sell some of it as fuel, but only the poorest of the poor in the shantytown beside the south docks would resort to such measures. Hardly the most wealthy clientele.

Again, Walther reflected upon the benefits of being a hunter. In addition to the bounty offered by the burghomeister, there was always a market for his catch.

From out of the darkness, a battered wooden sign swayed upon rusty iron chains. There was no lettering upon the board – few in this part of the city were literate – but the painted image of a hog's head did a serviceable job of proclaiming the sort of business housed within. Walther shifted the heavy sack from one shoulder to the other. Using the haft of the pole he employed in his work, he knocked against the door.

It was a few minutes before the door was tugged open. A balding, overweight man dressed only in his nightshirt stood blinking in the doorway, a foul-smelling candle clenched in his fist. He stared bleary-eyed at Walther. The rat-catcher knew he must present quite a sight, his wool garments caked in the filth of Nuln's sewers, his hands stained with blood, his face drawn and haggard from the long night crawling after rodents.

'Are you going to let me in?' Walther said, his tone gruff and impatient.

'Schill,' the fat man said, stepping aside to allow the rat-catcher entry. 'I've told you before to come by the back way,' the man grumbled as he closed the door behind his visitor.

'I'm in too much of a hurry,' Walther told him, blowing out the rushlight and stuffing the remains of the taper into a cowhide holster. 'Hunting was good tonight. I lost track of time.' He strode through the little shop, around bins of pig-feet and goat-ears, past racks of ham hocks and the plucked carcasses of chickens. With a sigh of relief, the rat-catcher set his bag down on a wooden counter at the back of the shop.

'In a hurry,' the fat man scowled, coming around the counter. He set the candle down beside a pair of bronze scales. Fumbling about behind the counter, he produced a number of tiny stone weights. 'You mean you've been dry too long.' He reached over and untied the twine closing the bag. 'You should talk Bremer into making you a partner with all the money you drop at the Black Rose!'

Walther's eyes narrowed with annoyance. Angrily, he drew the bag away. 'I don't go there to see Bremer and I don't come here to be lectured, Ostmann!'

'Have it as you want,' Ostmann apologised. 'Let's see what you have.' The butcher reached into the linen bag, removing the long furry body of a rat. He jostled the dead rodent for a moment in his hand, trying to estimate its weight before resorting to the scales. 'A big one. Might be sixteen ounces.' He cast a glance at the bulky bag. 'Are they all like that?'

Walther nodded. 'I said the hunting was good. Forty-three longtails and not a runt among them.'

Ostmann made an appreciative whistle, sliding the first rat over to the scales. 'I'm afraid I can't give you much coin,' he said. 'There's not too much demand for dog fodder…'

'You'll pay what you always pay,' Walther told him, reaching for the bag. Ostmann quickly laid a protective hand atop it. The rat-catcher drew back, waving his hand at the empty meat hooks hanging from the ceiling and the empty bins lined against the wall. 'I'm well aware of what you need. This talk of plague has made the burghers nervous. Count Artur has outlawed the transport of cattle from Stirland to try and keep it from spreading into Nuln. The guildmasters assure that they can buy enough Reikland beef to make up for it, but one look at your shelves makes me think otherwise. The burghers might be peasants but they aren't serfs. They want some meat with their supper.'

The butcher drew back, his face aghast. 'Surely you aren't suggesting…'

'I might do more than suggest,' the rat-catcher threatened.

Ostmann licked his lips nervously. He began drawing rats from the bag, setting each in turn on the scales, scribbling figures on a scrap of sackcloth. 'Care for something to eat while I tally this up? Some sausage?'

Walther gave the man a crooked smile. 'Ostmann, just because I catch them doesn't mean I want to eat them.'

# ━━◄ CHAPTER II ►━━

*Altdorf*
*Nachgeheim, 1111*

THE MEETING OF the Imperial Grand Council broke apart some hours later, disgruntled noblemen slipping back to their private manors scattered about Altdorf's Palace District, others retreating to their chambers within the Imperial Palace itself. There was no arguing with one of the Emperor's diktats and nothing but anger and frustration to be gained by trying.

Some of the dignitaries, however, felt enough resentment to accept the invitation of Prince Sigdan Holswig. The titular ruler of Altdorf, much of Sigdan's power was subordinate to that of Emperor Boris, leaving him with few duties and even fewer responsibilities. Since assuming the title from his late father, Sigdan's chief concern had become soothing the tempers of those who had felt the sting of the Emperor's decrees.

Situated overlooking the river, Sigdan's castle was a relic of older times. It was said to have been built by Sigismund II as a bulwark to command the approach to the Reik. In those distant days, Norscan reivers had been bold enough to sail their longships down the river as far as Nuln and Pfeildorf. It had been the river castles built by Sigismund II which had finally ended the depredations of the longships.

Gazing down from the lead-lined window overlooking the river, Dettleb von Schomberg could almost see the longships coming again, Snagr Half-nose sailing down the Reik with a fleet of berserkers to plunder and pillage the heart of the Empire. Only a few years ago, the nobleman would have found such a thing impossible. Now, he wasn't quite so certain. He'd just had a very forceful reminder that the greed of his Emperor knew no limits.

'Of course they will discharge their warriors,' Baron Thornig's voice drew von Schomberg away from the window. A dozen or so noblemen and their retainers were gathered at Prince Sigdan's table, picking at the remains of a roast boar and plates of pickled eel. 'What other choice do they have?'

'You make it sound as if you don't intend to discharge your own soldiers,' observed Palatine Kretzulescu. The Sylvanian dignitary looked even more drained and exasperated than he had in the Imperial Palace.

A wolfish grin spread beneath Baron Thornig's beard. 'I can speak for Graf Gunthar. He won't pay this criminal tax!'

'Don't think Boris will let him get away with that,' said Aldo Broadfellow. The halfling was sitting on a large cushion, massaging his hairy feet. He glowered at his toes. 'Why that man insists on my wearing boots when I see him…' he grumbled to himself.

'The half-man speaks the right of it,' cautioned Count van Sauckelhof. 'Try to keep a schilling from Boris's purse and he'll lay siege to the Ulricsberg.'

'With what?' Baron Thornig growled. 'He's made it

impossible to retain an army big enough to do the job!'

'Don't think he hasn't thought of that,' von Schomberg said as he returned to the table. 'Boris has already granted a dispensation to Westerland and Drakwald in recognition of their ongoing travails.'

Van Sauckelhof drained his goblet of wine in a swallow. 'I half expected him to make us pay for each barbarian,' he snapped.

Kretzulescu caught the old knight's meaning, his face growing even more pale. 'You mean Drakwald?'

'He's a Hohenbach,' von Schomberg said. 'He could be expected to demand a certain loyalty from his homeland.'

'He hasn't shown any particular inclination to help the Drakwalders,' Prince Sigdan said. 'He even sent the Reiksmarshal home before the beastmen were entirely exterminated. That doesn't sound like a man with any great devotion to his birthplace.'

'Or it shows a man too shrewd to let emotion stand in his way,' suggested von Schomberg. 'While Drakwald is without a count, the province remains a protectorate of the Imperial Crown. All of its wealth belongs to the Imperial Treasury.' The knight turned and nodded at Count van Sauckelhof. 'If Snagr Half-nose had been a bit more successful, there might be two provinces in the same situation.'

Van Sauckelhof slammed his fist against the table. 'Of all the outrages! Renting rooms in the Imperial Palace to commoners, allowing the gentry to buy new titles for themselves, these were villainies enough, but if what you say is true, then our Emperor is nothing more than a blackhearted traitor!'

'Have a care!' Prince Sigdan exclaimed, anxious at the turn the conversation had taken.

'Why else would he refuse to bestow the title upon

Duke Konrad?' Baron von Klauswitz asked. 'Why else would he tell Boeckenfoerde to disband the army before its job was done? The Reiksmarshal had orders to make certain the beastkin weren't annihilated!'

'That's not true!' The objection came from a young man in the white tabard of a knight, a member of the Reiksknecht. Baron von Schomberg had brought Captain Erich von Kranzbeuhler with him to the Imperial Palace as his adjutant. Always impressed with the captain's forthright manner and honourable character, he hadn't thought twice about bringing him to Prince Sigdan's castle.

'The Reiksmarshal is a loyal man and a fearless soldier,' Erich continued, unperturbed to have the attention of so many of the Empire's leaders focused upon him. 'If the Emperor was using him, then it was from deceit.' The young knight bristled at the incredulity he still saw on the faces of those around him. 'Can anyone here say they haven't been forced to do the same?'

Count van Sauckelhof smiled. 'One of Boeckenfoerde's officers has been carrying on with a shepster employed by my wife. It seems he was complaining about the Emperor giving them orders to finish the campaign before Mittherbst, then going and drawing off most of their cavalry to guard the Bretonnian frontier.' The Westerlander shook his head. 'I'd think such deceptions would be unnecessary if the Reiksmarshal was another of the Emperor's sycophants like Ratimir and that peasant Kreyssig.'

'What does it matter one way or another?' Kretzulescu declared. 'The problem right now isn't the army. It's this damn head tax or war tax or whatever the Emperor wants to call it! In Sylvania we've had three poor harvests in a row and enough ill omens to put a curse on Taal himself! I can name a dozen villages that have fallen prey to illness and half a dozen more that have been abandoned by both lords and serfs!'

'Things stand much the same in the rest of Stirland,' Baron von Klauswitz commented, a haunted look creeping into his eyes.

'Plague?' Prince Sigdan asked, giving voice to the dreaded word. It seemed to echo through the hall, sending shivers down the spine of every man at the table.

'Shallya have mercy,' von Schomberg whispered, invoking the goddess's protection against the fearsome spectre of pestilence and disease.

*Skavenblight*
*Nachgeheim, 1111*

A COLD, CLAMMY smell wafted through the darkened halls. Furtive shapes scuttled and scurried against the ancient stone passageways, squeaking and chittering as they crept through the shadows. The rats clawed their way through piles of rags, swam through scummy puddles of swamp slime, prowled across jumbles of old bones and tumbledown masonry. They leapt across the many holes pitting the crumbling floor or swarmed across the stout cables spanning the worst of the gaps.

The entrancing scent of food drew the ravenous vermin deeper into the primordial gloom. They ignored the rank odours of the creatures which called the maze-like confusion of halls and galleries home. A starving scavenger learned to become bold around even the most rapacious predator.

It was the boldest of the rats who scurried along the wall towards the alluring smell. The rat hesitated a moment when its beady eyes spotted two flickers of green flame rising from the darkness ahead. But hunger soon overrode caution and the big grey rat hurried on towards the source of the smell.

The lump of blackened cheese was lying just within the glow cast by the nearest of the lights. Again the rat hesitated, but again its hunger drove it onwards. It hurried towards the beckoning cheese, leaping the last three feet to sink its fangs and claws in the enticing feast.

As soon as the rat lighted upon the cheese, a great furry hand snapped out from the darkness, closing about the animal and its prize. The rat squealed in terror, writhing in its effort to sink its fangs into the flesh of its captor. Its captor, however, gave the rodent no chance to retaliate. With practised ease, a clawed thumb pressed down upon the rat's head, snapping its neck.

Krisnik Sharpfang stared down at the quivering carcass in his paw. Beady red eyes, hideously similar to the rat's own, gleamed with hunger. Long fangs, monstrously enlarged versions of those in the dead rodent's mouth, gnashed together in an expression of savage triumph. Whiskers twitched, ears shivered, a long naked tail lashed against the slimy wall. Uttering a famished whine, the skaven began to nibble at his catch.

'Save-save some cheese,' snapped a voice from the darkness.

Krisnik froze in mid-chew, turning a hostile glare at the speaker. Illuminated by the green glow of the farther worm-oil lamp was a black-furred ratman, his brutish frame encased in a hodgepodge of steel plates and strips of iron mail. A thick-bladed broad-axe was clenched in one of the creature's paws.

'Catch-take more rat-meat with cheese,' the second skaven hissed.

Krisnik wolfed down the bite he had taken, then

hurriedly closed his paw around the haft of his own broad-axe. 'My-mine cheese,' he snarled. 'My-mine rat-meat!'

The other skaven bared his fangs in a murderous leer, his claws clenching tighter about the grip of his weapon. His greedy antagonist glared back at him. The two ratmen, armed and armoured for battle, took each other's measure. The second skaven reluctantly backed down, casting a worried glance at the massive steel-banded door behind him. Krisnik noticed the gesture, his former bravado evaporating in a shudder of fright. Almost sheepishly, he tossed the hindquarters of his catch to his comrade.

It wasn't that he was worried about fighting the other guard. He was bigger and stronger than his comrade, and better with the axe. Besides, if he wasn't, there was that trick he'd learned about swatting an enemy's groin with the flat of his tail. No, it wasn't fear that made him relent; it was simply a matter of recognising the dignity and decorum which was proper for a ratman of his position. A warrior entrusted with the protection of the Shattered Tower didn't lower himself to squabbling over morsels of cold, gamey rat-meat.

Especially when the Lords of Decay would expect to find two guards exactly where they had been posted. It didn't appeal to Krisnik to consider what they would do should they find one of their guards missing. Clan Rictus had enough ways of dealing with traitors and shirkers, all of them hideous and unspeakable. He didn't need to think about how much nastier the imaginations of the council members might be.

Taking the tiniest nibble from his sliver of cheese, Krisnik darted a furtive look at the massive door. He was thankful the door was as thick as it was. Whatever the Council of Thirteen had been discussing for so long was nothing for his ears! The Lords of Decay took great pleasure displaying the bodies of spies when they were through mutilating them. Several score decorated the spires of the Shattered Tower at present, but the rulers of skavendom were always able to find room for more.

Krisnik shivered in his armour. Maybe joining the elite Verminguard hadn't been such a good idea after all. Which one of his jealous rivals had arranged to put him into such a predicament, he wondered?

EERIE GREEN LIGHT cast strange shadows across the enormous hall, rendering its immensity a patchwork of darkness and illumination. The light streamed from a pair of gigantic crystal spheres bound in cages of iron and supported upon great pillars of bronze. A confusion of wires and hoses drooped from the pillars, writhing along the stone floor until they vanished into a huge copper casket. A wiry skaven, his fur dyed a deep crimson where it was not scarred with burns, scrambled about the casket with frantic, jittery motions. His gloved paws flew across levers and hastily adjusted valves, causing the green light to flicker and small bursts of glowing gas to billow from vents in the bronze pillars.

The warlock-engineer bit down on a curse as the mechanism resisted his efforts. The warp-lantern was a new invention, the latest in the techno-sorcery of Clan Skryre. A lamp that created light not from rat dung or worm-oil, but from warpstone itself! A magnificent creation that would illuminate the whole of the Under-Empire and bring much profit to the warlock-engineers – if they could only get the thing to work right!

Glaring through his goggles, the technician growled at the scrawny skavenslaves locked inside the generator, forgetting for the moment that his snarls were wasted. The slaves were blind, deaf and mute, a precaution against their learning any of the council's secrets. Angrily, the warlock turned back to the copper casket, stabbing his claw against one of the buttons. A spark of blue electricity crackled from a coil set at the top of the generator cage, shocking the slaves and jolting them into motion. The slaves began scrambling inside the cylindrical cage, their momentum causing it to revolve. The energy of their terrified efforts raced along the wires, feeding the warp-lanterns and causing the green light to stabilise.

Tugging nervously at his whiskers, the warlock-engineer glanced across the cavernous hall to the great table where the masters of all skavendom were gathered. His glands clenched as his eyes roved across the concentrated gathering of evil and villainy. In all the Under-Empire, there were no skaven more fierce or ruthless than these twelve. As Luminary of the Shattered Tower, it was his duty to provide light for these merciless monsters, that they might better see their surroundings and so be assured that none of their rivals had broken with custom and brought assassins into the sacred confines of the Grey Chapel.

The Luminary darted an anxious glance at the supreme overlord of Clan Skryre, the cruel Warpmaster Sythar Doom. The wizened Sythar was hunched in his steel-backed chair, his paws folded against each other, his fingers stroking the copper wires embedded in his scarred fur. Sythar's face was a patchwork of skin grafts and iron plates, his eyes a pair of enchanted rubies three sizes too big for their sockets and held in place by a confusion of sutures and stitches. There was a compact power-plant hidden somewhere beneath the Warpmaster's flowing black robes, connected to the thick black cable implanted into the underside of his jaw. When his withered lips pulled back to expose his metal fangs, blue sparks crackled about his teeth. It was a vivid reminder to all around Sythar that he had survived several attempts to murder him and a promise that the next attempt would be quite costly to his killers. The power-plant was wired to his heart and should that organ stop beating the result would be quite explosive.

WARPMASTER SYTHAR DOOM didn't seem to notice the flickering warp-lights or the Luminary's efforts to stabilise them. His attention was fixed upon the other skaven seated about the council table, his ruby eyes gleaming as each facet focused upon a different ratman. In the deadly maze of schemes and intrigues that formed council politics, it was dangerous to ignore any of them. The weaker Lords of Decay were forever scheming to rise higher in the hierarchy of the Under-Empire; the stronger were equally determined to ensure that they retained their positions. Sythar cast a covetous look at the Twelfth Throne, a trickle of drool causing his metal fangs to throw sparks.

There were twelve seats upon the council. Here, within the Grey Chapel, the seats were arrayed about an ancient oaken table, each throne radiating outwards from the great stone chair which was the Black Throne, the thirteenth seat set aside for the Great Horned Rat. The most powerful Lords of Decay occupied the thrones to the left and right of their god, the first and twelfth seats. That on the right was the Seerseat, always occupied by the Seerlord, master of the grey seers and grand prophet of the Horned Rat. It was the Seerlord's function to implement the edicts of the council and to interpret the will of the absent Horned Rat. Supposedly above the bickering and politics of the skaven clans, the Seerlord was as ambitious and greedy as any ratman and used his position to further his own power, exploiting the vacant Black Throne to give himself a double vote whenever the need arose.

Seerlord Skrittar was going to need that double vote now. The fact pleased Warpmaster Sythar. The priest had dominated the council for far too long and it was time that he was put into his place. The bells fixed to Skrittar's long horns tinkled as the grey skaven tried to suppress the tremors of rage rushing through his body. With his ruby-eyes, Sythar's vision penetrated the oak table to see the Seerlord's tail lashing angrily against the side of his throne.

How it must vex the prophet to have all his careful alliances and treaties crumbling before his eyes! And to have them swept aside by the Seerlord's most hated enemy, the bloated Arch-Plaguelord of Clan Pestilens, Poxtifex Nurglitch IV, only made the spectacle even more delicious!

'The man-things fight among themselves,' the whisper-thin voice of Blight Tenscratch rasped through the shadows. A creature as twisted as his noxious clan, Blight was the despised ruler of the bug-breeding Clan Verms. Worm-oil was only a small part of his clan's fortunes, their real wealth coming from exterminating infestations of fleas and ticks, infestations most ratmen believed Verms themselves had caused.

'Now is the time to fight-slay,' Blight hissed, slapping one of his scabrous paws against the table. 'Kill all man-things and take their land!'

'The man-things won't fight each other if given a common enemy,' the sharp tongue of Shadowmaster Kreep slashed across Blight's words. Leader of Clan Eshin, Kreep commanded the most vicious cadre of killers and assassins in the Under-Empire, making his one of the most feared names in skavendom. Sythar thought it was a shame Kreep had allowed religious fervour and steady bribes to make him Skrittar's lap-rat.

'They will set aside their animosity to fight us,' Kreep pronounced, raising one of his black talons. 'We cannot fight all of the man-things.'

'Then why did we send Deathmaster Silke to kill the Vilner-man? Just to help stupid beast-meat?' The angry snarl came from Rattnak Vile, High Vivisectionist of Clan Moulder. The burly Rattnak was twice the size of Kreep, with immense paws tipped in steel talons within the Master Moulders had grafted to their clanlord's bones. Rattnak's eyes were glazed from the frequent overuse of warp-dust, and his posture was always that of a cornered beast ready to pounce. Kreep's paws vanished into the folds of his cloak, closing about whatever weapons he had hidden there. Unless the assassin had coated his blades in very powerful poison, Sythar didn't rate his chances against the monstrous Rattnak.

'Man-things fight, man-things die,' the sepulchral moan of Warlord Nekrot sent a shiver through the room. Though he occupied a lowly place upon the council, the ghoulish master of Clan Mordkin presented a terrifying aspect, his fur bleached to the colour of polished bone, his armour adorned with the skeleton of his predecessor. Clan Mordkin had reached prominence during the wars against Nagash the Accursed and they had been obsessed with death and decay ever since. Nekrot's black eyes gleamed from the skull-mask he wore, his fangs bruxing as he contemplated the death and destruction of an empire. If it came to war, the other council members would think in terms of plunder and loot, but Nekrot would care only for how much killing his clan would get to do.

'Boris-man now Emperor,' stated Raksheed Death-claw, glowering from within his red hood, his face obscured by a strip of scarlet cloth. Murderlord of Clan Skully, Raksheed was the bitter rival of Kreep, envious of Clan Eshin's power and prestige. He could always be counted upon to vote against Kreep and by extension, Seerlord Skrittar. With many warrens underneath the sands of Araby, it was also in Skully's best interests to maintain favourable relations with Pestilens and their extensive Southlands powerbase.

'Yes-yes,' agreed General Bonestab, the steel-encased warlord of Clan Grikk. 'My spies tell me Boris-man hated much-much by man-things. With no leader, man-things not fight!'

'Dwarf-things more problem than man-things!' snapped Warlord Manglrr Baneburrow, commander of the teeming hordes of Clan Fester. 'Dwarf-things kill Graug-dragon, now try to steal Fester-warren in Karak Azgal! We must crush-slay all dwarf-things!'

'We will kill-slay all dwarf-meat.' The words came in a venomous hiss. The eyes of the council turned towards the Twelfth Throne and the malignant creature seated there. Lord Vecteek the Murderous, Warmonger of Clan Rictus, preened his silky black fur as he leaned back in his stone chair, plundered from the dwarf-halls of Karak Ungor. Clad in a suit of steel plates that sported an array of spikes that would have shamed a rose bush, Vecteek let his piercing grey eyes linger upon each of his rivals. Even those who habitually sided with Clan Rictus squirmed under the Warmonger's scrutiny.

'The dwarf-meat will be slaughtered,' Vecteek pronounced, 'but first we will enslave the humans. We will use their fields and their herds to make us strong, to feed new armies. Then we will annihilate the dwarf-things.'

'The man-things are still too many,' insisted Kreep. 'We will lose too many fighting them. We will be too weak to conquer dwarf-things.'

'Who said we will fight them?' Vecteek chortled, his wicked laugh echoing through the Grey Chapel. 'Arch-Plaguelord Nurglitch has brought us a new weapon.' Vecteek extended his claw, gesturing for the Poxtifex to speak.

Nurglitch reared up in his seat, his corpulent mass undulating in a loathsomely boneless fashion. The Arch-Plaguelord was cloaked in a decayed habit of leprous green cloth, split in many places where the diseased ratman's buboes had swollen past the raiment's ability to restrain. Great thorns sprouted from Nurglitch's spine and shoulders, dripping a foul green sludge from their tips. Clouds of black flies swarmed over his rotten mass, crawling about the tattered hood which cast his face into shadow. When he spoke, the plaguelord's pestilent breath sent squadrons of flies dropping to the floor.

'Glory to the magnificence of the Horned One,' Nurglitch coughed, 'in His true aspect,' he added, shifting his hooded face towards Seerlord Skrittar. 'By his divine grace, we, His true servants, have discovered the most blessed of His contagions!' Nurglitch unclasped the heavy tome he wore chained about his neck, pulling away mouldering pages until he exposed a hollow within the book. His warty paw emerged clasping a glass vial. The other Lords of Decay cringed away from the plaguelord, each waiting for one of the others to leap from his seat and start a rush for the many exits hidden within the Grey Chapel's walls.

'The Horned Rat brings to us a new holy plague!' Nurglitch chortled, brandishing the vial aloft. His boast did nothing to ease the fears of the other lords. The slicing voice of Vecteek, however, reminded them that there were other things to fear.

'Coward-trash!' Vecteek snarled. 'Sit-stay! Hear-listen!

The plague is harmless to our kind. It will only kill man-things.'

First among equals, Vecteek's word was law among his fellow Lords of Decay. It wasn't belief, but obedience, that kept the council in their seats. Only the connivance of the Verminguard could have allowed Nurglitch to bring his poison into the Shattered Tower, and no ratman in Clan Rictus was insane enough to dare such a thing without Vecteek's permission. As they stared at the vial, the council members saw not only the power of Pestilens, but the dominance of Rictus. The reminder wasn't a pleasant one.

'How do we know it will kill man-things?' Rattnak Vile asked. His lips curled away from his fangs. 'How do we know it will not kill skaven?'

Vecteek rose from his seat, clapping his paws together. At the sound, a gang of Verminguard came slinking into the Grey Chapel, wheeling a great glass cage ahead of them. Inside the cage, a motley confusion of scrawny ratmen and dirty human slaves moaned and whined, clutching weakly at the transparent walls of their cell. The assembled Lords of Decay shifted uneasily as they noted the markings on the pelts of the skaven locked inside the cage, finding a representative from each of their clans among the captives. One piebald ratman even displayed tiny horns, making him resemble the grotesque grey seers.

Another signal from Vecteek and Nurglitch oozed out from his chair and approached the cage. The plague priest dragged open a tiny portal, then dropped the little vial into the cage. The vessel shattered as it struck the floor, expelling a black fog into the cage. For a moment, the captives were lost within a veil of darkness. Then the veil fell away as the fog dissipated, condensing into a black soot. The skavenslaves continued to paw madly at the glass walls, squealing in terror. The human captives, however, lay strewn about the floor, their flesh marked with weeping sores and suppurating buboes.

'No sickness,' Nurglitch coughed. 'Plague is for manthings. Won't kill ratkin. My apprentice, Poxmaster Puskab Foulfur, test new plague on many man-things. Nine of ten die!'

The statement brought greedy glitters to the eyes of the assembled ratmen. Nine of ten? The humans would be so decimated that even if they were united they would pose no threat at all to the hordes of the Under-Empire! The ratmen would be able to sweep the humans aside and claim the surface for their own! Fat from the plunder of the man-things' empire, they would be stronger than ever in the history of skavendom!

Sythar's tail twitched as he studied Nurglitch. The plaguelord was a zealot, a religious fanatic whose clan had once tried to enslave the entire Under-Empire. If the plague priests truly had a weapon of such potential then the power of Clan Pestilens would grow beyond measure. He cast an envious glance at the Twelfth Throne. Wresting the seat away from Warmonger Vecteek would be hard enough, but to usurp control of it from Clan Pestilens might be impossible. He turned his gaze across the table to Seerlord Skrittar. As much as it galled him, Sythar would have to side with the grey seer when things came down to a vote.

'I have seen the effectiveness of Puskab's disease,' Seerlord Skrittar declared, leaving unsaid whether such intelligence had come from sorcerous visions or flesh-and-blood spies. Nurglitch growled as he heard the grey seer bestow credit for brewing the disease upon his apprentice, an insult made all the more vexing for the truth behind it.

'This new plague has the potential to leave our

enemies helpless, to decimate them in their thousands,' Skrittar continued. Sythar waited for the grey seer to twist these seeming strengths into reasons why the council must oppose Nurglitch's new weapon. Instead, the grey seer shocked the other Lords of Decay by endorsing the contagion.

'The Horned Rat displays His beneficence in strange ways,' Skrittar said, tilting his head towards the empty Black Throne, almost as though he were listening to some unseen speaker. 'He has overlooked the... eccentricities of Clan Pestilens and through them bestowed upon us the weapon which shall bring about the long-prophesied ascendancy!' The prophet-sorcerer turned towards Vecteek, bowing his head. 'We should ask the council to vote. I say we endorse this new weapon and use it immediately against the man-things!' Again, Skrittar cocked his head towards the empty seat. If needed, there was no mistaking which way the Horned Rat would cast his vote.

Vecteek stared suspiciously at the Seerlord. At the moment, Vecteek seemed to be considering using his Verminguard and stopping whatever scheme Skrittar was hatching before it could start. However murdering the Seerlord was one of the few things beyond Vecteek's power. It would give the many enemies of Clan Rictus the justification they needed to band together and over-throw the Warmonger. Nothing was more guaranteed to incite the rabble of skavendom like a holy war.

'This new plague will achieve more than a hundred armies,' Vecteek said. 'The Boris-man has made the man-things divided and suspicious. That will make them vulnerable to the plague. Before they know what is happening, it will be upon them. Because they are divided, they will not be able to stop its spread.' His black paw clenched into a fist. 'They will be broken and beaten before our first warrior leaves the tunnels!'

With both Seerlord Skrittar and Warmonger Vecteek supporting the plan, the vote was purely ceremonial. In the end, only Warpmaster Sythar and Great War-lord Vrrmik of Clan Mors opposed the plan. Sythar couldn't stifle the feeling of alarm that coursed through his glands every time he caught a sniff of Nurglitch's gloating putrescence. The new plague might benefit all of the Under-Empire, but there was no question the plague priests would reap the dragon's share of the plunder. Of course, there was the possibility he was certain had occurred to every warlord on the council: if Pestilens could make a plague to kill man-things, certainly they could create another one to turn against their fellow skaven. Whatever they were up to, Sythar was determined that Clan Skryre would be watching and waiting.

Warlord Vrrmik's opposition was less complex – there was no creature above or below the surface he hated more than Grey Lord Vecteek. Sythar wondered if that would be enough to make him an ally against Clan Pestilens when the time came. Because there was no question the new plague would do what Nurglitch promised.

The uncertainty lay in what would happen after.

*Nuln*
*Nachgeheim, 1111*

THE BLACK ROSE sat perched along a hilly road in the riverside section of Freiberg. From its threshold, a patron could stare straight down the street to the clear waters of the Reik and see the grey rocky spires of Helstrumoog, the little island rising at the joining of the rivers. The distant spires of the abandoned Cathedral of Sigmar were visible in the morning light, deserted since the great fire that had claimed the old Grand Theogonist and much of Wissenland's Sigmarite priesthood. Beyond the ruined temple stretched its farmlands and pastures, desolate and unused after months of bickering among the nobles over who had the greater claim to lease the now tenantless land.

Walther sighed as he looked down the road. Nuln was a city in the grip of change. Emperor Boris had removed the capital to Altdorf following his ascension, removing the lustre from the place that had been called the 'jewel of the Empire'. When Grand Theogonist Thorgrad was elected as head of the Sigmarite faith, he had stopped reconstruction of Helstrum Cathedral and relocated the seat of the temple to Altdorf. In the space of only a few decades, Nuln had lost its position as centre of both the Empire's secular and spiritual worlds. A feeling of malaise and bitterness gripped the hearts of Nulners, an impression that their greatness was past and all that was left to them was a slow slide into decay and ruin.

The rat-catcher shook his head. There was nothing he could do about Nuln's lost glory. That was for Count Artur and the Assembly to worry about. His own problems gave him trouble enough. They might not be the sort of thing to vex a baron or a duke, but to Walther they were more important than the Great Mysteries of Verena.

Dawn found the Black Rose almost deserted. The bushy-bearded Bremer was tending the bar, cleaning out clay tankards and leathern jacks. A few lamplighters and chimney sweeps were scattered about the tables.

The real custom happened between sunset and midnight, when sailors and stevedores trooped up the hill from the docks and companies of students descended from the Universität. Then the place would be a bustling confusion of songs and jests, of hard-drinking river-traders and brawny lumpers, their clothes reeking of fish.

Walther preferred it quiet. He was used to silence, the stillness of the sewers where the only sounds were the crackle of his rushlight and the furtive skitter of the rats. Noise, the racket of too many people crammed into a small place, was to him a frightful thing. Sometimes he was happy that people shunned the company of a rat-catcher. It made it so much easier.

Except in one area. Walther's pulse quickened as he looked out across the tavern and spotted the woman making her way from the kitchen with a platter of black bread and frumenty. His eyes fixated upon her shapely figure, upon the way her body pressed itself against the simple wool kirtle and linen apron she wore. Even in the tavern's gloom, her long golden tresses seemed to shimmer like pieces of the sun. He watched as she rounded one of the tables, setting the platter before the grey-faced militiaman seated there. Walther's gaze darkened when the soldier made a grab for the woman's waist.

'Just a little kiss, Zena,' the militiaman suggested, starting to rise from his chair. The woman placed her hands on his shoulders, pushing him back down.

'None of that, Meisel,' she scolded him and twisted away from his clutch. 'Eat your porridge and be content with a full belly.'

Meisel frowned at his meal. 'I'll miss your cooking, Zena,' he said. 'Almost as much as I'll miss those big blue eyes,' he added with a wink.

'Leaving us, Herr Meisel?' Bremer called out from behind the bar.

Meisel shifted his chair around so he could face the bar. 'I've been discharged,' he said. 'Me and a hundred like me. Emperor Boris has placed a new tax for every dienstmann a lord retains.' He dipped his spoon into the bowl of frumenty. 'The nobles are scrambling to cut their expenses.'

'They'll cry a different song if the goblins come again,' Bremer cursed. 'Or if the beastmen decide to come down from the Drakwald. Then they'll be begging you fellows to take up arms again.'

The militiaman clenched his fist. 'They'll be begging before then,' he swore. 'There's a knight named Engel who is organising a march on Altdorf. We're going to petition the Emperor himself and make our demands known!'

While Meisel and Bremer continued their exchange, Zena retreated back towards the kitchen. Walther knew she detested talk of politics and religion, of anyone wasting their time arguing about things over which they had no control. She might endure the groping fingers of a drunken dock-walloper, but she couldn't abide a beerhall agitator.

Walther intercepted Zena just as she reached the kitchen door. 'Zena,' he whispered, catching her by the string of her apron. She spun around, her hand raised to strike her accoster. When she recognised the rat-catcher, her expression softened from anger to annoyance.

'Schill,' she sighed. 'Of course. No night is complete without being pawed by a ratman.'

Walther winced at the reprimand, releasing the apron string as though it had suddenly been transformed into a hissing serpent. 'I didn't mean…'

'You never mean anything,' Zena said. Her eyes dropped to the rat-catcher's hands, becoming hard when she saw the blood on them. 'You might have washed a bit before coming here.'

'I'm sorry. A few of them nipped me tonight,' Walther explained, trying to wipe his hands clean on the rough wool of his breeches.

'One of them is going to gnaw off your fingers,' Zena warned him. 'I've told you before you should find better work.' Her eyes softened when she saw the ugly gash Walther's efforts had reopened. 'Oh! One of those filthy things *is* going to bite off your fingers!'

The rat-catcher made no protest when Zena unwound her scarf and ministered to his wounded hand. The sting of his torn flesh was nothing beside the warm rush that pounded through his heart.

'No hunter is completely safe from his quarry,' Walther said. 'It is just one of the risks he accepts.' He reached down, cupping Zena's chin in his hand, lifting her face until her eyes met his. 'I'm doing it all for you. I'll make enough to support you, to raise a family.'

Zena pulled away, her expression becoming angry again. 'A penny a tail?' she scoffed. 'You'll raise children on a penny a tail?'

Walther smiled, reaching to his belt and removing the coins Ostmann had paid him. An exultant feeling filled him when he saw Zena's eyes light up at sight of the silver. She snatched them from his hand and stared at them in wonder, almost as though she couldn't believe they were real.

'That's just the beginning,' Walther assured Zena. He was thinking of the steadily increasing numbers of rats he'd been seeing in the sewers. He was also thinking of Ostmann's empty shelves and the embargo against Stirland.

Gently, the rat-catcher closed Zena's fingers around the coins and kissed her hand. 'Don't worry,' he told her.

'The happy times are coming.'

## ➤ CHAPTER III ➤

*Middenheim*
*Kaldezeit, 1111*

SNARLING WOLVES GLOWERED down upon the oblivious men, stone fangs bared. The flickering fire of an enormous hearth cast weird shadows across the lupine gargoyles, the shifting play of light and dark lending the marble wolves a semblance of savage life.

Far below the stone wolves, two men sparred across a polished wooden floor. The boards creaked and groaned as heavy boots stamped down on them, as thrust and parry whirled the combatants along the empty gallery. The clash of steel against steel rang through the concourse.

One of the combatants was a middle-aged man, lean of build, his close-cropped hair in retreat, his thin moustache displaying a scattering of grey. His face was thin and hard, his eyes as sharp as the edge of a knife. He wore a simple leather tunic, his only affectation being the golden pectoral that hung about his neck. He wielded his sword with suppleness and surety, his every move bearing the cool confidence of long experience.

His opponent was much younger, little more than a boy. Thick black hair hung to his shoulders, catching in the high collar of his garment. Unlike the simple tunic of the older man, the boy's gypon was extravagant, stripes of silver thread woven into the burgundy cloth, gold buttons crisscrossing the breast. An enormous buckle, cast into the profile of a running wolf, fastened a belt of dragonhide about his waist. The scabbard which hung from the belt was gilded across most of its length and engraved with elaborate scrollwork.

The boy's face was handsome, stamped with all the finer qualities of noble blood and careful breeding. There was pride in his deep blue eyes and a swagger to the curve of his mouth that betokened an innate confidence that needed neither practice nor experience to engender it. The will to accomplish was enough to embolden the boy and drive him to success.

His swordsmanship displayed a less refined, more primal style than the studied motions of the older man. It was emotion rather than skill which governed his blade, but such was the fire of his passion, the quickness of his reflexes that his guard was impenetrable, his attacks avoided only by the narrowest margin.

The older swordsman smiled as he twisted his wrist and blocked a slash from his adversary's blade. 'That would have been an impressive feint – if you had intended it as such,' he told the boy.

A smirk tugged at the corner of the boy's mouth. 'I don't need feints to sneak past your blade, old man.'

The other swordsman smiled back, rolling his blade across the back of the boy's sword and stabbing the point towards his breast. His foe dropped and shifted, swatting the thrust aside with the pommel of his own weapon. The older fighter nodded, impressed by the move. 'Nice work. I'd think you'd been studying the tricks of the Estalian diestro – if I didn't know you have no patience for books.'

The boy jabbed his sword at his foe's left arm, then turned his entire body so that he followed through with a rolling slash at the man's right leg. Both attacks crashed against the other swordsman's intercepting blade.

'Why read if there's nothing more to learn, van Cleeve?' the boy quipped.

The old man snorted with amusement, then brought his boot stamping down, not upon the floor, but upon his adversary's foot. The boy danced back in surprise. For an instant, his guard was down. It was all the opening his instructor needed. The point of his sword pressed against the youth's belly, the cork cap sinking into the cloth of his doublet.

'If all you want to do is get killed, then there's nothing more I can teach you, your grace,' van Cleeve said.

Laughing, the boy brought his sword whipping around in a stunning display of speed and flourish, the edge pressing against his instructor's neck. 'That is a mortal wound, but not immediately fatal. We die together, old man.' Smiling, he withdrew his blade, pausing to remove the nub of cork before returning it to its scabbard.

Van Cleeve sighed as he attended to his own weapon. 'I think his excellency the Graf would take small comfort from knowing his only son dispatched his assassin before he died.' The swordsman shook his head. 'You have an impressive natural aptitude, Prince Mandred. If you would only apply yourself to the science of the sword…'

Mandred frowned. It was an argument he had heard many times and one that he didn't appreciate, especially since it was a train of thought van Cleeve shared with his father. 'Techniques and schools of sword would ruin me. Tame a wolf and you dull his fangs.'

'A tame wolf lives longer,' van Cleeve observed.

'A wild wolf is happier,' retorted the prince. Van Cleeve could see he would make no points sparring with his student's wit. Clicking his heels together, the Westerlander bowed to the prince and withdrew from the gallery. Mandred waited only until the swordsman was out of sight before turning and dashing down the stairway at the far end of the gallery.

His sparring with van Cleeve had been frustrating today and the prince had been impatient to extract himself from the duel. There were more important things than sword practice going on within the halls of the Middenpalaz. Noblemen and dignitaries from across the city had been arriving all day. Something big was going on and he was determined to learn what it was.

Stealing through the brooding halls of the palace, Mandred avoided the most populous corridors. Using side passages and circling through empty chambers, he avoided encountering the small army of peasants who maintained the Graf's household or the armed guards who saw to the royal family's protection. The only one who noted his passing was Woten, the hoary grey wolf-hound lounging in one of the banquet halls, but the dog was more interested in the warmth of a blazing hearth than Mandred's activities. A wag of the tail was all the notice he paid the boy.

Creeping along the heavy, stone-walled corridors, Mandred reached his destination, a little waiting room adjoining the Graf's council chamber. There was a secret to the room, one which only a few people knew. A painting set into the wall could be tilted outwards upon a hinge once a hidden catch had been unlocked. Behind the painting was a pane of cloudy glass. It corresponded with a large mirror in the council chamber, but the reflective surface was only upon the outside. From the waiting room, a person could peer through the glass and observe whatever went on in the other room. The whole thing was dwarf-work, as attested by the sharp runes carved into the edge of the glass. Mandred wondered about the trick behind the spyhole but had long ago given up on puzzling it out for himself. Dwarfcraft or witchcraft, it was enough that the trick worked.

Gazing into the council chamber, Mandred could see twenty or so of the city's noblemen seated around the circumference of the Fauschlagstein, a great stone table carved from a single block of Ulricsberg granite. Among the city's notables, he could see the glowering visage of Grand Master Arno Warsitz, his great red beard drooping against his chest; the stern countenance of Ar-Ulric, High Priest of the White Wolf, his wolfskin robes matching his snowy hair and the milky eye staring blindly from the right side of his face; Thane Hardin Gunarsson, chief of Middenheim's dwarfs, his wizened face pulled into a perpetual frown. Beside such grim councillors, Graf Gunthar looked cheerful and vibrant, his dark hair swept back, his long houppelande of ribbed kersey flowing about him, the dark blue of the loose gown contrasting with the sombre blacks and russets of his council.

Any impression of cheer, however, did not reach to the Graf's eyes. They were ringed by dark circles, their sapphire depths haunted by worry.

'We are agreed then,' Graf Gunthar told his councillors. 'Middenheim will not be weakened to placate the diktats of a corrupt Emperor. We will not dismiss our soldiers and we will not empty the city treasury to pay an unjust tax.'

The statement brought nods of affirmation from the assembled nobles. Thane Hardin stroked his blond beard and scowled at the gold-grubbing effrontery of the manling Emperor. Even the worst gold-crazed dwarf wouldn't have dreamed up such a crooked scheme as Boris's plot to tax the human *Dienstleute* out of existence and leave his Empire disarmed and defenceless.

Graf Gunthar paced about the table, studying each of his advisors in turn. 'You are all aware what defying Emperor Boris could mean. He might raise an army to seize what he feels is owed to him.'

'Let him try,' growled Grand Master Arno, clenching his fist. 'The Drak-rat will never breach the Ulricsberg.'

'He wouldn't have to,' cautioned Viscount von Vogelthal, the Graf's chamberlain. 'He could simply lay siege to the mountain and cut us off from the rest of Middenland. Whatever the quality of our warriors, Emperor Boris can field more than us.'

Graf Gunthar nodded, agreeing with the chamberlain's observation. 'That is why I have decided that we must lay stores against any punitive actions the Emperor might take. We must levy the farms and freeholds around the Ulricsberg, double their harvest tax. I want the storehouses full to bursting before winter sets in. We can depend upon Emperor Boris to wait until the spring before mounting a campaign in the north, but every day after the thaw he stays in the Reikland will be a boon from Ulric.'

'The raugrafs and landgraves won't appreciate having their obligations increased,' objected Duke Schneidereit.

'We face an emergency,' Graf Gunthar snarled at the duke. 'If we are to survive, every man must make sacrifices.' He stopped pacing about the stone table and rested his hands against the cool granite surface. 'To that end, I have issued orders that the Sudgarten and

Konigsgarten are to be dug up. The ground is to be used as farmland. Whatever seed we can spare is to be sown at once, before the first frost.' He sighed as he looked across the worried faces of his advisors. 'It might not help us if Emperor Boris strikes fast, but if he delays, we may just bring in a crop before his army lays siege to the Ulricsberg.'

Many of the nobles nodded grimly at the pragmatic decision. They would grieve for the loss of the parks with their colourful shrubberies and flowers, but they would grieve even more if starvation descended upon their city.

'There is another concern we should consider, your highness.' All eyes turned upon the aged Ar-Ulric when the high priest spoke. He was much more than simply another of the Graf's advisors. As the chief authority of the cult of Ulric, he was the most powerful priest in Middenheim, venerated by Ulricans across the Empire as the representative of their god upon the mortal coil.

Ar-Ulric rose from his chair, his one-eyed gaze sweeping across the chamber. 'There is plague in the outlying provinces, in Sylvania and Stirland. If the disease spreads beyond their borders, into Talabecland and Hochland, or our own Middenland, then we must be prepared for refugees.'

'We have already taken in three thousand Westerlanders,' grumbled Viscount von Vogelthal. 'And another two thousand Drakwalders. The city can't hold any more squatters.'

'Nor will it,' Graf Gunthar declared. 'We must protect Middenheim. Accepting those fleeing from enemies is one thing, but there is a point when mercy becomes irresponsible.' He hesitated, collecting his thoughts, weighing the responsibility for his decision. 'No, Your Eminence,' he told Ar-Ulric, 'Middenheim will not harbour refugees from the plague. Any trying to climb the causeways, any setting one foot upon the Ulricsberg, must be cut down like dogs. Anyone seeking entry into the city must be sequestered at the foot of the mountain.'

Ar-Ulric bowed his head. 'If that is your decree, then do I have your leave to inform the Temple of Shallya of this decision? The priestesses will want to know and make their plans accordingly.'

'You have my leave,' Graf Gunthar said. 'But you may also warn the temple that anyone who attends refugees will not be permitted back into the city. I will make no exceptions. Not even for a priestess.'

Shocked by the cruelty of his father's decree, Mandred drew away from the spyhole, swinging the hinged painting back into place. It sickened him to think his father could be so unfeeling, to abandon the sick and the desperate, to turn his back upon those who needed help.

He had always admired his father's wisdom, but wisdom was nothing without compassion.

When he was Graf, Mandred swore he would be both wise and compassionate. He wouldn't be a cowardly tyrant like his father.

*Altdorf*
*Kaldezeit, 1111*

THE WIND BLOWING across the Reik into Altdorf had a cold sting to it, a reminder to all who felt it that the autumn was swiftly fading and that Ulric was already spreading his claws to claim the world. It would be a hard winter for the capital. Frightful rumours of poor harvests in Stirland and Sylvania had been given some veracity when the nobles of Pfeildorf and Wissenburg began to complain to the Emperor about the almost negligible amount of wheat and millet being exported down the river. Most of what trade had emerged from the provinces had gone no farther than Mordheim and Talabheim. Solland and Wissenland, their agriculture devoted principally to raising sheep and making wine, had become desperate to stock supplies for the winter. Food prices in Nuln had soared, diverting the harvest of many a Reikland lord southwards, away from the traditional markets in Altdorf.

The prospect of a hungry winter, however, was compounded in the last weeks of Brauzeit. It was then that the diktat of Emperor Boris against the *Dienstleute* bore its ugly fruit. Discharged from the service of their noble lords, unable to find work to sustain themselves, the dispossessed peasants had mobilised under the leadership of a grizzled old firebrand named Wilhelm Engel. A veteran of many campaigns, a soldier who had served as adjutant to generals and warlords, Engel organised his people with military precision and discipline. In those last weeks of Brauzeit, he led five thousand starving soldiers into the streets of Altdorf to seek redress from the Emperor in whose name they had fought.

From across the Empire, from every province, the *Dienstleute* continued to come. Every morning, a delegation from Engel would appear before the marble gates of the Imperial Palace with a petition, a request to treat with the Emperor and plead their cause before him. Engel's demands were straightforward: bread to feed his men, work to sustain them.

Weeks later, Engel's delegates were still seeking their audience with the Emperor. The 'Bread Marchers', as the discharged *Dienstleute* had come to be called, took to the fields and meadows of Altdorf, constructing shantytowns from wattle and thatch. The largest of these took shape in the wide expanse of the Altgarten, overwhelming the tranquillity of the park with a labyrinth of squalor and poverty. Altdorfers contemptuously named the place 'Breadburg', and cursed both it and the scruffy squatters who infested it.

The presence of so many rootless and desperate men was a cause of concern to the inhabitants of Altdorf. The little family farms which helped sustain the city were the constant target of poachers and thieves. Herdsmen took to keeping their livestock inside their homes; granaries began to resemble armed camps with companies of guards patrolling around them night and day. For days, the people of Altdorf shuddered at accounts of the von Werra stables – the stablemaster's entire stock being rustled in the dead of night. Cookfires shining from the squalor of Breadburg told the rest of the story.

From the towers of the Reikschloss the extent of the shantytown could be viewed in full. Patrolling the battlements of their fortress, the knights of the Reiksknecht watched as the numbers of Engel's Bread Marchers continued to swell. As more and more of the park was razed to make room for the expanding morass of shacks and hovels, the knights felt a coldness settle about their hearts. From their vantage, they could see the terrible menace that was growing right inside the city walls.

Baron Dettleb von Schomberg felt the tension in the air as he took his morning constitutional. Three circuits of the castle walls had been his habit since taking the position as Grand Master of the Reiksknecht. He felt that the combination of exercise and fresh air was conducive to good health and a clear mind. This morning, however, he was making his fifth circuit of the wall and still his thoughts were filled with dread.

Von Schomberg's heart went out to the Bread Marchers and their cause. He felt a great sympathy for these men who had lost the security of their homes and positions. At the same time, he could not afford to ignore the threat these desperate, starving men represented to the peace and security of Altdorf.

Lost in his thoughts, von Schomberg didn't see Captain Erich von Kranzbeuhler until he almost walked straight into the young knight.

'My apologies, my lord,' Erich said, snapping to attention.

Von Schomberg gave the knight a tired smile. 'Entirely my fault,' he said, then uttered a dry chuckle. 'I should thank you. If not for your intervention I might have walked right off the parapet.'

'Scarcely the heroic death worthy of the Grand Master,' Erich replied, falling into step beside von Schomberg as the baron marched towards the edge of the parapet. The baron gazed out across the slanted roofs of Altdorf, concentrating his eyes upon the jumbled confusion of Breadburg.

'There are many things beneath the dignity of the Reiksknecht,' von Schomberg sighed. 'But I fear we will be called upon to do them just the same.'

'The Bread Marchers?' Erich asked, following his captain's gaze. 'Surely that is a problem for Schuetzenverein?'

Von Schomberg shook his head, his expression turning even more grim. 'Perhaps at one time the city guard could have handled Engel's people, but the problem has grown too big for the Schueters.' He slammed his palm against the cold stone of the parapet. 'By Verena! Why didn't Prince Sigdan take steps to stop this!

Thousands of starving men swarming into his city and he does nothing!'

'Perhaps he didn't have the heart to turn them away,' Erich suggested. 'These aren't a rabble of vagabonds; these are *Dienstleute* discharged by their lords without thought or provision. Men who risked their lives trying to keep the Empire safe.'

'I share his sentiment,' von Schomberg said. 'Except for the officers, every knight in the Reiksknecht is a dienstmann, a vassal of Emperor Boris. I am not unfamiliar with the travails of belonging to such station, but a leader cannot allow sentimentality to cloud his judgment. Engel's people should have been turned away.'

'Maybe the decision wasn't Prince Sigdan's to make,' Erich suggested. 'Increasingly, the Emperor has come to view Altdorf as his own personal suzerainty. If it was his will to have the Bread Marchers repulsed, he would have ordered them removed by now.'

Von Schomberg lifted his eyes, staring out past the Altgarten, past the Great Cathedral of Sigmar to where the Imperial Palace sat upon its hill surrounded by its megalithic dwarf-built walls. The golden pennants of Boris Hohenbach fluttered from the spires of the palace, proclaiming to all and sundry that the Emperor was in residence. Safe behind the high walls of his palace, surrounded by his cronies and sycophants, it was just possible that the Emperor really was oblivious to the unrest gathering right on his doorstep.

The baron's face contorted into a grimace of pain. There was another possibility, one that von Schomberg found much easier to believe. The Emperor was exploiting the crisis, allowing it to escalate. He thought back to the meeting of the Imperial Council and the outrage expressed by the dignitaries over the new taxes being imposed across the Empire. Special dispensation had been granted to Drakwald and Westerland, in recognition of the unrest in those lands. Conspicuously, the Emperor hadn't extended such dispensation upon Altdorf and the Imperial Army. The *Dienstleute* who composed most of the troops would be taxed just like any other peasant, the monies levied to be applied to the Imperial Treasury.

For all his abuse of power, Emperor Boris was still answerable to the electors who had given him that power. He had made it his practice to play one province against another, ensuring that every elector had an enemy he hated more than his Emperor. He further ensured that his word and his power were the only thing preventing these smouldering hatreds from blazing up into outright warfare.

Now, however, it seemed he was playing a different game. Emperor Boris was using the distress of certain provinces to create a state of dependency between them and himself. Only by the largesse of Boris Goldgather would Westerland be empowered to reclaim Marienburg, only by his consideration would Drakwald recover from the depredations of the beastkin. Another emperor, a new emperor, might not be so sympathetic to their plight and impose upon them the same obligations as the other provinces.

It was a bitter kind of loyalty Boris would gain, but it was the only sort he would trust – a loyalty built upon need and dependence rather than respect and admiration.

The Bread Marchers. Von Schomberg could understand what the Emperor wanted with them now. Each Bread Marcher was a displaced soldier, one less sword in the arsenals of the other provinces. But his scheming went still deeper. Drawing the desperate men to Altdorf, to the Imperial capital, Boris intended to exploit them still further. He was deliberately allowing the shantytowns to grow. He was encouraging the despair and lawlessness taking hold of the city.

When the time came, when Boris was certain the size and scope of the thing would be unmistakable, then he would act. He would send out his soldiers to put down the rioters. The streets of Altdorf would run red with blood, the blood of valiant men who only months before had fought for the same Empire which would cause their doom. Afterwards, the bloodshed would be enough to silence the Emperor's critics. He would have all the justification he needed to exempt the Imperial Army, Altdorf and perhaps even the Reikland itself from the head tax on their *Dientsleute*.

Von Schomberg turned away from the parapet. 'The Emperor will act,' he assured Erich. 'He will act when there is no other choice but violence so that none can gainsay him. He will call out his Kaiserjaeger and his Reiksknecht and send them out to ride down starving men.'

Erich's expression sickened at the image the Grand Master conjured. 'Surely it won't come to that! Knights don't ride down defenceless men!'

Von Schomberg locked the young captain's eyes in a cold stare. 'We have guaranteed our honour through service to the emperor. Every knight of the Reiksknecht is sworn to obey the emperor without question and Boris is our Emperor. If he calls upon us to ride down the Bread Marchers, then that is what we will do!'

'It will mean a massacre,' Erich stated, shaking his head in disgust.

'Yes,' von Schomberg said, turning away to resume his walk along the battlements.

'It will mean a massacre.'

* * *

### Bylorhof
### Kaldezeit, 1111

SHOUTS AND HOWLS resounded through the town. Peasants thronged the streets, gathered together to watch the macabre procession creeping through Bylorhof. Twenty men, their naked bodies glistening with sweat and blood, struggled through the muddy lanes. Before them they pushed a hideous altar mounted upon the bed of a wagon. It was a ghastly, semi-human effigy, the eidolon of Bylorak. The marsh god's statue was a monstrous thing carved from green stone, a squat, broad-shouldered man-like thing with a gaping, toadlike mouth and a single hideous eye set into its forehead. Marsh reeds formed the eidolon's hair and swamp moss served it for a beard. In its left hand it held a fish. In its right, a human skull.

The men pushing the idol through the streets weren't part of Bylorak's priesthood. Most of the under-priests were dead and the chief priest had fled to a hermitage somewhere in the marsh, abandoning his temple. In his absence, fanatics of the ancient religion had taken it upon themselves to act. They had broken down the doors of the temple and stolen the image of their god, that Bylorak might witness the devotion and faith of his disciples.

Through the streets the procession crept. At every sixth step, the men pushing the idol would stop. Crying the name of their god to the heavens, they would lash themselves viciously with scourges. The whips ripped at their flesh, spattering the street with blood. After some minutes, the flagellants would stop and resume their march through the town.

Frederick van Hal watched the procession with a feeling of horror. Some of the flagellants were men he knew, pillars of the community. Terror of the plague had driven them into the madness of fanaticism. Viewing the gods of the Empire as weak and impotent, they had turned back to the old gods of the Fennones. The Black Plague had brought a second disease to Sylvania. A plague of unbelief.

The priest of Morr could almost sympathise with the desperation of the peasants. They had watched their priests and priestesses die all around them, unable to stop the plague, unable to bring the beneficence of the gods to the stricken community. If Shallya and Morr would not protect their own servants, then what hope was there for a simple commoner?

Such was the attitude of the laity, but to a clergyman, things were not so simple. Frederick understood that the gods worked through faith, that at those times when all hope was lost was when it was most important to cling to faith. The gods tested men, tested the strength of their will and determination, for only through ordeal could the true quality of man be revealed.

The priest pulled his robe tighter about his chest as a chill swept through his body. Such were the ways of benevolent gods, but there were other gods as well, gods of such malevolence as to make the cyclopean Bylorak seem beneficent and kindly. These gods were ancient and utterly malignant, daemonic things lurking just beyond the light, forever straining to cast down the world of men. Frederick had learned much of such gods when he had studied in the great librarium of the temple in Luccini, eldest of Morr's temples in the Old World.

He had learned more when he assumed the duties of high priest at the Bylorhof temple. There was a reason he had been chosen for that duty, why the lectors decided to install an outsider to this temple. The old priest, a Sylvanian, had been removed for practising the most obscene heresies. He and all his possessions had been consigned to flame, his very name purged from the temple records. The selection of a Westerlander to replace the apostate was to be a declaration that the previous infamy had been scoured from the temple.

It hadn't, of course. The peasants still looked upon the temple of Morr with horror and made the signs of other gods when they passed Frederick in the street. The temple of Bylorak had revived the old rites, disposing of the dead in the mire of the marsh so that none need pass beneath the gateway of Morr's garden. Baron von Rittendahl's wife, upon her passing, had been interred within the castle crypt without ceremony, the infamy of Frederick's predecessor making it impossible for von Rittendahl to have a Morrite ritual – if he even wanted one.

Father Arisztid Olt had left an indelible legacy behind him… and more. When the Black Guard had come for the apostate and consigned him to the pyre, they had missed the most prized of the heretic's possessions. Beneath the temple, in the oldest crypts, Olt had maintained a secret library – a collection of forbidden tomes and occult grimoires that eclipsed even the Luccini temple's collection of arcane lore.

A dream had led Frederick to the hidden library. Morr was god of sleep as well as death and employed dreams to guide his servants. It was a sacrilege for a priest of Morr to ignore any dream. When Frederick's dream showed him the old crypt and the secret door, he had taken it as a sign from his god. When he descended into the crypt, he found everything as it had been in his dream. When he followed the winding marble corridors, he followed in the steps of his dream-self. When he reached up to brush the beak of the obsidian raven carved into the face of a pillar, he could see the spectral hand of his dream-self. When the entire pillar sank into the floor, exposing a hidden doorway, Frederick knew what he would find.

It had been ten years since that discovery. It was the reason Frederick appreciated the spiritual doubts and fears of the peasants, but it also gave him an understanding of the folly to which such doubt and fear could lead. The gods could fail men, but men could also fail their gods. Evil times need not be a token of good gods, but a sending of evil ones to tempt men into the clutches of Old Night.

Frederick stirred from his recollections, staring with rising anger as he watched the flagellants lash themselves, as he noted the rapt fascination, the hopeful desperation of the spectators. Bylorak was an abomination, a relic of days when men crawled before inhuman masters. There was no salvation to be found by grovelling before the marsh god, only a path to depravity and destruction. Better to perish of the plague than live in such obscenity!

'Stop this!' Frederick cried out, stepping into the street. He brandished his staff, holding it before him, blocking the way. The wagon shuddered to a stop, the cyclopean visage of Bylorak glaring down at him. The flagellants came out from behind the wagon, their scourges slashing into their own backs, their voices raised in moans of outrage.

'Defiler!' one of the fanatics wailed, his lips flecked with foam. 'You dare stand before his sight!'

'Bylorak watches us all!' shrieked another flagellant. 'He sees us, for we are his children! He hears us, for we are his children! He helps us, for we are…'

Frederick advanced upon the shouting flagellant. 'You are fools, bowing to a stone effigy and worshipping a monster! All men die, but while they live they must do so with decency, with honour.'

The flagellant twisted away, prostrating himself before the eidolon. 'He helps us, for we are his children!' Tears rolled down the fanatic's face as he pressed his lips to the webbed feet of his god. Frederick moved to pull the man away, to restore some dignity to the naked wretch. But as soon as he reached out, his body recoiled in pain. A stone struck him in the cheek, slashing his pale skin. A second stone crashed into his side. The priest retreated as more stones came flying at him.

The barrage came not from the flagellants but from the peasants lining the street. The procession had stirred their hopes as nothing had in the past weeks and now they were aroused to violence by Frederick's effort to save them from themselves.

'Go back to your carrion, jackal!' one woman cried. 'Are you so eager to fill your garden? Is Olt's pup trying to outdo his master?'

The jeers and the barrage of stones increased, driving Frederick into flight. Rocks pelted his body at every step, dung and offal from the gutter plastered his robes. By the time he reached the safety of a covered pigsty, the priest's body felt like one big bruise. It took him a moment to appreciate that he owed his respite not to the security of his refuge, but to the shifting attention of the mob.

Distracted to violence against the priest, the peasants of Bylorhof were once again under the spell of the flagellants. The fanatic who had kissed the idol's webbed foot was still crouched before the wagon, but now his naked body had turned black. From head to foot, the flagellant was covered in pitch. The priest's eyes widened in horror as the kneeling man began to cry out to Bylorak, begging the marsh god to forgive the desecration caused by Frederick. A second flagellant approached the praying man, a flickering rushlight clenched in his fist.

The pitch-coated flagellant ignited like a torch, his prayer rising in a single scream. The stunned spectators maintained an awed silence as the surviving flagellants circled behind the wagon and pushed the grinning idol over the blazing husk of their late comrade. Even from his vantage point, Frederick could hear the crack of the man's bones beneath the wheels.

The priest hobbled away from his ignominious refuge while the crowd was still fixated upon the macabre procession. He shook his head sadly. There was one thing the gods could not save man from. That was man's own folly.

It was something Frederick van Hal knew only too well.

## ⤙ CHAPTER IV ⤚

*Nuln*
*Kaldezeit, 1111*

DESPITE THE THICK wool coat he wore, Walther Schill found himself shivering as he walked along Fox Street on his way to the Black Rose. He'd be thankful for a good warm fire and a nice pot of ale, anything to drive the cold from his bones.

Winter had descended upon Nuln with the fury of an invading army. Wissenland was infamous throughout the Empire for its unforgiving winters, but this one was announcing itself with all the savagery of the White Wolf. Frost coated every brick and stone, the streets were a slush of snow and ice, dagger-like icicles dangled from every eave and cornice. The wind swirled between the buildings like a slinking predator, withering the faces of the unprotected with blasts of frozen malignance.

How different from the sewers, Walther thought. It was easy to forget it was winter down there in the hot, humid dark. Perhaps it was that very fact which had caused the numbers of rats to swell. Perhaps it was the cold that had forced the vermin below, seeking shelter in the damp warmth of the dwarf-built tunnels. Whatever the cause, their numbers had increased to such a state that Walther had purchased three ratters and been compelled to take on an apprentice. Hugo Brecht wasn't the most likely lad, but there was a natural boldness to him that made up for his lack of experience.

Walther stifled a sniffle as he strode past a chandler's shop and passed a huddle of ragged beggars. He closed his ears to their piteous pleas for alms. It was something that was becoming easier to do with each passing day.

Nuln was almost like a city besieged. Rumours of plague in Stirland had proven out and all commerce with the province had been suspended. Count Artur had tried to make up the loss in trade by making new compacts with noblemen in Reikland and Talabecland, but these overtures had yet to bring food into the city. Wissenland and Solland, provinces given primarily to producing wine and wool, could offer little in the way of supplies no matter the price. It was joked grimly that when the burghers agreed to pay a lamb's weight in gold, the Wissenlanders might agree to send mutton instead of wool.

The threat of famine was becoming real enough that the Assembly had increased the bounty on rats, offering three pennies a tail. The storehouses and granaries were too important to suffer the menace of vermin burrowing their way inside and despoiling the stores. For a population faced with the possibility of rampant sickness, starvation was a complication it could not afford to entertain.

The plague. Walther shuddered at the very thought. He'd been in the Black Rose one night when a sailor had described its effects. His ship had been docked in Mordheim when a Sylvanian merchant had been discovered with the disease. The man had looked scarcely human, his body blotched with ugly black sores that dripped filth with every breath he took. The city watch had quarantined the merchant's house and the entire block around it. The sailor had been lucky to slip away before the cordon was closed.

The Black Plague they were calling it. Spread by evil vapours, some said, while others claimed the hex-magic of witches was responsible. Whatever the cause, one thing could be agreed upon. Wherever the disease established itself people died. Not one or two, but by the bushel. The pyres outside the walls of Wurtbad, it was said, could be seen days before a ship came within the harbour.

The first incidences of disease had appeared in Nuln over the last few weeks despite the embargo against Stirland. Entire households in Freiberg and Handelbezirk had been placed under quarantine and the priests of Morr had been commanded to report any plague deaths to the Assembly. Mobs of militiamen, often without official sanction, prowled the streets looking for anyone who might be hiding symptoms of the disease.

Commotion in the neighbouring street drew Walther's attention away from his fears about the future. Peering down an alleyway into Tanner's Lane, he could see many people running along the street, their passing marked by the glow of rushlights and oil lamps.

'Something's going on over there,' Hugo remarked, a factual if not particularly insightful observation. He shifted the bag of dead rats slung over his shoulder and stared his mentor in the eye. 'Should we go see what that's about?'

Walther deliberated for a moment. Rumours and stories were easy enough to come by, but this was a chance to see for himself what was happening. A sensible man could only trust half of what he heard, and less than that if his source was a sailor. But what he saw with his own eyes – that was different. That he could trust.

'Let's go,' the rat-catcher decided, checking to see that the cowhide pouch where he put the tails of his quarry was secure. People were becoming desperate enough to steal just about anything, and from just about anyone.

The two men hurried down the alley, the terriers trotting along beside them. Once they were in Tanner's Lane, Walther could see that a large crowd had gathered about one of the street's many tanneries. Even from a distance, the angry murmur of the crowd had an ugly and murderous quality about it.

'Quick,' Walther hissed under his breath, breaking into a run. The crowd was showing every sign of degenerating into a mob. Before that happened, he wanted to find out why. Racing ahead of Hugo, who had managed to trip over one of the terriers, Walther was in time to see a body being carried from the tannery by several men in the leather aprons of tanners. Like the pallbearers, the body lying upon an improvised litter of uncured horsehide was garbed in a long leather apron and carried the pungent stink of a tanner. The neck of the corpse was twisted and savaged, a great mess of torn skin and bloodied flesh.

'It was them that did it,' a voice from the mob snarled.

'They cut old Erwin's throat,' growled another.

Other angry shouts rose from the mob. Some of the men attacked the little fence outside the tannery, pulling out wooden stakes to employ as makeshift cudgels. Others pried stones from the street, brandishing them in their fists as though wielding Count Artur's Runefang.

'They did it!' a nameless voice cried out. 'They murdered Erwin because he was well and they weren't!'

'Sick in flesh, sick in soul!' cried out another, and the

shout was taken up by others in the mob. Yelling and screaming, the crowd drifted away from the tannery, marching down the lane towards a little stone house with a red cross marked upon the door.

Walther knelt beside the now forgotten corpse, the dead man in whose name the mob had abandoned itself to violence. He folded the cold hands across the body's breast, then leaned forwards and examined the neck.

'They're crazy!' Hugo exclaimed, joining Walther by the body. 'They'll kill somebody!' he added, gesturing with his pole at the amok mob.

'Right as usual,' Walther said, peering intently at the gashes in the tanner's throat.

'Aren't we going to try to stop them?' Hugo asked.

Walther gave his apprentice a piercing stare. 'They won't listen to reason. Not now. When faced by a mob like that, you have three choices. Become part of it, be a victim of it, or stay the hell out of the way.'

Hugo turned his head, watching as the mob threw torches onto the roof of the house. 'Maybe... maybe they really did kill this man,' he tried to convince himself. 'Maybe what they're doing is right.'

'They're murderers,' Walther told him. He pointed his thumb at the tanner's throat. 'This wasn't cut. It was bitten. Gnawed.'

Hugo stared in shock at the body, unable to believe what he'd heard. 'Bitten? We're in the middle of Nuln! What kind of animal would be able to do this in the middle of the city and sneak away?'

The rat-catcher didn't answer him. He was staring instead at the three little black dogs. Each of the ratters was trembling, their fierce little hearts filled with a conflicting mix of eagerness and fear. Their ears were flat against their heads, their bodies tense, poised for the attack. Despite the heavy odours of the tannery, the dogs had caught the scent of the man's killer. What was more, they recognised it.

Walther rose to his feet and whistled for the dogs. Despite the evidence of his eyes, he wasn't ready to believe. It was insane to even consider such a thing. If he was right, then Erwin had been killed by a rat, his throat gnawed to bits by the chiselled fangs of an enormous rodent, a monster the size of a full grown sheep! He wasn't ready to permit the existence of such a horror!

Yet, as he walked away from the tannery, as he turned his back on the little stone house engulfed in flames, the rat-catcher's mind mulled over what such a night-marish creature could mean to him.

There was a lot of money to be made catching normal rats. How much more might there be in hunting down a giant?

*Middenheim*
*Kaldezeit, 1111*

MIDDENHEIM WAS UNIQUE among the city-states of the Empire, rising high above the forests and meadows of Middenland. The entire city was built upon the flattened stump of rock the dwarfs called *Grazhyakh Grungni* – Grungni's Tower. Men called it the Fauschlag and the Ulricsberg, believing that once it had been a great mountain sacred to the god Taal. God of the wild places, Taal governed nature with his wife Rhya and a congress made up of all the animals. Because of the creature's craft and guile, Taal expelled the wolf from this congress, an act which incensed Ulric. To bring peace between the gods, Taal gave his sacred mountain to his brother. In a fit of rage, Ulric struck the top of the mountain with his axe, shattering it and leaving the flattened stump behind.

The dwarfs had helped the ancient Teutogen tribes to settle upon the flattened peak, providing the humans with a natural fortress unrivalled in all the Empire. Over the centuries, four great causeways were built, rising from the plains below to converge upon Middenheim from each direction. Mighty walls were erected about the perimeter of the stump, forming an impregnable barrier against any enemy. For over a thousand years, Middenheim had stood inviolate, a bastion for humanity in the wild northlands.

Prince Mandred toured the battlements of the Ulricsberg, feeling the brisk mountain wind whip through his fur cloak. He often walked the battlements, enjoying the view the walls afforded. He could look out across the sprawl of Middenland, picking out the keeps and villages scattered across his father's forested realm. Early in the morning, the mist obscured everything, making it seem as though the city was adrift upon a sea of cloud. Then would come that magical moment when the rising sun burned away the fog and the realm suddenly stood revealed before his eyes.

Normally, Mandred found that moment the most enchanting vision in the world, but today the sight was blemished, corrupted by feelings of guilt and shame. As the fog burned away, he could see the squalid cluster of tents and shacks sprawled at the base of the Ulricsberg between the northern and eastern causeways. Ar-Ulric's prediction that the plague would spread had been borne out. Thousands of refugees had abandoned their homes, fleeing before the approach of the dreaded Black Plague. From places as far apart as Solland and

Nordland they came, hoping to escape the creeping contagion. Some came because of the perceived strength and invulnerability of the Ulricsberg, many more came because Middenheim was the holy city of Ulric and they hoped to gain their god's protection by being close to his great temple and the Sacred Flame.

Hope had drawn these people here, but that hope had been betrayed by Graf Gunthar. Mandred felt a cold rage building inside him every time he thought about his father's cruel decree. There was enough room atop the Ulricsberg to shelter the refugees. The springs deep within the mountain provided Middenheim with more than enough water. True, food would be a problem, but through careful rationing that obstacle could be overcome. Many of the noblemen could do with skipping a few meals.

It galled Mandred to think of his father as such a callous tyrant. Even from the height of the city walls, the squalor and misery of the shantytown was obvious. The refugees had been condemned to a slow and shameful death, a death of neglect and starvation. The toll once the snows came would be hideous.

Mandred's jaw tightened. He had reached a decision. Turning upon his heel, he called for his bodyguard, a hulking bald-headed knight named Franz. The boisterous dienstmann was the prince's constant companion; ostensibly his protector, he seldom had the stamina to deny Mandred's impetuous decisions. Graf Gunthar had often reprimanded the knight, decrying him as the prince's accomplice rather than his guardian.

'Fetch our horses,' Mandred told the knight. 'I'm going for a ride.'

An uneasy expression came across Franz's face. He could see the direction of the prince's gaze when Mandred had been looking down from the battlements.

'Surely you're not going to Warrenburg, your grace.'

Anger flashed in the boy's eyes. 'What did you call the refugee camp?' he demanded.

The hulking Franz looked away, his face darkening with embarrassment. 'The soldiers call it "Warrenburg", your grace. Because it's all confused and disordered. Like a rabbit warren.'

'These people have suffered enough,' Mandred said. 'I don't think their dignity needs to be insulted any more than it already has.'

'Yes, your grace,' Franz hastily agreed, clicking his heels together in stiff, soldierly fashion. 'But I must ask why your grace wishes to go down there. It isn't the sort of thing a prince should be doing.'

'Those people came here looking for help,' Mandred told the knight. 'Now they have been betrayed and abandoned. Someone has to let them know they haven't been forgotten, that not everyone up here is blind to their suffering.'

'His highness won't be happy, your grace,' Franz said.

'You let me worry about the Graf,' Mandred said. 'Just have the horses ready.'

MANDRED FELT PROUD as he rode towards the East Gate, proud to defy the unjust position adopted by his father, proud to be standing up for the dignity of his fellow man. There was a time, he knew, when Graf Gunthar would have been proud too. He could still remember the day when his father had stripped a despotic raugraf of his lands and title for the crime of abusing his peasants. The Graf had explained his actions to his son, observing that no matter how high a man's station, he had to remember that he was still a man and answerable to the gods for his actions. The most noble house could make itself baser than the lowest virgater by its own deeds.

How base, then, had the Graf made his own house by abandoning the refugees? How much greater was his crime than that of the cruel raugraf?

Mandred would set things right. As much as it was within his power, he would atone for his father's cruelty. But first he had to see for himself first-hand the situation in the refugee camp. Perhaps if he reported to his father the way things stood, he could make the Graf appreciate that these were people, not some faceless complication to be dismissed with a wave of his hand.

Franz was visibly uneasy as they rode through the market district towards the massive gatehouse which opened onto the eastern causeway. The bald knight kept looking over his shoulder, staring off in the direction of the Middenplatz and the Graf's palace. Mandred felt a twinge of sympathy for his bodyguard. Franz had always been a loyal retainer, devoted to Mandred but obedient to the Graf. Never before had the prince placed him in a position where he had to choose between his loyalties. It made him happy to know Franz had sided with him.

The prince saluted the guards stationed at the gate. 'Raise the portcullis,' he called down to them.

The soldiers looked nervously at one another. The sergeant in command of the gate advanced towards Mandred's horse. 'Your grace, his highness the Graf has ordered that no one is to leave the city.'

'That order doesn't apply to me,' Mandred said, adopting his most imperious tone, a tone of such arrogance that it brooked no defiance. Every peasant was born to obey such a voice, to defer to the superiority of their noble lords. The sergeant was no exception. Turning back to his men, he started to give the order to raise the gate.

What stopped him was the sound of galloping horses.

Through the cobbled streets of the market district, a squadron of cavalry came thundering towards the gate. The snowy wolf-pelts and crimson armour the knights wore marked them as White Wolves. At their head, his dark blue robe fluttering about him, rode Graf Gunthar himself.

The sergeant saluted as the cavalry drew rein before the gate, but he went ignored by the Graf. His face crimson with anger, the Graf walked his horse between Mandred and the gate. 'What do you think you are doing?' Graf Gunthar snarled.

For an instant, Mandred cowered before his father's wrath. Then the thought that right was on his side put steel back into his spine. The prince stared defiantly into his father's eyes. 'I'm doing what you should have done,' he said. 'I'm going down there and helping the refugees.'

Mandred wasn't sure what kind of response he expected, but it wasn't the one he got. Graf Gunthar's face went white, his eyes shined with horror. Before Mandred could react, his father's hand smacked against his face with such violence the prince was nearly knocked from the saddle.

'Get back to the palace,' Graf Gunthar snarled, his voice trembling. Mandred stared in confusion when he heard that tone. It was the voice of a man on the edge of panic. He looked at his father, noticing his body shivering under the rich blue robe. He'd left the palace in such haste he hadn't even paused to don a cloak against the winter chill.

Remembering why his father had left the palace, all sympathy drained out of the prince's heart. 'I won't,' he growled back. 'Someone has to help those people.'

Colour rushed back into the Graf's face. His body stiffened as anger swelled up inside him. 'You'd like to bring them inside our walls?' he challenged. 'Bring all those sick people up here, pack them in with our own, shelter them in our own homes? And when they bring the plague into Middenheim what will you do then? What will you tell *our* people when they lie sick and dying in the streets? What will you tell *our* people when they throw their dead over the Cliff of Sighs?'

More than the slap against his face, the Graf's words made Mandred reel. The prince shook his head, stubbornly trying to defy the ghastly logic of his father's words.

'Our duty is to our own people,' Graf Gunthar told him. 'Not to strangers.' His expression softened, he reached to grip his son's shoulder. 'Believe me, if we could help those people without endangering the city…'

Mandred shook off his father's hand, his mind refusing to accept the grim reality the Graf had resigned himself to. He had done his father an injustice when he had called him a tyrant. He wasn't cruel. He was scared.

But that still didn't make him right.

Without saying a word, Mandred turned his horse and started back into the city. Franz followed behind him. The boy scowled at his bodyguard. There was only one person who could have told his father about what he was doing.

'You don't have to come with me,' Mandred told the knight. 'I'll behave myself now. You can stay with my father.'

Bitterness and a feeling of betrayal poured venom into Mandred's voice as he galloped ahead of Franz.

'You've shown me where your loyalty lies.'

* * *

*Skavenblight*
*Kaldezeit, 1111*

THE STINK OF stagnant water and swamp seepage created an atmosphere almost sufficient to blot out the rotten odour of the plague priest. Within the confines of the stone-walled vault, the smell of the ratman's mouldering green robes and mangy fur was enough to turn the stomach of even another skaven.

Perched atop a heap of broken masonry, Warlord Krricht pressed a blood-soaked rag to his nose in an effort to stifle the reek. The dozen armoured storm-vermin surrounding the warlord weren't so fortunate, coughing and wheezing as their keen noses rebelled against the stink.

The plague priest cared nothing for the discomfort of the other skaven, his warty lip pulling away from his fangs in an expression of contempt. The simpering flea-lickers of Clan Mors were no true children of the Horned One. They were ignorant of the true face of the Horned Rat, unable or unwilling to embrace the pernicious glory of their god. They would learn, however. Like the rest of skavendom, they would join the Pestilent Brotherhood or they would perish.

Poxmaster Puskab Foulfur pulled back the tattered hood of his habit, exposing a face hideous with decay. The patchy remnants of once-white fur were darkening into a jaundiced yellow. The bare flesh of his cheeks was rotten and leprous, strings of muscle gleaming wetly where the skin had peeled away entirely. A pair of crooked antlers sprouted from his scalp, stained with filth and pitted with decay. Only the priest's eyes seemed alive, shining from the shadows of deep sockets, blazing with a fanatic intensity.

Warlord Krricht shifted uneasily upon his perch. He had selected this meeting place because he could arrive early and claim the high ground. Skaven respected height – they were naturally subservient to those who could look down upon them. In any negotiation, it was the wise ratman who assumed a dominant position without a single word being uttered or a single drop of musk being vented into the air.

Unfortunately, Puskab wasn't fazed by the warlord's dominant position and as for the musk of supremacy, even if Krricht had secreted it there was no chance the diseased priest would smell it over his own filthy odours. The warlord looked anxiously at his coughing bodyguard, grinding his teeth at their display of weakness in the face of the plague priest. He had counted upon them to present a formidable sight, to cow Puskab with their menacing presence if all else failed. They were a dozen to the three plague monks which had accompanied Puskab, that should have been enough to intimidate the representative of Clan Pestilens. Instead, his stormvermin made a pathetic spectacle of themselves instead of bracing up and performing their duty!

Krricht took another whiff of his bloody rag and stared down at Puskab through watery eyes.

'We have heard much-much about the great Poxmaster,' Krricht said, his voice drifting between a squeak and a growl. 'Man-things call new pestilence "Black Plague". It will kill much-much. Leave man-things ready for conquest.'

Puskab leaned his bloated bulk against the knobbly wooden staff clutched in his leprous paw. He peered up at the warlord through malicious eyes. 'Why Clan Mors seek-want squeak-speak with Vrask Bilebroth?' he snarled.

Krricht lashed his tail in amusement. For all their show of religious fanaticism and zealous devotion, Clan Pestilens was just as grasping and selfish as any other skaven, their ranks rife with rivalry and petty ambition. Bilebroth was Puskab's chief rival – the spies Krricht had hired couldn't quite agree if Puskab had stolen the secret of the Black Plague from Bilebroth or if Bilebroth had tried to steal credit for the new plague from Puskab. For his purposes, it didn't really matter. It was enough that the feud was there and waiting to be exploited.

'Clan Mors wants a friend in Clan Pestilens,' Krricht explained. 'We didn't want to presume upon so renowned a skaven as Poxmaster Puskab, so we approached a lesser priest instead.' The warlord bobbed his head in an appeasing gesture. 'Great Warlord Vrrmik says even the Council of Thirteen speaks of Puskab Foulfur.'

Was that a flicker of alarm that passed through the plague priest's yellow eyes? Krricht twitched his whiskers in amusement. Even the feared Puskab knew fear at mere mention of the Lords of Decay. Grey Seer Skrittar's actions at the council meeting had aggrandised Puskab at the expense of Arch-Plaguelord Nurglitch. Hardly the sort of thing to assure Puskab's position as Nurglitch's favourite.

'What does Mors-meat want-want from Pestilens?' Puskab growled.

'Alliance,' the warlord said, gesturing with his bloody rag at his warriors and Puskab's plague monks. 'Mors offers warriors to help Pestilens. You will help us by using the Black Plague against the dwarf-things.'

Puskab's decayed lips exposed his blackened fangs in a sneer. 'Lord Vecteek tell-say use-use plague against man-things. Council vote to do what Vecteek say-tell!'

'Vecteek claim-want too much power!' Krricht hissed. 'Takes name-title of Grey Lord. He thinks he is better than council. Thinks Rictus-rats should rule all Under-Empire!'

A wracking cough shook Puskab's bloated frame. It took Krricht some time to realise the plague priest was laughing at him. His fur bristled as he realised the filthy monk was mocking him.

'Clan Rictus powerful. Mighty. Best warriors. Many black-furs.' Puskab's bulk quivered with renewed amusement. 'Clan Mors not so powerful. Not so many black-furs.'

'You could change that,' Krricht hurriedly squeaked. He waved his claw through the air. 'Change-fix plague so that it will sick-kill Rictus-rats. Break Vecteek! Vrrmik take much-great power without Vecteek. Share-gift some-much to Clan Pestilens.'

Puskab's yellow eyes narrowed with suspicion. Krricht licked his fangs, waiting to see how the plague priest would react to such treasonous words. Clan Pestilens might be disinterested in helping Mors overwhelm the dwarfs, but no skaven could ignore the promise of a better position on the council.

'Vecteek is friend-ally of Pestilens,' Puskab snarled. The fat monk backed away from Krricht's perch, his black teeth still threatening the warlord. 'Lord Nurglitch plan-plot much-much to sick-kill man-things. Rictus have many-strong warriors to conquer-take surface.' A hacking laugh oozed up from Puskab's belly. 'Mors not so many-strong.'

The plague priest let his last barb echo through the vault as he and his entourage made their retreat. Krricht glared after them, his fangs grinding together. It was tempting to leap down and cut the diseased vermin to ribbons, but too many within Clan Pestilens knew about the meeting and where to place blame should the Poxmaster fail to return.

Which was why Krricht had already made other plans. The crux of his pact with Vrask was the removal of Puskab. That was the real purpose of this meeting – to determine if Puskab might prove a better ally than Vrask. Now that the plague priest had made his mind known, Krricht would simply fall back on the original plan and fulfil his agreement with Vrask.

The warlord growled at two of his stormvermin. Chittering maliciously, the armoured warriors scurried away, darting down one of the narrow side-tunnels connecting to the vault. Krricht watched them go, lashing his tail in vicious anticipation.

Poxmaster Puskab would never sniff the Pestilent Monastery again.

PUSKAB FOULFUR STALKED along the dank, mucky tunnel, his splintered staff tapping against the bare earthen walls. The doleful chant of the monks accompanying him shivered through the stygian darkness, singing the praises of disease and decay. The rustle of rats creeping through the refuse littering the corridor was the only other sound.

The plague priest's mind turned over the treacherous proposal made by Warlord Krricht. The hatred and rivalry between Clan Mors and Clan Rictus was well known. Several times the warlord clans had clashed in open conflict, great armies of stormvermin making war in the tunnels and burrows of the Under-Empire. But there were times when the two clans had cooperated as well, conspiring together to crush some third clan between their combined strength. There was a great danger in trusting too much in the antagonism between them.

Krricht had been much too forthcoming about the supposed scheme to unseat Vecteek. True, he had made it sound like nothing but the slip of an excited tongue, but Puskab wasn't believing the subterfuge. The warlord's body posture had been too restrained, too controlled to make his careless excitement believable. The 'slip' had been deliberate. The question was, what had Krricht hoped to gain by it?

Puskab ran a claw across his chin as a new thought occurred to him. The meeting had been arranged between Krricht and Vrask, but what if they had intended Puskab's acolytes should intercept the messenger? What if they had planned on Puskab, not Vrask, leaving the Pestilent Monastery?

Vrask was ambitious and impatient, unwilling to wait for the Horned One to acknowledge his worthiness. The scheming efforts of Seerlord Skrittar to turn the Arch-Plaguelord against Puskab might have inspired Vrask to begin his own intrigues. With Puskab out of the way, Vrask would become Poxmaster and chief architect of the Black Plague's further development.

The plague priest's ears curled up against his skull. From the way Krricht had talked, it seemed Mors was aware of what shape the further development of the Black Plague would take. Pestilens had created a plague that would target humans. The next step would be to refine its properties so that it would strike down other races as well. Dwarfs, goblins, beastkin... and naturally any skaven that refused to accept the true aspect of the Horned Rat. Spies might have learned of the plague monks' intentions, but there were few spies who could survive the noxious atmosphere of the Pestilent Monastery for long.

No, there was another possibility. Vrask might be trying to cultivate allies outside Clan Pestilens and the

Pestilent Brotherhood. It was just possible he had disclosed plans for a wider-reaching plague to Krricht.

Which again left the question of why Vrask would want Puskab to meet with Krricht.

The plague priest whipped around, his staff clenched in his paws, his bloated body heaving as his frightened heart hammered in his chest. His eyes darted about the dank tunnel, gazing suspiciously at every darkened niche and shadowy hole. He snarled a warning to his entourage, stilling their cough-squeak chant.

There was a very good reason why Vrask would want Puskab to make the journey from the Pestilent Monastery. Uncertain if Puskab still enjoyed the favour of Nurglitch, Vrask needed a partner from outside to eliminate his rival.

Puskab now viewed the tunnel around him through the lens of paranoia. This far below the streets of Skavenblight, the corridor should be alive with skaven hurrying about their business. In winter, cold descended upon the surface, making the swampy lanes slick with frost and ice. But below, warmed by the fecund heat of thousands of ratmen, the tunnels retained an almost stifling heat. There should be hundreds of skaven scurrying through the corridor, squeaking and shoving as they hurried between warrens. Even allowing for the instinctive fear and abhorrence most ratmen displayed towards Clan Pestilens, there should have been at least some traffic present.

The plague priest raised his nose, sniffing for any trace of what had caused the other skaven to shun the tunnel. His mind raced with thoughts of warlock-engineers rigging the corridor to collapse or packmasters unleashing rabid wolf-rats into the passageway. Whatever was set to happen, news of it had spread among the skaven of this district and caused them to avoid the tunnel.

Puskab forced a slobbering orison from his throat, drawing upon the profane power of the Horned One. The air about his body began to grow murky, surrounding him in an aura of green smog. The rats creeping along the corridor squealed in fright as the scent of Puskab's magic reached them, fleeing as quickly as they could from the plague priest's presence.

'Swords,' Puskab hissed at the monks with him. The word had scarcely left his mouth before the tunnel was filled with fierce battle cries. From a dozen hidden holes and concealed pits, a mob of snarling skaven spilled into the dingy worm-light of the passage. They were ragged, hideous creatures, with scraggly fur and pallid skin. Scraps of filthy cloth and tatters of rusty mail clung to their scrawny frames, while stone-axes and bone knives were clenched in their paws.

The attackers had taken pains to smear themselves in dung to mask their scent, but the plague monks did not need to smell their foes to recognise them. Each of the attackers was malformed, huge flappy ears drooping from their skulls and enormous black eyes bulging from their faces. There was no mistaking the cave-rats of Clan Skrittlespike. Their kind dwelled in the warp-mines far beneath Skavenblight, eking out a troglodyte existence far from sun and surface. It was rare for them to ever venture higher than the under-warrens, and even then they did so only to scavenge supplies or steal pups from the brood-mothers of more prosperous clans.

Puskab snarled as the cave-rats rushed towards him. It seemed Vrask wasn't the only one who didn't want to be blamed for the Poxmaster's murder. Krricht must have taken pains to engage the swords of Skrittlespike's warriors. Already despised and outcast, the cave-rats didn't have anything left to lose by murdering such a renowned skaven.

There was only one problem with Krricht's plan. He had underestimated the strength of the Poxmaster.

Puskab stretched forth his claw, pointing his rotten fingers at the foremost of the charging ratmen. A sickly glow gathered about his fingers, then shot forth to pierce the cave-rat in breast and belly. The attacker crumpled, his fur turning pale and leprous where Puskab's spell had struck. The stricken ratman cried out in terror, but his shriek was cut short as the skaven behind him trampled his body underfoot.

The spell had accounted for one cave-rat, but there were a dozen more to take his place. Fear of Puskab's magic was not enough to overwhelm fear of their own clanlord. The plague priest's spells might strike them down one by one, but the clanlord's wrath would claim them all. In their craven hearts, each of the cave-rats was secure in the belief that it would be a comrade and not himself who would fall prey to the Poxmaster's magic.

In focusing upon Puskab, the ratmen made a critical mistake. The spell had killed only one of their number, but it had done something more. It was a physical manifestation of the power of the Horned Rat, a reminder that the path of Clan Pestilens was the true faith. The noses of the plague monks twitched as the smell of divine disease erupted from Puskab's fingers. Their ears filled with the anguished howl of the dying cave-rat, their eyes fixated upon the fast-spreading leprosy.

Before the cave-rats could reach him, Puskab's entourage was leaping into their path. Foam flecked the muzzles of the enraged plague monks as they lashed out against the goggle-eyed skaven. With the maniacal zeal of fanatics, the green-robed ratmen brought their rusty blades crunching through fur and flesh. The anguished whines of the wounded rose in a shrill cacophony, echoing through the empty tunnel.

The enormous ears of the cave-rats were too keen to endure their own shrieks. Their faces twisted in expressions of agony, their paws clapping against their heads in an effort to blot out the sound. Though they outnumbered the plague monks four to one, the cave-rats were unable to withstand the frenzied resistance of the robed skaven. Their attack faltered and they began to retreat down the tunnel, leaving their dead and dying strewn across the floor.

Puskab watched the havoc with narrowed eyes. It was all too easy. Much too easy. There was a reason why Clan Skrittlespike was despised and outcast. It was because they were weak. No matter how desperate, no murder ring would depend upon them to finish…

The plague priest whirled about just as a brown-furred ratman brought his sword chopping towards his neck. Puskab's staff intercepted the blow, the serrated blade of his adversary digging deep into the wood. His attacker snarled at him from beneath the brim of a steel helmet, his beady red eyes narrowed with hate. The powerfully built sword-rat brought one of his feet slashing upwards, kicking at the Poxmaster with his claws.

Puskab chuckled wickedly as the ratman's claws raked harmlessly against the mail hauberk he wore under his green robes. Like most skaven, the sword-rat hadn't given enough thought to what might be hidden under a plague priest's robes. His effort to disembowel Puskab thwarted, the skaven thrashed about, trying to free his sword from the plague priest's staff.

He discovered the deed to be more difficult than it should have been. The ratman strove with all his might to wrench the sword free, but instead there was only a grinding sound. Flakes of brittle red rust trickled from the edge of his blade. Horror filled the skaven's eyes as understanding began to assert itself. He glanced down at his foot, gazing in disgust as the fur began to peel away, as the exposed flesh began to ripple with decay.

Puskab chittered with loathsome laughter as his would-be killer tried to flee. The skaven was experiencing first-hand the protective magic that had been summoned by the Poxmaster's orison. The green smog surrounding Puskab was a concentration of the Horned One's putrid majesty. Harmless to true believers, but corrosive and deadly to all infidel-meat.

The sword-rat whined in terror, abandoning his corroded blade and moving to disengage from Puskab. Before he could flee, the plague priest's staff whipped around, cracking the skaven across the jaw. The rotten bone, weakened by Puskab's magic, shattered like an eggshell. The stricken ratman wilted to the floor in a quivering heap as he choked on his own blood.

The blade of a halberd came chopping down at Puskab, snapping the tip of one of his antlers and missing the bloated priest's head by a matter of inches. Puskab leapt back, moving with a frantic ease that belied his corpulent bulk. He found himself staring up at a snarling ratman looking down at him from a hole in the ceiling. No scrawny cave-rat from Clan Skrittlespike, but another brawny brown-furred warrior. It seemed Clan Mors had employed the cave-rats as a distraction and scapegoat, leaving the actual murder to their own stormvermin.

Puskab decided to show the vermin-meat the price of such arrogance. As the halberdier dropped down from his hole, the plague priest's voice croaked out a glottal incantation. Green fire flared from his eyes, the air filled with the repugnant sound of buzzing flies. The armoured stormvermin struck out with his halberd once more, trusting that the long reach of his weapon would keep him safely away from Puskab's corrosive aura. He did not reckon upon the priest's other spells.

From the very walls of the tunnel, writhing streams of maggots emerged. In the twitch of a whisker, their wormy bodies moulted, transforming into a legion of hairy flies. Clouds of the vile insects took wing, swarming about the stormvermin, ignoring his shrieks of pain as they bit into his flesh. The halberd clattered to the floor as the ratman tried to flee, his body now carpeted with gnawing flies. Blinded by the swarm, he crashed into the wall, toppling to the floor in a screaming heap. If there were other sword-rats lurking above the ceiling, the agonies of the halberdier made them reconsider challenging the plague priest's sorcery.

Puskab Foulfur watched his enemies with vindictive amusement. So would die all his enemies – slowly and in great pain. The suffering of these would be but a prelude to what would come.

# ⫷ CHAPTER V ⫸

*Altdorf*
*Kaldezeit, 1111*

THE SCENE OUTSIDE the *Kaiseraugen* was one of white tranquillity. The roofs of Altdorf were powdered with snow, the icy banks of the river shining like a field of diamonds in the early-morning sun. Tiny figures moved about upon the frozen docks, unloading cargo from the few ships still travelling upon the Reik. So small and frantic, they seemed like busy little ants.

Emperor Boris dismissed the men from his thoughts. Shifting his shoulders, snuggling his body deeper into the nest of warm furs draped about his throne, he restored his attention to the men seated around the table. Lord Ratimir was just finishing a particularly long-winded and tedious summation of the state of the Empire.

'Half of the provinces have had a poor harvest this year, either through war or pestilence,' Ratimir concluded. 'Disease has run rampant among the peasants in six provinces, spreading faster than it could be contained. Many fiefs have been left without enough men to gather the harvest, forcing them to leave crops to rot in the fields. Worse, this misfortune has attracted vermin in unprecedented numbers... Mice and rats which gorge themselves in the abandoned fields and then turn their appetites upon such food stores as have been collected.'

Boris waved a jewelled hand, motioning his minister of finance to silence. 'Exaggerations,' he sneered. 'A petty effort to cheat the Imperial Treasury. I want excise men sent into each province – outsiders, not natives – to evaluate the situation in each district.' A cunning smile spread over the Emperor's face. 'Have taxmen from Nordland sent to evaluate Middenland, ones from Sylvania to inspect Stirland.' He chuckled when he saw his smile infect Lord Ratimir's lean features. He didn't need to tell the minister to have provinces that already shared bad blood between them to police the accounts of the other. It would serve a twofold purpose. First it would ensure that each province would have its yields exaggerated by the inspectors dispatched by the enemy court. Whether such yields existed or not, the provinces would be taxed for them and the blame for this excess burden would fall upon the rival province, not the Emperor. Second, if a famine did develop, the Emperor could point to his tax records to show that ample supplies had been harvested and shift the responsibility over to greedy local lords engaged in speculation and hoarding.

'There is another problem, your Imperial Majesty.' Adolf Kreyssig rose from his seat, removing a scroll from a wooden tube as he approached the Imperial throne. 'My Kaiserjaeger have discovered not less than six incidents of plague in the last two days. We have been able to remove the infected peasants to Mundsen Keep without even the Schueters taking undue notice. It is not uncommon for us to remove peasants for interrogation.'

'Then there is no problem,' Emperor Boris said.

Adolf Kreyssig shook his head and opened the scroll, unveiling a map of the city. 'I'm afraid there is, your Imperial Majesty. The cases of plague we have found were in the vicinity of the south docks, the Niederhafen district; all of the victims were sailors of one stripe or another. That part of the city is cramped and overcrowded. Whatever fell influence brought the disease here, we can only assume that others have been exposed. It is only a matter of time before more incidents of plague begin popping up.'

'What are you suggesting?' Lord Ratimir asked. 'That we burn down the Niederhafen district? Do you have any idea how much commerce enters the city from those docks?'

'The plague may be entering the city from those docks,' Kreyssig countered. 'I have warned you that ships from Stirland and Talabecland should be turned away.'

'Your point is noted, commander,' Emperor Boris declared. The scheming gleam was back in his crafty eyes. A bejewelled hand drummed against the arm of his throne as his mind turned over the possibilities that now occurred to him.

'I do not think you understand the potential here, Kreyssig,' the Emperor said at last. He leaned forwards in his seat, pointing a finger heavy with rings at the commander of the Kaiserjaeger. 'You didn't find those people in the Niederhafen. They turned up near the Altgarten. The plague isn't entering Altdorf from the docks, Engel's rabble have brought it with them.'

Kreyssig's head dipped in a grim nod. 'I will have my men attend the peasants we have detained. It will look as though they died of the plague. We will leave the bodies close to Breadburg, conspicuous enough that someone will find them sooner rather than later. A bit of public fear will lend justification to future activities.' Like Grand Master von Schomberg, Kreyssig was well aware that the Emperor was only biding his time before unleashing his knights against the Marchers.

'Do not allow the panic to go too far,' Emperor Boris cautioned. 'I must be seen to be boldly leading the way, not reacting to the demands of peasants and petty lordlings. A day or so, then we ride against Engel's rebels.'

'I will have the Kaiserjaeger ready,' Kreyssig declared, snapping his heels as he saluted the Emperor.

'Notify the Reiksknecht as well,' the Emperor ordered. 'Get the Schuetzenverein too, if you think they will be needed.' Boris waved aside the objection forming on the commander's lips. 'I don't want Engel's protest merely broken. I want an atrocity. I want a massacre. I want the Altgarten painted in blood. I want such a slaughter that it will make the Imperial Council scream in outrage.' The Emperor chuckled as he settled back against the cushions of his chair. 'It will be regrettable, but with more troops, such a massacre could have been avoided. Enough soldiers could have controlled the situation without bloodshed. The carnage could have been avoided.'

'You will ask that Altdorf be granted a dispensation?' Kreyssig asked.

The Emperor's laughter swelled to a malignant thunder. 'After their cries of outrage over the massacre, none of those crowned fools will dare deny my request!'

'What about the plague, Your Imperial Majesty?' Ratimir wondered.

All warmth left the Emperor's eyes. 'When Commander Kreyssig wipes out Engel's rabble, there will be no more plague.

'Is that understood?'

* * *

It was late in the evening before Adolf Kreyssig returned to his home, a plaster-walled townhouse in the wealthy Obereik district. Directing a stiff salute to the squad of black-liveried Kaiserjaeger standing guard outside the building, the officer mounted the narrow flight of stone steps and entered his home.

Kreyssig's mind was awhirl with the conspiracy he'd become involved in. It was a measure of the confidence the Emperor placed in him that the execution of his plan had been entrusted to the commander of the Kaiserjaeger. He took a cruel pleasure from that display of trust. While barons and counts waved their airs and titles in his face, the Emperor himself recognised the capabilities of a mere peasant, choosing Kreyssig, not some pompous duke, to safeguard the city. He had been chosen over the highborn von Schomberg to lead the attack against Breadburg.

He had worked many years to build the Kaiserjaeger up into the force it had become, but now all of his toil was beginning to pay off. The only obstacle to his ambition was his status as a commoner, but Kreyssig had plans to remove that obstruction from his path. Baron Thornig of Middenland was the key to increasing his station. Kreyssig's spies had uncovered certain indiscretions from the baron's days in Nuln, indiscretions that would, at the very least, heap infamy upon the Thornig name. Fortunately for the baron, he had a very pretty daughter of marriageable age, Princess Erna. The Middenlander was proving to be stubborn, but eventually he would come to see that the only way he would safeguard his position would be to give Kreyssig his daughter's hand.

The commander smiled as he imagined himself elevated to the ranks of the nobility. Absently, he noted his valet awaiting him in the vestibule leading off the entryway. The short, fat functionary was visibly agitated, his face flushed with excitement. Kreyssig thought at first that Baron Thornig had finally come around, but there was too much anxiety tugging at the valet's thick features for whatever was bothering him to be good news.

'What is it, Fuerst?' Kreyssig demanded.

'Commander, I have been waiting for you for hours,' the valet stammered. He raised nervous eyes to the ceiling, seeming to stare through the timber planks to the floor above. 'The bell in your sitting room, the one you told me to always listen for, the one you said to wake you no matter the hour should it ring...'

'Yes, Fuerst,' Kreyssig growled, losing patience with the peasant.

Fuerst folded his hands across his belly, and stared apologetically at his master. 'The bell started ringing four hours ago.' He cringed when he saw the sudden fury that leapt into the commander's eyes. 'I sent runners to find you, but nobody knew where you had gone.' The valet found himself speaking to Kreyssig's back as his master rushed down the hallway.

'Someone said they thought you had possibly gone to Mundsen Keep,' Fuerst explained as he followed after Kreyssig. His master jogged through the hall, crossing through a lavishly appointed dining room and into a stone-walled kitchen.

'Mundsen Keep is clear across the city,' the valet said, still talking to his master's back. 'And by the time the messenger got there, you had already...' Fuerst blinked as Kreyssig opened the door to the root cellar, stepped inside and slammed the portal in his face. He could hear the commander lock the door behind him, then his heavy boots tromped down the stairway into the cellar.

Fuerst frowned, mystified by his master's actions. Timidly, he pressed his ear against the door. After a moment, he thought he could hear voices. One belonged to his master, but the other was a shrill hiss. Although he couldn't make out any words, the tone of that hissing voice sent the valet's flesh crawling.

It was some minutes before the voices fell silent and he heard Kreyssig's boots tramping back up the stairs. Fuerst hurriedly stepped away from the door, snapping to attention as his master emerged from the cellar.

'Fetch some runners,' Kreyssig told Fuerst. 'Ones that know their job better than the buffoons you dispatched earlier. I want to send new orders to the captains of the Kaiserjaeger.'

'Is something wrong, commander?' Fuerst asked, unable to restrain his curiosity.

Kreyssig nodded his head. 'The Emperor has ordered an attack against the Altgarten rebels,' he said. 'It appears there are traitors within the Reiksknecht who intend to stand with the rebels.'

Fuerst's eyes went wide with shock, his mouth gasping in disbelief. 'What… what will you do?'

There was a cold glint in Adolf Kreyssig's eyes.

'Kill them all,' he said.

*Bylorhof*
*Kaldezeit, 1111*

FREDERICK VAN HAL paused at the threshold of his brother's house. His eyes focused a grim gaze upon the red cross daubed across the door. Nearly every house in the street had similar markings as the plague rampaged through Bylorhof, but the priest had clung to the hope that the Black Plague would spare his family. Now that hope was gone.

The priest stretched forth his pale hand and rapped against the marked door. He waited a moment, listening to the snow settle upon the thatch roofs, watching rats creep along the gutters, smelling the charnel stink of sickness rising from the town. He shivered beneath his black robe, feeling the warmth draining out of him. Annoyance flickered across his dour features and he knocked again.

The door slowly opened. Rutger van Hal stood in the entryway, his hair rumpled, deep circles under his eyes. Always a robust, virile man, Rutger had become almost as pale as his priestly brother. He mumbled an apology to Frederick, then started to close the door. The priest jabbed his staff against the portal, holding it in place.

'Do not think you can keep me out,' Frederick snarled. He slapped the palm of his hand against the cross. 'Not because of that.'

Hardness flared into Rutger's tired eyes. 'One of us has to live,' he growled. The priest pushed his way past the merchant, shaking the snow from his shoulders as he stepped inside the house.

'Yes,' Frederick agreed. 'One of us has to live.' His sharp eyes fixed upon Rutger. '*You* are the one.' He raised his hand to stifle the protest he saw forming on his brother's lips. 'My place is here, Rudi. I have read much. I know more than just how to put people in the ground and consign their spirits to Morr's keeping. Whatever help I can give you, it is yours. Do not worry about me. Every day I am exposed to the plague. If I was fated to die by the Black Plague, it would have taken me by now.' The last statement was made with a twinge of anguish. The plague had wreaked havoc through Bylorhof's temple of Morr. All of the under-priests and two of the templars had fallen victim to the plague. The other survivors had cast off their robes and fled the town, leaving Frederick as the sole custodian of the temple.

'If it was me…' Rutger began, then stopped himself before he could say more. 'I'm sorry, Frederick, but Aysha doesn't want you here.' He started to pull the open door wider. The priest's staff cracked against the portal, slamming it closed.

'Is she sick?' Frederick demanded. There was a harshness in his voice that hadn't been there for years, a harshness that surprised even himself. Aysha had made her choice long ago. That question was settled. He had no right to worry over the woman who was now his sister-in-law.

'No,' Rutger answered, his voice a hollow gasp, his eyes shining with dread. 'It's Johan.'

Frederick's heart went cold when he heard the name of his nephew spoken in such a tone. However confused his feelings towards Aysha, he knew he had the right to love his nephew. 'Where is he?' the priest asked. He didn't wait for an answer. The moment Rutger raised his eyes and stared at the ceiling, Frederick was marching towards the stairs.

'You can't go up there!' Rutger yelled, hurrying after the priest. 'Aysha doesn't want you…'

Frederick rounded on his brother, transfixing him with an icy stare. 'She made that clear in Marienburg,' he said. 'This isn't about her, or me. This is about Johan and saving his life.' The priest stormed through the little parlour, brushing past the porcelain and ivory the van Hals had preserved from their Westerland home. He started to mount the steps leading to the upper floor, but stopped when he found someone descending the stairs.

It was a ghoulish figure that met Frederick's uplifted

gaze, a plump-bodied man with scrawny limbs, his mismatched frame draped in a wax-coated cloak. The man's face was hidden behind a wooden mask, its face pulled forwards to form a bird-like beak. Narrow green eyes squinted from behind the mask's glass lenses.

The priest had never met this grotesque creature, but he knew him just the same. After their ineffectual courting of heathen gods had failed, the people of Bylorhof had turned to a new foolishness to save themselves from the plague. They had sent to Wurtbad for a plague doktor, one of the so-called physicians who specialised in treating the Black Plague's victims and combating the spread of the disease. In response to their frantic call, Dr. Bruno Havemann had descended upon the town like a human vulture.

'We are all interested in saving the boy's life,' Havemann's muffled voice declared. 'But the Black Plague needs more than prayers to defeat it.' The plague doktor gestured with the copper-headed rod he held in his gloved hand, indicating the priest's staff. 'In Wurtbad and Altdorf, even the priestesses of Shallya have been unequal to the task. I fear that if the Goddess of Mercy cannot help, then what aid can we expect from the Lord of Death?' Havemann shook his head, the beak of the mask bobbing up and down as he did so, sending the aroma of vinegar and cloves wafting about the stairway. He shifted his gaze to Rutger. 'No, we must look to science to defend ourselves from this scourge. You did right, Herr van Hal, when you summoned me. The boy is very sick, but with proper care, it is my conviction that he may be saved.'

Rutger's tired eyes lit up when he heard Havemann's words. He rushed past Frederick, running to embrace the physician who had restored hope for his son. The doktor cringed from the merchant's outstretched arms, fending him off with the point of his rod. Recalling the plague doktor's abhorrence of physical contact, an abashed Rutger kept his distance.

'What must we do?' he asked in a sheepish voice.

The sight of his brother meekly deferring to Havemann brought Frederick's blood to a boil. Angrily he slammed the butt of his staff against the steps. 'Rudi! You're not going to listen to this charlatan!'

The crow-faced mask shifted its stare back onto the priest. 'Science can save the boy,' Havemann stated. 'Can you say the same of your god?' The plague doktor returned his attention to Rutger. 'I will need to prepare certain elixirs which must be given to rebalance the humours in Johan's body. The plague is caused by black spiders, their poison is what brings the disease. It will be necessary to bleed the boy and drain the poison from his veins.'

The plague doktor paused, his shoulders sagging as a deep sigh left his body. 'All of this will be time-consuming and expensive,' Havemann apologised.

Rutger's hand fell to the money pouch on his belt. The merchant didn't count the coins he withdrew, but simply held them out to the physician. Frederick noted with bitter amusement that Havemann wasn't so reluctant to touch his brother's hand now that there was money in it.

'The boy is resting now,' Havemann said, his gloved hand closing about Rutger's silver. The plague doktor rolled his wrist in a subtle effort to gauge how much he had been given. 'Frau van Hal is with him. He should be given some broth when he wakes, but absolutely no meat. It might attract more spiders.'

Rutger climbed past Havemann, running through the upper hall to his son's room, forgetting entirely the two men he left behind. Frederick couldn't see the triumphant smile on Havemann's face as the plague doktor continued his descent, but he knew it was there just the same. As he neared the bottom of the stairs, Havemann stared into Frederick's face, waiting for the priest to step aside.

'Take your money and forsake this imposture,' Frederick warned.

'You sound like all priests,' Havemann sneered. 'It doesn't matter what god you serve, all of you resent progress and science. You allow faith to stand in the way of reason.'

'Faith can move mountains,' Frederick countered. The plague doktor's eyes narrowed with anger. Using his rod, he shoved the priest out of his way.

'How is faith at curing plague?' Havemann asked as he stalked from the home.

Frederick turned to watch the doktor's retreat. 'Harm my family,' he said, his voice a hollow whisper, 'and you will find out what a man's faith can do.'

*Skavenblight*
*Kaldezeit, 1111*

MEGALITHIC IN ITS proportions, the Abattoir was a relic of the dim past. Constructed from gigantic columns of limestone, the structure existed as a series of towering arcades piled one atop the other, circling around a central arena. In the time before the Thirteenth Hour, the structure had been at the heart of the human civilisation which once ruled over this land and had built the great city from whose ruins the decayed splendour of Skavenblight had arisen. The amphitheatre had been designed to seat tens of thousands of spectators, a testament to the power and expanse of its human builders.

What games and spectacles, what pageants and plays had once drawn crowds to the arena the lords of Skavenblight neither knew nor cared. Even the name of the structure had been lost in the dust of time. Its new masters had given it a new title, one that better reflected its new purpose. It was the Abattoir.

An arena that could seat sixty thousand humans was inconsequential to the masters of Skavenblight. Atop the stone arcades they had ordered new tiers to be constructed, rising ever higher above the limestone, each succeeding layer more rickety and ramshackle than the last. In their religious zeal, the ratlords demanded a further seven layers to be built above the arena, bringing the total to the sacred thirteen. The expansion made it possible to cram half a million squealing, squeaking skaven into the galleries. A deranged mass of braces and supports struggled to restrain the chaotic jumble of carpentry – rarely succeeding for long. With terrifying regularity portions of the wooden scaffolds would collapse, spilling hundreds of ratmen to their deaths. Twice in its history, the entire Abattoir had rumbled and groaned as all of the wooden tiers came crashing down.

Such catastrophes were taken as a matter of course by the skaven. Any disaster which affected someone else was of little concern to the individual ratman. The service provided by the Abattoir was too important to the denizens of Skavenblight to do without. For the weak and the downtrodden, the Abattoir offered an escape from the drudgery of their lives. For the more successful ratmen there was gambling and the thousand other vices that nestled close to the arena. For the Lords of Decay there was security, a novelty to distract the teeming hordes of Skavenblight and make them forget their hungry bellies and flea-infested fur.

Puskab Foulfur rested upon one of the stone seats lining the third ring of arcades. The limestone was worn smooth from generations of skaven crawling over it and the plague priest had to fight against the sensation that he would simply slide off and go careening down into the lower levels. He knew it was only a trick of the mind, that he was in no real danger. The dangerous seats were those below, close to the arena floor, well within the grasp of any beast or slave that managed to escape.

The plague priest lifted his grotesque face and scowled as a little body went hurtling earthwards from one of the upper tiers. He cringed as he waited to hear the groan of timbers and the snapping of ropes, but no such sound drifted down to him. The superstructure wasn't collapsing – it was simply that one of the ratmen swarming about the cheap seats had taken a misstep and fallen. Or had been pushed, which was actually more likely. A network of posts and crossbeams rose above the stone arcades especially to intercept such falling bodies lest some prominent skaven be crushed by one of the hurtling wretches. The posts, however, didn't always block a ratkin's fall. Puskab breathed a bit better when he heard the crunch of the ratman's body a few hundred yards to his left.

After escaping from Clan Mors's killers and the intrigues of Vrask Bilebroth, it would be ignominious to be killed in a stupid accident. Or was that just what it would appear to be? Puskab squinted up at the wooden scaffolds, trying to gauge whether it would be possible to aim a body launched from such height with any degree of accuracy.

Puskab gnashed his fangs together. He was being

paranoid. Vrask was gone, fleeing Skavenblight with his tail between his legs. Puskab had escaped the trap Vrask had laid for him. Knowing how Nurglitch would react to this attempt upon his favourite disciple, Vrask had fled before any action could be taken against him.

Still, Puskab was unwilling to feel too secure. Vrask possessed friends in high places, friends who had warned him before Puskab's acolytes could come looking for him. And the traitor had allies outside Clan Pestilens. There was no saying how deep Vrask's ties with Clan Mors ran, or how much he had promised them. Depending on what Krricht might hope to gain, the zeal with which his sword-rats might pursue Puskab could be considerable.

For this reason, Puskab had come to the Abattoir, to cultivate his own allies beyond the confines of the Pestilent Brotherhood. If Krricht had more to fear than the displeasure of Clan Pestilens alone, he might forget whatever compact he had formed with Vrask.

Squeaks of excitement shuddered through the Abattoir as hundreds of thousands of ratmen greeted the activity unfolding on the arena floor with bloodthirsty glee. A great pit had opened up in the sandy surface of the arena, exposing a patch of impenetrable blackness. The skavenslaves mopping up the blood and offal from the last event screeched in terror, scrambling towards the little iron gates set into the wall. Their wails grew even more despondent when they found the gates firmly shut, callous guards jeering at them from behind the bars.

From the pit, that which the slaves feared crawled into view and a hush fell across the spectators. The creature was as big as a bear, its ghastly body covered in shiny black plates of chitin. Eight clawed legs sprouted from the sides of a squat, elongated body. Immense arms tipped with hideous pincers protruded from the front of the monster. The beast's face stretched across the front of its body without even the semblance of a head. Two clusters of lustrous eyes gleamed with a ruby glow above a gaping maw ringed with chitinous mandibles. Rearing from the monster's back, arching above its body, was a long muscular tail, its tip swollen with a dagger-like barb. Poison glistened from the tip of the barb, dripping down onto the creature's armoured back.

The hush passed. The crowd cried out in anticipation as the gigantic scorpion scuttled across the arena, charging straight towards the panicked slaves.

'Magnificent, yes-yes,' chortled the ratman seated above Puskab. Blight Tenscratch, Wormlord of Clan Verms, rested his twisted body in a high-backed chair, attended by a gaggle of tawny-furred slaves and ringed by a phalanx of armoured warriors. The wormlord seldom missed an arena fight. Next to worm-oil and beauty-ticks, the arena represented the most prosperous of Clan Verms's ventures. The bug-breeders produced a loathsome menagerie of horrifying abominations for the Abattoir. None were so popular with the crowd as the giant deathwalkers.

Puskab kept his voice indifferent, all trace of intimidation from his posture. 'It is scary-nasty, Most Murderous Tyrant.'

Blight chittered with laughter, raising a crooked arm and gesturing at the giant scorpion. The arachnid had reached one of the slaves, gripping the doomed ratman in its massive pincers while it stabbed its lethal sting into his chest.

'Only a demonstration,' Blight said. 'The real spectacle begins when that gate opens.' He pointed a claw at a massive steel-banded door set into the side of the arena just below the first row of the lower arcade. 'Clan Moulder promises something new. Something they think can beat my deathwalkers.' The Wormlord bared his fangs in a scornful sneer.

'Clan Verms very-much powerful,' Puskab agreed. He didn't add that they were also the most detested and abhorred of the Greater Clans, blamed for the legions of fleas and parasites that beset skavendom. 'That is why I want-like speak-squeak with your Despotic Magnificence.'

Blight's ears were masses of scar tissue, overwhelmed by the cluster of multi-coloured ticks which had fastened to them. Even so, they were able to flatten themselves against the Wormlord's skull, a gesture that bespoke the most condescending of humour.

'I know-know why Poxmaster Puskab wants to speak,' Blight said. From the arena, a shrill cry announced that the scorpion had claimed a second victim. 'Pestilens need-take help with plague-plan.'

Puskab's glands clenched as he heard Blight speak. If the skaven of Clan Verms knew how the plague was transmitted they could thwart all of Clan Pestilens's ambitions.

Grinning, Blight reached a gnarled paw to his neck, picking about the fur for a moment. He displayed the black flea he caught. 'This carry plague, yes-yes?' The Wormlord lashed his tail. 'My spies know plague monks want-buy many fleas. Not ratkin fleas, but man-thing fleas. Easy to guess-learn why.'

The crowd fell silent once more. Puskab shifted his gaze from the gloating Blight to watch as the wooden doors slowly drew apart, exposing a large cage. The thing within the cage was a monstrous brute, a hulking behemoth four times as tall as a skaven and covered from head to toe in shaggy brown fur.

'Packmasters call this ogre-rat,' Blight snorted. 'Deathwalker will eat well from its carcass.'

The plague priest wasn't so certain. When the door of the cage swung open and the brute lumbered out onto the field, its every step bespoke a primal strength and savagery. The ogre-rat slapped its clawed paws against its chest, snarling an unintelligible challenge to the monstrous scorpion.

'Clan Verms know-learn much-much,' Puskab said, letting a subtext of threat seep into his words. There weren't many skaven who pried into the diseased secrets of the plague monks. Even a Lord of Decay should know such a practice was unhealthy.

'We can help Pestilens,' Blight said, his eyes still fixed upon the floor of the arena. The deathwalker and the ogre-rat had closed upon one another and were now circling each other in preparation for the first attack. 'Verms breed better bugs than anyone in Under-Empire. Make stronger flea for Pestilens. Carry plague far-far. Infect many more man-things.'

Puskab shifted uneasily in his seat, uncomfortable that Blight knew so much about the Black Plague and how it was spread. 'I talk-speak to Arch-Plaguelord,' he said. 'Listen-learn if he like-like help from Verms.'

Blight clapped his paws together in glee. The scorpion lunged at the ogre-rat, its pincers ripping into the brute's flesh. He turned his gaze reluctantly back towards Puskab. 'You came here to help yourself, but I must have something in return. If you want-like Verms to protect you, then you must give something. I want to share in credit for the Black Plague. Impress Plaguelord Vecteek with the might of Clan Verms!'

'Arch-Plaguelord Nurglitch…'

Blight leaned back, blinking in surprise. 'I wonder at your lack of ambition. You are the Poxmaster, creator of the Black Plague. You kill-slay more man-things each day than a whole army of stormvermin! The council knows your name!'

The plague priest lowered his head, his mind awhirl with the Wormlord's words.

'Why talk-speak with Nurglitch?' Blight whispered. 'There can be only one Arch-Plaguelord on the council, after all. The other Lords of Decay are ready for a change.'

Puskab's glands clenched at the magnitude of what Blight was proposing. To sit upon the council! To be one of the Lords of Decay! It was more than he had ever dared dream, more prestige than he had ever prayed for! An alliance between Clan Verms and Clan Pestilens would make the spread of the Black Plague much easier and it would provide Puskab with the extra layer of protection he needed. But to betray Nurglitch, to allow the heathen Verms to share the credit for developing one of the Horned One's holy contagions... these were things he would have to meditate upon.

Blight leapt to his feet, cursing and slashing his claws across the snout of a nearby slave. He shook his fist at the arena below.

The ogre-rat had managed to free itself from the scorpion's pincers, its brawn such that one of the claws had been torn in half. Now the brute had its arms wrapped about the deathwalker's tail. While the arachnid scrambled to escape the hairy hulk's grip, the ogre-rat's powerful muscles flexed. With a ghastly popping noise and the rending of fibrous tendons, the brute tore the scorpion's tail from its body.

Blight snapped commands to his entourage, his taste for the Abattoir lost with the turn of battle. 'Think well upon my offer, priest,' he snarled down at Puskab. 'I will not make it again.' The Wormlord clashed his paws together and his retinue began to scurry for the closest exit.

Puskab turned his eyes back to the arena, watching as Clan Moulder's new monstrosity beat the huge scorpion with its own severed tail. The plague priest's rotten face pulled back in a gruesome leer. Hurriedly he scrambled after Blight Tenscratch.

The Poxmaster had decided he would accept Blight's offer of alliance.

# CHAPTER VI

*Altdorf*
*Kaldezeit, 1111*

ERICH VON KRANZBEUHLER shifted uneasily in his saddle, watching as the morning fog rolled in from the Reik. He could just see the trees of the Altgarten – those the marchers hadn't cut down – and the murky glow of campfires shining from the shantytown. The young knight reached down to his sword, his heart sickening as he felt the pommel between his fingers. He could not easily forget the motto engraved upon the blade of his sword. 'Honour. Courage. Emperor.'

Today he would betray one of those solemn oaths. He would ask the knights under his command to break faith with the vows they had undertaken. It was an enormous responsibility, one the young captain still wasn't sure he was equal to. He closed his eyes and prayed to Sigmar to lend him that strength.

'They don't really expect us to ride down our own soldiers, do they?' The whispered question came from the knight beside him, a tall, stalwart warrior named Aldinger.

For one of the Reiksknecht's veterans to ask such a question made Erich decide he had made the right decision. The only way the Reiksknecht could respect the first two oaths was to betray the last.

The captain peered through the grey veil, staring across at the massed ranks of cavalry. The entire strength of the Reiksknecht had been called out to supplement the Kaiserjaeger and the Schuetzenverein in quelling what had been termed 'rebellion' in their orders. The plan, as laid out by Adolf Kreyssig, was for the Reiksknecht to spearhead the attack, with the Kaiserjaeger and Schueters following on the flanks. The commander had made his intention clear. The knights were to drive Engel's rebels into the river. No quarter was to be given.

Grand Master von Schomberg's face had grown pale when he read the orders, but it had only made him even more determined to defy the Emperor. The plans he had discussed with his officers were much different from those Kreyssig had drawn up. The Reiksknecht would lead the charge, but only for a hundred yards. Once their backs were to the trees, they would turn about and stage a counter charge against the Kaiserjaeger and the Scheuters. It was hoped the surprise attack would throw the other forces into such confusion that they would disperse and retreat into the city.

After that, Engel and his people would have to fend for themselves. The Reiksknecht would have their own problems. The plan was to withdraw into the Reikschloss. There were food and provisions there to endure a lengthy siege. The longer they held out, the more embarrassment it would cause Emperor Boris and bring unwanted attention to the reasons why the Emperor's most loyal order of knights had turned against him.

Erich turned around, trying to find Grand Master von Schomberg in the fog. He could just make out the figure of Othmar, the Grand Master's standard bearer, but he couldn't see his leader. It was just as well. If he saw doubt in the old baron's eyes, he didn't know what he would do.

'Ernst,' he called, looking over to see if his adjutant was close. He saw the burly knight lift a gauntlet to his visor in reply. 'Stay close to me,' Erich told him, pointing at the horn tied to the dienstmann's belt. 'I may need to signal changes in formation after we begin the charge.'

Again, the spectre of doubt tugged at Erich's mind. Could he really go through with this? Was he really going to betray a direct command from his Emperor?

Still fighting his inner daemons, the sound of pounding hooves brought a curse to the captain's lips. Some fool had started the charge early! Up and down the line, he could hear the other officers shouting in confusion, wondering who had given the order. Grand Master von Schomberg's fierce tones barked out, ordering the rest to support the knights that had started the attack.

Like a single creature, the twenty knights under Erich's command urged their warhorses into a gallop. The steel-clad destriers lunged forwards, charging out from the plaza where they had mustered into formation. Erich felt the thrill of the charge course through his veins, saw the fog break apart before his leaping steed.

Then, disaster! The plaza which had only a moment before echoed with the clatter of charging knights now descended into a bedlam of screaming men and horses. Animals crashed to the earth on broken legs, crushing their riders beneath them as they floundered upon the cobblestones. Men hurtled through the air as their mounts threw them, smashing into the earth like plummeting gargoyles. It was like listening to the roar of an avalanche, the maddened shriek of a volcano.

Erich's horse buckled beneath him, pitching onto its side. The only thing that saved the captain from being pinned beneath his animal was the second floundering horse that reared up and pushed his own animal away. He was able to drop down from the saddle of his stricken destrier, scrambling away before the flailing hooves and hurtling bodies of the other warhorses could smash him down.

Like a great steel rat, the knight scurried away from the grotesque bedlam. As he did so, Erich saw the cause of the havoc. Under cover of the fog, someone had strewn spiked caltrops across the mouth of the plaza, leaving a field of jagged iron to impale the hooves of anyone trying to ride out.

He ripped his sword from its sheath, his first instinct being to place blame upon the obvious enemy. Wilhelm Engel and his Marchers! The scum had done this, used this churlish trick to cripple the Reiksknecht's horses and maim the Reiksknecht's men! Well, if Emperor Boris wanted a massacre, then Erich would be happy to oblige him now!

Then the captain saw the furtive figures stealing out from the buildings facing the plaza, peeking down from the rooftops and slinking down alleyways and side-streets. Kaiserjaeger! The horrible truth dawned upon Erich. It had been Kreyssig's men who had strewn the road with caltrops. Many of them had been hunters and woodsmen, they would have the skills to sneak in and leave such a hideous surprise under cover of the fog!

In the hands of each of the black-clad soldiers the slender curve of a bow was held at the ready. The Reiksknecht inside the plaza were hopelessly surrounded; the only way open to them lay across the field of caltrops and the bodies of their own injured comrades.

Kreyssig had plotted well. Somehow he had learned of Grand Master von Schomberg's intention to stop the massacre. With murderous planning, the commander had neutralised an entire order of knights. Screams rising from the Altgarten, raging fires blazing from the squalor of Breadburg showed that Kreyssig had even reserved enough of his forces to still carry out his original mission.

'Knights of the Reiksknecht,' a grating voice called out. 'Lay down your weapons and submit to the Emperor's justice!'

Erich could see the archers draw back their arrows, taking aim at the trapped knights. He looked around him for something, anything he could use to help his comrades. All he found was Aldinger trying to pull himself out from under the writhing body of his horse. A caltrop had stabbed through the flesh of his hand, three others piercing the body of his horse. Erich made his decisions at once, rushing to the knight's aid. Maybe he couldn't help the men in the plaza, but he could help Aldinger.

As he helped the pinned knight lift the body of his horse, Erich kept his gaze fixed upon the plaza. Grand Master von Schomberg was both brave and bold. He wouldn't submit meekly to a tyrant.

'Sigmar will be my judge!' von Schomberg's voice rose in a defiant shout. At his order, the knights in the plaza spurred their horses towards the caltrops, forcing the huge animals out from the trap, urging them to trample the bodies of wounded men and horses.

The command to loose arrows was given. The shrieks of horses and the screams of men rang out from the plaza as the volley struck. Others, however, came thundering out into the road. Many of the knights fell, the hooves of their horses punctured by the spiked caltrops, but others fought their way clear. Archers rushed over the rooftops to shoot them down, but the effort was too late. Erich could count at least twenty knights galloping away into the growing dawn, scattering into the streets of Altdorf.

He dragged his eyes away from the scene, closing his ears to the moans and cries of injured men. His arm supporting Aldinger's weight, he led the wounded dienstmann into the shadow of an alleyway. He leaned the injured man against the plaster-covered wall.

The Kaiserjaeger would be coming soon, looking for survivors. There was only one way to foil such expert trackers. Erich knelt to the ground, brushing away snow until he uncovered the stone cover of a sewer drain. It took him valuable minutes to pick away at the grime caked around the cover. While he worked, he could hear the Kaiserjaeger moving among the fallen Reiksknecht, evaluating each of the wounded. A ghastly gurgle told when they found a knight they thought too injured to stand trial.

The cover came free just as the Kaiserjaeger began searching the field of caltrops. Hastily, Erich lowered Aldinger down into the reeking warmth of the sewer. The captain followed a moment later, dragging the lid back into place before dropping down into the darkness.

Just as the lid settled into place, Erich heard the voice of the Kaiserjaeger officer again.

'Leave that one,' the officer snarled. 'Commander Kreyssig will want him no matter how beat up he is. It isn't every day you get to hang a Grand Master.'

\* \* \*

*Nuln*
*Kaldezeit, 1111*

'WE LIVE IN an age of science and reason, not idiotic superstition!'

The statement was given voice by Lord Karl-Joachim Kleinheistkamp, a wrinkled old man, his bald head unconvincingly covered by a horsehair wig, the buttons on his broad coat displaying a veneer of tarnish and smut. He affected the pompous confidence of a man secure in his authority and with no time for anything that did not fit neatly into the world described in his books and papers. All in all, Kleinheistkamp was typical of the Universität's professors.

Walther was discovering that frustrating fact. Kleinheistkamp was the third professor he'd managed to lure to the Black Rose and he was the third to openly laugh at the rat-catcher's story. He cast a despairing glance towards Zena, but all she did was shake her head and vanish into the kitchen. Hugo might have been more sympathetic if he wasn't too busy trying to teach the three ratters how to sit up and beg.

Bremer wore a big smile though, happily refilling the professor's stein at every opportunity. Walther winced each time he saw the taverneer grab for Kleinheistkamp's mug. For an old man, his lordship had a prodigious capacity, especially when Walther was paying. It seemed a noble title wasn't enough to keep some people from guzzling another man's beer.

'What you describe is simply impossible!' Kleinheistkamp declared, wiping foam from his moustache with the back of his hand. 'This is an enlightened age! We know now that there are rules to spontaneous generation. A salamander is created by fire, flies generate from unburied corpses, but higher forms, things like cattle and swine, must be created in the proper manner. We know that maternal impression causes malformations in offspring, not the diet or habits of the mother as simple herb wives would have it. We know that a cockatrice is spawned from the egg of a rooster exposed to the rays of Morrslieb and that it is not, as our less educated forebears would have us believe, the result of a serpent having congress with a hen.'

Walther could feel the veins pounding in his forehead. The professor had been prattling on like this for the better part of an hour, straying into subjects beyond either his ability or his desire to follow. 'That is all well, my lord, but about the rat...'

'Such a creature is impossible,' Kleinheistkamp said, tapping the wooden counter by way of emphasis. Bremer decided to take it as an appeal for the stein to be refilled. 'A rat as large as you describe would be crushed under its own weight! It wouldn't be able to move, much less launch itself at a grown man and bite out his throat!'

'I've hunted rats all my life,' Walther growled back. He held his hand out so that the professor could see the scars. 'I know what a rat bite looks like.'

Kleinheistkamp smiled and shook his head. 'I know you think you know what you saw,' he explained, his voice adopting the condescending tolerance of a parent teaching a child. 'But I'm afraid you just don't have the understanding to make a judgement of that sort. Isn't it more likely that the vigilantes were right? Somebody cut the fellow's throat and your imagination did the rest. You are so accustomed to seeing the violent handiwork of vermin that you unconsciously made a similar creature responsible for the tanner's murder.'

The old man took a long pull from the stein and rose from his chair. 'I grant that the mob was impetuous blaming plague victims, but I guarantee that a human malefactor was responsible. Robbery, not monstrosity, was behind the tanner's death.'

Chuckling under his breath, Lord Kleinheistkamp tottered off. Walther felt his stomach turn as he watched the pompous old man leave. The professor had marked his last chance to get somebody at the Universität to listen to his story. Entertaining the scholars while they smugly dismissed what he had seen with his own eyes had cost the rat-catcher the better part of twelve schillings. He would be weeks recouping the loss.

Bremer reached out to clear away Kleinheistkamp's mug. The taverneer squinted at the stein as he lifted it. 'His lordship left a bit,' he said, turning towards Walther and offering the mug to him.

'Drink it yourself,' Walther hissed, clenching his fist in frustration. Bremer shrugged and downed the rest of the professor's drink.

'They're fools,' Walther snarled. 'Blind idiots who won't believe anything unless it's written down in one of their precious books! They wouldn't accept this monster as real unless it crawled up and bit them in–'

'Then why keep bothering about them?' Zena demanded. There was colour in her cheeks, a tremble of anger on her lip. She knew as well as Walther how much he had gambled on the scholars. The loss of money was one thing, but the loss of hope was something she knew the rat-catcher couldn't afford. 'The Universität aren't the only ones who would want to buy such a beast.'

Walther stood, glaring at Zena, all the pain of his dashed dreams rising to his tongue. 'Who else would buy the thing? Ostmann? At a penny a pound?'

Zena glared back at the rat-catcher, her own anger rising. It wasn't just Walther who was depending upon a windfall from the monster. Against her best judgement, she cared about him. His defeat was her defeat. And she wasn't going to allow that to happen.

'Why not sell it to Emil?' she asked, pointing a finger at Bremer behind the bar. The bearded taverneer backed away, a frightened look on his face.

'You two fight all you want, but leave me out of it,' Bremer said.

Zena wasn't going to let her employer make such a gracious retreat. 'You're always saying you want something novel to drum up more business,' Zena told him in an accusing tone. 'What could be more perfect than this? A genuine monster for people to come in and gawp at!'

Bremer rolled his eyes. 'I was talking about dancing girls, not giant vermin. Who'd feel like eating staring at a huge rat mounted over the hearth?'

'I thought the idea was to sell drinks,' Walther countered, warming to Zena's idea. 'Just thinking about this giant makes me want a jack or two to steady my nerves.'

The taverneer came forwards, resting his elbows on the counter, one hand scratching his beard. 'There's something to be said for that,' he conceded. 'A man would want a drink after looking at something like that.' A hard glint came into his eyes and he stood back, turning his gaze from Walther to Zena and back again. 'I'm not making any promises, understand. But if Walther can get this monster, I'll have it stuffed and stood up right here on the bar. If it brings in any business, I'll split the profit seventy-five twenty-five.'

'Fifty fifty,' Walther objected. 'Remember, I'm the one actually going down there to get the thing.'

Bremer spit into his palm. 'Done!' he exclaimed,

offering his hand to the rat-catcher. Walther spit into his own hand and clasped the taverneer's, sealing the deal in the old Wissenland way. Zena withdrew hastily to the kitchen, leaving the two partners to discuss the details of their agreement.

'Herr Schill,' Hugo's quite voice broke into the discussion. The rat-catcher turned to see his apprentice sitting by the fire. He'd managed to get all three of the terriers to stand up on their hind legs and wave their forepaws at him like street beggars. Walther felt annoyed by the interruption, much more so because it seemed Hugo wanted to show off a trick an addle-witted child could have taught the most moronic mongrel.

Hugo, however, had a different reason for interrupting his master. Gesturing at the begging terriers, he said something that sent cold fingers closing around Walther's heart.

'If we're going after this giant,' Hugo said, 'won't we need bigger dogs?'

*Middenheim*
*Kaldezeit, 1111*

THE MOUNTAIN WIND whipped snow against the walls of Middenheim. A layer of ice and frost caked the jagged cliffs, transforming the entire Ulricsberg into a frozen pillar, the lights of the city shining from the heights like a phantom aurora.

The guards patrolling the benighted battlements huddled in their fur cloaks, cradling the skins of ale that were their best protection against the cold. The gibbous face of Morrslieb smirked down at them from the blackened sky, casting its sickly glow over the city. The moon's cleaner, more wholesome brother Mannslieb was in retreat, slinking towards the horizon, abandoning the field to the eerie gleam of its ill-favoured companion.

Dozens of sentries patrolled the walls of Middenheim, each tasked with a different section of the battlements. It was dreary, thankless work, especially in the dead of night with a snow flurry sweeping the mountain. Not one of the soldiers didn't wish himself warm in bed, a bottle of Reikhoch in his hand and a buxom tavern girl at his side.

Such visions, however, did little to cheer the men tasked with guarding the sleeping city. They tried to console themselves by considering everything that could jeopardise their comrades who were enjoying the taverns and bawdy houses of Middenheim's Westgate district. There were the cutpurses and pickpockets, always waiting for an opportunity to steal from a soldier too deep in his cups. There was the menace of drunken dwarfs, ever ready to take umbrage at the slightest remark and with the brawn to back up their short tempers. And there was the more recent menace, the whispers that a few of the district's denizens had come down with the plague.

For most of the soldiers patrolling the walls, rumours of the plague were disconcerting, but they placed no especial importance upon them. For the two soldiers whose patrol consisted of the stretch of wall between the west and south gates bordering the Sudgarten, such stories were much more. Other guards quieted their fears by telling themselves Graf Gunthar's decree made it impossible for the plague to reach the top of the Ulricsberg. These men knew otherwise.

'Halt and be recognised!' one of the soldiers challenged as a shape lurched out of the darkness. His halberd trembled in his hand.

'A friend,' an oily voice coughed. From the gloom, a heavy-set man emerged into the moonlight, his body bundled in a thick bearskin cloak, his head concealed beneath the folds of a fur-lined hood.

The challenging soldier relaxed when he recognised his clandestine benefactor, Oskar Neumann. He withdrew his menacing halberd, leaning the weapon against the ground. Anxiously he grasped Neumann's gloved hand. The clink of silver rewarded the brief contact.

The other sentry came forwards, likewise accepting a small leather purse from Neumann. A sour expression crossed the guard's face as he juggled the purse in his hand. 'It feels a little light,' he complained.

'It is the same as it has always been, Herr Schutze,' Neumann's greasy voice bubbled.

A malicious curl came to Schutze's lip. 'Yeah, but the risks aren't exactly what they were before.' Again he juggled the purse in his hand. 'About double what they were when we agreed to this.'

Neumann shook his hooded head. 'You want more money?'

Schutze stared into the dark shadow where the man's face was hidden. 'The captain has been asking questions. People say there's plague down in the slums. People are wondering how it could get there.'

'I thought you were doing this out of a sense of compassion,' Neumann sighed. 'I thought you were doing this to help those poor souls down in Warrenburg. I thought the money was just a secondary concern.'

Schutze laughed. 'You thought wrong, Oskar. It's all about the money. Don't tell me you aren't making a nice bit of silver off these people you're smuggling up here. If you don't want to lose out, just start asking more from your "poor souls" down there.'

Neumann shrugged his broad shoulders. 'I ask nothing from those I help except their discretion. My motives are purely altruistic. By helping these people, I am doing only what my faith demands.' A tinge of sorrow crept into his croaky voice. 'If, however, you are only interested in money, then you shall have it.'

Schutze smiled as another pouch of silver appeared in Neumann's left hand. As he reached out to take the money, however, he didn't notice the man's other hand. Before he could understand what was happening, a slender dagger punched into his side, sinking between the joins of his armour just under his armpit and stabbing deep into his heart. The soldier gasped once, then crumpled to the ground.

'You aren't going to give me trouble, Herr Brasche?' Neumann asked, the bloodied dagger still in his hand. 'I should hope that our arrangement can continue, despite this unpleasantness. Greedy men are a liability. They are… indiscreet.'

Brasche forced his eyes away from his comrade's lifeless body. There was no mistaking the threat in Neumann's oily voice. Even if he wanted to, he knew it would do no good to oppose the smuggler. With Schutze gone, he was alone now, while Neumann had an entire gang lurking somewhere nearby in the darkness.

'What will we do?' Brasche asked.

Neumann bent his burly body downwards, lifting Schutze's body off the ground as though the armoured soldier weighed no more than a child. 'When we are finished here, we will pitch Herr Schutze over the side. By morning, the snow will have buried him. You will report to your officers that he abandoned his post during the night.' The smuggler chuckled, taking the pouch of silver he had used to lure the soldier to his death and tucking it into the dead man's boot. 'Even if they find him, they will think he slipped and fell.'

Brasche shuddered at the callous way Neumann draped the body against the crenellations. Footsteps and the clatter of equipment drew his attention away from the macabre scene. Neumann's gang, seven men wrapped in a mismatch of furs and wool, came slinking along the wall. Four of them carried thick loops of rope over their shoulders, the other three struggled under the bulk of an enormous basket.

The soldier watched in fascination as the gang slapped together the pieces of a wooden windlass and fastened the coils of rope to it. The other ends they connected to the basket. In short order, they had the apparatus ready. The basket was lowered over the side of the wall, beginning its descent to the ground far below.

'It is a noble calling,' Neumann said, coming up beside Brasche. 'Too rich for noble blood.' The hooded head turned, staring up at the sky. 'There are several hours yet. We should be able to retrieve a dozen before it becomes too light to work any more.'

Brasche shifted uneasily, remembering all too well how the smuggler had murdered Schutze without a moment's hesitation. Still, he had to ask the question that was plaguing him. Just like Schutze, he had assumed Neumann was doing this because he was being paid to do it.

'You make me grieve for mankind,' Neumann answered. 'Have we sunk so low that we cannot understand a motivation higher than our own base needs? I told your comrade the truth, Herr Brasche. I take nothing from the people I help. The knowledge that I have lifted them up from the squalor and misery and set them free in the warmth and safety of the city is all the reward I need.'

The hooded head turned towards Brasche, fixing him with an unseen stare. 'We are doing the god's work, you and I. One day, all Middenheim will understand the importance of our work.'

# ⤙ CHAPTER VII ⤚

*Altdorf*
*Ulriczeit, 1111*

ERICH PRESSED BACK against the stone wall of the herbalist's shop and watched as three men in ragged clothes
ran down the street. Despite their scraggly looks, there
was some trace of military precision in the way they
moved. Erich decided they must be survivors from
Breadburg, *Dienstleute* who had escaped the massacre.

At least for a time. While the knight watched, he
saw three militiamen wearing the armbands of the
Schuetzenverein come around the corner with bared
swords, clearly in pursuit. As the two fugitives came
past the herbalist, a pair of men in the black cloaks and
tunics of the Kaiserjaeger drifted out from the mouth of
an alleyway. One of them drew a sword from his belt,
the other crouched in the street and took aim with a
crossbow.

One of the rebels screamed and crashed into the
snow, the iron spike of the crossbow bolt protruding
from his chest. The second rebel hesitated, lingering for
just an instant over his fallen friend. In that moment

of indecision, the three Schueters came upon him, one from each side. The dienstmann's only weapon was a hatchet, but the soldier employed it viciously, slashing open the arm of one militiaman and gashing the shoulder of a second before the Kaiserjaeger swordsman came upon him from behind and ran him through. The stricken rebel wilted into the snow, collapsing across the body of his slain comrade.

Erich carefully crept back into the gloom of a sidestreet. It wasn't the sight of violence that made him retreat. In the weeks since the Bread Massacre, Altdorf had played host to countless such scenes. Many of Engel's men had escaped the destruction of their camp, going to ground in the city. Plague had erupted in the poorer quarters, clearing out entire blocks of hovels. Ample space for desperate men to hide.

The Kaiserjaeger and the militia were untiring in their efforts to root out the rebels and street fights were the usual routine when they found their quarry. Poorly equipped and almost always outnumbered, the rebels still refused to surrender.

Serving with the *Dienstleute* of the Reiksknecht had vanquished any illusions Erich had that courage and valour were qualities exclusive to the noble classes. Still, he was impressed with the stubborn determination shown by Engel's peasants. In the face of certain death, they refused to give up their honour. A man couldn't ask for better from a comrade-in-arms.

He frowned as that thought came to him. What he had witnessed boded ill for his own comrade-in-arms. He had thought to secure woundwort and other curative roots from the herbalist to tend Aldinger's wounds. But the sudden appearance of the lurking Kaiserjaeger had shown him the folly of such an idea. The Kaiserjaeger knew some Reiksknecht had escaped their trap, and they knew some of the knights would be wounded. It was only natural that they would be watching any place that might offer succour to an injured man. Erich realised he was indebted to the luckless rebels. If not for them, he would have walked right into the Kaiserjaeger ambush.

Stealing down the narrow street, his eyes watching every shadow for enemies, Erich quickly put distance between himself and the herbalist. After a lifetime of drill and battle, playing the part of hunted animal was a unique experience for the knight. One that he vowed he would make Kreyssig pay for.

A barren patch of street devoid of snow marked another entrance to Altdorf's maze of sewers and subterranean culverts. The heat within the vaulted tunnels was enough to melt the snow that settled upon the hatch-like stone covers. Indeed, very often it was the only way to spot them, so cunningly had the dwarfs blended them into the cobblestones.

Erich crouched in the street, looking around to ensure he was unobserved. With the populace in a panic over the quickly spreading plague, there were few people on the streets, but the captain was cautious just the same. Only when he was certain he was alone did he lift up the stone lid and drop down into the murky darkness.

A simple rushlight lit his way once he was in the dank sewer. Erich crushed a perfumed cloth to his nose as he walked along the ledge bordering the stream of effluent coursing beneath the street. He took some comfort in the very loathsomeness of his surroundings. No one wanted to think about the sewers, dismissing the disgusting channels from their minds. Wilfully forgotten by most of the inhabitants of Altdorf, they made a perfect road for men who couldn't afford to be seen.

Bloated rats scampered away from the flicker of the

knight's light, splashes rising from the culvert as the rodents decided to swim away from the intrusive glow. Erich felt his gorge rise in disgust at the skulking vermin. The rats of Altdorf had grown bigger and braver this winter, sneaking into houses stricken by the plague to gnaw at the bodies of the dead. The priests of Morr had gone so far as to hire rat-catchers to guard the mortuaries and ensure the departed were consecrated into the keeping of their god with all of their fingers and toes still attached.

Erich's insides squirmed at the thought of those creeping brutes waiting in the darkness, biding their time like vultures before swarming over a man's body and stripping it to the bone. Well had they earned the epithet of Khaine's lapdog, for only the god of murder could have affection for such noxious scavengers. In all the world, there was nothing more repulsive than a rat.

The knight shuddered as he saw dozens of beady little eyes staring at him from the darkness ahead. The broken-down wall had become something of a landmark to him, a signpost letting him know he was near his hideout, but never would he grow accustomed to the horde of rats that nested among the shattered bricks and crumbling masonry.

As he approached the eyes withdrew, slinking back into their holes and burrows. By the time he was close enough to see the wall, the only trace of the rats was a long scaly tail vanishing into the gap between two stones. Erich shuddered just the same. He didn't need to see the vermin to know they were there.

Watching.

Waiting.

The knight hurried on. A few hundred yards past the broken wall he stopped, turning to his left and following a narrow brick-lined tunnel. When the dwarfs had first built the sewers for Emperor Sigismund, they had burrowed into many natural cavities and passageways under the city. Rather than go around such fissures, the dwarfs had simply incorporated them into the construction, leaving occasional cross-tunnels opening onto the main culverts. Over time, as the cellars and vaults of the city above became ever more extensive, many of the old tunnels were breached. Often such openings were sealed up again, but sometimes, when it suited the purposes of the builder's patron, these hidden tunnels were allowed to remain connected.

The refuge Erich had withdrawn to after the Bread Massacre possessed such a cellar. For several years he had enjoyed the companionship of Lady Mirella von Wittmarr, a ravishing beauty much favoured by Prince Sigdan. The lavish townhouse she inhabited was maintained by the prince's generosity. Lady Mirella was quite happy to return that generosity, though Prince Sigdan was liberal enough not to mind if she had her own entanglements outside their affair.

Erich had to suck in his breath to fit through the narrow fissure opening into Lady Mirella's cellar. It still amazed him that he had been able to squeeze Aldinger's bulk through such a tight passageway.

A torch was burning in the stone-walled cellar. Erich saw one of Lady Mirella's servants, an old retainer named Gustav, sitting beside the pallet where Aldinger lay. The peasant was applying some sort of compress to the knight's injured hand. His brow rose in surprise at the sight, unaware that Gustav knew anything about medicine and even more surprised that Lady Mirella had failed to mention such an important fact.

Then a frightful thought occurred to him. Perhaps, moved by pity, Mirella had sent Gustav to a herbalist or a barber-surgeon. If she had, then there might be a platoon of Kaiserjaeger even now surrounding the townhouse.

'Why the long face, captain?'

Erich's hand dropped to his sword as he spun around to face the speaker. He hadn't been aware of the men sitting there in the shadow of a wine rack. He was about to call out a challenge when one of the men leaned forwards into the light. He relaxed his hold on his sword as he recognised a fellow knight – Othmar, the Grand Master's standard bearer. The man beside him was another knight, a grizzled veteran named Konreid.

Erich bounded over to the knights, clapping his arms about them in a fierce embrace. 'How did you black-guards escape the Kaiserjaeger?'

Othmar grinned at the question. 'Konreid here jumped the caltrops. I always said his horse was part pegasus.'

'This idiot tried to fight his way out,' Konreid groaned. 'He looked like a hedgehog with all those arrows caught in his mail! Eventually even he realised the Kaisers were going to keep shooting him until one of their arrows did for him.'

'So I turned my horse around and charged right through a wall,' Othmar continued. 'Smashed right through a kitchen, a sitting room and most of a ves-tibule before my horse went through the front wall. There was a whole squad of Kaisers waiting on the other side, but they were so shocked when I came bust-ing through, by Ranald's purse, they're probably still standing there with their mouths hanging open!'

Erich laughed at the knight's daring escape. 'By Sig-mar, it's amazing to see you two, but how did you ever find us?'

'You can thank your lady for that,' Konreid said. 'You

know the Kaisers took the Reikschloss?' Erich nodded, aware that the fortress had been captured by the Emperor's forces only a few hours after the Bread Massacre. 'Well, without the castle to fall back on, a few of us decided to try for Prince Sigdan's manor. The prince was always a keen supporter of the Reiksknecht, but not so vocal about Goldgather's policies as to be someone Kreyssig would be watching.'

'There are ten of us staying with Prince Sigdan,' Othmar said. 'Including Seneschal Boelter. There's a physician too, a doktor named Grau who got caught up in the Bread Massacre. He's been tending Ernst Kahlenberg.'

'Ernst was pretty bad,' Konreid interjected. 'If not for Grau, he would have died.'

'Grau is who gave us the medicine and herbs for Aldinger,' Othmar said.

'Then we all owe him a great debt,' Erich declared.

Othmar shook his head grimly. 'The good doktor doesn't seem too keen on our gratitude. In fact, he's pretty eager to clear out of Altdorf. Says he will as soon as Ernst is out of danger.'

Konreid shot the other knight a look of disapproval. 'I think it is the talk not the company that bothers him.'

'What do you mean?' Erich asked.

'You know the Kaiserjaeger captured the Grand Master,' Othmar said. His voice dropped to a whisper. 'The Emperor has ordered his execution. They're keeping him in the Imperial Courthouse.'

'Tell him the rest,' Konreid prompted.

Othmar's face split in a broad smile. 'Prince Sigdan has a plan.

'We're going to rescue the Grand Master!'

\* \* \*

*Bylorhof*
*Ulriczeit, 1111*

A WHITE SHROUD was wound about the little body when Frederick van Hal next set foot in his brother's house. The priest placed a black rose upon Johan's breast, a ritual intended to protect the young spirit from daemons and witches until the departed soul could be guided into the keeping of Morr. It was an expensive gesture; black roses were always rare and the plague had driven demand for them to unprecedented levels. They could only be used once. The flower would be burned when Frederick conducted Johan's last rites, the boy's spirit freed with the smoke, freed to be gathered by the ravens of Morr.

Frederick looked up from the body of his nephew, staring at the parents who survived him. Rutger's face was a piteous display of anguished guilt, the face of a father who blamed himself for not doing enough. The pain carved upon the man's features would never be erased, it was a brand he would carry with him always, a token of the black spot in his heart.

Aysha had an even more tragic appearance. Her pretty features were collected and refined, her lips pursed in a staid expression. She might be patiently listening to the latest of Guildmaster Patrascu's long-winded speeches, or watching her husband haggle with a shepherd over the quality of his wool. There was no emotion in her face, only a terrible resignation. Frederick shuddered when he looked at her eyes, for the emptiness he saw there was so absolute there wasn't even a place for sorrow. The eyes of a corpse had more life in them.

'Thank you for coming, Frederick,' Rutger said, each word quivering as it left him.

'How could I not come?' the priest said. He placed a hand upon the grieving father's shoulder. 'I would not leave him for the corpse collectors, to be dumped into their cart like a slab of meat. While it is in my power, Johan will have all the dignity a van Hal deserves.'

'And when the time comes, will you do the same for us?' Aysha's voice was as careful and precise as the rigid poise of her face.

Frederick bowed his hooded head. He didn't want to discuss such things. He had just lost one member of his family. He didn't want to talk about losing the others. Rutger and Aysha were all he had now. He didn't want to think about them being gone.

Yet he knew he must. He knew they must. The Black Plague was merciless and rapacious, a prowling wolf that glutted itself not with a single victim but with an entire household. Where the plague struck once, it soon reared its monstrous face again.

Frederick placed his hand upon Johan's head, feeling the cold flesh of the boy through the shroud. For all of Dr Havemann's vaunted knowledge and skill, the plague doktor had failed to save his patient. The barbaric treatments Johan had suffered had been for nothing.

A hideous suspicion suddenly flashed through the priest's mind. His hand tightened about the shroud. His intense gaze swept across Rutger and Aysha. In their pain, they would have accepted whatever Havemann told them. Even if they doubted, they wouldn't know what to look for.

Before he could question his action, Frederick ripped the shroud from Johan's body. Aysha shrieked, her composure broken at last. Rutger wailed in disbelief, lunging at his brother. The priest held him back with one hand while pointing at the corpse with the other. 'Look!' he snarled.

Rutger peered past the priest, staring down with uncomprehending eyes at the pale, unmarked skin of his dead son. In his grief, his mind would not make the connection Frederick wanted him to see. He turned an imploring gaze upon the priest, beseeching him without words.

'There are no marks,' Frederick declared, raising the rigid arm to expose the armpit, rolling the head from side to side to emphasise the smooth, unblemished skin. 'The stains of the Black Plague are not here. I have seen enough of it to know the traces it leaves behind.' The priest's speech faltered, dropping to a sorrowful whisper. 'Whatever sickness Johan contracted, it wasn't the plague.'

Rutger bit his knuckles to silence the moan of horror that rose from his throat. Aysha said nothing. She was again the imperturbable wife, her face like a wooden mask, her eyes empty as a puppet's. Turning upon her heel, she sedately withdrew from the room. A few moments later, her footsteps could be heard mounting the stairs.

Rutger waited until the sound of Aysha's steps faded along the upper hall, then he leaned close to his brother. The merchant's jaw was set in an expression of grim determination. 'How did my son die?'

Frederick shook his head. It could do no good to tell Rutger. There was only pain in that knowledge, and Rutger had been hurt enough. Ignoring the question, he pulled the shroud close over Johan's body and started to fold the dead hands over the breast once more.

Rutger clasped Frederick's hand, crushing it in a maddened grip. 'How did my son die?' he repeated.

'Don't ask me that,' Frederick told him, trying to pull away.

'How did my son die?'

Frederick's heart sickened as he heard the frantic appeal in his brother's voice. Perhaps not knowing would be a damnation as terrible as the truth. But he doubted it.

'Too much blood was leeched from Johan,' the priest said. 'There wasn't enough left to sustain him.'

Rutger twisted away, falling to his knees and being noisily sick, every fragment of his being revolted by what he had learned. And what it meant.

Never in all his life had Frederick felt more ashamed for being right. Even when he'd uncovered the patron's deceitful bookkeeping back in Marienburg, an incident that had precipitated his exodus from Westerland, being right had never filled him with such regret. He'd said the plague doktor was a charlatan and a scavenger. Now Rutger understood that the priest had been right.

'Havemann killed him,' Rutger muttered, repeating it over and over, his voice rising from a hollow whisper to a vicious snarl.

Frederick listened to his brother's outburst with the deepest concern. He groped through the corridors of his mind for something, anything, to say to him that might ease the pain and guilt he felt. But for all his education, for the thousands of books he had studied, for the dozens of secret rites and esoteric rituals he had learned, there was nothing to be said. Some grief was too well-fed to be appeased. Like a winter storm, it was something that had to be endured, not avoided.

A crash from upstairs stirred Rutger from his anguish. He lifted his face upwards, staring at the ceiling for a moment, a look of bewilderment on his face. Then what little colour was left in his features drained away and a groan of soul-stricken despair shuddered from the merchant's lips. 'She knows,' he gasped. Rutger turned and glared at the priest. 'Don't you understand – she knows!'

Rutger didn't wait, but dashed from the room, taking the stairs in a mad scramble as he raced to confront a horror he knew he was already too late to thwart. Frederick lingered behind him for only a moment, puzzling over the import of his brother's words. Then in a chill of understanding, the priest pulled up his robes and raced after Rutger.

The plague doktor had killed little Johan through his barbarous fakery – but it wasn't Rutger who had sent for Bruno Havemann. It had been Aysha!

Frederick was only a few steps down the hall from the door to what had been Johan's room when the house was shaken by a piteous wail. The heart-wrenching sound came from just inside the room. It took every speck of courage the priest possessed to cross into that chamber. Like his brother, he knew what he could expect to find. Only now there was no question it was too late to stop the tragedy from unfolding.

Rutger sat upon the floor in the centre of the room, bawling like a small child, the beautiful figure of his wife clenched in his arms, her golden hair spilling across his shoulders.

And just a few inches away, lying where it had fallen from Aysha's lifeless hand, was a fat-bladed knife, its edge coated in blood.

*Skavenblight*
*Ulriczeit, 1111*

THE BURROWS OF Clan Verms were derisively known to skaven of other clans as the Hive. Few of them understood how fitting the name was. The earthen walls of the warren were obscured behind crawling masses of insects, the muddy floor was a morass of wriggling life, immense cobwebs dripped from the low ceiling. The air was hot and foetid, stinking of unclean life and the foulness that sustained it. Every inch of the stronghold seemed to have been given over to the cultivation of every manner of scuttling vermin.

Puskab Foulfur shuddered as he prowled the murky tunnels, thankful that the pestilential blessings of the Horned Rat killed most of the insects as soon as the creatures dared take an interest in him. The lower orders of life were always the first to succumb to corruption. Still, there were some things that proved hideously resistant to the plague priest's sacred mantle of disease. The most persistent was a strain of transparent gnat with an aggravating high-pitched buzz and a perverse obsession with crawling into noses.

The gnats had much in common with their creators. The skaven of Clan Verms were all obsessed with their loathsome livelihood. It went far beyond the simple dictates of commerce and megalomania. They didn't see their insects as a means toward an end, but rather a purpose in themselves. To breed ever stronger, ever hardier varieties of beetles and spiders, to create new colours of flea or bigger kinds of ticks, such matters formed the meat of the mania that gripped Clan Verms.

The deranged rabble were much too far gone to appreciate the divinity of disease the way Clan Pestilens did. They would never understand the holy truths of corruption. Their kind would never embrace the one true aspect of the Horned Rat.

But they would make useful instruments of the Horned One just the same. For the moment, it did not matter if Verms believed. It was enough that they obeyed.

Puskab stepped around a pool of stagnant water, its surface alive with mosquito nymphs, ducking his hooded head as a huge yellow spider swung down from the roof of the tunnel. A word of power, a gesture of the plague priest's paw and the arachnid shrivelled into a husk.

Ahead of him, Puskab could smell the comforting reek of pestilence and decay. It was only the most humble echo of the Pestilent Monastery, but it was enough to relax his glands. A few days of effort and he had made the cave Blight had placed at his disposal into a little patch of diseased corruption fit for a plaguelord.

The cave was aglow with the light of dozens of worm-oil lanterns, but the fug exuded by the oil was masked by the pungent smoke rising from several bronze incense cauldrons. Even the crazed ratkin of Clan Verms understood the wisdom in keeping their lice and beetles away from Puskab's laboratory.

Puskab chittered maliciously as he marched past the armoured skaven flanking the entrance to his lair. They were big black-furred bruisers, their bulks stuffed into mail that looked to have been fashioned from the chitinous plates of enormous bugs – perhaps from Blight's vanquished deathwalker or its spawn. The guards lowered their heads and exposed their throats in a gesture of submission as the plague priest passed. Puskab wondered how much of their servility was genuine and how much was show. There was a delicate line between the roles of bodyguard and jailor.

The plague priest dismissed the question for the present. His eyes gleamed with joy as he gazed across his laboratory. Dozens of low tables had been erected, each provided with shallow trays built from the brain-pans of skulls. In each tray, a sliver of rotten meat floated in a toxic cocktail of unguents and poisons combined in exact accord with the seven hundred and thirty-first psalm from the *Liber Bubonicus*. Only the most exalted of plague priests were granted such knowledge – any creature of lesser standing would contract Crimson Shivers from merely reading the formula.

Puskab was one of the exalted. He had brewed the solution within a thrice-cursed kettle and spoken the secret words as he stirred the mixture. Now each of the little trays with their tiny islands of festering meat would provide a breeding ground for the bacillus he had developed. The invisible vapours of the Black Plague would gather about the meat, forming mouldy patches upon its surface.

Staring out over the tables with their hundreds of trays, Puskab felt his heart flutter with delicious terror. Here, in this one room, were enough plague germs to kill every man-thing on the surface! If there were a way to distribute it evenly and quickly, the skaven could annihilate the humans in a single night.

Unfortunately, it wasn't that simple. The Horned Rat demanded ingenuity and cleverness from his disciples, and so he had imposed a flaw upon this most divine of plagues. The Black Plague by itself couldn't be spread. It needed a host, a creature to act as its vector.

Puskab turned away from the tables, strolling past a series of cages built into niches in the wall. Hordes of rats glared back at him with their beady eyes. The rats weren't the plague's vector, however. They were simply hosts for the creatures that would carry the plague. The fur of each rat was crawling with fleas of the hardiest and most fecund breed developed by Clan Verms.

In his first experiments, Puskab had been careful to use only human hosts. The fleas that infested man-things had no appetite for the blood of rodents, eliminating any chance the disease could be spread to the skaven.

What Wormlord Blight demanded, however, was something far different. He wanted to alter the Black Plague so that it could be used against other skaven. What the Lords of Decay were doing to the humans, Blight intended to do to rival clans. It was a thrilling display of the most murderous and uninhibited ambition!

Of course, Puskab was under no delusion that Blight could be trusted to honour their agreement. The army of assistants Blight had provided him were always trying to ferret out the secret of creating the plague. If Verms could gain that secret, their need for Clan Pestilens would evaporate. But the deception went farther than that. Puskab was aware that his supposed subordinates were continually sneaking insects into the laboratory, furtively testing them to see which strains could survive close proximity to the Poxmaster. It didn't take much imagination to guess what the objective of such experiments was.

Puskab bared his fangs at the leather-robed ratmen scurrying around the tables. None of them returned his gesture. Even alone, a plague priest was too formidable a foe for such cringing coward-meat.

Puskab regretted that he had been unable to bring a small pack of plague monks with him into the Hive, but as Blight told him, a secret was best kept by one tongue. It would have made the plague priest's position precarious to have his fellows around. It might give Blight ugly ideas about his new ally.

The plague priest's nose twitched as the aroma of the Wormlord struck his senses. He looked towards the doorway, watching as the twisted Blight Tenscratch and his retinue of sword-rats and lickspittles came trooping into the laboratory. Blight had draped his crooked body in a billowy robe of soft cloth he claimed was woven by worms. He held a little gold sphere in his paw, its sides split by narrow vents. As he approached, the Wormlord shook the ball, disturbing the beetle trapped inside and causing it to exude a sulphurous musk.

'The work proceeds?' Blight inquired, whiskers quivering with anticipation.

Puskab gestured across the laboratory to the cages. 'Much-much work still,' he answered. 'Horned One make-give plague to use-kill man-things.'

A low growl rattled about at the back of Blight's throat. 'But you can change-fix. You promise-say plague can kill-slay skaven!'

'Need-take time,' Puskab confessed. He turned to a little wooden box, holding it so that Blight might see the pile of curled-up fleas lying inside. 'Need-find flea that can live-carry Black Plague.'

'We will find the flea,' Blight hissed. 'If we have to stop the worm farms and turn them into flea ranches, Clan Verms will find what you need.' A crafty look crept into the warlord's eyes and his fangs clashed together. 'You must change-fix,' he told Puskab, 'or Clan Verms will not help you against Nurglitch-traitor.'

Puskab's black teeth showed in a menacing leer. 'Nurglitch powerful-strong! Too strong-mighty for Clan Verms!'

Blight reacted with a squeaky laugh. Waving his paw, he motioned for part of his retinue to come forwards. First was an armoured sword-rat shoving a trembling skavenslave ahead of him. Then came a sinister white ratman holding a big iron box. Finally, a pair of lean, wiry skaven brandishing strange worm-oil torches with long handles and a curious metal cup to cover the paws that gripped them.

'Watch-learn,' Blight commanded. As he spoke, the sword-rat ran the edge of his blade across the back of the slave's legs, hamstringing the wretched creature. As the stricken ratman collapsed, the white skaven set his box on the floor. Setting a heavy paving stone in front of the box, the white ratkin pulled a metal door upwards.

At first the motion made no sense to Puskab. The white-fur had opened the box but the stone still obscured whatever was inside. Then the plague priest's nose registered a sharp, acidic smell. While he watched, smoke began to rise from the stone and a low sound, like the sizzle of grease dripping onto an open flame, reached his ears. Before his eyes, the centre of the stone began to melt away. Soon a dark hole yawned at the middle of the stone and a cluster of hairy black legs emerged into the light.

The thing was a spider, a huge tarantula as big as Puskab's fist. The abomination scuttled out from the hole its venom had bored through the stone, rearing upwards on its back legs, its forelegs and pedipalps quivering in the air. The collapsed slave shrieked in terror, but his crippled legs buckled beneath him when he tried to rise. Before the ratman could crawl away, the spider lunged at him. What the spider's acidic venom could do to flesh was enough to sicken even a plague priest.

While the tarantula was still slurping up the melted flesh of the thrashing slave, the ratmen with the torches sprang into action. Displaying an agility honed by long practice and deadly necessity, the acrobatic skaven scurried around the spider, jabbing at it with their torches. At first the mindless arachnid simply reared back, waving its forelegs at its tormentors, but soon it gave ground, recoiling from the hot breath of the torches.

Using the oil-lamps like goads, the two skaven drove the spider away from its meal and back into the metal box. As soon the tarantula was inside, the white ratman slammed the door shut.

'We have many diggerfangs,' Blight boasted, savouring the effect his display had on Puskab. 'They will solve problem of Nurglitch. Burrow through walls of his sanctum. Eat him alive.

'Then Puskab Foulfur will be Arch-Plaguelord.'

# —◀ CHAPTER VIII ▶—

*Altdorf*
*Ulriczeit, 1111*

THE COURTS OF JUSTICE, the Imperial Courthouse of Altdorf, was a gigantic stone fortress, crouched almost in the very shadow of the Emperor's Palace and facing towards the Great Cathedral of Sigmar. Its grey walls were built from massive blocks of ashlar, great bartizans looming out into the wide square that Altdorfers had grimly named the Widows' Plaza. Soldiers in the gold-chased liveries of the Palace Guard patrolled the walls of the Courthouse. Dozens of halberdiers flanked the gatehouse, their weapons kept at the ready, their faces alert and resolute. From the heights of the Tower of Altdorf, the great round bastion rising above the Courthouse, a score of archers were held in reserve, men chosen for their unerring skill with the bow.

Such were the visible guardians of the fortress. Erich knew there would be others once they were actually inside. Traps and tricks devised by Emperor Sigismund's dwarf engineers, as well as whatever new surprises Emperor Boris and his minions had added since. Everything had been done to ensure there was no chance of escape for those languishing in the dungeons below the fortress. Erich only hoped nobody had put as much thought into people wanting to break *into* the Courthouse.

The young captain shifted uneasily in the black robe he wore over his armour. As a concession to speed and mobility, the knights had adopted simple suits of brigandine instead of their scale mail. Erich couldn't shake a feeling of vulnerability with only a cuirass of boiled leather with a few plates of steel woven between its layers. Even more uncomfortable, however, were the robes that formed their disguise. Wearing the raiment of a priest of Morr wasn't the sort of thing that cheered a man's spirits. There was just a chance that the god of death might take offence and decide to summon the perpetrators to his realm to discuss the transgression.

Erich shifted his gaze away from the forbidding Courthouse to inspect the disguises of his comrades. Even with the black robes, he thought they looked too big to pass for Morrite priests. 'This isn't going to work,' Erich grumbled.

'Have faith in Sigmar, my son,' admonished the man at the head of the procession, the only one who actually looked the part of a priest. That was only natural, since the man *was* a priest. Erich didn't know who he was; he'd kept his face hidden in the folds of his hood and Prince Sigdan had only introduced him as 'an ally from the clergy'. By the man's frequent invocations of Sigmar, however, Erich guessed he didn't belong to the temple of Morr.

The priest set his hand against Erich's arm, tugging at the coarse cloth of his robe. 'People see only the habit. They hold Morr and his servants in too much dread to look too closely at the man beneath the hood.' He nodded his head emphatically. 'That is the key we will use to set your Grand Master free.'

Erich took the priest's suggestion and silently asked Sigmar to pour conviction into his heart. While he was at it, he snapped his fingers to invoke the luck of Ranald. On an enterprise like this, the good favour of the god of tricksters couldn't hurt.

Five knights and a priest. It was a ridiculously small force to try to storm the Imperial Courthouse. The Bread Marchers had tried it with two hundred men and been slaughtered. The very audacity of trying it with this few men gave the captain pause. Yet it was the very impossibility of their mission that gave them their best chance of success.

Emperor Boris, in a fit of rage, had ordered Reiksmarshal Boeckenfoerde to muster the Imperial Army and move against Talabheim. The city-state had offended His Imperial Majesty by breaking off all contact with Altdorf – a precaution against the plague and risk of contamination. Incensed at the audacity of Talabheim's grand duke, Boris had ignored his generals and his advisors, dispatching the army to forcibly reopen the Talabheim markets, despite the logistical hazards of a winter march. The Emperor's detractors said it was the loss of tax revenue rather than Talabecland food shipments that worried the greedy Goldgather.

To muster an army big enough to lay siege to Talabheim had required employing peasant conscripts and drawing down the Altdorf garrison. In that fact lay the reason Erich hoped that once inside the Courthouse they might be able to free Baron von Schomberg. As formidable as the troops on the walls appeared, Boris's ransacking of the garrison meant there would be far fewer guards on the inside.

The six men in the sombre robes walked towards the

gatehouse. The guards posted around the portcullis drew away as the Morrite clergy came near, conversation dying away as they shifted uneasily towards the reassuring solidity of the wall behind them. A nervous-looking soldier wearing the armband of a sergeant stepped forwards to accost the approaching priests.

'You have business within the Courthouse, father?' the sergeant asked.

The disguised Sigmarite clergyman bowed his head and addressed the soldier in a hollow voice that was midway between a snarl and a whisper. 'I fear we have business throughout Altdorf, brother. The Black Plague has visited many and set many souls wandering. We are kept quite busy bringing the restless spirits peace and consigning them to the grace of Morr.'

Already anxious, the sergeant's face went a few shades paler at mention of the Black Plague and the suggestion of ghosts of victims haunting the Courthouse unless they were laid to rest. It was a combination that killed any other questions the soldier might have had. He gestured to the troops in the gatehouse above, and the portcullis began to rise. Nervously, the sergeant waved the priests forwards. The Sigmarite crossed his palms over his breast, making the sign of Morr's raven. The knights following behind him copied the gesture as they passed the sergeant.

'They will be keeping the Grand Master in the tower,' Erich whispered to the priest.

'Indeed,' the Sigmarite said. 'The dungeons will still be crowded with Bread Marchers. Even the plague can't kill them fast enough to suit Commander Kreyssig.'

Erich could feel his heart pounding against his bones as the invaders entered the inner bailey and stole through the winding passages of the Courts of Justice. Everywhere plaster statues of Verena in her aspect as goddess of justice glowered down at them, her right hand raised and holding a cornucopia for the innocent, her left lowered and holding a grinning skull – death for the guilty. It was a forbidding image, one that became ever more oppressive the more often the knights encountered it. Erich's skin crawled, an icy trickle seeping along his spine. It was as if the goddess herself glared at him from the stern visage of her statues, promising that this trespass would not go unpunished. Verena, wife of Morr; because justice often demanded death.

It took a supreme effort of will for Erich to extricate himself from the toils of the superstitious dread that held him in its grip. Fortunately they had encountered no human opposition. The guards within the Courthouse seemed just as eager to ignore the grim procession of Morrite priests as those at the gate. Not until they reached the barred entrance to the Tower of Altdorf did they encounter serious opposition. The sentry behind the gate was more attentive than his fellows, with a frustratingly keen level of discipline.

Erich quickly assumed control of the conversation when he saw that morbid platitudes weren't going to get the door open for them. Pushing the Sigmarite aside, Erich lowered his voice to a conspiratorial whisper.

'Commander Kreyssig sent us,' he told the guard. 'He wishes us to offer the prisoner the grace of Morr. I need not tell you that in order to receive that grace, he must unburden himself of sin. The commander was quite interested in hearing that confession.'

The guard behind the gate nodded in understanding, but he still had his suspicions. 'One of you may pass,' he said. 'It needs only one set of ears to listen to a traitor's words.'

Erich shared a look with his fellow knights. As

soon as the gate was pulled open, he stepped across the threshold. For an instant, the guard's attention shifted to the priests he had told to stay outside. In that moment of distraction, Erich struck, seizing the guard's neck with one hand and the edge of the gate with the other. Savagely he brought the two together with a sickening crunch. The guard didn't utter a sound, he just collapsed in the doorway.

The others rushed into the tower, closing the gate behind them and dragging the stunned guard behind the curve of the structure's spiral stairway.

'Othmar, take Josef and spike the trap leading up to the guardroom,' Erich said, his voice falling into his accustomed tone of command. 'The last thing we need are all of those archers walking in on us. The rest of you will look for the Grand Master. Subdue any guards, but only kill if it is absolutely necessary.'

The knights quickly separated, hurrying to the tiered levels of the tower. Such resistance as they found was quickly vanquished. Erich winced at each conflict, fearing that the sound would alert the garrison, but here the ponderous construction of the Courthouse served them well. The thick walls smothered all noise. This close to the Imperial Palace, silence was an essential. Emperor Boris found the cries of his captives disturbing.

It was Konreid who located Baron von Schomberg's cell. Erich knew something was wrong when instead of freeing their Grand Master, Konreid came went to find his captain.

'The Grand Master says he won't go,' Konreid reported, tears in the old veteran's eyes. It was with a sad desperation that he led Erich and the Sigmarite priest to the tower room where von Schomberg was imprisoned.

The Grand Master was thin, a pale shadow of the nobleman who had led the Reiksknecht through countless battles and had dared to defy a tyrant over a matter of conscience. He lay sprawled upon a bed of straw, his only garment a threadbare linen gown. His cell stank of filth, ugly black rats scurrying about in the dark corners. A pot of brown water that looked to have been dredged from the bottom of the Reik rested on the floor beside the captive's bed. A wooden slop bucket was the only other accoutrement. If not for the rush-light Konreid had wedged between the bars of the cell door, the Grand Master would have been consigned to complete darkness. No window marked the walls of his cell.

Erich took one look at his leader and felt a cold fury blaze up inside him. His knuckles cracked as he gripped the bars, jostling the door in its frame, testing the strength of its construction. It was solidly built, but it wasn't going to stop him from freeing the Grand Master.

'Stop,' the wheezing voice of Baron von Schomberg arrested his attack on the door. 'That will serve no purpose. You must leave me. It is important that you leave me.'

The young knight peered through the bars, wondering what delusion gripped his master. He could not imagine what tortures von Schomberg must have endured at the hands of Kreyssig's minions.

Feeble as he was, the Grand Master was still sharp-eyed. He could read the thought he saw etched upon Erich's face. 'No, I am not mad. But there are bigger things to concern you than preserving my life. Boris Goldgather has become a tyrant. If he isn't stopped, he will tear down the Empire with his greed. You must find others, gather an alliance to depose him. That is the only quest left to the Reiksknecht now!'

Erich shook his head. 'We will do all that,' he vowed,

pressing his shoulder against the door. 'And you will lead us,' he grunted as he tried to force the barrier.

'I will be more valuable to your cause as a martyr,' von Schomberg declared. 'I am to be beheaded in two days by Gottwald Drechsler, the Scharfrichter of Altdorf. My death is intended to make the other nobles cower in fear before Emperor Boris. You must make my death have a different meaning. You must make it a lesson that none of them are safe, that if he dares execute the Grand Master of the Reiksknecht, then he will dare even greater outrages. You must make the great and the powerful understand that they can only be safe if they rise up against this tyrant!'

'Prince Sigdan is already with us,' Erich told von Schomberg, trying to make his master see that his martyrdom wasn't necessary.

'You will need more than just the Prince of Altdorf,' the Grand Master said.

'They have other allies,' the Sigmarite priest declared. Throwing back the hood of his robe, Sigdan's nameless clergyman friend revealed the face of Arch-Lector Wolfgang Hartwich. Erich and Konreid stood in stunned silence, never suspecting that the second-most powerful man in the Sigmarite temple had been their accomplice.

Hartwich came to the door, smiling kindly at the Grand Master. 'You see, there is no reason to make this gesture. You can help this great cause much more as a living soldier.'

A ragged cough shook von Schomberg's frail body. 'It is too late for that, father,' he said. 'That choice has been taken from me.' Panic shone in the Grand Master's eyes as Erich made another attempt to force the door. 'No!' he commanded. 'Stay outside! Do not come near me!' His voice dropped to a mournful whisper. 'Death sits here beside me. The Black Plague.'

'You… you have the illness?' Erich asked, instinctively recoiling from the door.

Grand Master von Schomberg nodded his head sadly. 'At first Emperor Boris wanted to save my execution for the anniversary of his accession. Now he fears I will die before the Scharfrichter can take my head with his sword.' The prisoner's thin hands clenched into fists. 'But I will survive that long. I must survive that long.'

Erich turned away from the cell door, his hand reaching for the sword hidden beneath his priest's robes. He relaxed slightly when he saw Othmar and Josef come rushing into the hallway. The troubled expressions on their faces made it clear there wasn't any more time to debate the question.

'The archers know something is wrong,' Othmar reported. 'We could hear them trying to smash open the trap. It won't be long before one of them decides to shout down to the courtyard for help.'

The captain turned back to the cell, a bitter taste in his mouth. Snapping to attention, he saluted the sickly von Schomberg. 'The Grand Master has decided that he can best serve our cause by remaining here,' Erich told the other knights. Othmar looked ready to object, but the sad resignation he saw on his captain's face made him realise there was something more, something that made rescue pointless.

'Get the others,' Erich ordered. 'We can use the cellar beneath the tower to gain entrance to the dungeons.' The other knights nodded. They had studied the floor-plans of the Courthouse carefully before setting out. The dungeons connected to an older network of cat-acombs, which in turn led back into the dwarf-built culverts. The underground route had been too risky to effect entrance to the tower, but with the alarm raised, there was nothing to lose using it to escape.

'Sigmar's strength be with you,' von Schomberg called out to his knights as they reluctantly left him to await his doom.

'We will not forget your sacrifice, Grand Master,' Erich vowed.

*Nuln*
*Ulriczeit, 1111*

GAINING ACCESS TO poor old Erwin's tannery wasn't especially hard. After the man's murder, the place had become shunned, more for the belief that plague victims had done the crime than any fear of the crime itself. A belief was taking hold that the plague was spread by the sickly breath of the diseased. There was a chance that the sickly exhalations of the killers might be lingering in some dark corner of the building. No one wanted to take any chances.

Walther wasn't sure if he believed the plague was spread that way. What he was sure of was that Fritz hadn't been killed by anyman, sick or not. His killer was a monster, a rat bigger than a sheepdog, with fangs like daggers. People might laugh at him for believing in such a beast, but when he caught the giant, he would drag it out into the light of day and make his detractors eat their words.

The tannery was a filthy shambles. Housed within a boxy building with mud-brick walls and a floor that was depressed a good three feet below ground level, the tannery had acquired a thin scum of ice along much of the floor. With none to maintain the place, run-off from melting snow in the street had seeped into the building to form a crust of dirty brown frost. The big clay pots where the tanner stored the acids he used to cure hides still exuded the stench of urine despite being frozen solid. A motley confusion of half-cured goatskins and ox hides drooped from ropes suspended from the ceiling while a stinking heap against one wall denoted skins Fritz had never gotten around to.

Rats had, however. The pile of skins showed every sign of being rifled and pillaged by the vermin. Pellets littered the floor around the hides, scraggly scraps of fur and hair were strewn about. Any hint of flesh clinging to the skins had been plundered by the marauding rodents. Nor had the animals contented themselves to the meagre pickings left by the tanner. Several dozen rat carcasses were lying frozen to the floor, their skins turned inside out as their cannibalistic comrades stripped them clean. Walther had no idea how a rat managed to so utterly devour another rat. He was fairly certain he didn't want to know.

More important than the common vermin, however, had been the spoor of the giant. Walther had spotted a few of the monster's paw-prints in the ice and the terriers had uncovered a rat pellet as big as his own hand. It was obvious the giant had marked out the tannery as part of its range. The giant would be back to forage, and the rat-catcher would be ready for it.

A dozen box-like traps had been set up around the tannery. One thing Walther had always noticed about rats was their tendency to scurry in straight lines, keeping one flank against a wall at all times if possible. Playing upon that verminous habit, he placed his traps against the edges of the walls, far enough away from any holes or windows the giant might use to creep into the building that it wouldn't get suspicious. Each of the traps was the product of his own design, operating upon a counterbalance that would use the giant's own weight to trigger it. The rodent would slink into the box to retrieve the scrap of beef placed inside as bait. The increased pressure would tip the counter-balance and release the taut bowstring suspended above the box. Walther knew the design would work. He'd spent several hours adjusting the counterbalance after normal-sized rats sprang some of the traps. The bow-string had sliced the inquisitive vermin clean in half.

'Aren't you going to arm the rest of the traps?' Hugo asked when Walther rejoined him in their hiding spot between the wooden vats Fritz had used to soak the hides after curing them.

The rat-catcher sighed as he climbed down between the vats. He pushed away the affectionate welcome of the terriers and explained to his apprentice for the fifth time why some of the traps weren't armed. 'A rat is a clever brute,' he reminded Hugo. 'The traps will be new to him. He'll study them a bit when he sees them, sniff about and then play it very careful. Now, if he nips inside real quick, he might get away. So I leave the traps closest to the windows and holes baited but unarmed. That way he can get inside and treat himself to a bit of beef. It'll make him figure the other traps are safe too. And that'll be his last mistake.'

At first Hugo nodded, but then he began to shake his head. 'I don't see how this giant can get inside unless we leave the door open. The windows are too narrow and those holes you are talking about wouldn't let Alex wiggle through.' Hugo patted the head of one of the rat-ters, provoking a frenzy of tail-wagging.

Walther sighed again and explained again some of the peculiarities of a rat's physiology. 'A rat's skull isn't solid,' he said. 'The whole thing can dislocate, sort of collapse inwards so the vermin can squeeze into tight places. If its flattened skull can fit, then the rest of the brute will follow. I've seen one-pound rats crawl out of holes no wider than my thumb. Our giant has lots of options to get back in here if he has a mind to.'

The explanation seemed to sink in this time. Hugo's eyes roved across the walls of the tannery, staring at the narrow windows and peering into the dark recesses of the holes in the plaster.

Walther left his apprentice to his vigil, turning his attention to the cold meal Zena had prepared for him. A bit of rye bread, an almost shapeless nub of cheese and a sausage that he prayed hadn't been bought from Ostmann. Not the most lavish supper, but it was the thought that counted.

As he moved to take his first bite of the bread, Walther's face turned upwards. His hand froze before it could reach his mouth. His eyes bugged in shock. A grim pallor spread across his skin.

Staring down at him with beady red eyes was a creature spawned from a madman's nightmare. Squatting among the rafters, its whiskers twitching, its hideous naked tail dangling obscenely from its hindquarters, was the giant rat. The smells of the tannery must have hidden its presence from the dogs and the rat-catcher's labour with the traps had kept his own attention focused downwards, not upwards. How long the wicked thing had been sitting up there, watching Walther and Hugo, it was impossible to say. Perhaps it had been the smell of his supper that had lured the giant from whatever hole it had been hiding in. Whatever the circumstances, Walther was getting his first glimpse of the monster he had taken it upon himself to track and trap.

Hugo's words about needing bigger dogs came back to him as an unheeded premonition. The rat seemed to Walther's eyes to be as big as a pony, its back arched, its fur standing out in angry bristles. Its ghastly fangs, those chisel-like teeth which had visited such horrendous damage upon Fritz, glistened in the darkness.

The traps were a joke! This brute would never fit inside one of them! With those fangs it could gnaw its way clean through even if it did get caught. The bowstring wouldn't make a scratch on all that bristly brown fur.

Walther was about to whisper a warning to Hugo when one of the terriers, noticing the rat-catcher's fright and following the direction of his gaze, looked up and saw the giant. A low growl rumbled from the dog's throat.

The giant rat's beady eyes gleamed from the shadows, its hideous fangs clashing together. Walther had half-expected the monster to flee when the dog growled at it. For a second, disappointment flickered through his heart, fear that his quarry would escape.

Disappointment evaporated as stark terror raced down the rat-catcher's spine. The giant wasn't scampering off. Instead it launched itself from the beam, leaping straight at the littler dog. Horror flared through Walther's mind as the verminous body hurtled past him, its bristly hair and scaly tail brushing against his cheek. The colossal rodent struck the terrier head-first, the momentum of its leap sending both itself and the dog crashing against one of the vats, knocking it over.

A sickening yelp escaped from the little dog before its life was crushed between the rat's snapping fangs. The monster held its victim by the neck, shaking its own head from side to side to dig its fangs deeper into the terrier's throat. Blood sprayed from the mangled dog, steaming on the icy floor.

Without thinking, the stunned rat-catcher struck out at the marauding rat. Walther's pole cracked against the brute's flank. The giant didn't even squeak in pain as it dropped the dead dog and spun around to bare its

fangs at the man who had dared attack it. Blood dribbled from the giant's whiskers, flecks of foam oozed
between its sharp teeth. There was an almost calculating
malevolence in the rat's eyes as it glared up at Walther.

The rat-catcher cringed away from the monster's gaze,
his mind reeling with horror. The image of Fritz with
his throat torn out, the loathsome thought of the can-
nibalised rats with their innards eaten away and their
skins turned inside out, these came crawling through
his brain like black prophets of doom.

The giant was tensing itself to leap at the paralysed
rat-catcher when the brute was suddenly struck from
the side. This time it cried out, an angry chirp that
sounded like steel scraping against steel. Hugo jabbed
at it a second time with his pole and the brute spun
around, springing at the man without any warning.
Hugo screamed as the giant's weight tore the pole from
his grip and the fangs stabbed into his hand.

Hugo's scream snapped the remaining ratters from
their fright. Snarling, the two dogs fell upon the giant,
one seizing an ear in its jaws, the other darting in to
snap at the rat's belly. The giant ripped away from
Hugo, turning on these new attackers.

While the monster was busy trying to fend off the
dogs, Walther drove in upon it. A thick hunting knife in
his hand, he came at the brute from behind, stabbing
its back again and again, thrusting the blade deep into
the vermin's flesh. Pained squeaks streamed from the
rat as blood bubbled from its wounds. A terrible frenzy
came upon it, enabling it to shake free of the dogs and
drive Walther away with a lash of its naked tail.

The effort came too late to do the giant any good. The
rat had taken too much damage; Walther's knife had
pierced past ribs to puncture the brute's lungs. Wheezing, panting, it hobbled a few paces, then slipped on

the icy floor. The dogs were on it in an instant, tearing at its throat and avenging their fallen comrade.

Walther shook with excitement, that curious alchemy of terror and jubilation familiar to any victorious soldier. 'We did it!' he shouted, his voice so loud they might have heard him back in the Black Rose. 'Get ready, Bremer! You're going to have a heart attack when you see what I've brought you!'

The rat-catcher turned towards his apprentice. Hugo was sitting on the floor, hugging his arm against his side. Walther clapped him on the shoulder. 'Did you hear! Our fortune is made!'

Hugo nodded weakly, then his face contorted in a grimace of pain. 'Very… nice… Herr Schill,' he muttered. 'But… do you think… you could… get my fingers… out of its mouth…'

*Middenheim*
*Ulriczeit, 1111*

'YOUR GRACE!'

Franz's cry had Mandred clenching his teeth. It was bad enough that he had been unable to shake his bodyguard, but now it seemed the knight was determined to let everyone in the Westgate district know that the Prince of Middenheim was walking the streets.

Mandred pulled his wool cloak a bit closer and ducked into the closest alleyway. For a moment, he thought about ducking out the other end of the alley but then decided that Franz would only catch up to him again. Or maybe the buffoon would start asking around the neighbourhood if anybody had seen the Graf's son prowling about.

When Franz appeared at the mouth of the alley, Mandred grabbed him by the collar and pulled him up against the wall. The knight's hand fell to the grip of his sword, but quickly relaxed when he recognised the prince's features beneath the brim of the battered fur cap.

'Your grace,' Franz said, trying to affect a stiff salute within the narrow confines of the alley.

Mandred rolled his eyes and sighed. 'You do understand that I'm trying to go unnoticed,' he reminded the knight.

A bewildered expression came across Franz's stony features. 'Of course, your grace,' he said. 'You made that clear when we left the palace.'

'Then can I ask you to stop addressing me as "your grace"?' Mandred snapped. 'And stop bowing and saluting every time I look twice at you. We're supposed to be ordinary peasants, nothing more.'

Franz nodded. 'Yes, your grace.'

Mandred felt an ache growing at the back of his skull. Rumours of refugees sneaking into the city had reached the palace, accompanied by rumours that incidents of plague had started cropping up in the poorer sections of the city. Graf Gunthar had already dispatched troops to investigate the rumours, even going so far as to request Thane Hardin send some of his dwarfs down into the old Undercity to see if someone had found a way up through the tunnels. His father would put a stop to the stream of refugees once he uncovered the source. Mandred was determined to keep that from happening.

No outsider could possibly manage to sneak into Middenheim without help, a native of the city who knew how to get around the Graf's guards. Mandred was going to find that someone. Find them and warn them before his father could step in and stop the flow of refugees.

If he could only find one of the refugees and convince them of his sympathy, then Mandred might be able to learn who was helping them. But so far he had had no luck in finding anyone who didn't belong in the city. And the longer he looked, the greater the chance that Franz's blundering would give his presence away.

'Perhaps we should go and check the Pink Rat again, your grace?' Franz suggested, licking his lips at the thought of the notorious tavern.

Mandred closed his eyes and whispered a prayer to Ulric for guidance, or at least the self-control to keep him from strangling his own bodyguard.

The prayer for patience, it seemed, went unheeded, but a cry for help came drifting down the alleyway. It was the sort of appeal Mandred would have responded to anyway, but a thrill coursed through his body as he recognised a foreign tone to the shout. He opened his eyes and stared up into the grey sky. 'Thank you, Wolf Father,' he said before sprinting down the alley in the direction of the shout.

'Your grace!' Franz called after him.

Mandred didn't slacken his pace. The cry hadn't been repeated. Instead it had been replaced by the crash of steel and the inarticulate snarls of fighting men. The prince drew his own sword. He might have donned a simple horsehide sheath as part of his disguise, but the sword was the same keenly balanced dwarf blade with which he fought his duels with van Cleeve.

Through the maze of alleyways and side-streets, Mandred pursued the sounds of conflict until he burst out into a little square with a stone fountain at its centre. Dilapidated timber longhouses, their tile roofs groaning beneath a heavy snowfall, bordered the square on every side. Snow was piled high against their walls, almost to the very eaves, and a thick layer of snow carpeted the ground inside the little square. At once, the prince noticed the bright crimson splotches marring the ground.

Three men were sprawled in the snow, blades and bludgeons lying beside their bodies. Four ruffians in wool breeks and rough cowhide cloaks circled a lone fighter dressed in a heavy black cloak and wielding a fat-bladed broadsword.

It took Mandred only a moment to decide which side of the fight to make his own. 'If it takes four of you rats to fight one man, maybe you've taken up the wrong vocation,' the prince shouted. The combatants turned in surprise at his cry.

'There were six of them when they started,' the man in the black cloak boasted, his accent clipped and guttural, the mark of a Reiklander's voice.

'Stay out of this!' one of the cowhide ruffians growled. He gestured with an ugly iron bludgeon at the Reiklander and again at the third body lying in the snow. 'This scum has brought the Black Plague into the city!'

'So you thought you'd avoid the plague by getting into a swordfight?' Mandred said. He smiled with cool confidence at the four thugs. 'A fine idea. I'll be happy to oblige anyone who thinks six against two is honourable combat.'

'Take the meddler,' the thug with the iron club growled at two of his companions. 'Hans and I will finish the outlander.'

The ruffians separated into pairs. While the man with the club and a brutish thug wielding a crooked longsword converged upon the Reiklander, Mandred found himself opposed by a scar-faced rogue gripping an axe and a wiry villain armed with a horseman's mace. Just from the way they came at him, the prince decided that the maceman was the more experienced of the two and therefore the more dangerous. Before his foes could quite get to either side of him, Mandred lunged forwards, seeking to take the maceman by surprise.

The villain drew back, but not quite with the shock Mandred had hoped for. Instead of leaving himself defenceless, the man twisted aside from the prince's sword and delivered a hurried swipe of his mace that glanced off the boy's shoulder. Had it landed more squarely and with more force, the blow might have staggered Mandred and left him open to a more conclusive attack. As it was, the prince's body was simply jostled to one side, throwing his balance off for a fleeting instant.

Even that brief interval might have been too long if the axeman had been a more competent fighter. Instead the ruffian was still trying to get his mind around Mandred's sudden attack. The prince didn't give the man the chance to gather his wits. With the maceman momentarily on the defensive, Mandred swung around and slashed at the other ruffian. His sword rasped through the thug's knuckles just beneath the head of his axe. The man shrieked as blood spurted from his maimed hand and severed fingers tumbled into the snow.

'Ranald's teeth!' the maceman roared, swinging his weapon at Mandred's head. 'You'll pay for that, churl!'

The prince easily ducked under the swipe, bringing his sword in a downward sweep that sliced across the ruffian's thigh. 'You'd better flee before you really get hurt,' he taunted the thug.

The maceman's face contorted with rage. Snarling, he flung himself at Mandred, bringing his mace hurtling downwards with enough force to shatter the prince's shoulder. Unfortunately, he signalled the attack a little too broadly. As his arm came rushing down, his foe was darting forwards, thrusting the point of his sword into the ruffian's throat. The mace fell into the snow as the thug clasped his wound, trying to stop the blood gushing from a severed artery. He staggered towards the fountain, then collapsed into the frozen pool.

Mandred wiped the gore from his blade and looked over to see how the Reiklander was faring. There was a fourth body lying in the snow now, and a cowhide thug fleeing down an alleyway. Like the prince, the Reiklander was cleansing the blood from his sword with the cloak of his fallen enemy.

'One down and one in retreat,' the Reiklander said, nodding behind Mandred where the maimed axeman could be seen creeping along a little side-street. 'Seems we are evenly matched, friend.'

Mandred shook his head and sheathed his sword. 'You forget that you accounted for two before I even got here.'

A troubled frown came onto the Reiklander's face. The tip of his boot kicked against the body the ruffians had described as a foreigner. 'This one was mine too. Defending myself against him was what brought those jackals.' He chuckled grimly. 'Like any scavenger, they smelled blood.'

The prince stared down at the dead man. His clothes had a Solland cut to them and his boots were of raw wool, something rarely seen in the north. 'Why did he attack you?'

'He was afraid I would talk to the wrong people,' the Reiklander answered. A sharpness came into his eyes. For the first time Mandred appreciated the fact that the foreigner still had his sword drawn. 'He was right. I do intend to talk to the wrong people.'

Mandred stared hard at the Reiklander. He appeared

to carry himself with a military bearing, not surprising in a man who had just killed four enemies by himself. The clothes he wore were rough, an assortment of furs and wool such as any peasant might cobble together to survive the winter, but the sword in his hand was clearly a blade of quality, the surface etched with elaborate scrollwork. The overall impression was that, like the prince, here was a man trying to present himself as being of a much lower station than the one he belonged to.

'Who would the wrong people be?' Mandred asked.

'Anyone interested in refugees and how they are getting into the city,' the Reiklander answered. His body grew tense beneath the black cloak, his eyes watching Mandred for the slightest flicker of hostility.

'If I told you I was one of the wrong people, would you lower your sword?' the prince asked. He shrugged his shoulders when the Reiklander kept his blade at the ready. 'As you would have it, but it strikes me that you could use a friend right now.'

The Reiklander relaxed slightly. 'You have my gratitude for helping me against these jackals, but I am afraid I must make my own way. I need to see Graf Gunthar.'

Before Mandred could react to the Reiklander's startling statement, there was a commotion in the alleyway behind him. Sword drawn, his face distorted by panic, Franz came rushing into the square. The knight drew up short when he saw the bodies strewn about the snow. He darted a vicious look at the Reiklander who returned it in kind, then focused his attention on the prince.

'Your grace, are you all right?'

Franz's slip had the Reiklander blinking in shock. 'Your grace?' he echoed the bodyguard.

Mandred ripped the tattered hat from his head. 'Prince Mandred of Middenheim,' he announced.

The Reiklander snapped his heels together and bowed to the prince. 'Sir Othmar, late of the Reiksknecht, at your service, your grace.'

'Well met, Sir Othmar,' Mandred said, setting aside for the moment how and why a knight from the Reiksknecht had made the journey all the way from Altdorf to Middenheim. For the moment, he was only interested in finding out who was smuggling refugees into the city. More importantly, making that discovery before Graf Gunthar.

'Now that introductions are out of the way, perhaps we should discuss what you wanted to see my father about. And why people are trying to kill you.'

# ⤜ CHAPTER IX ⤛

*Altdorf*
*Vorhexen, 1111*

THICK STORM CLOUDS rendered the sky above Altdorf almost as black as night. A conspiracy of ravens circled above the Imperial Palace, their croaks echoing through the streets of the city. Many of the superstitious city folk hid in their homes, hiding from the eyes of Morr's corvid messengers. With the Black Plague abroad, none wanted to tempt the grim god.

Only in one place was the city alive. A great crowd had gathered in the Widows' Plaza, nobles and peasants alike drawn to the spectacle of the Grand Master's execution. Never in the long and renowned history of the Reiksknecht had the order suffered a charge of treason. Never had a man of such heroic reputation as Grand Master Dettleb von Schomberg been condemned to the ignoble fate of public beheading.

The crowd gathered about the Widows' Plaza gabbled excitedly among themselves. After the frightened solitude many of them had endured for so many weeks in an effort to escape the plague, this excuse to forget caution, to ignore peril had been seized upon with a desperate recklessness. A carnival-like atmosphere was the rule, peasants and nobles alike laughing and singing. Vendors circulated among the crowd, hawking withered fruits and scabby vegetables for grotesquely inflated prices. Halflings manoeuvred wheeled pushcarts through the mob, selling roasted rats to anyone willing to place frugality ahead of prudence. Unlike the fruits and vegetables, there was no shortage of rats in Altdorf.

All around the plaza, the black-liveried soldiers of the Kaiserjaeger were out in force, halberds and crossbows at the ready. Commander Kreyssig himself stood with a small retinue of officers and guards beside the wooden platform at the centre of the square. The low born Kreyssig bore a triumphant smile as he surveyed the mass of humanity that had gathered to watch the execution. It was more than the destruction of a traitor – it was the moment of his personal triumph. By proving Baron von Schomberg a traitor, by getting the Reiksknecht disbanded and outlawed, he had created a gap in the power structure of Altdorf, a gap he and his Kaiserjaeger would quickly fill.

Still smiling, he lifted his eyes from the babbling crowd, staring towards the Imperial Palace. Beneath the circling ravens, he could see the balcony which had earned the epithet of the Traitors' View. From here, a denizen of the palace could stare straight down into the Widows' Plaza and observe the executions. Emperor Boris was there, resplendent in his sable robes of state, the golden crown of Sigismund the Conqueror resting snugly about his head. Kreyssig chuckled inwardly. He was glad the Emperor had turned out to watch the execution. He'd arranged to provide his Imperial Majesty with quite a show.

The crowd fell silent as the gates of the Imperial Courthouse were raised. A phalanx of soldiers emerged, flanking a small wooden cart. Crouched inside the cart, his thin arms tied behind his back, his body shivering underneath the shabby linen robe he wore, was the man everyone had turned out to see. Grand Master von Schomberg, on his way to keep his appointment with fate.

Behind the cart marched the sinister Scharfrichter, the Imperial Executioner himself, Gottwald Drechsler. Dressed in black, his head hidden beneath a leather mask, he strode through the plaza like some primordial daemon. The Sword of Justice, a monstrous claymore nearly as tall as a man, was balanced across his broad shoulders, its pommel shaped into a leering skull of silver, its blade etched with curses and maledictions to damn the soul of those who felt its bite.

Kreyssig exulted in the hush that had come upon the crowd. He could fairly smell the fear rising from them. And in Boris Goldgather's Altdorf, fear was power. Von Schomberg would make an object lesson to the others, an example of what they could expect if they dare defy the Emperor… or Adolf Kreyssig.

Drechsler mounted the steps to the scaffold, resembling some inhuman fiend rising from the Pit. As he reached the platform, he threw off the hangman's cloak he wore, exposing a musculature of such proportions that it would have looked more at home on an ogre. Every inch of the Scharfrichter's chest was swollen with muscle, his every motion sent a thrill of raw power rippling down his massive arms. Cheerless black eyes stared out from the holes in Drechsler's hood, seeming to judge every face they happened to glance at, warning them that they too might feel the bite of the executioner's sword.

Von Schomberg had to be helped from the cart, a task delegated to two prisoners from the dungeons. The Grand Master sagged limply in their grasp, his body wracked by a fit of coughing as they carried him onto the scaffold. No priest waited upon the condemned man. After the attempted rescue, Kreyssig had forbidden anyone contact with von Schomberg.

The doomed man was half-dragged, half-guided to the wooden block at the centre of the platform. He was made to kneel before the block, to rest his head against its notched and stained surface. A leather strap was fitted over his shoulders, securing him to the block and making it impossible for him to pull away.

The Scharfrichter hefted the immense Sword of Justice, holding it overhead and circling around the scaffold so that all in the crowd could see. Then, with a savage gesture, he plunged the blade into the earth at the base of the scaffold, hurling the huge sword as though it were a boar-hunter's javelin. The spectacle brought gasps of astonishment from the crowd, both for the display of strength exhibited and for the breach of custom. Drechsler turned his cold eyes towards where Kreyssig and his officers waited.

For an instant, a tremor of uncertainty swept through the crowd. Was the Scharfrichter refusing to carry out the execution? Hope flickered into tremulous life in the minds of those who sympathised with the Reiksknecht and what they had tried to do.

Then that hope was smothered, crushed underfoot by the inventive cruelty of a despot. From among Kreyssig's officers, a sergeant of the Kaiserjaeger emerged. In his hands the soldier carried a huge double-headed axe.

It was not enough to kill von Schomberg. Kreyssig intended to humiliate him, to disgrace him before the eyes of all Altdorf. Tradition was clear, the law was firm.

Nobles were executed beneath the blade of a sword. Only peasants suffered the kiss of the axe. It was a distinction understood by highborn and commoner alike, an insult even the lowest serf could understand.

Taking up the axe, Drechsler circled the scaffold once more. When he finished his third circuit of the platform, he turned towards the prisoner and the wooden block. Lifting up the axe in both hands, he brought its gleaming edge flashing down. A collective gasp rose from the crowd.

Screams of horror filled the Widows' Plaza. The axe had missed, at least in part. Its keen edge had gouged the side of von Schomberg's neck, but had failed to decapitate him. The stricken captive thrashed about in his bindings, a ghastly gurgle issuing from his mangled throat. Blood spurted from his wound, spraying across the scaffold.

The Scharfrichter leaned back, resting his hands across the butt of the bloodied axe. For the better part of a minute he waited while his victim writhed in pain. Then he took up the axe once more, bringing it sweeping down in a murderous arc.

There would be no need for a third blow.

For a moment, silence gripped the Widows' Plaza once more. Kreyssig grinned at the effect the deliberately botched execution had had on the crowd. They would remember this, and they would fear suffering a similarly infamous end.

Then a voice cried out, loud and clear. 'Shame!' the voice shouted, and the cry was taken up by others, growing into a roar of outrage. Kreyssig had overplayed his hand. The travesty he had made of von Schomberg's execution had incensed, not cowed, the crowd. The Kaiserjaeger struggled to contain the furious mob. Bricks and stones clattered about the scaffold as the enraged people of Altdorf tried to avenge the hideous death of a martyr.

Under the barrage, Kreyssig withdrew into the protection afforded by the thick walls of the Courthouse, the Scharfrichter and the officers of his Kaiserjaeger following close behind him. Before he withdrew into the gatehouse, however, the commander looked back at the Imperial Palace. Horrified anger flared through his heart. There was no one standing on the Traitors' View. Emperor Boris had retreated back into the palace, distancing himself from Kreyssig and his misfired attempt to terrorise the people of Altdorf into submission.

Adolf Kreyssig could see all he had worked for slipping through his fingers. He would get it back. Whoever he had to denounce, whoever he had to imprison or execute, he would get it all back.

*Bylorhof*
*Ulriczeit, 1111*

THE SEPULCHRAL SILENCE of the temple of Morr was broken only by the sputter of a peat-moss lamp. Black shadows stretched across the marble-walled mortuary, throwing the fluted columns into sinister relief. The ebon statue of a raven peered down from its perch above the gateway connecting the chamber to the sanctuary itself, its beak open in a soundless cry. Darkened alcoves gaped in the walls, urns of incense smouldering in niches built into their sides, fighting a losing battle against the reek of death rising from the corpses stacked within.

The mortuary was filled beyond capacity. Even with the full complement of priests the temple normally possessed there would have been no way to keep pace with the decimation wrought by the Black Plague. By himself, Frederick van Hal was overwhelmed. In his blacker moods, he could almost be thankful for the slow slide back into heathenism many of the Sylvanians had abandoned themselves to. If not for the bodies dumped into the marsh, the dead would be piled not only in the niches, but everywhere in the mortuary and out in the sanctuary itself. There was simply too much work for one man, however much he pushed himself.

At the moment, however, Frederick wasn't concerned with the dead townspeople lying in the niches, awaiting the rites that would commend them to the keeping of Morr. He wasn't concerned with the dozens of newly dead the corpse collectors would bring him in the morning. He was concerned only with the piteous figure stretched out upon the stone table at the centre of the mortuary, its long blonde tresses fanned out around its still-beautiful face.

By custom and stricture, he should never have brought Aysha here. A suicide was a damned soul, a thing cursed by Morr and abandoned to the infernal hells of his murderous brother Khaine. The Sylvanians believed that the flesh of a suicide attracted ghouls from their forest lairs. The proper thing to do was to bury such a wretch in the middle of a crossroads, a great stone stuffed in the corpse's mouth and the bones of its legs broken with a spade.

Frederick cared neither for custom or stricture. This was Aysha, his sister by marriage, a woman who, if he had remained in Marienburg, might have been even more to him. He was willing to commit sacrilege for her, to spare her anguished spirit the indignity of a nameless grave. For her, he was willing to do even more.

The priest looked over at the black candles laid out

around the body. It had taken him most of the day to make those candles, a labour that still made his gut churn with disgust. He glanced over at the darkened niches, picturing the mutilated bodies hidden in the darkness. It was blasphemy for a priest of Morr to do such a thing, but the books of Arisztid Olt had been adamant regarding the corpse-candles and their necessity to the ritual.

Frederick stepped away from the table, slapping his hands together in nervous agitation. He had long studied the tomes of Olt's secret library, studied them when he should have consigned them to the flames. Until now, he had never been tempted to exploit that occult knowledge. He had considered the esoteric secrets with the detached appreciation of a scholar. He had never intended to put such obscenities into practice.

It was heresy for a priest of Morr to even contemplate what Frederick was doing. If they hadn't been taken by the plague, the Black Guard would have executed him for even thinking about such a thing. The servants of Morr had a connection to death and the world beyond the mortal plane, but the magic Frederick thought to invoke was something else entirely. It wasn't part of death, but a blasphemous attack upon it. It wasn't a connection to the world beyond, but rather a violent assault upon the gateway between planes.

With a moan of despair, Frederick rounded upon the table. His arm was raised to sweep the candles to the floor, to turn away from this heresy before he committed the ultimate sacrilege. But his eyes focused upon the pretty features of Aysha. Conviction faltered and temptation flooded into his heart. Instead of dashing the candles to the floor, he took a rushlight and ignited the hempen wicks. One by one, the corpse-candles sputtered into stagnant life, their eerie blue flame seeming to increase rather than lessen the darkness of the mortuary.

The priest circled to the foot of the table, staring up at Aysha's shrouded form. He placed the edge of a stone knife against his palm, cutting deep into the flesh, gritting his teeth against the pain. With his own blood, he drew a symbol upon the floor, tracing from memory the ancient Nehekharan hieroglyphs. From a wicker cage, he retrieved a red-breasted wren. Sacred to Taal, killing a wren was an affront against the gods of nature. Frederick paused only a moment, then snapped the bird's neck, tossing the pathetic body to the rats creeping among the corpses.

Frederick could feel the mortuary growing colder, a chill that was somehow more profound than the mere bite of winter. It was a chill that seeped down into the soul itself, the clammy clutch of dark magic and Old Night. He could almost see fingers of darkness reaching through the shadows, drawn to his rites of blasphemy and horror. He hesitated as he stared down at the last object required by Olt's spell. The priest gagged at the thought of what he must do. Only the thought that he had come too far to hesitate now steeled him for the perversion. In one swift motion, he scooped up the gelid bit of flesh, trying not to visualise the empty socket from whence it had come, and popped it into his mouth. His body rebelled as he swallowed the abomination; he clamped his bleeding palm across his mouth and forced the sickness back down.

At once, the darkness came rushing in. Frederick could feel it pawing at his robes, slithering against his skin. The hairs on the back of his neck prickled and his face felt as though it had been plunged into the maw of an ice troll.

Frederick shook himself from the sensations crawling

across his body, from the frozen talons clawing at his soul. He stared again at Aysha and from his lips streamed the harsh notes of an ancient tongue, the language of vanquished Khemri whose streets were dust a thousand years before the birth of Sigmar.

The peat-lamp sputtered and died, leaving only the blue flames of the corpse-candles and the sickly light of Morrslieb streaming through the mortuary's single window to illuminate the room. Frederick's flesh turned to ice as the eldritch emanations summoned by his spell came rushing in. Rustles and squeaks heralded the fright of rats as they scurried away from the fell energies summoned by the priest.

A cold glow suffused Aysha's corpse. From her pursed lips, a smoke-like wisp began to rise. Seeping into the atmosphere like an uncoiling snake, the glowing mist assumed the rough semblance of shoulders and head, the faint echo of limbs and torso. Only the most fevered, deluded imagination could have said the ghost bore the slightest resemblance to the woman it had been. It was a thing of shadows and reflections, a memory and nothing more.

Frederick smiled as he looked into the face of Aysha. Forgotten was the horror and blasphemy. All that mattered was her presence and the chance to speak to her one last time.

'Aysha,' the priest whispered. The wisp shifted slightly as the name was spoken.

A thin, rattling voice, like the scratch of talons against glass, hissed through the room. 'There are doors that must not be opened,' the phantom words took shape in Frederick's mind. 'Powers that must not be invoked. Beware of calling that which you cannot dismiss.'

Frederick stared into the ghostly visage, doubt flickering through his heart. The enormity of this sacrilege pressed against him, squeezing him like the grip of a python, crushing the breath from his lungs. For any man to draw upon this unholy magic was crime enough, but how much worse was it for him, a priest of Morr, a man dedicated to the sanctity of the grave?

'There are sympathies of spirit and mentality that must never be made,' the ghost warned. 'Do you wield the Power or does it wield you?'

Frederick closed his eyes, refusing to accept the spectre's warnings. He knew what he was doing. It was evil, abominable, but it would only be this once. He would never draw upon this magic again. He would have no use for it. Just this one time, this once so he might speak to Aysha one last time. Just this once so when his time came, his soul might find peace.

The priest opened his eyes again, gazing into the cold wispy image of Aysha. Grimly, Frederick exerted his will over the ghost, forcing its doleful tidings to subside.

'Why have you called me?' the apparition demanded.

Frederick leaned against the table, remembering only at the last moment Olt's precaution about not stepping out from among the symbols he had drawn upon the floor. 'I had to see you, had to speak to you. I had to let you know.'

'There is nothing to be said to the dead,' the ghost admonished.

'I had to let you know what I felt,' Frederick persisted. 'I had to tell you I have never stopped loving you. I know you had to marry Rutger, I know it was the right thing for you. I have never begrudged that decision and I have always been indebted to him for what he did. Both for you and for me.' The priest turned his face towards the sanctuary. 'I have placed Johan in the mausoleum of the templars, the most sacred place in the garden. He will be at peace there. Your body will rest there as well. I won't let them take you away.'

The wisp shifted once more, at once seeming to swell and diminish. 'You should not have called me. Johan and Rudi are waiting. They beckon to me. You should let me go to them.'

Frederick shook his head, tears in his eyes. 'Every time I saw you, every time I saw Johan, I thought of what could have been. I like to think that I could have made you happy. I want to think I would have been a good father to Johan.'

'He belongs to Rudi,' the ghost spoke. 'He is waiting with his father. You must let me go.'

The priest slumped away from the table, the magnitude of the ghost's statement twisting in his gut like a knife. All these years, he had believed Johan to be his own. He had never dared speak of the matter with Rutger, had never pressed the point with Aysha. He had always believed it was for the best if Johan never knew. It had been a privation of the soul, to look on in silence, but his quiet suffering had given Frederick the strength to go on. Now that his pain was revealed to be a lie, all that was left was a terrible emptiness.

Through the melancholy of his mind, an alarm began to flash. Frederick stared hard at the ghost's formless face. It was the second time she had spoken of Rutger waiting for her. But his brother was alive. He couldn't be waiting...

'Why do you speak of Rutger as one of the dead?' Frederick demanded, horrified anger contorting his face. 'My brother is alive! He is alive!'

'Rudi waits for me with Johan. They beckon to me.'

Terror filled Frederick's heart. He had left Rutger only the night before, when his brother had helped him bring the bodies to the temple. It was impossible that the plague had struck the merchant down in so short a time. Rutger was all the family he had left now.

'How is it that my brother waits in the realm of Morr?' Frederick demanded.

The wisp wavered. For an instant the eyes of Aysha gleamed from the flickering shape, imploring the priest to relent. Frederick squeezed his hand into a fist, sending more of his blood dribbling to the floor, strengthening the black magic he had evoked.

'Rudi went to seek justice for our son,' the ghost answered. 'Havemann was ready for him.'

Frederick's body sagged as the ghost's words pressed upon him. The corpse-candles sputtered and died. As they winked out one by one, the ghostly wisp drained back into the body laid out upon the table.

'The line has been crossed,' the spectral voice whispered. 'Sympathies of spirit and mentality have flung open the gate that can never be closed again.'

The priest didn't even notice the apparition's retreat. He was thinking of his brother.

And the man who had murdered him.

*Middenheim*
*Ulriczeit, 1111*

NIGHT ONCE MORE cast its sinister pall over the roof of the Ulricsberg, the clean light of Mannslieb warring against the ugly glow of Morrslieb for domination. The watchfires upon the walls of Middenheim stood stark against the black sky, clearly marking the locations of gatehouses and guardtowers. Smaller lights, flickering as they passed behind the battlements, revealed the lanterns of patrolling sentries.

From the Graf's private hunting preserve, the little

garden forest called the Ostwald, Mandred studied the revolving patrols. The prince crouched beneath the boughs of a snow-covered fir tree, waiting for the token Othmar had described, the beckon that would summon the smugglers to the wall.

'You said we were going to get more men,' Othmar whispered at the boy's ear. Unlike Franz, the Reiklander was managing to refrain from invoking Mandred's title. The fact that the prince had stubbornly refused to inform his father of this venture had grated against the knight's sense of duty and it was hard for him to keep a touch of resentment out of his voice.

'We aren't sure they're going to be there,' Mandred whispered back. 'We can get help later if we need it.'

Franz rubbed his calloused hand across his bald head, sweeping away the snow that had settled on his scalp. Anything touching his head made the knight uncomfortable – snow, rain, hats, even his own hair had been sacrificed to his sensitivity. At moments of stress or when his mind was anxious, that was when his scalp was at its most irritable.

'I don't like this, your grace,' Franz coughed. 'It might be wiser to tell the Graf what is going on.'

Mandred shot his bodyguard a stern look. It was enough of an irritation to have the Reiklander questioning his plan; he didn't need one of his own subjects voicing doubts.

The prince was about to call Franz to task when a sudden change in the pattern of the lantern on the wall above the Sudgarten drew his attention. Instead of continuing along the regular route, the light suddenly came to a stop. Up and down it rose as the sentry holding it signalled to someone in the city below. The gesture was repeated thrice, then the light went out. If someone didn't know what they were looking for, there was little chance of noticing the irregularity.

'Looks like your friends will be heading for the wall,' Mandred told Othmar. 'You said they used ladders to climb up to the battlements?'

The Reiklander nodded. 'That is how they brought us down from the wall,' he said. 'It stands to reason that would be how they got up there.'

Mandred stepped out from the cover of the fir, knocking snow from its branches. 'Let's see if the ladders are there. Then I'll know better how to proceed.' The look Othmar gave him made it plain to the prince that he still thought the Graf should be informed and more men sent to deal with the smugglers. Mandred felt a twinge of regret that he had to deceive the knight. In the little time he had known Othmar, he had been impressed by the man's integrity. He rationalised the deceit by reminding himself that there were bigger things at risk than a single knight's pride. The lives of countless unfortunates down in the shantytown were what was really at stake.

The three men crept through the garden forest, picking their way into the hedgerows and flower beds of the Sudgarten. Vast swathes of the park had already been ripped apart, cleared of trees and shrubs, getting the ground ready for the plough once the spring thaw came. The torn-up earth made Mandred think of a battlefield, the piled dirt evoking images of earthworks, the deep furrows resembling jagged trenches. It was a resemblance that made the prince uneasy. Middenheim was his home. The thought that war might soon be battering at its gates was not a pleasant one.

The bells were tolling in the temple of Shallya, the closest of Middenheim's temples to the Sudgarten. There were no priestesses left in the temple; they had all taken Graf Gunthar at his word and left the city to tend the sick down in the shantytown. Only a single deacon had remained behind to maintain the temple and ring the bell, to remind the people of Middenheim that even without her priestesses, the goddess was still with them.

Such was the clamour of the bells that Mandred didn't hear Othmar when the knight called to him. The Reiklander had to grab his arm to get his attention. He followed Othmar's hand as the knight gestured towards the wall. As he had promised, a pair of tall ladders were leaning against the barrier. They were peculiar looking constructions, made of a soft white pine and with strangely spaced rungs. It took Mandred a few moments to realise what they were – trellises from the ruined park. The smugglers had scavenged them from the debris and lashed them together with ropes to create their ladders. It was an ingenious idea. When they were finished they could simply cut the trellises from one another and dump them back with the other debris from the park. No need to worry about dragging the things to and fro, the trellises would be waiting for them on the junk pile the next time they were needed.

'Now we tell the Graf, your grace?' Franz asked, anxiety in his voice, one hand rubbing his head.

'Now we go up there and see who it is,' Mandred said, still trying to play for time. He turned a commanding gaze upon each of the knights. 'If we send for help and they don't come in time, at least we will know what these smugglers look like.'

'There were seven of them when I was brought up the cliff,' Othmar reminded the prince. 'And you'll have to take into account the sentries they've bribed.'

'We're just going to have a look,' Mandred promised. 'They don't even have to know we're there.' He felt guilty lying to these men, but he didn't have time to make them see his point of view. Mandred's motives were pure, but he knew from past experience that some men were too cynical to believe in simple humanity.

Franz led the way to the ladders, Mandred's one concession to his bodyguard's incessant demands for caution. The prince followed close behind, with Othmar climbing up the second ladder. The Reiklander had described in some detail the arduous climb, made all the more difficult by the irregular spacing of the rungs. Even so, Mandred found himself panting by the time they reached the top of the wall.

No light shone upon this section of the battlements. The bribed sentries had doused their lantern, leaving the smugglers to work by the light of the moons. This, it seemed, was more than sufficient. Mandred could see where a crude windlass had been constructed, thick ropes uncoiling from it to drop down over the side of the wall. Somewhere below in the darkness would be the basket Othmar had described, perhaps even now bringing another clutch of refugees over the cliffs.

Three men dressed in a motley assortment of furs attended the windlass, grunting with effort as they gradually brought the ropes winding back around the timber spool. Two soldiers in the livery of Wallwardens watched the operation, worry etched upon their faces. Another pair of men in cloaks paced back and forth, their every move betraying an attitude of wary vigilance.

There were two other men present. Like the sentries, they seemed intent upon watching the smugglers working the windlass. One was a broad-shouldered, stoutly built man, his head covered by a bearskin hood. There was an unmistakable air of authority about him; even without Othmar's description, Mandred would have marked the man as the chief of these smugglers.

The chief's companion was a little fellow, wiry and

nervous, his scrawny body covered from head to toe in a ragged robe of dyed wool. He capered about the chief, seemingly unable to keep still, his head twitching from side to side beneath the folds of his hood. Mandred took an instant dislike to the little man, finding his every gesture somehow disturbing and repulsive.

'We should get your father now,' Othmar whispered.

Mandred glanced aside at the knight. Now was the time to act. He would have only one chance to show his companions how wrong they were. He only hoped they would give him the opportunity to make them understand. 'Follow my lead,' the boy told the two knights. Before either of them could react, Mandred strode boldly towards the smugglers, his hands open at his sides.

'Peace,' he called out as the two smugglers detailed as lookouts spotted him and came running forwards. Mandred noticed that each of the men had a sword in his hand. 'I am not here to interfere.'

The prince's appearance drew the attention of the chief smuggler. The broad-shouldered man turned away from his observation of the windlass. His face lost in the shadows of his hood, the fur-cloaked man marched forwards. The bribed soldiers and the little man in the wool robe followed behind him.

'That is a good way to get your gizzard slit,' Neumann's oily voice intoned. 'You shouldn't scare people in the dark.'

'People who are doing things the Graf doesn't like, don't do them in the light of day,' Mandred countered, fixing his face in a companionable smile. A perplexed look came upon the face of one of the soldiers when he heard the prince speak, the look of a man who has recognised something but can't quite place it. Mandred knew he had to convince the smugglers of his sincerity before the soldier remembered where he had heard his voice before.

'I have heard about your operation,' Mandred continued. 'I wanted to see if I could help.'

Neumann chuckled as he heard the offer. There was an unpleasant cruelty in that laugh. The smuggler raised a gloved hand, gesturing behind Mandred, pointing a finger straight at Othmar. 'That man led you here,' Neumann grumbled. 'I cannot abide indiscreet people.'

'I asked him to bring me here,' Mandred said, hoping to divert Neumann's attention. 'If not for him, you might be talking to the Graf's men instead of me.'

The statement was a mistake. It seemed to jog the memory of the perplexed Wallwarden. 'Prince Mandred!' he exclaimed.

The two smugglers who had been closing on Mandred backed away in alarm, but Neumann only laughed. It was a low, evil mockery. 'The prince,' he hissed. 'And he wants to help us.'

The soldier who had identified Mandred rushed to Neumann's side, clutching at the smuggler's arm. 'That is the prince!' he repeated. 'You wouldn't harm his grace!'

Neuman swung around, a dagger springing into his hand. 'Watch me,' he snarled, stabbing the blade into the soldier's body with such force that it tore through the mail links and buried itself in his ribs. The dying soldier's fingers tightened in the folds of Neumann's cloak, dragging it from the smuggler's body as he slumped against the battlements.

Mandred's eyes went wide with horror as the smuggler's face stood exposed. Neumann's head was an oozing mass of sores and scabs, wormy strands of black hair scattered in patches across his scalp. A mouth, fat and puckered like that of a fish, drooled from the man's right temple, its greasy slobber draining into the atrophied stump of an ear. The face itself was leprous and swollen with rot, jaundiced eyes staring piggishly from folds of dead skin. A pair of rotten teeth, like the fangs of a snake, gleamed from a lipless mouth.

'With you as hostage,' Neumann growled, wiping the soldier's blood from his dagger, 'the Graf won't lift a finger against us.' The mutant's eyes glowed from his decayed face as evil thoughts swirled inside his skull. 'If he does, then the Prince of Middenheim will make a fine sacrifice to Grandfather Nurgle!'

Mandred's gorge rose as he heard the forbidden name of the Plague God uttered, feeling the sound burn inside his nose. The horrible truth dawned upon him. These men weren't mere smugglers, they were servants of the Ruinous Powers! The realisation was like a physical blow, all of his ideals and noble intentions withering before the baleful eye of the Plague God.

Had his father been right? Could only evil come from helping the refugees? Was compassion the weakness these diseased cultists had been waiting to exploit?

'Defend yourself, your grace!'

In his shock, Mandred wasn't even aware that one of the cultists was rushing him. Left on his own, he would have been too late to stop the man's descending sword. The blade seemed to chop down at him in slow motion, his eyes able to pick out every nick and notch in the corroded steel.

Then Franz was there, his sword crunching into the cultist's shoulder, dragging away both the enemy's sword and the arm that held it. The smuggler wheeled away, whimpering as thick gouts of blood spurted from his maimed body. Out of the corner of his eyes, Mandred could see Othmar fighting the other lookout, his training and skill quickly putting the cultist on the defensive. Even the surviving Wallwarden was taking a hand, flinging himself at Neumann and backing the chief cultist towards the edge of the wall.

A twitchy blur scrambled across the flagstones, ripping at Franz as the bald knight made to finish his enemy. He cried out in agony as a pair of crooked knives slashed through his legs. He crashed to the ground, rolling in pain, his sword thrusting uselessly at the wool-robed cultist. A shrill, hideous titter sounded from the villain as he darted in and stabbed one of his knives into Franz's knee.

'Get away from him, you scum!' Mandred roared. Sword in hand, he rushed at the slinking killer. The cultist sprang away at the sound of his voice, displaying an unbelievable agility and speed. Mandred chided himself for shouting. If he'd kept quiet he might have taken the fiend by surprise.

The prince had no time to think about his mistake. With a snarl, the wiry cultist leapt at him, whipping the wool cloak from his shoulders as he did so. Mandred was forced to duck the flying garment, then hurriedly brought his sword whipping up to block a descending knife. The other knife glanced across his side, catching in the heavy furs the prince wore.

Mandred barely noticed the pain of the cut along his ribs. For the second time, the boy was horrified by the shape hidden beneath a cultist's robes. The thing attacking him was utterly inhuman, more beast than man, and the most debased fusion of the two he had ever seen. Its face was pulled into a long, verminous snout, its hands were claw-tipped paws and its body was covered in mangy brown fur. The creature resembled nothing so much as an enormous rat.

The beastman gnashed its yellow fangs at Mandred, then jabbed its knife at his side once more. The prince twisted away from the stabbing blade, his free hand closing about the furry wrist. He felt his flesh crawl with revulsion at the contact. Utter disgust welled up inside him, overwhelming the careful discipline that had been drilled into him for years by instructors like van Cleeve. Howling, the prince brought his boot kicking up into the beastman's lean body. Its paw held in the prince's unyielding grip, the rat-creature could only partially twist away, taking the heavy boot against its leg instead of its belly.

The thing squeaked in pain, its scaly tail lashing out at Mandred as it tried to flee. The prince's sword came chopping down, severing the tip of the loathsome appendage. The smell of its own blood seemed to drive the beastman berserk. Chittering malignantly, the monster lunged at Mandred, knocking him onto his back with the snarling rodent sprawled across his chest.

Mandred saw the creature's arm twist, trying to bring its other knife into play. Pressing his boots against the flagstones, the prince pushed himself over, rolling onto his side and bearing the beastman with him. The creature squealed in panic as its hand was caught beneath the weight of both their bodies, the knife dropping from its numbed claws.

The panicked thrashings of the monster propelled both of them towards the crenellations looking out over the cliff. Mandred struggled to free himself from the monster's tenacious grip, its scrabbling claws trying to tear through his tunic. The prince screamed in pain as the rat-creature's snapping fangs sheared through the lobe of his ear.

Blood was streaming down the side of his face when the prince and his enemy at last crashed against the stone crenellation. Pressing his body against the solid stone, Mandred used it to gain extra leverage against his enemy. With his body anchored against the battlement, he heaved upwards with all his strength. For all its savage fury and ghastly speed, the rat-creature was sparsely built and weighed much less than a real man. Mandred's brawn broke the thing's hold, pitching it outwards between the crenellations. He saw its paws scratch desperately at the masonry as it hurtled head-first out into empty space. A shrill squeak of terror receded into the distance as the monstrosity fell towards the foot of the Ulricsberg.

Mandred's shaking hand pressed against the crenellation, using it to support himself as he regained his feet. He stared across the fortification, the flagstones splotched in black beneath the moonlight. All of the cultists were either dead or had fled into the night. All except for the burly Neumann. The chief cultist had ended the valiant effort of the guard who had turned against him, but not before the soldier had crippled one of the mutant's arms. Now he was looking for a way to get past Othmar's flashing sword, finding the effort easier in concept than execution. Every time the cultist tried to circle past the knight, Othmar would press him back with a sweep of his blade. Gradually, Neumann was being pushed back towards the battlements.

Mandred reached down to the bloodied ground, retrieving the discarded halberd of one of the soldiers. He shifted towards Neumann's flank, cutting off all possible chance of escape.

The mutant turned his deformed head, a sneer twisting his lipless mouth. Neumann gestured with his bloodied dagger at the windlass and the ropes hanging over the side of the wall. 'There are people in that basket down there, just waiting to be pulled the rest of the way up. Innocent people, like this indiscreet Reiklander.'

Mandred's blood went cold as he saw the cunning gleam in the cultist's eyes. Neumann was much closer to the windlass than anyone. One quick slash of the knife and he could send the basket crashing down the side of the Ulricsberg.

'We'll let you go,' Mandred said. He stared hard at Othmar. 'You understand? This… man is to go unharmed.'

The evil chuckle again bubbled from Neumann's lipless mouth. 'It is charming that you expect me to trust you.' His eyes narrowed with malicious spite. 'And utterly moronic that you would trust me.'

Before Mandred could even start to move, Neumann raked the edge of his dagger across the windlass, breaking the pin which restrained it. Faint screams rose from below as the unwinding ropes, free and unfettered, sent the basket crashing to the ground.

'Bastard!' Mandred snarled, charging at the gloating mutant. The cultist's body shuddered as the prince impaled him upon the spiked tip of the halberd. Hissing his defiance, Neumann tried to slash at the boy's face with the dagger, only the length of the halberd preventing his blow from landing. Before he could rear up for a second try, Othmar's sword hewed through the mutant's arm, sending both it and the dagger clattering across the battlements.

'You are all doomed,' the dying mutant chortled as he wilted against the flagstones. 'You can't even surrender. Because they've already won.'

Mandred pressed the halberd deeper into the cultist's body, sending a gout of blood bubbling from his mouth. The malicious light in Neumann's eyes slowly faded. The prince looked up as Othmar came beside him.

'Now can we see the Graf?' the knight asked.

## ⫸ CHAPTER X ⫷

*Altdorf*
*Vorhexen, 1111*

RATS SCURRIED THROUGH the rafters of the old warehouse while snow drifted down through holes in the roof. The bite of winter whistled through gaps in the walls, stirring up the thick layers of dust which lay everywhere.

The building had been shabby and poorly maintained even before its abandonment, owned by a Drakwald baron with a penchant for mercantile pursuits far beyond his finances. Since the ruination of Drakwald and the evanishment of the baron, the warehouse had been left to its own, quietly decaying into the riverfront. Even before the plague, Altdorf's dispossessed had shunned the place, seeking less dilapidated environs in which to ensconce themselves. Since the onset of the Black Plague, there were too many houses and manors devoid of tenants for anyone to look twice at a crumbling ruin.

Its very ignominy made the warehouse the perfect setting for a midnight rendezvous. Never had the riverfront played host to such an assemblage as now congregated under the tattered tile roof of the old warehouse.

For the best part of an hour, a cross-section of the Empire's lords and leaders had been discussing questions of loyalty and tyranny, of honour and conscience, of survival and destruction. Captain Erich von Kranzbeuhler, much as he had at that long ago meeting in Prince Sigdan's castle, maintained a cautious silence, content to listen and observe.

The ghastly execution of Grand Master von Schomberg had backfired upon Emperor Boris and his scheming confederates. Instead of subjugating dissent through terror they had created a martyr, a rallying point for the many enemies of Boris Goldgather and his grasping policies. Despite the plague and the chill of winter, demonstrations against the Emperor had popped up in every quarter of the city. Walls throughout Altdorf had been marked up with the image of the Imperial eagle, a noose wrapped about its neck. An armed mob had even broken into the residence of Lord Ratimir, forcing the minister to flee and seek protection within the walls of the Imperial Palace.

As Erich looked across the desolate warehouse, his spirit thrilled at the great men who had joined their destinies to the cause of justice. The cadaverous Palatine Mihail Kretzulescu of Sylvania standing beside Baron von Klauswitz of Stirland, the animosities of their homelands set aside in this moment of mutual crisis. Baron Thornig of Middenheim and his daughter the Princess Erna. Duke Konrad Aldrech and Count van Sauckelhof, lords of lands reduced to ruins by the politicking and opportunism of their Emperor. Even the diminutive Chief Elder Aldo Broadfellow, representing the halfling dominion of the Moot, was present. The halflings owed their independence to the old emperor, but that debt hadn't made them blind to the outrages of their benefactor's son.

Beside the noble lords and dignitaries of distant lands, the Arch-Lector Wolfgang Hartwich was present. With him, the Sigmarite priest had brought several commoners, representatives of the peasant trade guilds and men from Wilhelm Engel's scattered Bread Marchers. Sentiment against Emperor Boris wasn't confined to the noble classes, and as Hartwich had stressed, any effort to overthrow the Emperor would need to be a popular revolt, not something seen as being imposed upon the people by a clique of ambitious aristocrats.

'Then we are all of one accord,' Prince Sigdan announced, his eyes roving from one face to another. 'We have decided that Boris Goldgather is unfit to bear the title of emperor. His overthrow is essential to the continued survival of the Empire. We have decided that action must be taken against him and those loyal to him.'

Count van Sauckelhof shifted uneasily, his face growing pale. 'It must be clear that we will act only if there is no way to constrain the Emperor. If we could force him to accede to our demands in a way that would compel him to relinquish some of his authority…'

'A tyrant isn't to be trusted,' snarled Meisel, one of Engel's Bread Marchers. His hard gaze bored into van Sauckelhof's frightened eyes. 'You don't appease a snake, you crush its head. If that sits ill with you bluebloods, then leave the dirty work to those of us without title and position to protect.'

The dienstmann's harsh words brought cries of protest from several of the noblemen. 'This is unacceptable!' growled Baron von Klauswitz. 'I will support any move to depose the Emperor, but I will not lend my name to regicide!'

'Your stomach for treason has its limits,' scoffed Mihail Kretzulescu, clearly siding with Meisel's position.

Hartwich stepped forwards, waving down the tempers threatening to flare up. 'Assassination is not being discussed here. It is the preservation of the Empire, not the murder of the Emperor. Boris Hohenbach must be compelled to abdicate, but his person must not be harmed. You may count on the support of the Grand Theogonist, but only if it is understood that the Emperor's person is inviolate. The Temple of Sigmar cannot be an accomplice to murder.'

'It seems to me that the temple isn't doing much at all,' Duke Konrad complained. 'You tell us the Grand Theogonist will ratify Prince Sigdan as steward once Boris Goldgather abdicates, but what is the temple willing to do for us now, while we are struggling to make that event a reality?'

Hartwich shook his head sadly. 'All we can do is pray,' he answered. 'If the temple is seen to stand with a conspiracy against the Emperor, the followers of other gods may rally to Boris Hohenbach.' His eyes darted to Baron Thornig and his daughter. 'The cult of Ulric harbours resentment against the temple of Sigmar. That resentment might cause them to support Boris if the Grand Theogonist were to be seen as the instigator of his deposing. You must be seen as liberators, not usurpers, if the Empire is to be preserved.'

Baron Thornig's face wore a scowl, but the Middenheimer conceded the validity of Hartwich's concern. 'In Middenland, we hold that the Sigmarite faith is, at best, a beneficent heresy. Many of my countrymen hold even harsher opinions. There is no love of Boris Goldgather in Middenheim, but if Ar-Ulric thinks this uprising is an effort by the Sigmarites to impose a theocracy upon the Empire, he will denounce us. That would force

Graf Gunthar to join forces with Boris.' The ambassador from Middenheim ran his hand through his beard, eyes half-lidded as he contemplated the politics in the City of the White Wolf. 'We should dispatch a messenger to Graf Gunthar's court,' he suggested. 'The sooner Middenheim can be informed of what we plan, the greater Graf Gunthar's involvement, the more legitimacy Prince Sigdan will possess as steward.'

Erich stepped forwards, bowing to the assembled lords. 'Your absence would be noticed, baron,' he stated. 'It would be more prudent to send one of my Reiksknecht on this mission. My knights can be trusted with any confidence and will let no obstacle stand in their way.'

'A sound suggestion,' Prince Sigdan approved. 'If I may expand upon it, I say we send messengers not only to Graf Gunthar, but to each of the neighbouring provinces. Count Artur has left Altdorf to return to his own lands.'

'That could mean either Nuln or Wissenburg,' Hartwich pointed out. As both Count of Nuln and Grand Count of Wissenland, Artur maintained palaces in both cities.

'We send a knight to intercept Count Artur in both cities,' Count van Sauckelhof stated. 'Wissenland's support will be vital to keeping the river trade routes open to us once Boris has been deposed. If Count Artur intends to stand by Boris Goldgather, then it is in his power to starve Altdorf.' Sadness crept into his voice as he added, 'It will be some time before Marienburg can fulfil its old position as provider.'

'Knights must also be sent to Averland and Stirland,' Baron von Klauswitz said. 'We are no friends of Boris in Wurtbad, and there is no cause for Averheim to love him either.' He shot a sharp look at Mihail Kretzulescu.

'We can forward any appeal to Count von Drak if we think his inclusion is necessary.'

The Sylvanian dignitary smiled sourly. 'On behalf of the voivode, I thank you for your courtesy.'

'We must not forget Talabecland,' Duke Konrad said. 'The grand duke will surely support any move against Goldgather now that the Imperial Army is moving against him.'

'Why stop there?' Erich asked. 'Why not send word to the Reiksmarshal? He is an honourable man, a soldier who understands the difference between a just and an unjust war. If we approach him, he may side with us.' He could see the dubious looks on the faces of those around him. Defiantly, he returned those stares. 'There is nothing to be lost in trying,' he said.

'And much to be gained,' Prince Sigdan conceded. 'Very well, we shall appeal to both the grand duke and the Reiksmarshal. Perhaps the first fruit this conspiracy will bear is the prevention of a useless war.'

'That alone, your highness, would be enough to justify our cause,' Hartwich said.

'This is all well and good, my lords,' Meisel said, 'but we need men inside Altdorf. We need soldiers here and now, not away in Middenheim and Nuln. With the Imperial Army away, there will be no better time to strike!'

'What about the Bread Marchers?' Erich asked. 'How many of you can we count on?'

Meisel sighed. 'Not enough, I fear. We've been able to contact most of those who escaped the massacre, over four hundred men. But they've been hiding in the worst slums and shacks in Altdorf, constantly on the move to escape Kreyssig's spies. A lot of them are sick.' His eyes became like chips of ice. 'The plague,' he hissed, almost choking on the word.

'We don't need an army,' Prince Sigdan said. 'The right men in the right place will serve us better than a thousand swords. What we need is someone close to the Emperor. Someone who can get inside the Palace and inform us first-hand of his plans. There will be a time when it will be right to strike, when even a few men can seize the Emperor.'

'Then perhaps I can be that man,' Princess Erna said. The statement brought a grunt of amusement from Duke Konrad.

'Boris would have to be blind to take you for a man,' Konrad quipped.

Princess Erna scowled at the Drakwalder's jest. Before her temper could rise, Baron Thornig came forwards, placing a hand on his daughter's shoulder.

'Hear her out,' he said, his words heavy with regret and shame. 'There may be a way to slip one of our own into the heart of the enemy camp.'

Erna gripped her father's hand. Taking a deep breath, knowing that she wouldn't have the courage to repeat what she had to say, the princess hurried to make her proposal. 'For some time, Adolf Kreyssig has attempted to court me. He has spared no effort to secure my father's blessing, from the most vile threats to the most tempting gifts. At any time, my father could pretend to be swayed by Kreyssig's demands. As the wife of that monster, I could be the eyes and ears of this cause.' She could see the disgust on the faces of the men listening to her. 'Please,' she said, 'let me do this, let me make this sacrifice. All of you are willing to risk your lives, your names, your very legacies to depose a despot. Is what I risk so much more precious?'

'Your highness, you cannot allow this?' protested Erich. 'You cannot sacrifice this lady's virtue and honour this way!'

Prince Sigdan shook his head. 'No,' he said slowly. 'The very horror of the idea is what tells me Princess Erna is right. The enemy will never suspect her. She will be privy to confidences we should never be aware of otherwise.'

'But to ruin a lady's reputation?' the knight persisted.

Erna smiled at Erich's chivalry. 'When the moment comes, you may avenge me upon my husband,' she told him. 'The person of the Emperor may be inviolate, but a scheming creature like Adolf Kreyssig deserves only a nameless grave. Send him there, my dashing knight, and give all of his victims justice.'

Erich's hand tightened about the hilt of his sword. 'I will,' he vowed.

FROST CLUNG TO the stone walls of the cellar, twinkling in the glow of Kreyssig's rushlight as he descended the stairs. An angry squeak from the shadows reprimanded him for leaving the light unshaded. The commander of the Kaiserjaeger grinned at the distempered vocalisation. It was always a good thing to remind his sneaking friends of their place.

'What have you learned?' Kreyssig snarled, arresting his descent at the foot of the stairs. He didn't like being even this close to his subhuman confederates. They were useful, but that didn't change how disgusting they were.

'Prince-man meet with other-more traitor-meat,' a nasally voice hissed from the darkness. Kreyssig could just pick out the scrawny shape with its hunched shoulders and hooded face. Even that much left too vivid an impression upon him. Only once had he gotten a good look at his slinking associates, an incident that continued to haunt him in his nightmares. The Sigmarites were right to burn mutants if such horrors as what he had seen could spring from a collusion of corrupt souls. He promised himself that once these vermin had ceased to be useful to him, he would hunt them down and destroy their lairs.

'They spread-bring plague-cough,' the voice said. 'Make many-more sick-die. Weaken city-place, then make attack-slay!'

Kreyssig nodded as he heard his informant's statement. Useful spies, these skulking mutants, and they had provided him with the information that had made him the most feared man in Altdorf. There was no one they had failed to dig up dirt on, no secret they had failed to uncover for him. The revelation that Prince Sigdan was moving against Emperor Boris, and that the rebels were behind the plague, was something Kreyssig had long suspected.

'You can bring proof of this?' Kreyssig demanded. In the shadows, he could see the mutant's hooded head bobbing up and down emphatically. 'Bring it then. Whatever support the prince thinks he can count on will wither and die if he is shown to be the source of the plague.'

'More-more,' wheezed the mutant. Kreyssig's hair stood on end as the creature uttered a titter of ghastly laughter. 'Saw-scent Sigmar-man meet-seek traitor-meat. Haart-witch, say-called.'

Kreyssig's smile broadened. Arch-Lector Hartwich conspiring with rebels? It was almost too good to be true. For years he had struggled to find a way to put the temple of Sigmar under his thumb. Evidence of what had happened in Nuln hadn't seemed enough for what Kreyssig needed, but combined with evidence of a more recent scandal it would be just the lever he needed to bring the Grand Theogonist down to his level.

'Well done,' Kreyssig told his spy. 'Your Emperor thanks you for your service.'

A titter of inhuman laughter sounded from the darkness, then the mutant spy was gone, vanished back into the subterranean depths from whence he came.

Kreyssig turned and ascended the stairs with slow, deliberate steps. It was an effort not to run, to flee back into the clean world of light.

Yes, once these vermin had served their purpose, he was going to take extreme delight exterminating them.

*Nuln*
*Ulriczeit, 1111*

WALTHER LEANED AGAINST the counter inside the Black Rose, a pleased smile on his face. The tavern was a bedlam of activity, people clustered about the tables, gathered about the bar or simply squeezed into any corner where there was room enough to stand. Every fist was filled with the handle of a tankard. The rat-catcher had it on good authority that Bremer had been forced to send to other taverns in the neighbourhood for more beer and Reikhoch to replace what he'd sold.

It made sense. Nuln was in the grip of plague. There was no denying that fact now. Panic had settled upon the city. There had been a crazed culling of cats and dogs after a rumour started that the plague was being spread by the animals. Walther had lost his two ratters to a mob of terrified peasants, helpless to do anything but watch while the wretches beat his dogs to death – all the while crying out to Shallya to preserve them from the plague. In their fear, none of them bothered to consider that all life, even that of a little dog, was sacred to the goddess of mercy.

The prudent folk of Nuln had taken to barricading

themselves inside their homes, hoping that by sequestering themselves they could avoid contact with the disease. Others, without the affluence or temperament to be prudent, had thrown themselves into a frenzy of licentiousness, determined to indulge to excess before the shadow of Morr fell upon them. It was to such grimly exuberant clientele that the Black Rose and a hundred other taverns now catered, each struggling to capture the dragon's share of the wilfully reckless libertines.

Thanks to Walther's contribution to the Black Rose's ambiance, Bremer was taking in the dragon's share. The rat-catcher looked across the crowd, his eyes lighting upon the oak stand where the giant had been mounted. In a bit of irony, the brute had been stuffed by a tanner from Tanner's Lane. The tradesman must have possessed a touch of the thespian about him, for he had posed the giant rat in an attitude of such ferocious aggression that the first impulse of all who saw it was to recoil in alarm, ready to defend themselves from the snarling monster.

The rat was well and truly dead, of course. Scattered on the stand about its feet were the bones of its skeleton. The tanner had improvised a wooden frame to support the rat's skin, using only the creature's skull when he stuffed it. Two bits of ruddy copper served the thing for eyes, shining sinisterly whenever the light hit them just right.

The effect was a bit spoiled by the crude sign hanging about the rat's neck. Somehow a rumour had been started that rubbing the monster's fur was a charm against the plague. In an effort to protect his new attraction, Bremer had placed the sign around its neck. It didn't do any good. Most of his patrons couldn't read and those who could, mostly students from the now closed Universität, ignored it anyway. A few spots on the monster's hide were starting to look a little thin from the constant attention.

'I tell you this is too important to simply be relegated to being a freakshow attraction!'

Walther took a slow sip from his beerstein before deigning to continue his conversation with Lord Karl-Joachim Kleinheistkamp. The professor stood at his elbow, his brocaded hat clenched in his white hands, beads of sweat on his wrinkled brow. The rat-catcher savoured the desperate quality in the nobleman's expression.

'The Universität will pay… three crowns for the specimen,' Kleinheistkamp said, holding up his fingers. 'Three gold crowns,' he chuckled.

Walther joined in the professor's chuckle, clapping the old man on the shoulder. Kleinheistkamp frowned at the overly familiar gesture, but quickly forced a wide grin on his face. 'Three gold crowns. How many rats would you need to catch to earn that much?'

'One,' Walther said, taking another sip from his stein. He pointed across the tavern to the crowd circling about the stuffed giant. 'That one,' he elaborated. 'That beauty is bringing them to the Black Rose in droves and I get half of the profit. Now, if I had a similar arrangement with the Universität – whenever Count Artur decides it is safe to reopen, that is – then perhaps we might come to terms. You are going to charge admission, aren't you?'

All geniality faded from the professor's face. 'I want that specimen for scientific study, not for a bunch of peasants to gawp at!'

Walther shrugged his shoulders. 'Too bad. It looks like I'll make more leaving my monster right where it is.' A hard edge crept into his eyes as he watched

Kleinheistkamp angrily turn away and order a fresh drink from Bremer. 'Be careful, your lordship,' Walther said. 'I'm afraid you're paying for the drinks this time.'

Laughing at the baleful look Kleinheistkamp directed at him, Walther pushed his way through the crowd. Maybe it was the professor's ire, but suddenly it felt a bit cold inside the tavern. The rat-catcher was eager for the warmth of the fire. As he walked through the busy room, he found himself cheered and toasted by the patrons. Perhaps not quite as renowned as the monster he had killed, Walther had nevertheless become something of a local hero. For the rat-catcher, accustomed to being shunned even by the lowest dregs of society, all of the attention was more exhilarating than anything Bremer kept behind the bar.

The patrons gathered about the Black Rose's hearth cleared a spot for Walther. A big, broad-shouldered man with a warrior's bearing and a distinct Reikland accent even offered the rat-catcher a drink. Politely declining, the local hero nestled close to the fire and tried to warm the chill from his hands.

A different chill crept into his body when he noticed the object nailed to the back of the hearth, almost hidden by the roaring flames. The jawbone of a hog, its tusk black with soot. Folk medicine from the days of the Old Faith, a talisman against evil spirits and disease. There were many hearths decorated with such talismans these days, but the one in the Black Rose was there for a specific reason. There was a specific sickness the talisman was intended to alleviate.

Walther stared into the flames, his thoughts turning away from the busy crowd, from the congratulatory cheers. He was thinking of the little room down in the tavern's cellar and the man entombed there. The rat-catcher looked away from the fire, wondering if the

Reiklander was still around and if the offer of a drink was still open. Instead he found himself looking into Zena's pretty face. His pleasure at seeing her looking for him quickly faded. There was a fearful look in her eye and a tightness about her mouth. Over the last few days the chores of the tavern had increasingly been taken up by the other serving girls. Zena's attentions had increasingly been needed elsewhere.

Walther didn't speak, simply grabbing Zena's elbow and guiding her towards the kitchen. His retreat with the shapely serving wench brought jovial catcalls and lewd gestures from some in the crowd, but they ignored the rude humour of Bremer's patrons. Some things were too serious to bear distraction.

'Why did you leave him?' Walther demanded once they were in the kitchen. Zena cast a worried look at the cook and the kitchen boys. Catching the suggestion, Walther drew her into the larder and lowered his voice. 'You should be with Hugo,' he accused.

Zena winced at the anger in his voice. 'I can't do anything for him,' she said. 'What's wrong with him?'

'It's not that,' Walther growled. 'Ranald's purse! Do you think I'd ask you to look out for him if it was that! It's just a fever, an infection from that damn rat bite!'

Zena placed her hand against Walther's neck, drawing his face close to her own. 'It's more than that,' she whispered. 'He's getting worse. It's more than fever now.'

Walther pulled away, uttering a pained moan. His fist lashed out against a sack of potatoes, disturbing an ugly grey rat that was hiding in a cranny behind the bag. Squeaking, it scurried off to find a new refuge.

'He saved my life,' Walther said. 'When that thing turned on me, I couldn't move. I froze. I just stood there. If Hugo hadn't attacked it…'

The woman's arms closed around him, hugging him

to her body. 'You've done all you could for him. If he has the plague, there's nothing you can do.'

'I can get him a doktor. I have enough gold for that, even with Bremer cheating me on my cut. I'll get him a doktor.'

'And you think Bremer will sit still for that?' Zena scoffed. She jabbed her thumb at the door. The murmur of the tavern crowd was just audible. 'You think he'll risk losing the business you've brought him? How many of those people would be here if there was a red cross daubed on the door? They might scoff at death, but they won't go courting it!'

'Hugo saved my life! I won't abandon him! I'll find a way!' Walther reached beneath the fancy new tunic he'd bought, retrieving a fat purse stuffed with coins. 'Take these. Find a physician who will be discreet. We can do this without Bremer getting wise.'

Zena shook her head, but couldn't refuse the purse when it was pressed into her hands. Walther leaned down and kissed her. 'If you haggle, maybe there will be enough left for a new dress.' The remark brought a smile to her lips. Her eyes looked up into his. For a moment, all worry and fear was forgotten. There was only hope and love.

A harsh knock at the door broke the moment. Walther and Zena pulled apart as Bremer's frantic voice sounded from the kitchen.

'Schill!' the taverneer cried out. 'I need you! There's an idiot out here saying your rat is fake!'

Walther pressed Zena's hand. 'Take the money. Get Hugo a doktor.' He didn't wait for her to answer, instead turning and opening the door. A flush-faced Bremer stood just outside.

'You need to stop this idiot, or our agreement is off!' Bremer threatened.

Walther glared at his partner. 'Hans and Schultz are the roughs!' he snarled back at the taverneer, naming the two bouncers who had been hired on when business increased. 'Have them kick the fool into the street!'

'Look, I don't have time to argue or wait for you to finish fondling the help,' Bremer said, peering over Walther's shoulder at Zena. 'You either get this idiot to shut up, or we're through!'

Walther stared hard at Bremer. Something was wrong here, he could feel it in his bones. 'Why can't Hans and Schultz handle this?' he asked, menace in his voice.

Bremer backed away, all the bluster draining out of him. 'What are we going to do?' he wailed. 'That idiot is going to drive away business!'

Walther stalked past the taverneer, his anger rising with each step. 'If his argument is that that thing I killed isn't real, then I'm going to make him eat his words! Whoever he is!'

The rat-catcher brushed past the cook and kitchen boys who were peering into the tavern from the cracked door. The patrons had fallen silent, all conversation stifled by the agitated cries of a single shrill voice. Walther could see the crowd backing away from the oak stand. Suddenly no one wanted to be close to the dead giant or rub its charmed fur.

'This abomination is a cruel fraud!' the voice wailed. 'A hoax to gull fools into debauchery and licentiousness! You people should be ashamed of yourselves to be tricked away from your homes by such an absurd jest!'

Walther's anger swelled as he heard the sceptical words and sneering tone, all the humiliation of his appeals to the scholars returning to him. He reached behind the bar, retrieving one of the cudgels Bremer kept there to cosh drunks. The feel of the heavy club brought a vicious leer to his face. The patrons around him must have noted his demeanour, clearing a path for him without a word leaving his lips.

'Who says the giant is fake?' Walther snarled as he emerged from the crowd. There was a man pacing before the mounted monster. At Walther's challenge he turned. The rat-catcher groaned when he saw who the giant's detractor was. Captain Hoffmann Fellgiebel of the Freiberg Hundertschaft, that element of Nuln's city watch charged with policing the district. Suddenly it was very clear to Walther why the two bouncers wanted nothing to do with this particular trouble-maker.

Fellgiebel looked the surprised rat-catcher over. The captain's face was lean and hungry, his eyes close-set and with all the charm of a snake about them. One of his gloved hands caressed the pommel of the sword sheathed at his side, the other gripped a bundle of fresh posies, a safeguard against the plague. He shook the flowers in Walther's direction.

'You must be the charlatan himself,' Fellgiebel said, his voice like an audible sneer. 'I charge you to confess to these people the imposture you have committed so that they might return to their homes and turn their minds to more righteous pursuits.' The captain's eyes gleamed with malice. 'You will accommodate me,' he stated. A pair of men wearing leather jacks and the dagged black and yellow sleeves of the Hundertschaft came stalking forwards from their posts at either side of the tavern's entrance. Each of the men had a fat-bladed halberd in his hand.

The rat-catcher's anger faltered for a moment. Then the thought of how close he had come to dying, of Hugo and the man's suffering, poured fire back into his veins. Standing his ground, Walther glared back at Fellgiebel. 'I'm the man who killed that monster and had it stuffed, if that's what you mean.'

Fellgiebel blinked in shock. In this place, in this district, his reputation did not fail to precede him. Nobody stood up to him. They knew what would happen if they did. The captain's eyes became even colder and more reptilian. 'I think I heard you say it's fake.' He turned and cast his gaze across the crowd. 'I think they heard you say so too. Why don't you say it again so everybody can agree?' His thin lips pursed into a menacing grin. 'Say it while you still can.'

The two watchmen came marching towards Walther, their weapons lowered. A single gesture from Fellgiebel and they would use those weapons. Not to kill, Fellgiebel wasn't so crude as that. All of his men were quite good at using their halberds to maim and cripple. One living wreck of a man was worth more as an example to others than a dozen graves in the garden of Morr.

'He said it's real and he killed it.' The words were spoken with a gruff Reikland accent. Walther was no less surprised than Fellgiebel when a big blond-haired man stepped out from the crowd and slapped down the halberd of the nearest watchman with the bared sword in his hand.

'That was a mistake!' Fellgiebel hissed. The captain started to pull his own sword when the sound of steel scraping against leather sounded from all across the room. The big Reiklander, it seemed, had quite a few friends.

'Was it?' the Reiklander demanded. 'I think it is you who've made the mistake. That rat looks pretty real to me.'

'Stitched together from scraps,' Fellgiebel snarled back. 'I can get witnesses who will testify to that.'

Walther's anger swelled as he heard the captain speak. He could well imagine how Fellgiebel would get such testimony. The Reiklander clearly didn't have any idea what he was getting himself into, but Walther was going to put a stop to it. This was his fight and he wasn't going to let anyone fight it for him.

'Fake!' Walther shouted, slapping the cudgel hard against his palm. 'Stitched together from scraps!' He marched past Fellgiebel and to the oak stand. His arm trembling with fury, he raised the cudgel and brought it slamming down against the stuffed monster. The verminous fur tore beneath the blow, the bits of copper flying loose and clattering across the tavern. The bleached skull of the rodent crashed to the floor, bouncing once and landing so its fanged grin faced the watch captain.

'Tell me who made that for me!' Walther yelled.

Fellgiebel stared at the rat skull, colour rushing into his cheeks. Angrily, he turned away, whipping his cloak over his shoulder. As he stalked towards the door, a chorus of jeers and taunts followed him out.

Walther frowned as he considered the damage his anger had caused. The damage to the monster was one thing, but the humiliation of a man like Fellgiebel was another.

'It does me good to see that cur walk out of here with his tail between his legs.' The speaker was the big Reiklander. There was a beerstein in his hand. Walther was grateful when the man offered it to him.

'You shouldn't have interfered,' Walther said. 'It was my fight.'

'You looked like you needed the help,' the Reiklander said. His jaw clenched tight as he stared after the departed Fellgiebel. 'Besides, I didn't like his arrogant tone. It reminded me too much of the Kaiserjaeger back in Altdorf.'

Walther nodded his understanding. Even in Nuln,

news of the Bread Massacre and the Kaiserjaeger's role in the slaughter had spread. The rat-catcher looked at the Reiklander with a new appreciation. Maybe he had been one of Engel's Marchers. He might even know Meisel. He certainly had the look of a dienstmann about him.

'Walther Schill,' the rat-catcher introduced himself, laughing as he watched Bremer come racing from the kitchen to scoop up the rat skull before anyone could step on it.

'Heinrich Aldinger,' the Reiklander said, extending his hand. The smile faded from his face as he turned his eyes once more to the door. 'I worry that perhaps I did you no favour just now. That seems like the sort of man who will bear a grudge.' He sighed, a note of bitterness in his voice. 'That is the trouble with being a soldier. You are taught to fight and ignore the consequences.'

'Let me worry about the consequences,' Walther said, trying to force some levity into his tone. It wouldn't do to upset Aldinger. The man had meant well and, as the rat-catcher had said before, Fellgiebel was his fight.

However uneven that fight might be.

*Skavenblight*
*Ulriczeit, 1111*

Poxmaster Puskab Foulfur stared down at the quivering ratman, indifferent to the creature's agonies. Using a long brass rod, the plague priest poked and prodded the skinny skaven, lifting his arms and turning his head. A satisfied hiss rushed past Puskab's rotten fangs. Ugly black buboes clustered about the skavenslave's throat and armpits, syrupy treacle oozing from the swollen sores. The slave's breathing came in ragged, uneven gasps, flecks of blood staining his nostrils and whiskers.

'Good-good,' the plague priest pronounced. He withdrew the brass rod he had thrust into the slave's cage. Stalking over to one of the flaming braziers which flanked the entrance to the laboratory, Puskab thrust the end of the instrument into the fire. He held it there until the tip glowed and any trace of disease had been purged.

'The Horned One favours me,' Puskab declared. 'New-better fleas. Carry-bring plague fast-quick!'

The skaven assisting Puskab in his diabolical labours glanced anxiously at one another. Somewhere beneath their protective leather cloaks, glands tightened and the reek of fear-musk oozed into the air. They had been warned by Wormlord Blight what their fate would be if Puskab's experiments were to fail, but now they wondered if perhaps success wasn't even more terrifying.

Puskab scowled at the frightened ratmen. Unbelievers! Hedonistic little heathens! To be infected by one of the Horned One's holy plagues was a fate to be embraced joyously! Only in the fevered fires of disease could the soul of a skaven be judged! The inferior were destroyed, the superior emerged stronger than before, endowed with something of the Horned One's divinity and ferocity.

The plague priest stalked past his trembling assistants, peering at them with his rheumy eyes. Soon there would be only two kinds of ratmen in the world. The true believers and their slaves. Clan Verms would help to bring about that change. Willing or unwilling, they were now instruments of the Horned One's design.

The clatter of armour warned Puskab that he had guests. He turned away from the tables and faced

the entrance to his laboratory. A pack of burly warriors marched through the doorway. Behind them the
twisted shape of Blight Tenscratch lounged upon the
platform of a velvet-draped palanquin. Breeder-scent
wafted from the curtains and the smell of goat-cheese
and blood-wine was strong. From the smells lingering
about the Wormlord and the vicious expression in his
posture, it seemed some pleasant interlude had been
disturbed.

'I am told your work has succeeded,' Blight snarled,
baring his fangs.

Puskab gestured towards the cage where the infected
slave struggled to suck breath into his lungs. 'Early-
soon, but look-smell good-good,' he explained.

Blight's malformed body contorted at a grotesque
angle, his claws wrapped about a lead goblet. Furi-
ously, he flung the cup at the cage, spattering the slave
inside with blood-wine. 'Not-not this test-meat!' the
Wormlord snapped. 'What about the others? The ones
outside?'

Puskab's heavy frame wilted under Blight's enraged
glare, assuming a posture that was both abased and
alarmed. 'None-none,' he squeaked, pointing again at
the cage. 'This one first! Swear-tell by Horned One!'

'Bring the traitor-meat!' Blight growled. Before
Puskab could act the armoured ratmen pounced upon
him, seizing his flabby arms in their powerful claws.
The plague priest's assistants watched in excitement as
their fearsome master was dragged away into the darkness of the Hive.

PUSKAB WAS CARRIED to a vast cavern far beneath
Skavenblight. The air was moist and musty, stinking of
mildew and pond scum. His keen ears could hear water
dripping from the roof overhead, each drop landing

with a soft *plink* upon some loamy surface. The cavern was dark, its blackness so perfect that even the eyes of a skaven couldn't penetrate it. A snarl from Blight caused a green glow to gradually form. Puskab could hear the crackle of electricity and the laboured breath of panting ratmen. The first thing he saw was the bronze pillar and crystal cage of a Clan Skryre warp-lamp, a nest of cables leading back to an enormous treadmill.

The irony of Clan Verms employing one of Clan Skryre's warpstone-powered lamps wasn't lost on Puskab. The clan stood to lose a fortune in the trade of worm-oil should use of warp-lamps become widespread. Verms spared no opportunity to criticise the upstart warlock-engineers and argue against the safety of their erratic inventions. To find them using one of the very devices they were so vehement in denigrating brought an uncontrolled bark of laughter rushing past his fangs.

'Blind-worms not like smell-scent of worm-oil,' Blight explained, his face sheepish, his tone embarrassed. His lips pulled back in a vicious grin as he remembered who he was talking to and why. Imperiously, the Wormlord pointed across the cavern.

The floor of the cavern was, as Puskab had imagined, covered in a loamy surface, a mass of moss floating upon a great pool of foetid water. He could see things slithering through the sludge, just beneath the surface. Scrawny skavenslaves were wading through the muck, chasing after the things swimming around them. Sometimes they would dive into the morass to emerge with a writhing mass of slimy white flesh clenched in their paws.

Puskab knew the snake-like things to be blind-worms, an observation validated when he saw the slaves drag their catch to a floating workstation where a brawny brown overseer wrestled the flailing worms into a suspended harness. Other slaves equipped with wicked metal probes crawled under the hanging worms to tease milk from the soft tissues between each segment of the worm's body. The stinking ooze was collected in a motley assortment of buckets and bowls.

The plague priest had only a few moments to observe the procedure. His attention was forcibly diverted when Blight's guards shoved him into the pool. Puskab sank to his waist in the muck, thrashing about wildly until he appreciated the fact he couldn't sink any deeper.

'Explain,' Blight growled.

Ahead of him, floating some distance from the platform, was a pair of bodies. They were skaven, their lean frames still draped in the tatters of leather cloaks. Unmistakably, they had been Puskab's assistants. The way they had died was also unmistakable. Ugly black buboes clustered about their throats.

Puskab took a long look at the corpses, then rounded upon Blight, pointing a quivering claw at him. 'Your work-rats!' he coughed, spitting a blob of phlegm into the pool. 'Spy-meat! Traitor-meat! Listen-steal for enemies!'

Blight scratched at his whiskers, surprised by the violence and rage he saw on display. The plague priest was playing the part of injured party with impressive gusto. Enough so that the Wormlord waved aside his guards, intending to hear more before he had them hack Puskab to bloody giblets.

'Who would dare sneak into the Hive?' Blight asked.

'Eshin,' Puskab answered. The assassins were always the obvious choice when it came to infiltrators and spies. But perhaps they were just too obvious. The plague priest bared his fangs as he mentioned another possibility. 'Skully-sneaks,' he said.

Blight's ears curled back against his skull, his tail lashing the snouts of the slaves bearing his palanquin. A low hiss of hate rasped across his fangs. The murderlings of Clan Skully weren't so skilled as the killers of Clan Eshin, but they were close allies of Clan Moulder's beastlords. Of all the other clans, there was particular enmity between Verms and Moulder. The two clans both prided themselves on their ability to breed new and exotic creatures to serve the Under-Empire, but where the power of Verms was beginning to wane, that of Moulder was in the ascension.

'Spy-meat try to filch-steal plague-fleas,' Puskab explained. 'Not know-think that extra fleas crawl-hop into fur. Kill traitor-meat quick-quick!' The plague priest's corpulent body shuddered with a titter of laughter.

Blight's head bobbed from side to side as he considered Puskab's theory. It did fit all of the facts, but what decided him was that Puskab himself had remained in the Hive, well within the Wormlord's reach. If the Poxmaster were up to something, surely he wouldn't be so foolhardy as to linger around.

Still, it wouldn't do to let the plague priest grow too secure in his mind. 'Maybe steal-take for Mouldermaggots,' Blight mused. 'Maybe they spy for Nurglitch. Look-fetch Puskab back to the Pestilent Monastery!' A sadistic grin split Blight's face as he saw terror flash along Puskab's spine. The plague priest wasn't the only one who could think up disturbing theories.

'You need my protection,' Blight reminded Puskab. 'Nurglitch kill-slay quick-quick if you leave the Hive!'

Puskab bowed his horned head, the antlers brushing across the scummy surface of the pool. He turned and pointed a claw at the floating bodies. 'Stash-hide plague-dead,' he cautioned. 'Other spy-meat must not know-find!'

'Let them know,' Blight sneered. 'Soon Clan Verms will have the ultimate weapon thanks to you.' He clenched his claw into a fist, shaking it at the dark ceiling. 'Soon-soon all skaven grovel before Blight Tenscratch!'

'Or all-all attack-fight,' Puskab said. 'Plague-fear great-much. Keep-hide secret until ready-strong.'

Blight's eyes narrowed with cunning. The loathsome plague priest was right, it might be disastrous to let the other clans know what Verms was doing too soon. If the other clans rose up before Verms had enough of the bacillus and enough fleas to carry it...

'Fetch-burn!' Blight snapped at his guards, pointing his claw at the floating bodies. When they hesitated, he leaned out from behind the curtains of his palanquin, his voice a low whisper. 'Fetch-burn, or I'll burn you!'

The threat sent his guards splashing into the pool, stumbling over each other in their haste to reach the bodies.

Puskab watched them wade out, a sly glimmer in the depths of his yellow eyes.

# ⊸ CHAPTER XI ⊱

*Talabecland*
*Vorhexen, 1111*

BARON EVERHARDT JOHANNES Boeckenfoerde, Reiksmarshal of the Imperial Army, tapped his fingers against the scroll of parchment resting on the little wooden camp table. His face was inscrutable, his eyes half-lidded and with a faraway stare. The crackle of the fire burning in his tent's tin stove was the only sound.

'This is treason,' the Reiksmarshal said at length, his voice almost a whisper. His eyes fixed upon Konreid, studying the knight's face. 'I have sworn an oath to the Emperor. Every man in my army has done the same.' His hand rose from the table and pointed the golden head of his marshal's baton at the knight. 'The Reiksknecht took the same vow. We obey our Emperor. It is not for us to decide if his rule is good or bad, it is only enough that we perform our duty. That is all.'

Konreid stood at attention, feeling the winter cold clawing at his back through the canvas tent flap behind him. Except for Boeckenfoerde's adjutant, he was alone with the Reiksmarshal, a fact that gave him confidence even if the general's words weren't reassuring. By rights, he should have been arrested the moment he appeared at the army's encampment. Konreid knew that Emperor Boris had outlawed the Reiksknecht, a diktat that Boeckenfoerde couldn't help but be aware of. It would have been well within the general's authority to have him seized and executed on the spot. That he hadn't, that he had agreed to this conference, was all the proof Konreid needed to give him hope.

In his heart, the Reiksmarshal knew Boris Goldgather was a dictator and tyrant. If his conscience, if his sense of duty and honour could be overcome, if he could be made to see that his ultimate loyalty was to the Empire itself, not the man wearing the emperor's crown, then his support would be won.

'If we do not decide, Reiksmarshal,' Konreid said, 'then who will? Grand Master von Schomberg was every bit as loyal a man as yourself, yet he saw at the last that he had given that loyalty to a man unworthy of it.'

The Reiksmarshal shook his head. 'He swore an oath and he betrayed it.'

'For that, he was humiliated and murdered in the most obscene spectacle,' Konreid said, his voice becoming as cold as the wind at his back.

Boeckenfoerde's face became troubled. He rose from his chair, pacing across the tent's small interior. 'I have heard what happened,' he said regretfully. 'But it is not the Emperor's doing. It is those animals around him, that peasant Kreyssig and that usurer Ratimir.'

'They are the Emperor's men,' Konreid reminded. 'If he was so disgusted with them, they would not be there.'

'You are just a dienstmann,' Boeckenfoerde said. 'You don't understand politics, how the old families can wield their influence to force their way into positions of importance. I tell you, the Emperor doesn't believe in these sorts of things!'

'What sort of influence does the family of a peasant wield?' Konreid asked. 'Boris keeps Kreyssig because he finds the man useful. How many of the great families have resented the power and reach of the Kaiserjaeger, and the fact that a mere commoner acts as their commander?'

The Reiksmarshal silently returned to his chair, turmoil written across his face. 'I have taken an oath,' he repeated.

'And your loyalty has been betrayed,' Konreid insisted. The knight waved his hand, indicating the trembling walls of the tent, the snow drifting under the tent flap. 'This campaign against Talabheim is nothing more than greed and an abuse of authority. This army is nothing more than a gang of excise men dispatched to fill Goldgather's coffers!'

Boeckenfoerde lifted his gaze, staring into Konreid's eyes. 'You go too far. I will not listen to any more treasonous talk.'

Konreid kept his face impassive, but inwardly he felt a sense of exultation. The general's growing agitation was a sign that the doubts already inside his mind were rallying to the cause.

'He sends an entire army out in the dead of winter to force Talabheim to keep its markets open, to countermand the grand count's efforts to control the spread of the plague,' Konreid declared. His voice lowered to a contemptuous hiss, each word twisting like a knife in the Reiksmarshal's heart. 'Yet when he might have kept your forces in the field to preserve what was left of the Drakwald, what was his command? He demanded the army be disbanded, the soldiers sent home so that they might help bring in the harvest! More taxes to line his own pockets!'

'Enough!' the Reiksmarshal growled. His fist closed about the parchment, crushing it between his fingers. Slowly he rose once more, marching to the stove. He stared into the fire, then thrust the crumpled message into the flames.

'I was schooled in the teachings of Verena and Myrmidia,' the general sighed. He turned and smiled grimly. 'I was taught to value reason above everything. To understand why things are what they are and how to use the mind to change them.' He began to pace once more, the marshal's baton slapping against his leg with each step. 'I was also raised to hold every oath as sacred and inviolate. Reason demands I support your coup, honour dictates that I cannot.'

Konreid felt his stomach sicken at the general's decision. 'That is your final word?'

Boeckenfoerde looked from the knight to his adjutant waiting beside the doorway. For a moment, his eyes took on the faraway gaze of an augur. Finally, he turned and approached the table. Removing a quill from its inkpot, he began to scribe a letter. 'You may take this back to those who sent you,' a flicker of a grin crept onto the general's face, 'and whose names I do not wish to know. I can suspect who they are, and that is bad enough.'

The knight stepped forwards and took the letter from the Reiksmarshal. A look of embarrassment came upon him. 'I fear I cannot read,' Konreid confessed.

The Reiksmarshal stepped away, approaching a large map of the Empire stretched across the wall of the tent. 'I have agreed to meet your conspiracy halfway,' he said. 'I will not take up arms against my Emperor, but if he is deposed I will stand by the new Imperial Majesty you install.' He tapped the map with his finger. 'Further, your fears that you will inherit a war from

Emperor Boris… on that front I can be of more direct assistance. Right now, we are marching along the River Talabec. Our supplies come to us by ship. This offers the most direct route to Talabheim, but the risk of discovery is great. I shall decide that the risk is too great, and so I will reroute our march around the Great Forest and along the River Delb until we near the Howling Hills. Much of that territory has been depopulated by Khaagor Deathhoof, but the terrain is familiar to many of my officers. It is the more prudent course to follow, and some of my more cautious commanders have already advised me to take it.

'Of importance to your friends, however, the careful road will mean a two-month delay in laying siege to Talabheim. Your people will have two months to unseat the Emperor before I will be in a position to strike against Talabheim.'

Konreid bowed to the Reiksmarshal. 'Thank you, baron. Two months will see an end to Goldgather's tyranny. Your support will not be forgotten.'

The Reiksmarshal sighed and resumed his pacing. 'I rather fear it won't,' he said. 'Be sure when you stage your revolt, you get Kreyssig even if you can't get his Imperial Majesty. I'd rather not have that peasant in any condition to come looking for me.'

*Bylorhof*
*Ulriczeit, 1111*

THE DESOLATION OF Bylorhof struck Frederick more forcefully than ever before. Somehow, just knowing that Rutger and Aysha and Johan were out there, living their lives, had lessened the terrible reality. Now that they were gone, he appreciated fully how forlorn and devastated the town had become. Few doors failed to display the red cross scrawled across their faces. The dead lay piled against the walls, snow and ice plastering them to the street. There were only a few corpse collectors now that the town elders had stopped paying for the removal of the dead. The few who remained were little better than brigands, only bearing away those bodies grieving relations paid them to take away. Frederick saw one of these gangs load the dead children of a white-haired widow, taking several loaves of bread and a basket of vegetables as payment. The ruffians took their cargo only as far as the next corner, stopping their wagon and ditching the corpses in the snow as soon as they had pried the shoes off the dead feet.

Bylorhof's woes had been compounded by the town's noble lord. Locked within his castle, Baron von Rittendahl had seen to his own protection from the plague by engaging the services of a warlock. The enchanter's magic hadn't been powerful enough to keep the plague from the castle and in an ironic turn, he had been one of the first to die. Now the terrified baron had cut himself off completely, still hoping to escape the plague through seclusion. To ensure that seclusion, he had appealed to his feudal lord, Count Malbork von Drak.

Soldiers of the Nachtsheer, the mercenary troops of the von Draks, had arrived to impose a quarantine upon Bylorhof. Establishing armed camps just beyond the perimeter of the town, the soldiers ensured that no one entered or left the town. The bodies of those who tried were left hanging on a gallows as a warning to their neighbours.

Bylorhof was dying. Frederick could feel it decaying around him as he prowled the streets. He could almost see the ghosts of the departed hovering above their homes, beckoning to those left behind, beseeching them to forsake the suffering of life and embrace the oblivion of the grave. He could feel the preternatural chill of the tomb wafting down the lanes, roving like a hungry beast in search of prey. He could hear the mournful wails of the dead drifting away on the winter wind.

It was an effort to blot out the macabre visions, to deafen himself to the morbid wailing. Frederick wondered if this was some terrible legacy, a curse visited upon him for presuming to invoke the black arts beneath the roof of Morr's temple. He wondered if this was madness, reaching out with long claws to rend his mind.

He wondered if he cared.

The priest paused in his ramble. Ahead, at the top of the street, he could see a dark shape emerge from one of the houses, a house with a red cross painted across the door. There was no mistaking the grotesque mask of the plague doktor. Bruno Havemann, making his rounds, fleecing those desperate souls who could still afford his dubious services.

Frederick's hand tightened about his staff, his jaw setting in a rigid grimace of loathing. His family was dead, and this man was responsible. Havemann would answer for those deaths. Frederick would bring him to justice for his crimes, confront the people of Bylorhof with the true nature of the snake they had allowed into their midst.

The priest's pace quickened. Up ahead, the plague doktor noticed Frederick's rapid approach. The fat man with the scrawny limbs turned about, knocking frantically at the door he had just closed.

'Murderer!' Frederick snarled as he neared the plague doktor. 'Charlatan!'

Havemann swung around, whipping the copper-headed rod at Frederick's hooded head. The priest's staff blocked the blow and pushed Havemann backwards. The physician stumbled, falling onto the snowy street.

'I've done nothing to you!' Havemann cried, his words muffled by the mask, his hands raised to protect himself from the priest's staff.

'Nothing!' Frederick spat, his eyes shining with wrath. 'You've lied and cheated people who believed in you! You've killed the sick and the weak and preyed upon their families! You've murdered those who found you out!' The priest reached down, grabbing the front of Havemann's waxed cloak and dragging the man to his feet. 'You are a murderer and a fraud, Havemann, and by the gods, you'll tell everyone before they hang you!'

The door of the plague-stricken house swung open. A pasty, wizened man stood in the doorway, his tired eyes staring in confusion at the strange spectacle unfolding on his doorstep. Havemann turned his beaked face towards the startled peasant.

'Help! The priest has gone mad!' he cried.

The cry was enough. The sickly man launched himself across the threshold, flinging himself at Frederick. Arms, wasted and weak, struggled to restrain the priest, to free Havemann from his grasp. Frederick strove to shrug off the infirm peasant's pathetic efforts, but to do so would mean releasing his hold on the plague doktor.

The peasant was howling for help, his screams carrying across the deserted streets. In his panic, the peasant did not question Havemann's assertion, did not think that maybe it was the plague doktor, not the priest who was his enemy. There was a hideous tragedy – one of Havemann's victims fighting to protect his own tormentor.

From seemingly deserted houses a stream of peasants began to emerge. Withered by hunger, pallid from disease and seclusion, they were like a host of shades rising from a tomb, the merest echo of the vibrant community that had flourished here only a few months ago. Yet fear lent their wasted bodies strength, strength to race through the snow, to confront the man who persecuted the symbol of their one hope for survival.

Once before, Frederick had been driven from the streets of Bylorhof by an angry mob. Then it had been to protect himself from the rage of the peasants. Now he retreated to protect them from his own wrath. Looking at the wasted, sickly wretches, Frederick knew he could wipe the street with the entire mob. Not one of them, not five of them acting in concert, had enough strength to oppose him.

But that would not be justice. That would only compound the suffering Havemann had brought upon these people. They had endured enough. Frederick would not add to their misery.

Releasing his grip on the plague doktor's cloak, the priest turned and fled. He did not stop running until he was back within the sombre halls of the temple and within the sanctuary. He bowed before the altar, and before the image of his god, Frederick van Hal began to weep.

He wept for Rutger and Aysha. He wept for little Johan, who might have been his son. He wept for Bylorhof and its people. He wept for himself, for the things he had done and the things he had wanted to do.

A noise from outside stirred Frederick from his sorrow. Distractedly, like a person in a dream, the priest rose and stepped to the window. Before him stretched the headstones and monoliths of Morr's garden.

Frederick's senses snapped from their somnolence. His attention was riveted upon a strange figure walking among the graves. The priest rubbed at his eyes, unable – unwilling – to believe what he was seeing.

The trespasser was caked from head to toe in dried mud, a long rope fastened around its neck. The thing moved with a ghastly, shuffling gait, its head crooked against one shoulder, its left arm dangling brokenly at its side. By the ghoulish light of Morrslieb, Frederick could see the discolouration of the thing's wormy flesh, the ragged tears through which leathery muscle and bleached bone shone.

The thing moving among the graves wasn't a living man! It was some nightmare horror, a walking dead man, one of the cursed undead!

The thing seemed to sense it was being watched. It turned and lifted its rotten face, staring at the window with eyes that were blackened by decay. It was impossible that the thing could see with such eyes, yet as it stared at the window, its lipless mouth pulled back in a gap-toothed grin.

For Frederick, this was the ultimate horror. The priest cried out, crossing his arms over his face to blot out the hideous vision. His body swayed as his brain recoiled.

A moment later, Frederick lay prostrate upon the floor, shocked into unconsciousness by the abomination he had seen.

An abomination that slowly, clumsily, made its way towards the temple.

*Skavenblight*
*Ulriczeit, 1111*

EVEN THE PERFUME-BALLS, stuffed with honey and soaked in the most aromatic of insect ichor, couldn't blot out the stench of the Pestilent Monastery. Many of the skaven from Clan Verms had resorted to binding urine-soaked rags about their noses in an effort to block the reek of the plague monks and their perfidious stronghold.

Puskab Foulfur observed the precautions of his allies with undisguised scorn. The Pestilent Monastery was a holy place, saturated with the diseased power of the Horned One. The air, the floors, the very walls exuded the malefic energies of another world. There was no defying the might of a god! Those who dared trespass would be tested in the flame of fever and the cauldron of contagion. The worthy would endure, becoming stronger than they had been. The unfit would sicken and die.

The plague priest reflected upon that truism, the great truth which set Clan Pestilens above all skavendom and marked them as the only true servants of the Horned One. Where the other clans were corrupt and decadent, their leaders nothing but avaricious megalomaniacs, the plague monks prostrated themselves before the sacred judgement of their god. No pup was born to privilege, no clanlord could worm his way to authority and greatness beyond his right, no grasping warlord could selfishly retain power when his time was past.

All those who carried the scent of Pestilens passed through the purifying fire of disease. The greatest were those that endured the most lethal sickness and plague. Any plague monk who felt his devotion and purity was strong enough could embrace one of the Seven Lethal Poxes, sacred diseases imprisoned within great golden cauldrons. The cauldrons were bound with spells of darkest sorcery, crafted by the obscene toad-things of Lustria. The sacred vessels had been carried by the plague monks throughout their long exodus out of the jungles, becoming the most holy of relics. Any skaven of the clan, no matter how lowly, might petition to have himself immersed in one of the contaminated cauldrons. If he survived the resultant infection, his status within Clan Pestilens would increase. Puskab had braved three of the cauldrons, more than most plague priests. Few of the plaguelords themselves had submitted to more than four of the cauldrons. No skaven had ever survived all seven.

Puskab raised his nose, sniffing at the air, trying to catch the smell of the Scabrous Sanctuary where the cauldrons were kept. He would draw comfort from the familiar odour of his clan's sacred relics.

The distance was too great. Puskab had led his allies by an obfuscate and circuitous route into the inner sanctum of the monastery – a labyrinth of forgotten cloisters and disused passages. They had bypassed the moat of effluent which surrounded the stronghold. They had avoided the malarial maze where packs of half-living pus-bags roamed in fevered agony. They had crawled through the catacombs beneath the great dormitories where rabid poxbearers contemplated the forty-nine mystic symbols of the Final Pandemic. Through unused halls and forgotten corridors, Puskab led his allies, violating the secret knowledge entrusted to him as Poxmaster.

Wormlord Blight's suspicions that Nurglitch was moving against Puskab had given the plague priest the leverage he needed to goad Clan Verms into action. The dead ratmen found floating in the worm pools might have been traitors bought by Nurglitch for the express purpose of striking against Blight. While Puskab had been working upon a strain of plague transmissible to skaven, Nurglitch could have had other plague priests working upon the same problem. With more resources at their command, the other plague priests might have solved the problem first, using that knowledge to infect two of their spies in Clan Verms.

Blight had seemed indifferent to the theory until Puskab pointed out that if the infection was deliberate, it would hardly have been his doing. No ratman set fire to his own nest and if the Black Plague were to escape into the Hive, then Puskab would be just as much at risk as his allies. And if Nurglitch had sent traitors to infect Clan Verms, then it was a certainty the Arch-Plaguelord would try again.

It was this, more than anything, which had finally decided Blight to move ahead with the assassination of Nurglitch. Puskab had suspected the proposal was simply a ruse to draw him deeper into the toils of Clan Verms, that Blight had no intention of going ahead with such a dangerous plot. Now the Wormlord's paw had been forced. Killing Nurglitch had become a matter of survival, not bait to entice the loyalties of an ambitious plague priest.

Puskab grinned at the score of ratmen creeping down the narrow, earthen tunnel. White skaven carrying big metal caskets, their dyed fur proclaiming the dangerous cargo they bore. Brown skaven with the curious fire-prods that would drive the spiders to the attack. All of them moved with their backs hunched, their ears and tails low. They stank of fear and they were right to be afraid.

The catacombs they now travelled wound through the very walls of the Outer Temple. If they listened carefully, they could hear the abbots squeaking putrid psalms as they sawed off bits of their leprous bodies to place within reliquaries. These were the last guardians, the last ring of protectors before the Inner Temple and the sanctum of the Arch-Plaguelord himself.

There was no going back now. For any ratman outside the Pestilent Brotherhood to be discovered here was the ultimate in sacrilege. Such an outrage would bring frenzied packs of plague monks down upon them all. They would be slaughtered in an orgy of bloodshed.

So it was that when they reached the hidden doorway which connected the catacombs with the Inner Temple, none of his companions objected when Puskab used his magic to create a scout for them. Drawing upon his sorcery, the plague priest's body convulsed in a fit of hacking and coughing. A black mixture of vomit and blood spilled from his mouth, forming a pool of foulness upon the floor. As Puskab wiped the filth from his whiskers, the pool began to undulate, forming itself into shapes. Great hairy flies emerged from the mess, their faces pinched and somehow ratlike. Their clawed legs scraped against their translucent wings, drying them of the priestly sickness.

'Seek-see,' Puskab hissed at the flies. He pressed his paw against the stone which served as the catch for the hidden door. The flies buzzed away into the black corridor beyond.

'What will-will they do?' gasped Swarmleader Thaglik, ostensibly commander of the mission. The clanrat's eyes were wide with anxiety, his posture cringing and timid.

Puskab glowered at Thaglik. He pressed a claw against his eye, then against his ear. 'Spy-flies see-hear much-much,' the priest explained. 'I see-hear all-all.' He bared his blackened fangs in a savage display. If Thaglik had any more questions about the priest's magic, he kept them to himself.

For several minutes, the skaven huddled in the murky darkness, shivering at every sound. After a time, the buzzing of flies could be heard through the narrow crack Puskab had left open. Six hairy black shapes came whizzing through the opening, landing upon the plague priest's paw. One by one, the flies faced Puskab, buzzing and fluttering their wings, almost as if reporting to their master. As each fly fell silent, the ratman swallowed it, drawing back into his putrid body the noxious life his magic had spawned.

When the last fly vanished into Puskab's mouth, the priest turned to his companions. 'Safe-alone,' he snarled. 'Nurglitch pray-think in refectory.' The plague priest's eyes gleamed murderously. 'Spider-things burrow-chew wall! Scurry-hurry straight to Nurglitch!'

The bloodthirsty excitement shown by Puskab seemed to infect the others. The magnitude of what they had been tasked with had depressed and frightened them – every skaven half-believed that the Grey Lords were immortal and unkillable. But the vicious confidence displayed by Puskab fanned the embers of their own fragile courage. If it was possible to kill the Arch-Plaguelord, then they would be handsomely rewarded by Blight Tenscratch. More importantly, if they killed Nurglitch, then they would be able to leave the horrifying Pestilent Monastery.

The skaven scrambled out from behind the wall, emerging into a dank hall of stone. Each of the mismatched blocks looked to have been dragged down from the surface, appropriated by Clan Pestilens to construct their stronghold. It was a sensible precaution – earthen walls could be breached by the fangs and claws of other ratmen given enough time, but solid stone could thwart such intrusions. Unless, of course, the intruders had creatures such as the diggerfangs to help them.

Puskab pointed at one of the walls, marking it as adjoining the refectory where Nurglitch made his prayers. It was the only time when the Arch-Plaguelord would be alone, that hour when he made direct communion with the Horned One.

The ratmen of Clan Verms hastened across the hall, the white rats setting down their metal caskets, the brown rats lighting their worm-oil torches. Thaglik and the two skaven appointed as his bodyguards stood well away from the spider-handlers. For a skaven, the biggest part of being a leader was avoiding the hazards delegated to underlings. At the moment, keeping close to Puskab was preferable to any proximity to his fellow clanrats.

Puskab watched as the spider-handlers made ready to loose the diggerfangs, his tail twitching expectantly. He held his breath as the white ratmen pushed the caskets towards the wall and raised the lids. The uneven, disordered state of the wall made it impossible to press the cages flush against the stone, so as the tarantulas scuttled into view, the torch-bearers leapt into action, goading the arachnids with the heat of their prods. Under their merciless direction, the spiders attacked the wall, using their venom to burn their way into the stone. Soon a half-dozen smoking craters pitted the face of the wall, each of the holes marking the passage of a ferocious killer.

The skaven chittered softly to each other. Now that the diggerfangs were on their way, the destruction of Nurglitch seemed assured. The spider-handlers rested beside the cages, leaning against their worm-oil prods. After the tension of manoeuvring the tarantulas, the ratmen had slipped into a state of exhausted relief.

A squeal of terror snapped the skaven from their idleness. Spinning around, the ratmen watched in horror as one of their comrades quivered on the floor, a huge tarantula fastened to his leg, its acids eating away his flesh. From the other holes, more of the spiders began to emerge, rushing with eight-legged rapidity towards the stunned skaven. The spider-handlers rushed at the creeping arachnids with their torches, but the creatures barely flinched from the flames. Displaying mindless disregard for their own safety, the tarantulas kept on coming. Their hair singed by the torches, still the scuttling vermin charged at the ratmen. First one, then a second handler was dragged down by the enraged tarantulas.

The other ratmen threw down their prods and scurried back to the hidden door. The white skaven watched the retreat of their fellows for only an instant, then followed them in flight. Yipping like a gutted weasel, Swarmleader Thaglik hurried after his routed minions.

Puskab lingered behind, his fangs bared as he watched the spiders feast upon the fallen skaven. Somehow Nurglitch had discovered the murder scheme. Through magic or cunning, he had thwarted it. Blight was committed now. There could be no more half-steps in his feud with the Arch-Plaguelord.

Eyes glowing with ambition, his mind awhirl with future schemes, Puskab made his way to the hidden door. He paused for only a moment as the seventh fly conjured by his sorcery came buzzing down the corridor and landed upon his arm. Quickly he snatched up the insect and swallowed it. There weren't any eyes to see him, but Puskab was always careful in his intrigues.

Licking his fangs, the corpulent plague priest vanished into the secret passage. It wouldn't do to give Thaglik and his rodents too much of a head start.

*Altdorf*
*Vorhexen, 1111*

ADOLF KREYSSIG BOWED as he was conducted into the calefactory. Like the rest of the Great Cathedral, the chamber was magnificent in its air of opulence and grandeur. The walls were of gleaming marble, the floor a mosaic of contrasting black and white tiles. Great columns spiralled upwards to the heights of vaulted ceilings adorned with panes of stained glass. Tapestries depicting events from the life of Sigmar were displayed in abundance, only a handful betraying the sooty odour of relics rescued from the temple in Nuln.

At the centre of the chamber stood an analogion of wutroth, a massive copy of the *Deus Sigmar* resting upon the lectern's slanted shelf. To either side of the lectern, two enormous fires blazed, fed by a quartet of solemn monks dressed in sackcloth, their shaven heads tattooed with the mark of the twin-tailed comet. Behind the lectern, seated in a tall throne of carved cherrywood, sat the most powerful clergyman in Altdorf, Grand Theogonist Thorgrad.

The Grand Theogonist was an old man, his hair the colour of new-fallen snow, his eyes listless and weary, his wrinkled skin as thin as parchment and bleached to an almost leprous hue, looking somehow ghoulish in a setting of black priestly robes. A jade talisman clung to the priest's throat and about his finger he wore a matching ring. A corset of gromril, a fabulous girdle of dwarfcraft said to possess magical powers, circled his waist and upon the breast of his robe was woven the symbol of Sigmar's hammer, the legendary Ghal Maraz.

Kreyssig stifled an impious snicker when he noted the priest's proximity to the flames. It wasn't the chill of winter that lured Thorgrad to such a conflagration. One of the most widespread stories about the Black Plague was that it was caused by the bites of little black spiders. The common remedy for keeping the spiders away was a good stout fire.

'Thank you for receiving me, your holiness,' Kreyssig said, his tone more mocking than deferential. It was a distinction that did not go unnoticed. The monks hesitated in their tending of the fires, staring at him with scandalised astonishment. Thorgrad shifted in his chair, an ember of life flaring up in his weary eyes.

'Your insistence made a personal audience – how did you put it, commander – *advisable*.' The Grand Theogonist made the last word drip off his tongue like venom. 'I am in seclusion at present. Not to be disturbed. I am communing with Great Sigmar, meditating upon his holy creed and begging his aid in the crisis which besets our Empire. It will take divine aid to stamp out this plague which afflicts us in body and soul.'

A wry smile spread across Kreyssig's face. The only body and soul Thorgrad was trying to save from the Black Plague was his own. 'Forgive my disturbance of your meditation,' he said. 'However I came here not to impose, but to perform a service.'

Immediately Thorgrad's eyes narrowed with suspicion. 'To what does the Temple of Sigmar owe this sudden display of piety, commander?'

'Evidence has come to me that there is a conspiracy against his Imperial Majesty. The name attached to this ring of traitors is that of Arch-Lector Hartwich.'

The Grand Theogonist half rose from his chair, his body trembling with anger. 'You dare come in here and accuse one of Sigmar's most devout and pious servants of such…'

'I have my evidence,' Kreyssig snarled back. 'And I can get more, as much as I need. The threat of Drechsler's axe can be most persuasive.'

Thorgrad's anger intensified. 'The Temple of Sigmar is not answerable to secular authority, and especially not the authority of an ambitious peasant who would aggrandise himself through blasphemy!'

Kreyssig shrugged his shoulders. 'I feared that would

be your attitude. Laws can be changed, but why should we scandalise the entire Sigmarite faith because of one treacherous priest?' A cunning tone crept into the dienstmann's voice. 'Or is it only one treacherous priest?'

'Now you have the affrontery to accuse me!' the Grand Theogonist roared.

Kreyssig's eyes gleamed like slivers of steel. 'Not you, your holiness, but your predecessor. You see, I've heard some ugly rumours about Grand Theogonist Uthorsson. Some ugly ones about what happened to him as well.'

Thorgrad's face went pale. The priest's body collapsed back into his chair. He gestured to the attendant monks, motioning for them to leave the calefactory. Kreyssig watched them leave, triumph stamped across his smirking features.

'How much do you know?' Thorgrad demanded.

'The Verenan inquisitors down in Nuln were quite… inquisitive,' Kreyssig said. 'For some time they had been investigating the excesses of your predecessor. They mentioned Uthorsson as having a connection to something called *Slaanesh* and intimated that the outrages against propriety unfolding after dark in the Nuln cathedral were not so much an expression of degenerate proclivities but a sort of obscene religious ritual.' The commander's smile became almost reptilian. 'It was rather fortunate that a fire destroyed the cathedral and your predecessor before the Verenans decided to take matters into their own hands.'

The Grand Theogonist lost all appearance of power and authority, his shoulders slumping, his body wilting against the cushions of his chair. 'What is it you want to keep this information secret?'

'Only a small consideration,' Kreyssig said. 'Hartwich

is an enemy of his Imperial Majesty, but as a priest he becomes a special case. As you observe, I have no strict authority over him. You, however, do. I am not saying that you have to denounce him publicly as a traitor. You can do whatever you like, just as long as he is disposed of. Quickly and permanently.'

Kreyssig looked over the raging fires, his lip curling in a sneer. 'Say he died of the plague, if you like. There's a lot of that going around right now.'

The Grand Theogonist nodded, conceding to Kreyssig's demands. He was enough of a realist to know this was only the beginning, that the commander would exploit the secret shame of the temple as often as it suited his purposes. Blackmail was a crime without an end.

'What will you do about the other conspirators?' Thorgrad asked.

Kreyssig stepped away from the fires. 'They will be rounded up and disposed of. My spies are quite thorough. Even now, we have taken a man into custody.' He hesitated a moment, weighing whether he should disclose the name of his catch. Contempt for the old, frightened man perched between the flames decided him. Even if the priest grew the spine to warn the conspirators –allowing he knew who they were – their very effort to escape would reveal them to him.

'My Kaiserjaeger found a plague doktor down in the docks who had an interesting story to tell. It seems he was treating a certain peasant, a man who has been hiding from me for some time now. It took a little persuasion, but the physician eventually led us to the hole this peasant had hidden himself in.

'I have Wilhelm Engel,' Kreyssig stated, watching to see if Thorgrad displayed any special reaction. He was disappointed to find none.

'I have Wilhelm Engel,' he repeated. 'And through him, I will track down all of these traitors and put their heads on the Tower of Altdorf's roof.'

## ➤ CHAPTER XII ➤

*Altdorf*
*Vorhexen, 1111*

'I CAN MAKE the pain go away. I can make all the hurt and suffering stop. You can be whole again. Clean again. Why won't you let me help you?'

The words crackled through the black corridors of Mundsen Keep, reverberating from the frozen slime caking the filthy walls. Somewhere in the darkness a maniac began to giggle, his chains clanking against the bricks of his cell.

Wilhelm Engel clenched his eyes closed, trying to hold back the tears. Kreyssig's torturers had been at work on him, splitting open his diseased flesh with hot tongs, scalding his skin with boiling oil, piercing his fingers with copper nails. Somehow, through it all, he had kept silent.

Or at least given the Kaiserjaeger nothing better than inarticulate screams.

Now, however, the fiendish Kreyssig had unveiled a new torture. The torment of hope. The promise of life to a man already resigned to death.

Engel was strapped to a table, his mangled body held in place by long belts of leather. He could just raise his neck enough to see the hideous ruin the Kaiserjaeger had made of him, the raw glistening meat where his leg should be, the red wreck of his chest. He could also see the man who promised to undo everything that had been done to him. More than that – the man who promised to do the impossible. To save him from the plague.

It was easy to be brave when you were prepared to die. How much harder to die when you were offered a miraculous chance to escape death, to cheat Morr even as he reached out his bony hand to take you.

Karl-Maria Fleischauer, a scarecrow of a man, his face displaying hard angles beneath its thick growth of beard, his eyes glistening with an ophidian lustre. He wore an extravagant robe of silk, its foreign contours lent a further exotic flavour by the mystical symbols embroidered over its surface. Grinning moons and whirling stars, writhing dragons and fiery phoenixes, coiled serpents and roaring lions. Fleischauer, the pet warlock of Emperor Boris, a man both infamous among and feared by the peasants of Altdorf and common folk everywhere. The black arts were a thing to be shunned, their practitioners reviled and destroyed. Such sorcerers were debased, subhuman things, preying upon the innocent to call forth elementals and daemons, sacrificing the helpless to seal their unholy pacts with the Ruinous Powers.

Yet Fleischauer promised his magic could do something so wondrous that it was beyond even the priestesses of Shallya. He promised his spells could drive the plague from Engel's body.

'Perhaps you doubt my magic,' Fleischauer said, a tinge of hurt seeping into his grotesque voice. He ruffled his arms, throwing back the voluminous sleeves of his robe. 'I shall demonstrate. Then you will believe. You will know that you can trust my spells and my word.'

The frigid air of the dungeon became impossibly colder as the warlock worked his magic. Engel could feel the tears freezing to his eyelids, could hear the blood crystallising against his skin. His ears rang with the sinister sing-song incantation rolling from Fleischauer's lips.

Then, before his amazed gaze, Engel saw the buboes marring the pit of his arm growing smaller. The discolouration of his skin faded, his flesh becoming smooth and unmarked, flush with the ruddy glow of health and strength.

'I can take it all away,' the warlock promised. 'All you need do is tell Commander Kreyssig what he wants to know. Then I will take away the plague. I will fix all your injuries. You will be free. You will leave this place on your own two feet.' The warlock's hand brushed across the burnt, oozing mess where the iron boot had been used on Engel's right foot.

Engel's eyes rolled, a piteous moan of torment rising from his lips. He wouldn't break. He would stay strong. He owed that much to all the Marchers he'd brought to Altdorf, the men who had died because he had been naïve enough to think the Emperor was a reasonable man. He had to protect Meisel and the others, engaged upon their great work, fighting to depose a tyrant.

Against his will, he looked at the spot the warlock's magic had cleansed. Engel's resolve shattered. Before he was even aware, words were spurting from his tongue. He tried to stop himself, but it was an effort he knew he couldn't win. That part of him that was willing to die for the cause was too small beside the part of him that wanted to live. He heard his own voice telling the lurking Kaiserjaeger about Lady Mirella and her cellar. He damned himself as a traitor, falling silent before he could reveal any more than he already had.

Adolf Kreyssig's evil laugh told Engel that what he had already confessed was enough. The commander stepped out from the shadows, his cruel face lit up by the glow of victory. 'That is all I require, warlock,' he said.

Fleischauer wiped his brow with the sleeve of his robe. 'That is well,' he said. 'The enchantment is a taxing one to sustain.' As he spoke, the atmosphere in the dungeon became noticeably warmer. Engel could feel the change in the air, a lessening of the nameless dread crawling over his skin.

In its place came pain and horror. Searing agony coursed outwards from his chest. Craning his neck, Engel could see the buboes popping back into noxious existence as the warlock's illusion was broken. As he heard Kreyssig growl commands to the Kaiserjaeger, Engel knew he was worse than a traitor.

He was a fool.

ERICH LISTENED WITH growing disgust as Baron Thornig discussed the coming marriage of his daughter to Adolf Kreyssig. As hard as he tried, he couldn't accept the woman's shameful sacrifice. It was easy to get his head around the hazards of torture and death, even of disgrace. But something as unseemly as to exploit a woman's virtue simply to learn the enemy's secrets? It tainted the entire cause, took their noble purpose and dragged it through the mud.

Lady Mirella noticed the knight's disquiet. Detaching herself from the conversation, she drifted over to where he stood against the curtained wall of her sitting room. 'It disturbs you, such talk?'

The captain nodded, his eyes never leaving the chair where Princess Erna was seated. She was taking no part in the conversation, content to let Baron Thornig explain the arrangements that had been made, the nuptial vows that had been exchanged. No, he corrected himself. Content was too indifferent a word. One look at the princess made it clear she was anything but indifferent to her fate. Resigned was a better word to convey her sentiment. Resigned to her doom, a doom whose horror she fully appreciated.

'How can Prince Sigdan and the others seriously allow this?' Erich wondered. 'What will become of her?'

'If everything works out, she'll be a widow before summer,' Lady Mirella predicted.

Erich's jaw tightened. 'But everyone will still know. She'll still have his stink on her.'

Lady Mirella gave the young captain a curious stare. 'If I didn't know you better, I'd say you were jealous. Maybe her willingness to go through with this has aroused that knightly passion. Maybe you sense a kindred spirit, someone willing to sacrifice personal honour for the good of people who will never thank her, people she doesn't even know.'

The captain turned away, pulling at the heavy curtain, peering through the frosted glass at the street outside. 'I wonder when Konreid will be back,' he said, brusquely changing the subject. 'If we knew where the Reiksmarshal stands, we could make our plans accordingly.'

'And what are your plans?' Lady Mirella asked, resting her hand on the knight's arm. 'I mean beyond the overthrow. After Boris is deposed.'

Erich scowled as he heard the question. It wasn't something he'd considered before. 'Rebuild the Reiksknecht, I suppose. Try to get things back to what they were.' His body suddenly stiffened, his eyes fixing on a dark figure he'd glimpsed on the street. He had seen the man for only an instant before he ducked back behind a corner, but he was certain he'd been wearing the uniform of the Kaiserjaeger.

Even as he turned to warn the rest of the conspirators, Lady Mirella's manservant came rushing down from the garret. 'Kaiserjaeger!' Gustav gasped.

'What?' Prince Sigdan exclaimed. 'Where? How many?'

'In the street, your grace,' the servant said. 'At least a score moving to surround the house!'

'They must know we're here!' bellowed Duke Konrad. All the poise drained out of the nobleman, leaving only terror behind. 'We've been betrayed!' he shrieked, casting an accusing eye over everyone in the room.

'That's impossible,' grumbled Baron Thornig. 'Everyone who knew about this meeting is here!'

'Arch-Lector Hartwich isn't,' Mihail Kretzulescu observed.

'Wilhelm Engel knew about this place too,' Meisel confessed. 'He was too sick to come, but as leader of the Marchers, I felt he should know.' The statement brought a flurry of angry recriminations racing through the room.

'It doesn't matter who told them!' Erich barked, trying to shout down the others. 'What matters is that we get out of here before they can close the noose.' He let the curtain fall closed. A disturbing thought occurred to him.

'You say you saw only twenty Kaiserjaeger?' he asked Gustav. The peasant nodded. 'That's not enough to rush the building. Kreyssig may be a demented madman, but he's no fool.'

'What are you thinking?' Prince Sigdan asked.

Erich was already racing towards the kitchen and the

stairs leading down into the cellar. 'If he found out about the house, he may have found out about the cellar! The men in the street are just there to keep us in! The real attack will come from below!

'They're going to use our own tunnel to trap us!'

*Nuln*
*Ulriczeit, 1111*

WALTHER PACED ALONG the alleyway behind the Black Rose, his hands stuffed deep inside the pockets of his coat in an effort to defend against the cold, a thick scarf wrapped around his face to defend against the omnipresent stench of the streets. The snow falling from the sky was almost white, scarcely smirched by the smoke rising from the city's chimneys. For the first time he could remember, the city was blanketed in white, not the dirty grey of soot.

The image was beautiful, but it was a terrible beauty. The reason the snow was white was because there weren't enough fires left to stain it. There weren't enough people. Nuln was dying. By day the corpse carts prowled the streets, men already sick collecting those who were dead. Great pyres blazed at the heart of every district. The priests of Morr had been dying by the bushel, leaving no one to bury the dead. The only solution left was to consign the corpses to fire.

The city was breaking apart into two camps: those who blamed the plague on spiritual corruption and those who believed it was just an ordinary disease, no more selective about who it struck down than Reikflu. The religious-minded either kept to their homes, fasting and praying, or else prowled the streets in penitent mobs, lashing themselves with whips and preaching that the judgement of the gods was upon mankind. The threat of the world's ending, however, only made those less spiritually inclined increase the magnitude of their debauchery. 'Eat, drink and love,' was their mantra. 'For tomorrow, we feed the rats!'

Walther gritted his teeth as he considered the horror of such a toast. As the people of Nuln became fewer, the number of rats had swollen to fantastic proportions. With the cats and dogs culled by superstitious peasants, the vermin roamed the streets with unprecedented boldness. There had been hideous stories of rats creeping into cradles and gnawing the infants inside. Bodies left out in the gutter would be picked down to the bone in a few hours.

The rat-catcher shook his head. At one time he would have considered the ferocity and fecundity of the vermin as good for his business. He didn't feel that way any more. He appreciated the suffering of his fellow man better than before the plague had come. To profit from another's misery would make him nothing better than a parasite. Besides, the Assembly had stopped issuing bounties for rats. The problem was simply too big to solve that way. Like everyone else in the city, the nobles had resigned themselves to sitting back and waiting for events to run their course.

In the alleyway, a big black rat scurried through the snow, so confident that it didn't even twitch a whisker as it passed near the Black Rose. Walther watched the repulsive rodent wend its way towards the street, diverting its course only when it drew near a beggar slumped in a doorway. Apparently the wretch was still healthy enough to be a poor prospect for the rat's appetite.

'Herr Schill?' a muffled voice called out from the darkness. Walther turned away from the retreating rat and turned around. A gasp of alarm automatically escaped him. As the speaker stepped out from the shadows, Walther found himself confronted by a tall figure enclosed within a black gown of waxed canvas. A wide-brimmed leather hat fitted to a waxed canvas hood covered the man's head while a grotesque mask with a protruding beak concealed his face.

'You… you are the doktor?' Walther asked. The ghoulish apparition sketched a slight bow. The rat-catcher felt anger swell up inside him. 'You were asked to be discreet, not come dressed like a raven of Morr!'

The plague doktor shrugged. 'You cannot pay me enough to take any chances,' he said, his words all but smothered by his mask. 'The graveyards are filled with imprudent men.'

'Get inside, before someone sees you!' Walther hissed. He reached for the plague doktor, but the man brushed his hand away with the heavy walking stick he carried.

'I said I do not take chances.' The doktor pointed with his staff at the tavern. 'Lead me to the patient, but do it without touching. I try to limit physical contact when I can.'

Fuming at the plague doktor's condescending tone, Walther showed him through the tavern's side entrance. At this late hour even the Black Rose was without a crowd. The cook and his assistants had retired, leaving just Zena to attend the few patrons still abroad. She nodded when she saw Walther appear at the door, motioning that it was safe to come in. The rat-catcher and the plague doktor swept past her. Walther pulled open the trap in the floor and climbed down the ladder into the cellar below. Zena and the plague doktor followed close behind him.

The cellar was filled with casks of wine and barrels of beer, provisions Bremer was hoarding against the day when quarantine conditions would kill all traffic from the rest of Wissenland and force Nuln to survive on what was already within the city walls. Walther circled through the confusion of boxes, making for a faint glimmer of light at the back of the cellar.

A section of the room had been partitioned off by a ragged curtain, behind which Hugo lay sprawled on a pallet. In his fever, he had pushed away the mass of furs and blankets Zena had provided to keep him warm. Despite the frosty chill which gripped the cellar, Hugo's nightshirt was soaked with sweat, fairly plastered against his chest.

Walther shook his head sadly as he gazed down at his friend, then his lip curled back in anger. Several rats were circling around the pallet, gnawing away at the rushlights they had knocked down. One of the rodents had even started on the stem of the only light still held fast to its fixture. Walther shouted at the loathsome vermin, but the bold rats didn't so much as glance in his direction. Only when he started forwards and caught one of the rats with a kick did the scavengers retreat, fading into the blackness with instinctive ease. They didn't retreat far, their beady eyes gleaming from the shadows as they watched the people gather around the sickbed.

Walther hurriedly righted the remains of the rushlights, pushing them back into their stands with frustrated violence. 'Why weren't you watching him!' he snarled at Zena when he had the tapers lit once more. 'You should never leave him alone! The rats…'

Zena stepped to Walther's side, laying her hand against his chest. She knew he didn't mean the unjust accusation, that he was simply lashing out because of the helplessness he felt. He was powerless to stop Hugo's decline and that was something Walther couldn't accept.

While Zena consoled Walther, the plague doktor stood over Hugo, the glass eyes of his garish mask reflecting the fires of the rushlights. The invalid recoiled from the dreadful apparition hovering over him, but didn't have the strength to ward away the doktor's staff as it jabbed at his nightshirt. The copper talon at the end of the stick hooked the fabric of the nightshirt, peeling the garment back and exposing the sick man's chest. A smell of vinegar exuded from the bird-like mask as the doktor peered closer at his patient.

'Plague,' the physician declared, tugging his stick free from Hugo's clothes and retreating from the man's bedside. He turned his back to the pallet and concentrated on holding the copper talon at the end of his staff in the fires of the rushlights.

Walther's fists clenched at the plague doktor's callous attitude. 'Do something for him.' He pulled away from Zena's restraining arms. 'You're supposed to be a healer! Help him!'

The bird-like mask turned and the glass eyes fixed upon Walther's enraged features. 'I've heard too many pleas, too many threats, to feel anything. If you are appealing to the better angels of my nature, I'm afraid you are too late. They flew the coop months ago.' The plague doktor drew the copper talon away from the flame, inspecting the hot glow of the metal. 'After a dozen deaths, you learn not to care. After a hundred, you can't even if you wanted to.'

'You must be able to do something,' Walther growled.

The plague doktor looked past the rat-catcher and his woman, staring at Hugo's wasted frame. The physician's gloved hands drew a tiny clay bottle from a pouch on his belt. Grimly, he set it down on one of the boxes. 'You've paid me well, so I leave you this. It will make his going swift.' He tapped the neck of the little bottle. 'By

Verena, if I only had more of it. Enough for everyone.

'I won't inform the Hundertschaft about this,' the plague doktor said, his tone becoming harsh. 'By law, I am required to. By conscience, it is my obligation. But, I suppose it makes no difference. The gods have decided that we're all going to die. It is only a matter of time.' He turned away, walking back across the cellar towards the ladder. On his way, he snatched a bottle of wine from a rack against the wall. 'I'm going home to drink this and in the morning I will have forgotten I was ever here.'

Walther didn't move until the plague doktor was gone. His eyes were fixed upon the bottle the physician had left.

'Perhaps it is for the best,' Zena whispered.

The rat-catcher stormed across the cellar, his hand closing about the bottle. With an inarticulate howl of rage, he threw it at the wall, shattering it into a hundred pieces.

'There has to be a way!' Walther shouted. 'By all the gods, there has to be some hope somewhere!'

Tears were glistening in Zena's eyes as she heard the pain in her man's voice. Walther felt powerless to help Hugo. She felt powerless to help Walther.

From the shadows, the rats began to scurry back towards the rushlights.

*Middenheim*
*Vorhexen, 1111*

GRAF GUNTHAR LEANED back in his oaken throne and studied the foreigner his son had brought to the Middenpalaz. He tried to restrain the hostility he felt towards the man. Whatever the Reiklander's intentions, the knight had inadvertently led his son into danger. Mandred's excuses that it was he who had deceived the knight into taking such a risk had fallen on deaf ears. Grown men should know better than to bow to the whims of a mere boy, however great his noble station.

He had been tempted not to grant the audience at all, to have the knight sent into quarantine at once – or executed out of hand as Viscount von Vogelthal had urged. It was still a temptation. The Graf wasn't so power-mad that he couldn't forgive a man who defied his decree to further some noble cause. But the fear of the plague being unleashed inside Middenheim was too great to ignore. Even for this audience, he had commanded smouldering braziers placed at either side of where the knight stood in the hope that the pungent smoke would smother any pestilential fumes the Reiklander might have brought with him.

To his credit, Othmar had uncovered and helped destroy a hideous conspiracy. The plague cult could have brought destruction upon all of Middenheim – indeed, such could only have been their purpose. The Graf owed him a debt of gratitude for putting an end to the cult's activities. Indeed, that was the only reason he had agreed to meet with the man.

'Speak, while I am still of a mind to listen,' Graf Gunthar told the Reiklander. His deep voice echoed through the narrow confines of the audience hall. A much smaller chamber than the palace's council rooms and great hall, the vault-like room was used to receive dignitaries and visiting royalty in a more intimate and less public setting. The rich tapestries and fantastic hunting trophies lining the walls were intended to create a feeling of informality while at the same time reminding a guest of Middenheim's splendour.

Othmar bowed to the throne, careful to keep himself

between the braziers. A trio of armed guards were watching his every gesture. One false move and he would be expelled from the royal presence – alive if he was fortunate.

'Your highness, I have had a long and perilous journey to reach you,' the knight began. 'You know already of the difficulty just gaining entry to the city.'

'We are quite familiar with your flagrant violation of the Graf's decree,' von Vogelthal snarled. The chamberlain's face was pinched with loathing, but in his eyes was a terrible fear. A big brass pomander hung about his neck and every time he even glanced in the knight's direction, the viscount raised the ball to his nose and took a deep sniff of the aromatic spices locked inside.

Graf Gunthar motioned for his frightened chamberlain to be silent. What was done was done. Now that the Reiklander was here, the Graf would listen to what he had to say.

Othmar bowed his head in contrition. Catching the mood of the few advisors the Graf had brought with him to this audience, the knight hastily dropped the subject of his travels.

'I do not know how much you are aware of what is transpiring in Altdorf,' Othmar said. 'The situation as it is, I can imagine that news from the outside is scarce and much of what you have heard has probably been dismissed as rumour or fancy. I have been dispatched by my masters to ensure that Middenheim has a clear and accurate picture of what has happened and the course of action we hope to pursue.

'Boris Goldgather has shown himself to be a grasping despot unworthy of the title of emperor. In his ruthless drive to aggrandise his own wealth and power, he has increasingly perpetrated outrages upon his imperial subjects. The taxation of the *Dienstleute*, his callous massacre of starving men in the streets of Altdorf, the march against Talabheim, the abandonment of Drakwald, these are only the latest of his crimes. The Emperor's tyranny will break the Empire apart if it is allowed to continue.'

'We have heard that the Reiksknecht has already taken up arms against the Emperor,' Graf Gunthar said. 'That yours is an outlawed order, the lives of all its knights forfeit to the imperial crown.'

'That is only partly correct, your highness,' Othmar replied. 'The Reiksknecht was commanded to undertake the slaughter of defenceless men in open defiance of every convention of chivalry and honour. Grand Master von Schomberg refused to besmirch the reputation of the Reiksknecht by being a party to such a crime. For his stance, a warrant was issued for his arrest and the entire order was commanded to lay down its arms. We refused.'

'And now you plot against the Emperor,' von Vogelthal sneered. 'A hundred knights against the might of the Empire!'

Othmar bristled at the chamberlain's derision, his fist clenching at his side. Quickly he turned his gaze away from von Vogelthal and back upon the Graf. He didn't need to win the viscount's support. The only man in this room he had to appeal to was Graf Gunthar.

'We are not without our allies,' Othmar stated. 'You will understand that I cannot disclose their names, but I will say that they represent some of the most powerful men in the Empire. The tyranny of Boris Goldgather must be brought to an end.' Othmar looked about the room, studying the faces of the Graf's advisors, noting the scowls of distaste they wore. 'Would it help to know that I was sent here not by my Grand Master, but by your own Baron Thornig? He said that the sons of Middenheim would never sacrifice their freedom, that they would take a stand against the oppression of Altdorf.'

'One city against the whole Empire?' scoffed Duke Schneidereit. 'We would be swatted like a fly.'

'Not one city alone!' protested Othmar. 'Others would stand with you! It needs only someone to show them the way and all the provinces will rise up against this despot!'

'And you expect Middenheim to lead the way?' Graf Gunthar asked, his voice as cold as steel.

Mandred could sense the anger boiling up inside the Graf. Limping towards the throne, the side of his head wrapped in bandages, the prince appealed to his father. 'You know Sir Othmar to be a brave man, father. You can trust what he says.'

The Graf turned narrowed eyes upon his son. 'Liars can be brave men too,' he hissed, the meaning of his words causing Mandred to hide his face in shame. The Graf leaned back in his throne, shifting his cold regard back upon the Reiklander. 'It happens that I believe you,' he declared. 'I believe you mean everything you say. But tell me, will this noble cause make Nordland forget their schemes to wrest control of the Middle Mountains from my realm? Will it make Ostland stop stealing timber from my forests? Will it make the robber barons of Westerland stop raiding my villages? Will we forget all of our differences and unite against the only thing that holds us together?'

'Boris has schemed long to pit neighbour against neighbour,' Othmar said. 'He knows that by keeping the provinces divided he ensures his own rule. Tala-becland feuds with Stirland, Averland quarrels with Solland over the price of wool, Wissenland places an embargo upon Reikland wine.'

Graf Gunthar nodded his head. 'Then you do understand the impossibility of what you ask.'

Mandred turned back towards the throne. 'But father, you yourself said that Middenheim must prepare for the Emperor's armies to attack us!'

A pained sigh rumbled from the seated monarch. 'If the Emperor attacks us, we will defy him.' He stared hard into the face of his son. 'Don't you understand? What this man is asking of us is treason! To betray our oaths to the Empire! Saint or tyrant, Boris Hohenbach is our Emperor!

'I am sorry,' Graf Gunthar said, turning back to face Othmar, 'but what you ask is impossible. Middenheim will fight if it is attacked, but we are not traitors.' He motioned with his hand and an attendant in crimson livery blew a single note upon a curled hunting horn. This audience was at an end.

'Take Sir Othmar to the Cliff Tower,' von Vogelthal ordered. The Graf's guards motioned for the knight to follow them, taking pains not to come too close to the man. Bowing once more to the seated monarch, Othmar allowed himself to be led from the room.

'Is it necessary to lock him away like an enemy?' Mandred asked.

'Until we are certain he is not carrying the plague, he is an enemy,' von Vogelthal told the prince.

'He will be well looked after,' the Graf promised.

Mandred shook his head at his father's statement. 'And what about the people down at the foot of the Ulricsberg?' he demanded. 'Will they be well looked after?'

'The beastkin will soon solve that problem,' von Vogelthal said, then immediately regretted his snide remark when he found Mandred glaring at him.

'What does that mean, viscount?' the prince snarled.

'Our sentries have spotted beastmen gathering in the forest,' Graf Gunthar told Mandred. Unlike von Vogelthal, there was sympathy in the monarch's tone. 'When they feel their numbers are strong enough, they will undoubtedly attack.'

'And what are we going to do?' Mandred demanded.

'The only thing we can do,' the Graf answered. 'The only thing that can keep Middenheim safe.

'We let Warrenburg burn.'

## ━━❮ CHAPTER XIII ❯━━

*Altdorf*
*Vorhexen, 1111*

HIS HEART WAS pounding as Erich von Kranzbeuhler led the way into the cellar. It was not fear for himself that sent terror racing through his veins, but the knowledge that if they were caught then their cause would die with them. No one else in Altdorf would dare to stand against Emperor Boris after them. It was that thought which made his fist clench tighter about the hilt of his sword and made him pause at the door, listening for the slightest sound from below.

Erich looked back, instinctively seeking out Prince Sigdan, the leader of the conspiracy. He waited until the nobleman nodded his head, then he wrenched open the door and leaped down the short flight of stairs. He braced his feet on the cold stone floor, his body tensed for battle, his eyes scouring the darkness for the faintest hint of motion. The only sound was the rustle of rats creeping among the boxes and nibbling the straw scattered about the cellar.

A rushlight threw rays of illumination across the

cellar, driving the rats back into their holes but revealing no lurkers in black livery. Erich glanced back at the steps behind him, reaching back to take the burning rushlight from Baron Thornig.

'It doesn't look like they're here yet,' Erich said. 'We can thank Sigmar for that, at least!' The captain turned about, staring at the jagged opening to the tunnel. He frowned as he thought of asking aristocrats like Prince Sigdan and Duke Konrad to creep through the muck and mire of the sewers, and the idea of Princess Erna and Lady Mirella slinking through such filth turned his stomach. If there were a way to spare them such indignity... but, no, they would suffer far worse if they fell into Kreyssig's hands.

That is, those of them who hadn't already decided on such a fate. He felt his jaw clench as he imagined the lovely princess married to a reptilian peasant like Kreyssig. For a moment he hesitated, wondering if it wasn't better to make a stand of it and go down in a clean fight.

'What is it?' Mihail Kretzulescu asked. 'Why have you stopped?'

The darkness hid the twinge of embarrassment on Erich's face as he answered the Sylvanian. 'Thought I heard something,' he answered lamely. 'It must have been a rat.' Without explaining further, the knight pressed on, rushing along the cramped passage, following the mephitic reek of the sewer. Gradually the air became warmer, the moist unclean heat of the steaming channel of waste flowing beneath the city.

Erich hesitated upon the ledge, watching and listening. In the distance, he could just make out the sound of voices. They were faint and indistinct and in the echoing sewer it was impossible to tell which direction they came from. All he could tell was that there were a lot of them and there was a rattle of armour any time the speakers were silent. Only one group of armed men would have any business in the sewers. It was the Kaiserjaeger, come to close Kreyssig's trap.

'Which way, my lord?' asked Meisel, a notched blade gripped in the dienstmann's hand.

Erich agonised over the answer, turning his head left and right, desperately trying to decide which direction the voices were coming from. If they waited long enough to see the lights the Kaiserjaeger carried, then their own rushlight would be seen. They had to move before then, before Kreyssig had a chance to spot them. But if he made the wrong choice, they would run right into the villain's arms.

As he gazed into the murk of the sewers, Erich felt his skin crawl. Thousands of beady red eyes gleamed at him from the shadows, each burning with obscene hunger. Looking at them, he could picture his body lying in the effluent with a Kaiserjaeger sword through his gut and a horde of greedy rodents gnawing the flesh from his bones.

The knight froze as he noticed another pair of eyes watching him from the darkness. They were bigger than the rats' eyes, higher off the ground and with a disturbing impression of a lanky shape behind them. Yet they reflected the glow of the rushlight with the same crimson gleam as the rats around them, an unholy ember of malice and hunger. Erich felt fingers of ice race along his spine as he locked eyes with the sinister apparition.

Then there was no more time to think about the dreadful spectre. Imagination or nightmare, Erich tore his gaze from the dark figure, twisting around in answer to the cries of shock and horror rising from behind him. His first thought was that the Kaiserjaeger had stolen upon them from behind somehow. An instant later, he was wishing what had ambushed them was Kreyssig's thugs.

The walls of the sewer were alive with vermin, great bloated rats that scurried along the ledges and swam through the filthy channel. An army of squeaking, chittering rodents came swarming towards the fugitives. Meisel was shouting in disgust, using the flat of his sword to fend off the vermin scrabbling at his legs. Lady Mirella screamed as a black beast with enormous fangs gnawed at her shoe. Palatine Mihail Kretzulescu stamped frantically with his boots as a pack of squealing brutes rushed at him.

Erich lunged at the chittering horde, thrusting the rushlight full into the faces of the rats as they swarmed about the feet of Princess Erna. The horrified woman collapsed in his arms, her breath reduced to a terrified panting. The knight shifted her weight to his sword arm, pressing her against his shoulder as he waved the flaming brand across the snouts of the onrushing pack.

An anguished wail echoed through the sewer. Erich looked up to see the manservant Gustav clutching at his bleeding leg, a piebald rat gnawing at his knee. His mangled leg collapsed beneath him, spilling him face-first into the swarming tide of rodents. At once they were over him, a living carpet of gnashing fangs and flashing claws.

'We can't fight them!' Erich shouted, waving his sword and rushlight. 'Not with these! We have to run!'

'Run where?' demanded Prince Sigdan, trying to slash the vermin spilling around his feet with a jewelled dagger and a gromril sword. 'What about the Kaiserjaeger!'

'Khaine take the Kaiserjaeger!' exclaimed Duke Konrad, his arm covered in gore from where a rat had leaped upon him. 'Anything's better than being eaten alive!'

Erich spun around, noticing for the first time that the

way was clear to their left. For some reason there were no rats in this direction. Perhaps they had been scared off by the approaching Kaiserjaeger, but whatever the reason, he wasn't going to squander the chance to escape those verminous fangs! Yelling to his comrades, hugging Princess Erna tight against him, Erich led the frantic retreat.

The rats swarmed after them, chittering and squealing, raising such a deafening, monstrous commotion that the echoing voices of the Kaiserjaeger were smothered by the noise. Erich couldn't tell if they were moving closer to or away from their enemies. Nor did he care. All that mattered was to escape the horde of ravenous vermin.

For what seemed an eternity but couldn't have been more than a dozen minutes, the fugitives fled through the sewers. It was a shameful, terrified retreat. Warriors who had faced ogres and orc warlords across the field of battle fleeing for their lives before such tiny, miserable animals! Yet there was no fighting such a swarm. For every rat Erich might crush underfoot, ten would rush in to take its place. There were only two choices to make: run or be devoured.

Finally, when he felt his heart must burst from the exertion, when his breath was a burning agony in his lungs, when sweat streamed from his brow and blinded his eyes, the sewers suddenly fell silent. Erich paused in his headlong flight, daring to look back. He wiped the sweat from his eyes and blinked, unable to believe what he saw.

The rats were gone! One instant the sewers had been filled with a swarming horde of vermin hungry for blood, the next there was only the ancient masonry and brickwork. Against all belief, the entire horde had suddenly decided to abandon the chase!

'Where did they go?' Erna gasped in wonder, almost unwilling to believe the evidence of her eyes.

'Let's not stick around to find out,' Erich decided. His hand lingered against the silky smoothness of the princess's fingers, then, with deliberate gentleness, he led her to her father. The knight nodded grimly as he saw the gratitude in Baron Thornig's face. He didn't feel he'd done the princess any favours. What waited for her was every bit as repulsive as an army of hungry vermin.

'At least we seem to have avoided the Kaiserjaeger,' observed Count van Sauckelhof, trying to staunch the flow of blood from the bites marking his legs. 'But where are we?'

Meisel sheathed his sword slowly and looked about him. Gradually the dienstmann began to nod. 'I think we must be somewhere near the waterfront.' He jabbed a thumb at the mucky channel, indicating the fish bones sticking from the effluent, then he pointed down the tunnel. 'This should let out to the Reik soon. The flow is getting quicker and the air is just a little colder.'

'Who cares where it leads, so long as it gets us out of these damn sewers!' Duke Konrad grumbled.

'That, your grace,' Erich said, 'is the best damn idea I've heard all day!'

With unseemly haste, the small group of nobles and idealists hurried down the tunnel, eager for the clean air and the open sky. None of them looked back. None of them saw the gleaming pair of red eyes watching them from the darkness or heard the shrill, inhuman titter of laughter that rose from the lanky shape behind the eyes.

'FIND THEM,' KREYSSIG snarled, glaring at the Kaiserjaeger sergeant. The soldier executed a stiff salute and hastened back through the tunnel leading up into Lady

Mirella's cellar. Kreyssig scowled as he heard the shouts of the other men searching the sewer tunnels. Except for one dead man, they had found no trace of the conspirators. Even the corpse was useless, gnawed beyond all recognition.

'Commander,' a sharp voice hissed from the darkness. Kreyssig swung around, a dagger in his fist. He could just make out the shape crouched beside the rubble of a broken pillar. There was no mistaking that twisted, subhuman slouch. It was one of his mutant friends, the secret eyes and ears of the Kaiserjaeger.

Kreyssig kept his dagger ready, anger blazing in his eyes. 'They've escaped,' he snarled. 'For all your talk about knowing the sewers, the traitors escaped! If you'd led us here quicker, if you'd found a more direct route, I could have had them all!'

The mutant cringed before Kreyssig's wrath, pressing its ratty nose to the filthy ledge in a token of abasement. 'Forgive-mercy, great-terrible commander!' the mutant squeaked. 'Try-help, yes-yes, try-help much-much!'

Kreyssig resisted the urge to kick the cowering abomination's fangs down its throat. 'They've escaped,' he repeated.

The mutant reared up slightly, its eyes gleaming red in the light of Kreyssig's oil-lamp. 'Not all-all,' the creature hissed, its body straightening with pride. 'Catch-take one,' it reported. 'Kill-wound,' it added, its tone becoming apologetic. 'Crawl off to die-die. But find-take this before traitor-meat get away!' The mutant reached into its filthy cloak, removing a scrap of parchment from some hidden pocket. It reached out with its furry paw to give it to Kreyssig. The commander's face contorted in disgust. Angrily he pointed to the rubble, indicating the mutant should leave its prize there.

Kreyssig was annoyed by the failure of his subhuman

confederates. He was just beginning to think the
mutants had outlived their usefulness when he reached
down and retrieved the scrap of letter. As his eyes read
the fragmented sentences, he chuckled cruelly.

'This is good,' he said. 'Your people have done well.'
The mutant bobbed its head as Kreyssig complimented
it. He, however, had already dismissed the creature
from his thoughts. He was too busy thinking about the
letter and how he was going to tell Emperor Boris that
his most favoured general was colluding with a conspiracy to depose him.

First his marriage to Princess Erna, then his destruction of Reiksmarshal Boeckenfoerde's career. Great
things were ahead for Adolf Kreyssig.

There was no limit to where a man with his kind of
ambition could go.

*Skavenblight*
*Vorhexen, 1111*

Panic rippled through the streets and rat-runs of
Skavenblight. Every eye glistened with fear, musk
dripped from every gland. The stormvermin of Clan
Rictus and their thrall clans poured through the
sprawling confusion of dilapidated buildings and subterranean tunnels, viciously trying to maintain order.
No less than a dozen slave uprisings had broken out in
different warrens. Several lesser clans had exploited the
anarchy to pursue vendettas against rivals, ransacking
each other's burrows and slaughtering enemy breeders
and their pups.

The source of the unrest lay within the infested tunnels of Clan Verms. More ratmen had become victims

of the plague, and this time Wormlord Blight hadn't been able to keep news of the disease from leaving the Hive. The exuberance with which the Black Plague had been regarded as it decimated the man-things by the thousands now turned to absolute terror as the skaven came to understand the same plague might be loosed among themselves.

Blight Tenscratch had been present at the hasty meeting of the council. A vote had been taken to decide what measures must be instituted to control the plague. It came closer to any vote in the history of the council to being unanimous. Blight was the only one who was against the immediate seclusion of the Hive and the extermination of every living thing inside it. Only extensive bribes had allowed Blight to escape the fate of his warren. Except for himself and a cadre of cronies, the skaven dwelling in the Hive were to be sacrificed for the common good of skavendom.

By design, Puskab Foulfur was one of the few Blight selected to be spared. Each ratman allowed to escape the Hive had cost the coffers of Clan Verms dearly, but of them all it was the plague priest who Blight felt offered the most potential for reclaiming his lost fortune.

The Black Plague had struck almost immediately after the failed assassination of Arch-Plaguelord Nurglitch. Blight didn't think that was a coincidence. Puskab's theory that Nurglitch was using traitors to spread the disease among Clan Verms had been proven. But Clan Pestilens had been more subtle than Blight had given them credit for. Rather than move against Verms openly, rather than depend on the plague to wipe them out, Pestilens had instead turned the whole of skavendom against them!

\* \* \*

PUSKAB SCURRIED THROUGH the winding passages of the
Hive, keeping pace with the mob of chieftains. He
was careful to keep a particularly sharp eye on Nakkal
Blackfinger, the Treasure Hoarder of Clan Verms.
Charged with cataloguing and protecting the income
from worm-oil, Nakkal was among the most important
of Blight's functionaries. Even more so since there was
no question that the treasurer had skimmed a fair portion of the clan's profits for himself and squirreled his
loot someplace far from the Hive. Blight would want to
get his paws on that plunder, but to do that he would
need Nakkal alive. At least for a little while. If any
of the Wormlord's minions had been given accurate
instructions for how to escape the destruction of the
Hive, it would be Nakkal.

There were several groups of chieftains and warlords racing through the tunnels, abandoning their
underlings to the cruel fate that awaited them. The
others, however, had been given false trails to follow.
Their escape routes ended in tunnels bristling with
black-furred stormvermin and withering fusillades of
jezzail fire. The shrieks of those who had been betrayed
by Blight's deception echoed through the doomed
burrows.

Puskab was thankful for the Wormlord's foresight,
even as his glands clenched at the notion that his
group might likewise be hurrying to its own massacre.
The lesser skaven of Clan Verms were hardly content to
sit back and wait for death to claim them. Those that
had not thrown themselves into a mindless rampage of
looting within the main warren had gathered in large
packs, stalking after the refugee chieftains, hoping to
join them in escape.

Few skaven followed Puskab's group. The plague
priest had been viewed with fear and suspicion from

the first, but now he was shunned as the source of all their woes. Their panic hadn't risen to the point where they would forget their fear and try to attack the horned sorcerer; there hadn't been enough time for hate to put some mettle into their spines. Before it could, Puskab intended to be far away.

Down the cramped tunnels, the walls crawling with bugs of every size and shape, the skaven hastened. Sometimes their little group would dart into a side passage as a larger pack of refugees came rushing past. Once they waited while a gigantic scorpion, loosed from its cage, came scuttling down the tunnel, a half-eaten ratman clenched in its claws. Twice they were forced to retreat before the waddling bulk of a skaven brood-mother, an entourage of eunuchs and slaves trying to guide the brainless females to some place of imagined safety. The husky scent exuded by the frightened brood-mothers was enough to compel even a few of the chieftains to forget about safety and rush after the females, instinct driving them to protect the breeders despite their certain doom.

The crack of jezzails ahead announced that the refugees were nearing one of the dozens of egresses from the Hive. The sharp tang of skaven blood, the acrid smell of warp-powder and shot, the musky reek of fear-smell, all of these joined to form a stench peculiarly redolent of merciless despair.

The narrow tunnel widened as it climbed towards an archway of stone. Dozens of skaven bodies, some of them still twitching, lay strewn about the gateway. Beyond, a phalanx of Clan Rictus ratmen, hulking in their patchwork armour of plate and chain, stood with spears at the ready. Between the spear-rats, their red eyes shining maliciously in the flickering light of worm-oil lanterns, weedy Clan Skryre sharpshooters huddled. Each of them clutched a massive tube of steel in his paws, the front spitted upon a triangular firing rest which had been driven into the ground. The jezzails were taller than the ratmen who carried them and it took two skaven to pour powder and shot down their cavernous barrels.

Puskab's eyes narrowed as he saw the formidable cordon that had been thrown about the Hive. His magic would be useless against such numbers. He might slay twenty or thirty with a ball of burning putrescence, but after that his body would be shattered by the jezzails. His only hope now lay in his usefulness to Blight and whether the Wormlord had spoken truly about a way out.

'Tenscratch eat-slay traitor-meat!' Nakkal barked out, his voice shrill and terrified. It was the password that had been arranged between Blight and the fangleaders he had bribed. If the treachery had been discovered, or if the guards had reconsidered the agreement...

A scar-faced stormvermin, a battered human helmet crushed down about his skull, a nugget of glowing warpstone dangling from the lobe of his ear, stepped slightly forwards, pushing aside the spears of his henchmen. 'Late-late, fool-meat!' the fangleader snarled. He cast an anxious look over his shoulder, then waved his arm in imperious fashion. 'Hurry-scurry or stay-burn!'

The warning didn't need to be given twice. Puskab scrambled along with the Verms chieftains, shoving Nakkal out of his way as he reached the gap that had opened between the stormvermin. His haste was quickly justified. A sharp squeal sounded from somewhere up the tunnel – the cry of some unseen sentinel. In response, the fangleader's warriors closed ranks once more, blocking the escape of the slower chieftains. Callously, the fangleader growled a command. The stormvermin lashed out with their spears, skewering the refugees still before them. Those few who eluded the spears and tried to flee back into the Hive were shot in the back by the chittering sharpshooters.

Puskab could see the reason for the fangleader's sudden sense of duty. From the broad tunnel beyond the archway a great mob of skaven was scurrying into view. Foremost among them were a number of huge cask-shaped carts pushed along by packs of emaciated slaves. Riding atop the carts were groups of leather-clad ratmen, their paws and forearms covered in thick oilskins, their heads encased in weird fur masks that had been soaked in something that was at least partly vinegar to judge by the smell. The scent of Clan Skryre lingered about the masked skaven and each of them fussed about a confusion of brass wheels and ratgut hoses.

'Make way!' the fangleader snarled, casting a warning look in Puskab's direction. The plague priest did as he was told, scurrying aside as the weird carriages came trundling past him. A second pack of stormvermin followed, these bearing the red fur and scorched armour of Clan Volkyn. They fanned out as the bulky Clan Skryre carts passed through the archway and down the entrance into the Hive. Excited squeaks rose from the warriors as a ragged mob of skaven appeared at the far end of the tunnel. Anxiously they clashed swords against shields until the entire corridor boomed with the clamour.

The mob of Clan Verms skaven hesitated for only a moment, then gave voice to a savage howl. Like a crazed thing, the horde of desperate ratmen came charging down the passage. As they rushed towards the carts, the warlock-engineers mounted atop them began to work the machinery of their arcane contraptions. Some of

them fiddled with pressure valves while others worked
networks of pumps and windlasses. At the fore of each
cart, a strongly-built ratman raised a heavy hose with a
broad metal nozzle.

In response to the efforts of the warlock-engineers,
smoke began to rise from the mouth of each hose.
Then a tiny flicker of green flame sputtered into view.
It danced about the metal nozzle for only an instant
before it was drowned by a great rush of shimmering
emerald fire.

The charging horde shrieked as the green flames
washed over them. Ratmen leapt into the air, their fur
blazing, their flesh melting from their bones. Dozens
of them were reduced to piles of steaming meat in the
blink of an eye. Scores more wailed in agony, trying to
drag their mutilated bodies back into the darkness of
the Hive.

The warlock-engineers laughed at the havoc wrought
by their hideous weapon, the warriors of Clan Volkyn
cheered at the spectacle of burning bodies strewn
before them. Encouraged by the ease of the slaughter, the warlock-engineers shouted down at the slaves
chained to the sides of the carts, ordering the wagons
pushed deeper into the boundaries of Clan Verms.

'They will burn out every inch of the Hive.'

Puskab turned about, surprised to see Blight Tenscratch standing beside him. He had been so fascinated
by the display of Clan Skryre's admittedly heretical
techno-sorcery that he had failed to notice the scent of
the Wormlord and his remaining guards.

'Warpfire they call it,' Blight hissed. 'I am told it uses
a mixture of worm-oil and warpstone.' His head suddenly darted to one side, then the other, eyes searching
among the ranks of the Rictus stormvermin.

'Nakkal lost-gone,' Puskab said, guessing who Blight

was looking for. The plague priest felt a twinge of amusement as he stated that the chieftain had suffered an accident.

Blight's lips pulled away from his fangs. 'This is all that flea-sucking pimple-arsed Nurglitch's fault!' The Wormlord shook his fist at the roof of the cavern, muttering curses under his breath.

'We will-must try-try again,' Puskab said.

Blight fixed the plague priest with a crooked smile. 'We?' he snickered. 'No-no, not *we*! *You*!' The Wormlord's claw trembled as he pointed it at Puskab. 'You will kill-slay Nurglitch! Challenge him for his seat on the council! Take his place-pelt as Arch-Plaguelord!'

*Bylorhof*
*Ulriczeit, 1111*

WHEN FREDERICK ROUSED from his stupor, the monster was gone. Retrieving a spike-headed mace from the cells once inhabited by the templars, the priest made his way outside to inspect the temple grounds. The cold wind blew snow across the rows of graves, headstones vanishing beneath a mantle of white. In the distance, the mournful cry of a dog rose, invading the eerie quiet of the night. Mannslieb was nearly full now, the greater moon's silvery light eclipsing the sickly glow of Morrslieb.

By moonlight and rushlight, Frederick circled the temple, the heavy mace always at the ready. Snow crunched under his feet as he scoured the ground for any trace of the undead creature he had seen. If the thing had left any tracks, they had been obliterated by the new-fallen snow.

The priest uttered a nervous laugh. If the thing had been there at all. If it hadn't existed solely in his own mind. If he wasn't going mad.

Then Frederick's steps brought him to the side of the temple and the ornate window looking into the sanctuary. His skin crawled as he stared at the ground below the window. Sheltered by the eaves of the roof, the ground here had been spared the attentions of the latest snowfall. Pressed clearly into the snow were the marks of unshod feet, feet like none he had ever seen. Visible in the snow were the prints of toes, toes that were like scraggly claws. Toes from which all the flesh had been peeled away. As a final sign that the creature had been real, Frederick found a strip of decayed skin caught upon the window frame, left there when the undead horror had pressed itself against the glass and peered into the sanctuary.

Clenching the mace tighter, Frederick turned away from the window. His eyes scanned the silent rows of graves, wondering where the monster had gone. He felt an obligation to track down the abomination. Despite the heretical spell he had evoked, he still regarded himself as a priest of Morr and it was a priest's duty to bring peace to the restless dead.

The open door of the old vault swayed in the wind, banging against the carved granite walls. Frederick felt a chill run down his spine. There was no one who would have opened that door. Even the most desperate looters shunned the gardens of Morr, if not from fear of the plague then from the dreadful memory of Arisztid Olt and his frightful abuses of the cemetery.

Forcing himself towards the mausoleum took more courage than Frederick believed he had. At every step he felt the urge to flee, to retreat into the temple and cower behind the altar. His flesh crawled, his breath came in icy gasps, his hair stood on end. Every part of his being could sense the unnatural aberration which had preceded him and left the door swinging in the wind.

Somehow he managed to reach the mausoleum. The priest hesitated upon the threshold, gazing in silence upon the confusion of prints which had disturbed the centuries of dust inside the vault. Clumps of marsh grass and mud littered the steps as they descended into the musty darkness. Furtive sounds rose to scratch at the edge of his hearing and Frederick did not need to be told it was not the noise of rats.

Frederick started to pray to his god, then hesitated. After what he had done, the blasphemy with which he had profaned Morr's temple, he had no right to presume upon the god's benevolence. He had failed his god. Perhaps this was a test, a trial to redeem himself. If so, he was determined he would meet the challenge on his own.

The darkness wrapped itself around Frederick as he descended into the ancient vault. The illumination of the rushlight lessened with each step, as though the tomb resented the intrusion of its flame. As the light began to fail, raw panic threatened to overcome the priest.

Again the furtive shuffling sounds slithered across Frederick's ears. They were closer now, close enough to startle the priest. He had imagined his quarry to be deep within the catacombs by now, not lingering so near the entrance. Casting a worried glance at the doubtful flame of his rushlight, he strode towards the noise.

Before he had gone more than a few steps, a sweet, rotten stench struck his senses. From the gloom, a shape emerged into the faltering light. Frederick recoiled in shock as he found himself gazing into the decayed face of a Bylorhof peasant, the man's visage reduced almost to a skull by the ravenous attentions of marsh vermin. Worms writhed in the peeling flesh, the scaly carcass of a scavenger fish protruded from the creature's cheek, ugly water beetles crawled through hair matted with slime.

Frederick swung the heavy mace into the monster's hideous face. The rotten skull shattered beneath the terrified blow, spattering the wall of the crypt with stagnant muck and slivers of bone. The creature swayed for a moment, as though unaware its brain had been pulverised. Then the thing collapsed on the dusty floor.

Zombie! The grotesque word came unbidden to Frederick's mind. Walking revenants without purpose or motive, slinking horrors that were the antithesis of life and of death. They were the lowest form of undead abomination, mindless corpses devoid of either will or soul.

Yet, as Frederick's mind turned back to the dark lore of Arisztid Olt, a troubling thought came to him. A zombie was a thing that existed because of dark magic, it could thrive only at the direction of some outside force, some greater will to sustain its empty husk. Suddenly he understood why these things had appeared. Some terrible fiend had descended upon the graveyard, might even now be lurking among the tombs. Witch or daemon, it was summoning the unhallowed dead, drawing them from their watery graves.

The priest's heart pounded in his breast. Somewhere, in the black catacombs, a malevolent power was gathering its strength. It had to be stopped, stopped before it could threaten the town.

Frederick followed the sunken passages, the spiked mace held in a white-knuckle grip. His eyes struggled to pierce the gloom, strove to compensate for the increasingly poor illumination of the rushlight. The shuffling steps echoed ahead of him. He could tell they came from more than one source, but whether there might be a dozen or a hundred, he could not say. If fate favoured him, he might never need to know. There was only one enemy he had to face – the occult power that had summoned the zombies from the marsh.

On through the blackness the priest crept. Sometimes the decayed hulk of a zombie would loom out at him from the shadows. A blow from the mace quickly drove the things back, shattering decayed limbs and crushing rotten bones with each frantic strike. Frederick's skin crawled as he noted the unnatural way the zombies reacted to his assaults. Making no move either to defend or attack, the things simply wilted beneath his blows, staggering aside as he forced his way past them.

Perhaps their sorcerous master was as yet unaware of the priest's presence. Perhaps the fiend had exhausted its power resurrecting the dead and was now resting, trying to replenish its energies. Frederick hoped such was the case, that he could steal upon this malignance and destroy it before it was strong enough to oppose him.

Movement ahead arrested the priest in his tracks. Whatever was ahead of him moved with an energy and vitality absent from the shambling zombies he had encountered. Images of ghouls and vampires flashed through Frederick's brain. Again, he felt the urge to flee. Again, he forced himself to be brave. Whatever was ahead of him might still be unaware of him. He might still be able to take it by surprise.

Wailing an inarticulate cry, the priest charged into the blackness, the mace flying forwards in a brutally violent sweep. Frederick cried out in pain as the mace crashed against some unyielding force, sending tremors throbbing down his arm. Reeling from the injury, he thrust the faltering rushlight at his antagonist.

An incredulous smile crept onto Frederick's face as he looked ahead. There was no fiend in the darkness, only the smooth blackness of an obsidian pillar, a monument to some long-dead templar knight. The pillar was marked by a scratch, the best his mace could do when it had smashed into the immovable stone. The pillar had retained its polish down through the years, reflecting the glow of Frederick's rushlight and the man who held it.

Trying to attack the fiend who haunted the catacombs, Frederick had attacked his own reflection. The absurdity of the thing brought bitter laughter to the priest's lips.

His laughter died as the sounds of shuffling steps filled the passage behind him. Frederick's attack on the pillar might have been absurd, but it had borne terrible fruit. The zombies were aware of him now, guided to him by the malignant power of their master. He could see them groping their way into the light, faces purple with rot, swollen tongues protruding from mouths clenched in the final rictus of death.

Frederick shifted the mace to his uninjured arm and braced himself to confront the undead horde. 'Keep back,' he warned the creatures.

To his shock, the zombies stopped advancing. Like ghastly statues, the things froze in place, their lifeless eyes staring emptily at the priest.

Raising the mace, trying to encourage the rushlight to greater effort, Frederick took a step towards the waiting zombies. The undead monsters moved not so much as a muscle. A dreadful cold settled around the priest's heart, a suspicion so monstrous he refused to accept it.

'Let…' Frederick's voice failed him. Licking his trembling lips, he tried again. 'Let me pass.'

His mouth opened in horror as the ranks of zombies shifted, pressing their decayed bodies against the walls of the catacomb, clearing a path for the priest. The display of mute, unquestioning obedience sent a thrill of terror rushing through Frederick's soul.

Without a sidewise glance, Frederick ran past the zombies, fleeing with all haste from the vault and the awful discovery he had made.

He could run from the zombies, but Frederick could not run from the truth. The undead had been called by a terrible power, a force great enough to bind them to his will. *He* was the fiend who haunted the cemetery. *He* was the malignance that called the dead from their graves.

Frederick van Hal had surpassed the legacy of Arisztid Olt.

He was now the necromancer of Bylorhof.

## ✦ CHAPTER XIV ✦

*Altdorf*
*Vorhexen, 1111*

ARCH-LECTOR HARTWICH WALKED slowly into the calefactory. The priest was dressed in a coarse linen robe, a simple rope belt tied about his waist, his shaved scalp grey with ash. Across his palms, the symbol of the twin-tailed comet had been cut, his blood still clotted about the ceremonial wounds. To either side of Hartwich marched an armoured knight, the steel scales of their mail etched in gold, their white surcoats displaying the skull and hammer heraldry of the Knights of Sigmar's Blood, the templar guard of the Great Cathedral.

Before the humbled arch-lector, crouched in his chair between the roaring bonfires, Grand Theogonist Thorgrad stared sorrowfully at Hartwich. 'Have you contemplated your heresy?' he asked, his voice sounding more ancient than even his withered body should produce.

Hartwich raised his head. 'I beg your indulgence, your holiness, but it is not heresy and I shall not recant.'

Thorgrad leaned forwards in his chair. 'If you die with

wilful sin blackening your soul you will be denied the grace of Sigmar. Your spirit will be cast out, condemned to wander until the daemons of Chaos claim it for their own.'

'My heart is pure, your holiness,' Hartwich insisted. 'If I must die without ceremony, then so it must be. Sigmar will judge my deeds.'

A hint of pride crept into Thorgrad's eyes. 'A man may risk his life for what he believes to be right. It needs a saint to risk his soul for what he knows to be right.'

Hartwich rose from the floor, a puzzled expression on his face. Thorgrad laughed at the other priest's confusion, but it was a mirthless, weary laughter.

'When you say Sigmar will judge you, perhaps he has,' Thorgrad said. He gestured to the roaring bonfires, to the trappings of his audience chamber that had been removed to the calefactory. 'I am a frightened man. I am afraid to die. I am afraid of the plague. I am afraid to face Sigmar and answer for my crimes.'

Thorgrad reached to the neck of his robe, tugging it open, exposing the ugly black buboes. 'Despite all of my precautions, the plague has found me. I will die. I know that now. Like you, I must face Holy Sigmar and atone for my heresies.'

'Your heresies, Holiness?'

'Yes,' Thorgrad nodded. 'I was the Lector of Nuln, you know. I served under Grand Theogonist Uthorsson. I saw his slow decline into degeneracy, blasphemy and idolatry. I watched as he turned away from the light of Sigmar and embraced the darkness of Old Night.'

The Grand Theogonist sank back into his chair, tears in his eyes, a rattle in his voice. 'I was there when Uthorsson began to call upon the Prince of Pleasures. I stood by as he profaned the temple with the most unspeakable atrocities. I was afraid,' Thorgrad stared into Hartwich's eyes. 'Do you understand? I was afraid to speak out against what I knew to be an obscenity because Uthorsson was Grand Theogonist and I feared his power! I hid behind oaths and vows, telling myself it was not my part to question the acts of the Grand Theogonist. I sat by and watched as Uthorsson's outrages grew. I did nothing, Wolfgang, nothing to stop this vile degradation.

'I did act, in the end,' Thorgrad said. 'When it was forced upon me. When I understood that if I didn't oppose Uthorsson I would be branded as his accomplice. The inquisitors of the temple of Verena were investigating the rumours of midnight orgies and human sacrifice being committed in the cathedral. I knew they would uncover everything in time, and I understood that this was Uthorsson's plan – to put such a stain upon the temple that the Sigmarite faith would be discredited and dishonoured for all time. This was the great offering he wished to make to Slaanesh.'

Thorgrad's hands tightened about the arms of his chair. 'I stopped him,' he said. 'Before his shame could become something more than rumour and suspicion, I stopped Uthorsson.' A fanatical gleam filled the old priest's eyes. 'I waited until he and his filthy coven were practising their obscenities in the sanctuary. I locked them in, barring the door with cold iron that he might not call upon his daemons to set him free. Then I set fire to the temple. The flames consumed the defiled sanctuary and the foulness within!'

The strength drained out of Thorgrad and he slumped back against the chair. 'Is it wrong to murder evil? That is something only Sigmar can judge. Like you, I am willing to let him decide.'

Hartwich shook his head, trying to digest the revelation he had heard. Certainly there had been stories about some heretical taint upon Grand Theogonist Uthorsson's reign, but he had never imagined so monstrous an aberration, nor Thorgrad's role in ending the fallen priest's sacrilege.

'I admire your courage, Wolfgang,' Thorgrad said. 'I wish that I had possessed such valour when I needed it. But it is too late now. My fate has been decided.'

'And mine?' Hartwich asked. It was an impertinent question. He had already undergone the rituals preemptory to a religious execution. He already knew that such a resolution had been demanded by Kreyssig and Boris Goldgather.

Thorgrad smiled. 'Wolfgang Hartwich must die,' he said. He lifted his hand and pointed to a corridor leading out from the calefactory. 'He is lying in his cell right now, meditating upon his crimes against the Emperor. In the morning he will be consigned to the pyre.'

'I don't understand. What are you saying?'

'It is strange how much Wolfgang Hartwich resembled one of my attendants, the unfortunate Brother Richter, who has contracted the Black Plague. After the fire, I do not think even Commander Kreyssig will be able to tell the difference.' The Grand Theogonist smiled and gestured to a door at the other side of the room.

'Through that door, you will find raiment and provisions, my son. These good knights will see you clear of the city and accompany you where you need to go. I am sorry there is nothing I can do to help Wolfgang Hartwich and his cause, but I will trust you to honour his name.'

Hartwich kneeled before the dying Grand Theogonist once more. 'I shall make it my life's work, your holiness,' he said. 'By Sigmar's grace, I will carry on Wolfgang Hartwich's work.'

\* \* \*

*Middenheim*
*Vorhexen, 1111*

FROM THE WALLS of Middenheim, Mandred had a clear look at the squalid shantytown crouched between the causeways. Miserable little cook-fires rose from the tents and shacks, scrawny pigs and goats shivered inside ramshackle pens made of sticks and thatch. Sometimes there would be a flash of white among the squalor, the robes of a Shallyan priestess as she made her rounds among the sick. Over the weeks, the sight of a priestess had grown more and more infrequent. The prince tried to tell himself it was because they were kept busy inside the barn-like infirmary. He didn't like to think it was because they were succumbing to the very plague they were trying to stop.

Every day miserable caravans of wretched humanity came trudging through the snow. Most accepted fate and simply added their misery to the squalor of the shantytown. A few, however, made the long journey up the causeways. These were turned back at the bastions, warned that Middenheim was closed to all outsiders. Some few refused to accept this dashing of all their hopes, racing desperately past the bastions in a mad effort to storm the city gates.

Mandred always turned away before the mad fools were brought down by archers. A family of lepers who lived in a cave at the foot of the Ulricsberg would come later to clear the bodies away.

It sickened the prince to be able to see the suffering going on down below, to be so near and yet able to do nothing. His father had forbidden even the smallest intervention, telling his son that it was best to think of the refugees as already dead. He had to harden his heart against them. It was the only way to keep Middenheim safe.

Mandred refused to resign himself to such callous pragmatism. The Graf's obligation might be to the people of Middenheim, but he had another and greater obligation to his fellow man. To turn his back on these people diminished him, made him something less than human in Mandred's eyes. He had always been close to his father, but he no longer recognised the man who sat upon Middenheim's throne and wore the crown of Middenland.

A blur of activity at the edge of the shantytown drew Mandred's horrified attention. He watched as a pack of dark, shaggy shapes burst from the trees, charging towards a group of children at play. Before any of the adults could react, several of the children had been caught up by hairy claws and were being carried off into the forest. Mandred sobbed a prayer to Ulric, asking that the men rushing to stop the abduction would be in time.

For an instant, it seemed his prayer had been answered. Mandred whooped in triumph as a hulking refugee tackled a goat-headed monster, smashing the beast to the ground. The screaming girl squirmed out from the stunned monster's clutch. Before the brute could rise, the enraged man straddled its body and seized it by the horns. With a savage twist, he snapped the beastman's neck.

The triumph was short-lived. A second beastman charged at the heroic refugee, while a scraggly half-man circled around to grab the fleeing child. The hero clenched his hands into fists, refusing to flee before the goat-headed monster. The brute's harsh bray carried all the way to the mountain. Swinging its stone axe, the beastman cut the refugee down where he stood.

Mandred forced himself to watch the tragedy play itself out, to look on as the beastmen retreated back into the forest, dragging the dead with them into the darkness. None of the refugees pursued them, stopping well away from the trees and shaking their fists in impotent rage.

It was a scene that had repeated itself over and over in the past weeks. At first, the beastmen had been skittish, rushing out from the trees only when their prey was alone and darkness cloaked their actions. Each success had made them bolder, however, and their raids into the shantytown had become more and more frequent. Realising the refugees were sickly and largely unable to defend themselves, the beastmen had claimed Warrenburg as their own private hunting ground. Not an hour went by that they didn't rush out to snatch a child or drag a sick old woman from her bed. A hideous effort to placate the monsters with the bodies of the dead had only increased their lust for manflesh.

'Maybe the filth will catch the plague and die,' Mandred snarled aloud.

'They won't die off soon enough to do those people any good,' observed Arno Warsitz, the brawny Grand Master of the White Wolves. Like Mandred, the knight frequently toured the battlements, staring forlornly at the cluster of shacks at the foot of the mountain. 'The belly of a beastman is the toughest thing in the world,' he added, his face twisting with distaste.

Mandred slammed his fist into his palm. 'If we could just get weapons to them…'

'It wouldn't do them any good, your grace,' Arno said. 'Even if most of them knew how to use a sword or swing a hammer, they're too weak to use them.' He nodded his head sadly. 'Those people down there are beaten, and they know it. They're just waiting for the end now.' The Grand Master's eyes turned to the sprawl of the forest. It looked so beautiful, the firs covered in snow, icicles dripping from their branches. It was difficult to picture the monstrous evil lurking beneath such beauty.

'The beastkin won't wait long,' Arno said. 'Patience isn't something those brutes understand. What they do understand is strength and weakness. Once they realise that Warrenburg can't stop them and that we won't help, they'll come storming down out of the trees like the second coming of Cormac Blood Axe.'

The image of such a massacre brought a chill to Mandred's heart. 'We can't let that happen.' He stared hard into Arno's eyes. 'You understand, we can't let that happen.'

The Grand Master scratched at his beard. 'These monsters will be the dregs of their herds, the ones too weak or cowardly to join Khaagor Deathhoof's warherd. Any show of real force might be enough to break them. Let them come out of the forest, show their faces in the open and fifty good men would be enough to send them bleating into the hollows.'

'Find me fifty good men,' Mandred told Arno. Colour flushed to the knight's cheeks as he appreciated what he had been saying and how the prince had interpreted his words.

'Your grace, I was just thinking aloud,' the Grand Master protested. He pointed down at the causeway where the lepers were clearing away bodies. 'Anyone who goes out there can't come back. The plague can't be allowed inside the walls.'

'Take only volunteers,' Mandred said. 'Men who understand the risks.' He pointed at the bastion on the eastern causeway. 'Once the brutes have been routed, the men can take shelter in that bastion. There is food and drink to last the winter and staying there they will pose no risk to the city. The garrison can keep to the top floors of the tower and avoid any contact with the men who relieve the encampment.'

Arno nodded sombrely. 'I will get your men. They can be billeted in the Altquartier, their animals stabled in the horseyards.' A cunning smile spread across the Grand Master's face. 'If we are careful, we should be able to keep the Graf from finding out.'

Mandred gripped the old knight's arm. 'This is the right thing to do,' he told him.

The Grand Master smiled. 'I know, your grace. Sometimes the measure of a man isn't his wisdom, but his courage.'

Mandred sighed when he heard those words. They were the exact opposite of his father's philosophy. To him, cold reason was the only thing that could govern a leader's actions.

Mandred only hoped he could show his father how wrong he was.

*Altdorf*
*Vorhexen, 1111*

'DOES EVERYTHING MEET with your approval?'

The question was asked in a frantic, almost panicked tone.

Princess Erna turned away from her cursory inspection of the master bedroom, making no effort to hide her distaste. Adolf Kreyssig had spent a considerable amount furnishing his home – far more than his income as commander of the Kaiserjaeger should have allowed – yet his peasant background was betrayed in every chair, every table, every blanket and pillow. Gold could buy possessions, but it couldn't buy refinement and taste. Walking around the townhouse was offensive to her sensibilities. If she were in Marienburg and wandering about the tent of a Norscan jarl, she could have found her surroundings no less barbarous. At least the Norscan wouldn't have any pretensions about himself.

'No, it doesn't,' Erna told the manservant. Immediately she felt a twinge of regret as she watched Fuerst's composure crack. From a tremulous optimism, his entire bearing crumbled into dejection. It was like kicking an enthusiastic puppy and despite her noble upbringing, she felt guilty for being the cause of such disappointment. She laughed at the ridiculousness of so petty a thing causing her concern. Here she was, married to the worst monster in Altdorf and she was agonising over the sensibilities of a peasant.

'My lady?' Fuerst asked, his voice timid, his mind confused by Erna's sudden humour.

Princess Erna stepped away from the elaborately carved wardrobe dominating one wall of the room and strode purposefully towards the door. 'It doesn't matter, Fuerst. This is Commander Kreyssig's room. I won't be staying here.' She gave the manservant a friendly smile. 'I'll depend on your help getting one of the other rooms fit for me.'

'Of course, my lady,' Fuerst agreed, bobbing his head in obsequious fashion. His earlier disappointment was forgotten and there was an excitement in his face as he turned away. The excitement died as he faced the doorway. Quickly, he bowed before his lord and master.

Adolf Kreyssig leaned against the open door, his eyes glittering with an ophidian gleam. 'That won't be necessary, Fuerst,' he told his servant. 'My wife will be staying here. Where she belongs. With her husband.'

Erna's face turned crimson and she threw back her head in outrage, her long hair whipping about her creamy shoulders. 'I do not intend to linger among this… this squalor.'

'That *squalor* cost a lot of people a lot of pain,' Kreyssig said. 'Sometimes, people can be quite stubborn. Especially when they think they are better than… well, the man with the whip.'

The princess glared at her husband. 'Don't presume to threaten me, peasant,' she warned. 'I am not some schilling-a-tumble dock strumpet to be awed by your tawdry pretensions at society! I am the daughter of Baron Thornig of Middenheim, and you had best remember it! You've bought an option on a noble title, nothing more! And you had best remember it! Because a peasant born is always a peasant!'

Kreyssig turned his cold gaze on Fuerst. 'Out,' he hissed, stabbing his thumb at the hallway behind him. The manservant cast a shamed, apologetic look at Erna, then scurried from the room. Kreyssig closed the door behind him.

'I've bought the whole damn thing!' Kreyssig snarled. 'The title, the wife, and everything that goes with it!'

'Believe what you like,' Erna said, her voice a withering lash. 'But lay one of your filthy peasant hands on me, and you'll regret it!' The defiant words didn't keep a pallor from Erna's cheeks as she watched Kreyssig step away from the door and saw for the first time the coiled whip he'd been holding behind his back.

'Now I will tell you something,' Kreyssig hissed. 'In a little while you will be begging to have peasant hands on your noble flesh.

'Stubborn people always learn their place. Nobles just take a bit longer to teach.'

* * *

*Nuln*
*Ulriczeit, 1111*

THERE WEREN'T ANY answers in the stein of beer resting on the table but Walther stared into it as though all the secrets of the gods were to be found hidden within the foam. He'd lost count of just how many beers he had ordered since the plague doktor left the tavern. Sometimes he would call out to Bremer for an accounting, but whatever tally the proprietor rattled off it was soon forgotten by the rat-catcher.

That was the entire point. To forget. To forget about the man lying down there in the cellar. To forget about the reeking buboes spreading across his flesh. To forget that Hugo had saved his life. To forget that keeping the plague-stricken man here jeopardised himself and Zena and everyone who patronised the Black Rose.

Where were the gods? Walther hadn't led a good life, but he knew many people who had. Old Petra the midwife, for one, a woman so open-hearted that she would adopt any baby whose mother didn't want it. She had been as good and gracious and fine a person as could be found in Nuln. How could the gods allow the plague to strike her down? How could they let disease decimate her children, breaking her heart by inches and degrees even before the Black Plague stilled it forever?

If this was retribution, the vengeance of the old gods against those who had followed the creed of Sigmar, then why had this terrible curse not fallen when the Cathedral was still standing, when the music of the Grand Theogonist's parties had echoed across the city? Why had the gods stayed their hand until now, now when so many people needed their benevolence, not their judgement?

Or were the gods as powerless as everyone else? Walther took a long draught from his beer as he considered that terrible thought. The priesthood of Morr was all but exterminated in Nuln, felled by the plague lurking in the bodies they had gathered for burial. The priestesses of Shallya had likewise perished in droves, unable to combat the magnitude of the plague with their rituals and prayers. Many of the acolytes of Verena, trying to augment the ranks of the overtaxed barbers and doktors, had also sickened and died. Even the druids of the Old Faith, calling upon the magic of Rhya and Taal, had been powerless to protect themselves. The death of the high druid had sent the rest of the Old Faith's priesthood into retreat, scattering back into the countryside to hide in their sacred groves.

The world was crumbling all around him. Everything Walther had known and believed had been turned upon its head. It seemed impossible that such a chaotic upheaval could come about in so short a time. The luxurious greensward around the Universität had been overrun by refugees, transformed into a mire of tents and shacks. Count Artur, the bold 'Lion of Nuln', the city's great master and benefactor, had forsaken his home to remain at the Emperor's palace in Altdorf. The dwarf sewers, that wonder of engineering which kept the city pure and clean, had become a breeding ground for hordes of vermin, vermin that were unafraid of man.

It was all madness! Nothing made sense any more! Walther tipped back his stein, draining the last dregs from the cup. He started to wave to Bremer, then noticed Zena standing in the doorway to the kitchen. His cheeks flushed with shame. She wasn't some prudish Verenan, but just the same she didn't approve of a man who drank in some deluded effort to escape his troubles.

Anger flared up inside the rat-catcher. Who was she to disapprove of him! What else was there to do except drink! Drink and forget! Drink and forget.

Walther waved to Bremer, motioning for another stein. Zena stepped over to the bar and retrieved it from the taverneer, carrying it over to the table.

'No lash of the tongue?' Walther grunted when she set the beer beside his hand.

Zena stared down at him, pain etched across her face. Walther became sober almost at once. She started to speak, but he pressed his fingers to her lips. He didn't want to hear what she had to say. If he didn't hear it, then it wasn't real. It he didn't know what had happened, then it didn't happen.

Hugo! He'd been a stupid, naïve boy, something of a country bumpkin. But he'd been brave and loyal, and Walther had owed his life to him.

The rat-catcher pushed the stein away and closed his hand around Zena's. He looked up at her with eyes that had no hope in them, only a terrible emptiness. 'I'm sorry,' he told her. 'I should never have asked… never have risked…'

Tears rolled from the woman's eyes. 'He saved your life,' she sobbed. 'I was indebted to him too.'

Walther felt his chest swell. Old Night could take the rest of the world, if it would only leave him and Zena alone. He'd allowed himself to agonise over things that were beyond him, he'd allowed himself to be distracted by his sense of obligation to Hugo. None of it mattered. All that mattered was the woman he loved and making sure she was safe.

'Zena, I…'

The rat-catcher never finished what he was going to say. At that moment, the tavern door burst inwards. A squad of men in the rough brigandine armour and yellow sleeves of the Hundertschaft came rushing into the Black Rose. The few patrons tending drinks at this late hour cried out in fright and cowered before the menace of the soldiers' halberds and swords.

Captain Fellgiebel sauntered into the Black Rose like a wolf trotting through a flock of sheep. There was a merciless, vengeful smile on his lean face when he spotted Walther. He glanced over the other occupants of the room, frowning when he didn't see Aldinger the Reiklander.

'Herr Captain!' Bremer cried out, circling out from behind the bar. 'What brings the Hundertschaft to Lord Plessner's establishment?' It was seldom that Bremer invoked the name of his liege-lord, the nobleman in whose service the taverneer operated the Black Rose and paid a portion of the profit. For him to resort to such a tactic was evidence of the fear pounding through Bremer's veins.

Fellgiebel raised a gloved finger, making a warning gesture for Bremer to keep quiet. The captain turned and waved his hand at the stuffed rat. 'Remove that abomination and burn it,' he told his men.

Walther leapt to his feet and stormed towards Fellgiebel. 'You can't do that!' the rat-catcher snarled.

'Ah, the charlatan,' Fellgiebel hissed. He nodded and one of the watchmen drove the butt of his halberd into Walther's belly, knocking the wind out of him. As the rat-catcher doubled over in pain, Zena rushed towards him. A snap of Fellgiebel's fingers sent a guard to restrain her.

'You've been a busy dog, haven't you?' Fellgiebel sneered. He turned and watched as more of his soldiers marched into the Black Rose. There was a third man walking between the two guards, a man with a bloodied face and the torn remains of a long linen cloak. Walther groaned when he recognised the garment. Though he had never seen the man's face before, he was certain the prisoner was the plague doktor who had visited Hugo. Belatedly, Walther recalled the lone beggar who stayed out in the cold. Doubtless a spy for Fellgiebel, charged with watching the tavern.

'This establishment is hereby placed under quarantine!' Fellgiebel declared, removing a parchment proclamation from his sleeve. He shook the parchment at Bremer. 'You will nail this to your door and daub a red cross over every entrance and exit to this building. There has been plague in this place. No one here is allowed to leave for a period of thirty days. If any of you are seen upon the streets, my men have orders to cut you down on sight.'

Fellgiebel dismissed the entreaties and protests that followed his declaration. Still smiling, he watched his men remove the giant rat. Then he turned and stared down at Walther. 'You will return to the watch station with us,' he said. 'There are… questions that need asking.'

A cry of horror rose from Zena's throat. She struggled to free herself from the guard. 'It was my idea! All mine! Hiding Hugo was my doing!'

'Don't lie to him,' Walther coughed. 'He knows it was me. I'm the only one he wants.'

Fellgiebel's eyes were more snakelike than ever as he stalked towards the rat-catcher. 'Very sensible,' he said. The captain shifted his gaze to the frantic serving girl. 'We are only interested in the rat-catcher. She can stay.'

The watch captain's eyes became even colder as he hissed into Walther's ear. 'She can stay… for now.'

* * *

*Altdorf*
*Vorhexen, 1111*

THE MANGLED BODY slammed down against the old oak table, causing the legs to creak and sway. Gasps of startlement and shock coursed through the dingy room, the basement of a candle maker who had been stricken with the plague. No one's shock was greater than that of Erich von Kranzbeuhler. The features on the corpse's pale face were ones he had seen many times before. Konreid of the Reiksknecht had fought his last battle.

'Where did you find him?' the captain asked the man who had brought the body into the hideout. The morbid courier was a rough-looking man with a military swagger, one of Engel's Bread Marchers. He stared uncertainly at Meisel, the Nulner who in Engel's absence had assumed leadership of the dispossessed *Dienstleute*. Meisel nodded, motioning for the peasant to forget his suspicions and answer the nobleman.

'He was in the sewers,' the dienstmann said. 'The rats had been at him, but it was a Kaiserjaeger dagger that did for him.' He reached into the grimy wool tunic he wore and tossed a steel knife onto the table, its hilt bearing the heraldry of Kreyssig's enforcers. The dienstmann withdrew another item from his pocket, handing it to Meisel despite the man's lack of letters.

'He had that clenched in his hand,' the dienstmann reported. 'It looks like it was torn off.'

Meisel handed the scrap of letter across the table to Baron Thornig. The hairy Middenlander studied the murky ink, struggling to make sense of the faded letters. The muck of the sewer had effaced most of the writing, but he was certain it didn't match the message the conspirators had sent to Reiksmarshal Boecken-foerde. Then he uttered a sharp curse. Down near the bottom of the letter, partially effaced, was the general's signature.

'This is a letter from the Reiksmarshal!' Baron Thornig exclaimed. His outburst brought the other conspirators rushing to his side, eager to see what little there was of the missive. It wasn't a large group; only Palatine Mihail Kretzulescu and Count van Sauckelhof were present. Prince Sigdan was busy trying to get Lady Mirella out of Altdorf. Princess Erna was busy experiencing the nuptial bliss of her new life as wife to Adolf Kreyssig.

Erich pulled the scrap away from Kretzulescu's bony grip and studied the jagged tear, trying to judge how much of the letter was missing. The Kaiserjaeger dagger made it clear who had the rest of the letter. If they had enough of it…

'Two days ago a troop of Kaiserjaeger rode out from Altdorf,' Baron Thornig said. 'They might have been going to Talabecland. They might be looking for Reiks-marshal Boeckenfoerde.'

Erich crushed the remnant of the letter and stared down at Konreid's corpse. 'We have to assume they have. And depending on what was written on the rest of this letter, Kreyssig might know exactly who is conspiring against Boris.'

'What do we do?' Count van Sauckelhof asked, panic written across his face.

Erich stepped around the table, wondering if he had the authority to make such a decision. By rights, it was Prince Sigdan's prerogative to sound the call to arms. To take that responsibility would be to flout the prince's position and leadership. At the same time, to delay might be to give Kreyssig the time he needed to smash their uprising before it could even start.

'We have to put our plans into action at once,' Erich decided. 'Have Aldo's people get word to Prince Sigdan and the others. Meisel, you will muster as many of your Bread Marchers as you can reach. If we wait, we play right into Kreyssig's hands. So we won't wait. We'll seize the Imperial Palace tonight!'

The declaration seemed to terrify the other conspirators. For as long as they had talked about it, the magnitude of their plot, the fact that they were really going to storm the Imperial Palace, had never really sunk in. Now, faced with the imminence of history, their courage began to falter.

Erich gestured down at the body of Konreid. First the execution of Arch-Lector Hartwich, now the murder of the old Reiksknecht veteran. How much blood would it take to stop a tyrant's outrages? 'It is too late to back out now. Too many people have sacrificed their lives and their honour to bring us this far. We will not fail them now. And if that isn't enough, consider this. Right now, Kreyssig is reading the other half of this letter. He might be reading each of your names. If the thought of saving the Empire from a tyrant isn't enough to make you commit to this cause, then fear for your own lives is!'

Baron Thornig leaned against the wall, his eyes haunted, his breath coming in frightened gasps. 'There's another way. Erna is with that monster right now. If I told her to, she could eliminate any threat from Kreyssig.'

Erich rounded upon the baron, grabbing him by his tunic and hoisting him to his feet. 'We're not using your daughter as a murderess!' the knight snarled. 'All of us are committed to this cause! We won't back out now!'

'But we're not ready,' protested Count van Sauckelhof.

'Then we'd better get ready,' Erich snapped, releasing

his hold on Baron Thornig and turning his ire on the Westerlander. 'Because time is running out. Not only for us, but for the whole Empire.'

## ─⟨ CHAPTER XV ⟩─

*Altdorf*
*Vorhexen, 1111*

IN TWOS AND threes, grim-faced men began to gather in the streets and alleyways bordering the Widows' Plaza. They came with clubs and knives; hammers and axes; swords of every size, shape and condition; home-made spears and curved bows of Reikland elm wood. Muffled in fur cloaks and wool coats, the men braved the bite of a mid-afternoon snow flurry, using the falling snow to mask their approach and hide their numbers.

Meisel had drawn upon some three hundred survivors of Engel's Bread March and to this core of experienced warriors he had added as many of Altdorf's disaffected peasantry as he could muster. It was a considerable mob that moved against the Courts of Justice. Rumours that the popular Arch-Lector Hartwich had been executed on orders from Emperor Boris had found fertile soil among Altdorf's suffering masses. Men who had silently endured all of the Emperor's other diktats and abuses had found this last one insufferable. Now, it seemed, the Emperor was trying to extend his tyranny into the realm of the gods and that the commoners would not allow.

The watchmen high atop the Tower of Altdorf didn't notice the approaching mob until packs of armed men emerged from the drifting snow and began marching into the Widows' Plaza. At once they sounded the alarm bells, nocking arrows to bows. The officer in command of the archers hesitated, however, as the numbers of men in the square continued to increase. He didn't want to make the decision to provoke the unrest further by shooting into the crowd. Precious minutes were lost as he awaited orders from his superiors to tell him what to do.

By then, the choice of drawing first blood was taken from the soldiers in the tower. Bowmen among the mob took aim and loosed arrows at the watchmen patrolling the walls of the Imperial Courthouse. Most of the soldiers had already taken shelter behind the battlements on the fortress walls, but their adversaries down in the square included men who had stalked the borders of the Laurelorn Forest and who had hunted through the wilds of the Drakwald, men who had honed their aim and their eye to a degree never imagined by the martial schools of Altdorf. A half-dozen soldiers were struck down by the precision shooting, many of them pitching into the fortress courtyard, as lifeless as the flagstones they smashed against.

When the command to loose arrows was finally given, the archers in the Tower of Altdorf found that their enemies were prepared for them. The mob hefted crude palisades crafted from doors and shutters, many of them bearing the chalk-mark warning against plague scrawled across their faces. The arrows slammed into these wooden panels, but were unable to pierce the men sheltering behind them. The vengeful marksmanship of hunters and targeteers sent a pair of the tower's bowmen slumping against the narrow embrasures, arrows transfixing their bodies.

A great cry rose from the mob as a swarm of enraged humanity converged upon the scaffold at the centre of the square. Like a pack of rabid wolves, the rebels tore down the hateful platform, smashing it to splinters with their boots and bare hands when no other weapon was available. Perched atop the scaffold steps, Meisel shouted direction to his followers, ordering them to drag down the gibbet. Armed with the thick oak post that supported the gibbet, the mob swung back around and rushed at the massive gates of the Imperial Courthouse.

Alarm bells clattered, horns and trumpets blared as the besieged garrison announced its plight to the city. Drawn down to provide troops for Reiksmarshal Boeckenfoerde's march against Talabheim, the garrison commander knew he didn't have enough men to defend the fortress if the rebels should get inside. For the moment, the fools seemed content to use their improvised battering ram against the gates, but soon one of them would get the idea to employ ladders. When that happened, the Courthouse would be overrun. There weren't enough soldiers to protect the walls.

The defenders of the Courts of Justice cast frantic eyes towards the nearby bulk of the Imperial Palace. There were hundreds of soldiers inside the palace, the Emperor's own bodyguard and the elite Kaiserknecht. If those warriors would sally forth and break the revolt, then the Courthouse could be saved. Otherwise, Altdorf would play host to its second great massacre of the season.

ERICH WATCHED THE attack on the Imperial Courthouse, waiting with bated breath for the moment when the violence of the mob would throw the defenders of the fortress into a panic. From long experience, he knew how soldiers reacted to the reduction of their foundation, how any battle assumed monstrous proportions when they were called upon to fight without their accustomed strength. When Meisel tore down the gibbet and the mob used it for a ram against the gates, it was the tipping point for the garrison commander. Horns and trumpets, bells and drums sounded from the fortress, appealing to any and all for assistance.

The closest help at hand was the Imperial Palace itself. Turning his gaze in that direction, he could see the confused agitation of the Palace Guard. Back and forth they rushed, reporting to their officers, then hurrying back to strengthen the defences at the Palace gate. For some twenty minutes, things continued in this manner, then a sharp clarion call echoed over the roofs of Altdorf. The inner gates withdrew into the ceiling of the gatehouse, the outer gates swung wide and a great company of knights came thundering down the marble walkway, the hooves of their mighty steeds striking sparks from the stones. Erich knew that golden tabard, marked with the hammer and laurel heraldry. The Kaiserknecht, Boris Goldgather's personal retinue of knights, men who had been drawn not from noble families or the ranks of the *Dienstleute*, but rather foreign mercenaries who were bound to the Emperor by the only loyalty Boris understood: gold.

The captain of the Kaiserknecht shouted an order in his lilting, Bretonnian tongue and the riders behind him, with the precision of a machine, lowered the visors of their great helms. Each knight dipped his lance as he charged through the gate, then his huge destrier wheeled about and galloped through the streets towards the Imperial Courthouse.

Erich frowned as he watched the knights sally forth, wondering how long Meisel would be able to keep his rebels fighting against such awesome odds. Some measure had been made to delay the knights; barricades had been erected across many of the streets and marksmen waited on the roofs to snipe at their enemy. Still, as a knight himself, Erich knew the power of a cavalry charge and the psychological destruction it wrought even against disciplined troops. Many of Meisel's rioters weren't even that, simple peasants without any military experience. They would shatter like glass when the Kaiserknecht hit them. All Erich could hope for was that the knights would lose themselves in the thrill of slaughter. That when they realised they had been tricked, it would be too late.

'Now, or never, your grace,' Erich told the man beside him. Prince Sigdan nodded, but his expression was doubtful as he lifted his hands, the chains wound about them rattling against his armoured chest.

'Sigmar preserve us,' Prince Sigdan said.

'And let's not be too proud to ask Ranald for some help too,' joked Baron Thornig. The shaggy Middenlander looked more comfortable in his chainmail and wolfskin cloak than he ever had in his robes of state. His hairy knuckles closed about the haft of an enormous hammer. 'I still say you should let me have first crack at them.'

Erich laughed at the Middenlander's impatience. 'There will still be plenty to go around,' he promised.

'Unfortunately,' observed Duke Konrad, looking somehow incongruous in his battered scale armour with a bright blue felt hat crunched down around his ears. 'But at least we'll get inside if this works. Trying to pass off that unwashed Ulrican beast as a Kaiserjaeger wouldn't get us even that far.'

Baron Thornig's eyes glittered menacingly. 'When this is over, we should talk,' he growled. 'As Graf Gunthar's emissary, I'm authorised to negotiate with other provinces.'

'Enough talk,' Prince Sigdan declared. 'Those peasants won't keep the Kaiserknecht busy for long.' The reminder didn't have to be repeated. Four of Prince Sigdan's retainers, dressed in the armour and livery of the Kaiserjaeger, took hold of the nobleman's arms. Erich, wearing similar uniform with the addition of a sergeant's armband, took position at the head of the little procession.

The phoney Kaiserjaeger marched towards the gates of the Imperial Palace, herding the captive Prince Sigdan with them. Under his breath, Erich continued to whisper prayers to Sigmar. Now would be the most dangerous point in their plan.

The Palace Guard lowered their halberds as the men approached, suspicion on their faces. Summoning every ounce of command his voice could muster, Erich growled orders at the threatening guards.

'We have arrested the traitor named Sigdan for inciting a revolt against His Imperial Majesty, Emperor Boris,' Erich said. 'Make way so that we can conduct this malcontent somewhere he will be safe.'

The guards continued to glare suspiciously at Erich. The knight could see one of them glance at a small bronze alarm bell set into the corner of the little watch post.

'Why do you think those peasants are attacking the Courthouse!' Erich snarled. 'They think we're keeping Sigdan there and they want to free him! Now let us in before they learn their mistake!' Erich watched uncertainty grow on the faces of the guards. Before the soldiers could ask any questions, he decided to add a final remark to help decide them. 'If this traitor gets away, I will see to it you answer to Commander Kreyssig.'

The threat worked. The sergeant in command of the gate waved his arms, motioning for the soldiers behind the walls to open the gate. Erich grinned when he saw the sergeant repeat the gesture for the benefit of the troops in the gatehouse. In his haste to get the prisoner inside, the sergeant was forgetting the most basic security. He was opening both gates at once.

'I will tell the Emperor of your service,' Erich promised. Then the knight's armoured fist came smashing into the guard's jaw, dropping him like a poleaxed ox. Instantly the other supposed Kaiserjaeger were leaping into action, rushing towards the inner gate before the stunned guards in the gatehouse could close it against them. The rest of the troops watching the outer gate were dragged down by the stealthy figures who stole upon them from behind. Soldiers from Duke Konrad's retinue, these were men who had grown up stalking beastmen through the Drakwald. Sneaking up on the Palace Guard was child's play to them.

'Once we gain the inner courtyard we can use Sigismund's escape tunnel to get into the Palace itself,' Prince Sigdan said, casting off the chains that had been looped around his hands. Rulers of Altdorf in the long period when the emperor's court had moved to Nuln, Sigdan's ancestors had an intimate knowledge of the Imperial Palace from the days when it was under their stewardship. The old escape tunnel had become obsolete when the Palace was expanded beyond its original dimensions, but for some reason the passage had never been filled, simply bricked over. For a man who knew what he was looking for, it would be a simple task to open it up again.

Now that there was no need for subterfuge, the rebels came streaming towards the Palace. Some of them were Bread Marchers, but most were soldiers from the retinues of the conspirators themselves, Reikland swordsmen and Drakwald hunters, hairy axemen from Middenheim and grim halberdiers from Sylvania, archers from Stirland and flamboyantly attired sea-dogs from Westerland. Even a handful of halfling bowmen, Aldo Broadfoot's contribution to the fight, came rushing along with the rest.

Erich gave the heterogeneous brigade its orders, pointing them towards the gatehouse where Prince Sigdan's retainers struggled with the Palace Guard. The fake Kaiserjaeger already had the upper hand, but reinforcements would quickly decide the fight.

'Now if we can just get the Palace secure before Kreyssig brings his Kaiserjaeger here,' Palatine Kretzulescu commented, his voice dour.

Baron Thornig clapped the cadaverous Sylvanian on the shoulder. 'I shouldn't worry about him. That problem has already been settled.'

Erich felt his blood run cold as he heard the Middenlander's boast. 'What have you done?' he demanded.

The baron glared back at the knight, a smug smile on his face. 'Erna is doing her part,' he said. 'And when that peasant scum is gone, no one will worry about how he died!'

PRINCESS ERNA GASPED in pain as her husband's fist smashed against her cheek. Blood dribbled from the corner of her mouth. Staggering back, she made a dive for the dagger that had fallen to the floor. Kreyssig lunged at her before she could grasp it, seizing her by the hair and wrenching her away with a savage twist. Again his fist lashed out, connecting with her belly and driving the breath from her lungs. Far from satisfied, he brought his fist smacking across her chin. Only the hand buried in her hair kept her upright.

'My lord!' shouted Fuerst, rushing towards his master. 'Commander! You'll kill her!'

Kreyssig turned and glared at his manservant. Blood was dripping from a long slash along the side of his face. 'That's the idea,' he hissed.

Fuerst felt his gorge rise. A timid, even cowardly man, he had no stomach for bloodshed. That was why he had cried out when he entered his master's bedchamber to announce a messenger below. Princess Erna had been standing over his sleeping master, the dagger in her hand. The distraction of Fuerst's shout had caused her to falter for a moment, and in that moment, Kreyssig was able to roll away, his face suffering from a blade that was meant for his heart.

'You can't do that!' Fuerst protested, rushing forwards as Kreyssig punched his reeling wife once more. The manservant reached out to stop him, but trembled at the thought of daring to touch his master. Instead, he pleaded for the woman's life in the only way Kreyssig would understand. 'If you kill her, you will never inherit the title of baron. They will never let you keep the dowry Baron Thornig bestowed on you. You'll lose all the lands you would have inherited.'

Kreyssig's face contorted into an almost inhuman snarl. Contemptuously he let Erna crumple to the floor. 'Baron Thornig?' he hissed. 'That blue-blooded rogue was here today. He put her up to this!' His eyes took on a reptilian quality as he wondered why the nobleman had desired his death so soon after the wedding.

'Maybe it has something to do with the riot?' Fuerst suggested.

The glowering commander rounded on his functionary. 'What riot?' he snapped. 'Where? When?'

Fuerst backed away, flustered by his master's barrage of questions. 'An uprising outside the Courthouse,' he said. 'Not more than half past the last bell. There's a messenger downst–'

Kreyssig snarled in rage, springing towards his wardrobe. 'That is what this is about! They wanted me out of the way and used this witch to do it!'

Fuerst stared at his master, unwilling to believe his words. 'Nobody… no one would dare…'

Shaking a boot at his servant, Kreyssig explained the one thing that would give an enemy the courage to strike at him in such a way. 'They dare because they intend to remove the Emperor!' he declared. 'This riot is just a diversion!' He pointed his finger at Fuerst. 'Go tell that messenger to send word to all the Kaiserjaeger and any Schueters we can trust. The revolt isn't at the Courthouse! It's at the Imperial Palace!'

Eyes bugging from his face at the magnitude of what he was hearing, Fuerst scrambled downstairs to pass instructions to the messenger. Kreyssig continued to dress himself, already dreading he might be too late. He cast a hateful look at the unconscious woman strewn across the floor.

'Before this is over, my dear,' he said, 'you will wish Fuerst had let me kill you.'

*Skavenblight*
*Vorhexen, 1111*

THICK COILS OF pungent incense veiled the vast hall in a smoky haze. Worm-oil lamps cast sickly green light from a great chandelier suspended from the soot-stained ceiling, conspiring with the smoke to cast weird shadows flickering about the walls. From the floor, an enormous glyph blazed with sinister brilliance, its sharp angles shining with a hellish luminance that rippled with echoes of flame and ruination.

Puskab Foulfur abased himself as he stepped towards the glowing symbol, the sigil of the Horned Rat. Though it was a false mask, the plague priest knew it was expected that he should prostrate himself before the symbol of the skaven god. Here, at the very heart of the Shattered Tower, the grey seers held sway and were zealous in punishing anything that smelled of heresy.

Piety, devotion to the Horned Rat. It was the final of the Twelve Tests and, in a perverse twist, also the easiest of them. Perhaps the grey seers really did depend upon their god to smite down any unbeliever. Or perhaps Seerlord Skrittar didn't dare evoke some conjuration against Puskab and then claim it was a divine judgement. Whatever the case, the plague priest lifted his horned head and scurried across the floor, careful to carry himself with just the right mix of timidity and boldness the Lords of Decay would expect from a supplicant.

The plague priest scowled at the sigil as he stepped across it. One day Clan Pestilens would blot out the false superstitions of the grey seers. The plaguelords would reveal to the whole of skavendom the true aspect of the Horned One and cast aside once and forever the foolishness of deluded mystics. On that day, the ratmen would either bind themselves to the Pestilent Brotherhood, or they would be destroyed!

Taking a firm step across the angular horns of the sigil, Puskab lifted his eyes from the floor. The time of Clan Pestilens was coming. The Black Plague was already burrowing towards that day.

A raised dais dominated the far side of the hall. A

pedestal draped in grey cloth loomed at the centre of the dais. Surrounding it, just dimly visible in the hazy mix of smoke and shadow, were thirteen stone seats, great thrones each adorned with the symbol of the Horned Rat. The personal banners of the council members hung suspended above each seat, displaying a chaotic confusion of glyphs, pictures and trophies.

Few skaven were ever allowed to enter the Shattered Tower, the megalithic structure which dominated Skavenblight and the whole of the Under-Empire. Fewer still were granted a glimpse of this place, the Chamber of the Thirteen, the great hall of the Lords of Decay!

Puskab struggled to focus his vision upon the figures seated upon the dais, but the effect of the incense and the flickering shadows made the effort impossible. The council members were always wary of assassination and so took pains to obscure their presence even within their most inviolate sanctums. For all the plague priest's senses could tell, the creatures seated upon the dais might be no more than members of the Verminguard while the real Lords of Decay observed him from another room.

The plague priest scratched his muzzle while he waited for the masters of skavendom to acknowledge his right to stand before them. Anger briefly flickered through the ratman's savage heart, resentment that despite the great service he had done, despite his discovery of the Black Plague, he had still been treated like a common clanrat by these lurking schemers!

The Twelve Tests were designed to slay any skaven desiring to challenge the Council of Thirteen. One test devised by each of the Lords of Decay. Some were cunning traps, others took the form of mind-wracking riddles while still others were composed of the most unfair and one-sided contests the vicious brain of a skaven could devise. All were alike in one respect – unless the challenger knew what to expect each of the tests was impossible.

There was only one way a challenger could prevail and that was how Puskab had done it. Through the sponsorship of a seated lord, and the use of his network of spies and informants, the challenger might learn the secret of each test before he ever set a paw within the black depths of the Shattered Tower. Blight Tenscratch had revealed to Puskab the trick to each trap, the answer to each riddle, the solution to each contest. Through the Wormlord's connivance, Puskab had survived to make his challenge and demand a place among the council.

The figures upon the dais glowered down at Puskab for several minutes, their malignant scrutiny causing the plague priest to shiver and his glands to tighten. When they did deign to speak to him, it was the fierce tones of Warmonger Vecteek that boomed down from the shadowy thrones.

'Poxmaster Puskab,' Vecteek snarled. 'We are pleased with your gift-offering. The man-things wither under the Black Plague. Their cities rot from within. They cower inside their burrows and hide from their own neighbours. They shall be easy-meat for our armies!'

Puskab bowed before the dais, crooking his head so he exposed his throat in the proper gesture of submission. 'Happy-proud to serve-help great lords,' Puskab said. 'Black Plague kill-kill much-much. Many man-things sick-die! Bring-make glory to Horned One!'

'Too many die!' snapped High Vivisectionist Rattnak Vile. 'Leave none to catch-take! No slave-meat to grow food and dig tunnels!'

'And the plague strikes our own!' growled Warpmaster Sythar Doom. 'We have been forced to burn the burrows of Clan Verms because they caught your plague!'

Puskab quivered as the Grey Lords made their accusations. Any one of these tyrants could have him killed on the spot and none would be the wiser. He turned his eyes across the shadowy rim of the dais, trying to pierce the haze and appeal to his patron.

'The infection of the Hive wasn't the fault of Puskab Foulfur,' Blight declared, his voice a threatening growl. 'The Poxmaster has come here, braved the Twelve Tests to challenge the traitor who sits in our midst! He has come to topple this greedy maggot who has endangered all Skavenblight by his murderous schemes! The Horned Rat has allowed him into the Chamber of the Thirteen, that he may purge this council of the corruption within its ranks!'

The arguing Grey Lords fell silent as Blight's words echoed through the great hall. 'Is this true?' the hacking tones of Arch-Plaguelord Nurglitch rasped. 'Have you come here to challenge a traitor for his seat upon the council?'

Puskab raised his horned head, pulling the tattered hood back from his decayed face. 'Survive-win Twelve Tests,' he growled. 'Now-now want-take Thirteenth Challenge! Take-win name-rank of Lord of Decay!'

Hisses and snarls filled the shadows as the lords of skavendom reacted to the reckless effrontery of the plague priest's demands. Tradition and the convoluted politics of the Under-Empire dictated that Puskab had earned the right to make his challenge, but the villainous despots didn't appreciate the callous way he addressed them.

'Puskab is right,' Blight shouted down the other lords. 'The destruction of my warren demands justice! Challenge the traitor-meat! Remove his stink from the Shattered Tower!'

Puskab's lips pulled back in a feral grin, exposing blackened fangs and bleeding gums. 'Claim-fight traitor-meat who sick-kill Clan Verms! Claim-fight heretic-spleen who think-want poison-slay all skaven!' The plague priest raised his fat claw and pointed to one of the black thrones.

'Claim-fight Blight Tenscratch!'

*Bylorhof*
*Ulriczeit, 1111*

FREDERICK SAT IN a wicker chair, his back to the wall of the mortuary, his priest's robes pulled tight against the preternatural cold which surrounded him. He stared out across the morbid chamber. It was silent now; the gnawing and scratching of rats as they fed upon the dead had been absent these past few days. Even the vermin had been driven off by the fell energies converging upon the place. There was only one living thing in the entire graveyard now.

The priest stared at the stone knife resting on the floor beside his chair. Many times he had taken up that blade and set it against his wrist. Against the horror he had unleashed, death would be a welcome release. That is, if death was still an option for him. It lacked the same finality with which he had regarded it a week ago.

He raised his eyes from the knife and gazed upon the silent, unmoving shapes facing him. Frederick had ordered them here and they had come. He could order them to leave, and they would go. If he closed his eyes and pictured their arms raised in salute, the decayed arms would rise. His merest whim was unbreakable law to these zombies. Creatures with no will of their own, they were utterly enslaved to the necromancer's desires. Frederick found the concept alternately fascinating and abominable. His mind whirled with thoughts of power and emotions of blackest despair.

Necromancer. Another word from the tomes of Arisztid Olt, the title of the most reviled heretic of them all – the magician who pierced the veil between life and death, who drew his sorcery from the very emanations of the grave. One of the insane monsters who followed the forbidden arts of Nagash the Accursed.

Frederick tried to tell himself he wasn't such a creature, that a vast gulf separated him from an apostate like Olt. He knew the argument was a lie, a final desperate effort to cling to decency and morality, to keep faith with the gods he had betrayed.

There was a reason why, for all his cleverness, Olt had been discovered. The temple had been built upon a nexus point, a convergence of magical forces that magnified any act of sorcery. When Olt had practised his spells, he had opened a gateway he could not shut. The dark energies had swelled and grown until they could not be ignored. That had proven Olt's downfall. It had also proven the source of Frederick's curse.

When he had conjured the ghost of Aysha, the priest had opened the floodgates. The baleful emanations, once tapped, had refused to recede. They had spread, directionless and unfocused, acting upon the subconscious desires of the necromancer who had drawn upon them. Locked within his mind were all of Olt's spells and secrets, the knowledge of generations of sorcerers and witches stretching back to the sands of Nehekhara. In his slumber, his dreaming mind had evoked those spells and the directionless energies had brought them into being. Frederick's guilt and shame at being unable to save the people of Bylorhof from the plague had resulted in the unconsecrated dead rising again as zombies – a sardonic and aimless refutation of the Black Plague.

It was a feat to impress any warlock – conjuration without apparatus or gesture, magecraft by sheer force of will alone. Frederick had never imagined such ability to lie untapped within his mind. If he had, he should have killed himself long ago.

The necromancer scowled at the rotting zombies standing before him. He was tempted to tell them to jump in a lake, except that was exactly what they would do. There was no limit to their servitude. As an experiment he had ordered one of them to chew off its own arm. Neglecting to specify which arm, he had looked on in amazement as the zombie gnawed its way through each arm in turn.

Emperors and kings did not command such loyalty! Frederick shuddered at the hideous power he possessed. Yet might such horror not be turned towards benevolence? Must only evil arise from evil? He was still a decent man, moral and just. He could control this terrible power. He would not allow it to control him.

Frederick rose from his chair, stalking past his zombies. He faced one of the niches, the niches filled with the corpses of Bylorhof's dead. These bodies had failed to reanimate under the influence of the necromancer's subconscious. Shriven, protected by rituals sacred to Morr, these dead were already consecrated. The protection against evil had been enough to fend away his undirected magic. But what would happen, he wondered, if he were to wilfully concentrate his power upon one of these bodies?

The necromancer turned away. A snap of his fingers sent a pair of zombies shambling over to the niche.

Without uttering a sound, the undead reached into the corpse pile and dragged out the body of a young woman. Still acting upon their master's unspoken command, the zombies carried their morbid burden to the stone table, laying it prostrate upon the cold surface.

As he stared down at the dead husk, Frederick pictured Aysha's body lying there. For a moment, he felt a surge of regret. He almost desisted in the horrible experiment, but a tremendous desire to know, to understand the limits of his magic, pushed him on. Aysha was safe within the mausoleum, beside Johan and the templars of old. She had no part in this. There was only Frederick van Hal and some nameless bit of peasant carrion.

He closed his eyes, visualising the dark power, drawing strands of black energy and weaving them around the prostrate corpse. His lips moved in a whispered invocation, calling upon one of the Nine Names of Nagash. The foreign note of that name seemed to make the room tremble. Frederick could feel it crawling off his tongue, slithering like something alive across the mortuary to settle upon the dead woman's pale brow.

For a moment the necromancer could feel the corpse struggling to oppose his will. It was a fleeting defiance, brushed away as casually as a cobweb. Frederick opened his eyes and extended his hand towards the corpse. Clumsily, the dead woman began to rise from the slab. A thin smile of triumph flashed across Frederick's face. Even the protection of the gods wasn't enough to defy his power!

The necromancer returned to his chair, staring across his undead slaves. This was power, but he would not abuse it. He would use this magic in the cause of justice, a counterpoint to the cruel abuses of corrupt lords like Baron von Rittendahl and Count Malbork von Drak.

Frederick's eyes became cold and hard, his hands clenching around the arms of his chair.

There was too much injustice, too much suffering in Sylvania, but he knew just where he would start. The plague doktor, Bruno Havemann, murderer and charlatan. He would be made to confess his crimes.

And then he would answer for them.

## ━━❮ CHAPTER XVI ❯━━

*Altdorf*
*Vorhexen, 1111*

THE ABANDONED TUNNEL wasn't as abandoned as Erich von Kranzbeuhler had expected. After battering their way through the stone blocks concealing the entrance, the rebels had been surprised by a squeaking horde of black-furred vermin. After their experiences in the sewer, it was a shock that had them shrieking in disgust and horror. For a moment, the rats rushed at the startled men, but it was flight not fight that motivated the animals. Soon their scaly tails were seen darting into bushes and behind outbuildings.

The conspirators breathed a collective sigh of relief, but as they stared down into the blackness of the tunnel, they wondered if perhaps they shouldn't have stayed behind with the men holding the gates or the force staging a diversionary attack on the Palace doors.

'If it has been sealed up all these years, how did the rats get in?' Palatine Kretzulescu wondered. No one could give the Sylvanian an answer.

Erich took it upon himself to lead the way. Lighting

a whale-oil lamp provided by Count van Sauckelhof, the knight reluctantly entered the forbidding darkness. At once the dank reek of the tunnel engulfed him, a choking foulness that brought a cough rumbling from his chest. He felt his pulse quicken as theories about miasma as source of the plague rose unbidden in his mind.

The walls of the tunnel were ancient, displaying the rough masonry and brickwork of Sigismund the Conquerer's time. Bones and rat pellets littered the floor while cobwebs dangled from the vaulted ceiling. Here and there the bulk of a fallen slab of stone loomed in the darkness, a vivid warning that something more substantial than a cobweb might drop down into the passage.

As Erich crept through the tunnel, he found his thoughts straying to the daughter of Baron Thornig. The Middenlander had pressed upon Princess Erna first the role of spy and then that of murderess and assassin. It offended the knight's sensibilities to exploit a beautiful woman in such a fashion, however noble the cause. For her sake, he hoped that Erna would ignore her father's command.

A familiar stench brought an end to Erich's ruminations. Ahead, the knight saw a yawning pit, bricks scattered about it. The smell was that of the sewers, evoking once more visions of horror. Rats scampered about the hole, dropping down into it as they recoiled from the light of Erich's lamp.

Here at least was the answer to how the rats had gotten into a sealed tunnel. Part of the floor had collapsed into the sewers, which must run beneath the Imperial Palace. So much for the durability of dwarf architecture – though as he looked at the pit and the stones piled about it, he couldn't escape the idea that something was very wrong. The hole looked like it had been caused by something burrowing up from below rather than stones collapsing into a passageway beneath.

'We have to hurry,' Prince Sigdan cautioned. He cast a dubious glance at the pit, then laid his hand on Erich's shoulder and urged him onwards. 'Every minute we delay is another minute of Boris's tyranny.'

'And more time for the Kaiserjaeger to show up,' warned Baron von Klauswitz.

Baron Thornig's harsh laughter echoed through the tunnel. 'I've arranged to pull their teeth,' he boasted. 'Right now Commander Kreyssig is dining with Khaine in hell!'

Erich felt his blood boil at the baron's bravado. So lost was he in what he considered a clever bit of scheming that Baron Thornig seemed oblivious to the danger he had placed his daughter in. The knight half-turned to berate the Middenlander, but Prince Sigdan's silent urging kept him moving.

There would be time to settle all accounts once Boris Goldgather was deposed.

*Middenheim*
*Vorhexen, 1111*

THE WARBLING CLAMOUR of crude horns rose from the darkened forest, a feral din that seemed to scratch at the stars and to drag down the moon. The discordant notes had scarcely started to fade before a confusion of animalistic howls, bleats and screams pierced the night. From the battlements of Middenheim, archers loosed flaming arrows into the treeline. By the flickering light of the arrows, a bestial horde could be seen rushing from the woods.

An alarm bell sounded, echoed a moment later by the clarion call of trumpets all along the wall. It seemed a useless gesture. The inhabitants of Warrenburg had to be aware of the attack already. They didn't need the soldiers on the walls to warn them.

For hours the beastmen had been working themselves into a frenzy, the dull rhythm of their manskin drums pulsing from the forest, the growling chants of their savage shamans rising from the trees. There had been ample time for Grand Master Arno to gather his chosen men. Fifty knights in full armour, each of their steeds a gigantic warhorse clad in steel barding, mustered behind the portcullis of the East Gate.

At the clarion call of the trumpet, Arno raised his hand. Slowly the soldiers within the gatehouse began to raise the barrier. Arno watched the massive gate retreat into the roof of the archway with a fatalistic resignation. Once he went through that portal, he understood there was no coming back.

'I didn't expect you to lead the charge.'

The Grand Master turned in surprise at hearing the voice of Prince Mandred, though in hindsight he shouldn't have been. It was, after all, the boy's idea.

'I couldn't ask any of my men to risk themselves if I was too timid to go myself,' Arno explained. A troubled frown came across his face. 'You should stay behind, your grace. This is too perilous for the Prince of Middenheim.'

Mandred smiled at the knight's protest. 'If it is so dangerous, then we can't risk the Grand Master of the White Wolves.'

Arno laughed. 'Commander Vitholf can more than make up for my loss. The White Wolves might even be better off with him leading the pack.' The troubled look returned to the knight's face. 'There is only one Prince of Middenheim,' he said.

Mandred saw the Grand Master directing what he thought was a subtle signal to his knights. The prince watched as two of the warriors edged their horses closer to his own. Glancing at the rising portcullis, Mandred dug his spurs into the flanks of his warhorse.

'Let it never be said the Prince of Middenheim asked his subjects to do something he was afraid to do himself!' he shouted as his horse bolted forwards. Crouching his body low against the animal's neck, he was just able to clear the spikes jutting from the underside of the rising gate.

Grand Master Arno gawped after him in astonishment, then roared at his knights. 'You heard his grace!' Arno bellowed. 'Follow him to hell or victory!' Spurring his own horse onwards, the Grand Master copied Mandred's example, clearing the gate as it was still being raised. Behind him he could hear the thunder of hooves as the rest of the knights started after him.

The broadness of the eastern causeway gave the knights room to form ranks as they charged out from the gate. Above them, from the walls, the clarions sounded once more, singing out into the night, announcing the wrath of man to his inhuman enemies.

The beastmen had reached the hovels of Warrenburg, rampaging through the confused huddle of shacks with feral bloodlust. If they heard the trumpets sound, the brutes were too lost in their animalistic rage to care. The primordial hatred of beastkin for man burned in their savage hearts, feeding the fires of their fury. Not content to simply kill their victims, the raging beastmen mauled their victims, ripping them to shreds with tooth and claw. In their fury, they glutted themselves in an orgy of destruction.

Into this vision of atrocity, the warriors of Midden-heim charged. The tents and hovels of Warrenburg crumpled beneath the pounding hooves of their steeds, parting before them like wheat before a scythe. Refugees scattered before the knights, but the blood-mad beastkin stood transfixed, their savage brains flung into confusion by the sudden appearance of the warriors.

Warhammers came smashing down into horned heads, great axes clove through furred flesh, iron-shod hooves crushed bestial bodies. The name of Ulric rose in a fierce war cry as the White Wolves brought the vengeance of man to the marauding forest beasts.

Mandred was in the thick of the battle, spurring his huge destrier into the heart of the shantytown. His sword slashed across the face of a fawn-faced beastling as it gorged upon the body of a slaughtered woman. The creature clapped furry claws to its mangled eyes, bleating in agony. Another sweep of the prince's sword opened the monster's throat and sent it crashing into the snow.

A second beastman rushed at Mandred, a wiry thing with ox-horns and an almost human visage. It brandished a dismembered human leg, wielding the macabre trophy like a club. Mandred waited for the thing to come close, then put spurs to his warhorse, urging the destrier to rear up, to lash out with its front hooves. The flailing legs struck the charging beastman, hurling it back and snapping its ribs.

A braying war cry was Mandred's first warning that a third beastman was running towards him. It was a huge goat-headed monster, a rusted broadaxe clenched in its paws. The brute was charging towards him from the flank, at an angle where the prince wouldn't be able to reach it with his blade. He tried to wheel his horse around to meet the monster's rush, but even as he did so, he knew it would be too late.

Suddenly another rider appeared, crashing through the wall of a shack. The beastman was caught beneath the warhorse's pounding hooves, smashed to the ground and crushed underfoot. Mandred could hear its bones snap as the horse charged over it. He opened his mouth to thank his rescuer, then laughed in disbelief as he recognised the rider.

'Franz!' the prince exclaimed. 'What are you doing here? You should be in bed tending your wounds!'

'I don't need to stand to ride a horse, your grace,' the bodyguard answered. He rubbed his hand over his bald scalp. 'It was wrong to leave me behind,' the knight said.

'I was afraid you might tell my father,' Mandred said.

Franz smiled and shook his head. 'The Graf will learn about this foolishness soon enough.' He looked away, peering through the nest of shacks and tents. 'It seems they're running, your grace. We'll have to hurry if we want to claim a respectable contribution to the battle.'

Mandred grinned and brought his horse around. 'Let's make them wish they'd stayed in the Drakwald.'

THE BATTLE WAS a short but bloody affair. Fully a quarter of the shantytown was trampled by the time the beast-kin broke and fled. At least a hundred of the brutes had fallen before the charge, but behind them they left scores of dead and dying refugees.

The herd had been broken, however. Grand Master Arno didn't think they'd be back. It would take them a long time to lick their wounds and build up their courage. By then, perhaps, the threat of the Black Plague would be diminished enough for the Graf to allow the refugees inside Middenheim.

Jubilation at their victory was tempered by the

knowledge that it was a pyrrhic victory. Everywhere in the shantytown the marks of plague were in evidence. Dead bodies swollen with buboes, living wretches with black treacle oozing from their pores. Contagion was everywhere, the stink of disease omnipresent.

The knights knew that through their bold charge they had exposed themselves to the plague. Somewhere in the squalor of Warrenburg, the source of the disease lurked. None of the warriors could say for certain that its deathly touch had not reached out for him. None of them knew if he carried the seed of the Black Plague in his body.

Mandred looked up the causeway, staring at the grim edifice of the bastion. That would be their home now, locked away behind those grim grey walls. There they would await the judgement of the gods, wait to see if the justice of their cause was enough to guard them against the clutch of the plague.

A sombre silence gripped the knights as they slowly rode towards the bastion. Each of them wondered if he would ever leave the place alive.

Mandred struggled to find some words of reassurance to bolster their flagging spirits, but nothing seemed profound enough to honour their sacrifice. It was a sacrifice he was proud to share with such men.

The sound of a horn cause Mandred to turn his gaze away from the bastion. For a moment the fear that the beastmen had regrouped flashed through his mind. Then he recognised the notes of his father's hunting horn. Raising his gaze to the East Gate, he was shocked to see a company of cavalry slowly trotting their way onto the causeway.

At their head, resplendent in his blue cloak and gilded armour, rode Graf Gunthar.

\* \* \*

### Talabecland
### *Vorhexen, 1111*

REIKSMARSHAL EVERHARDT JOHANNES Boeckenfoerde rose from his chair as his three visitors were bowed into the general's tent. His adjutant, Nehring, offered to take the heavy cloaks from the visitors, but they declined his overtures with a brusque shrug.

'We have come from Altdorf,' the foremost of the men announced.

The Reiksmarshal gave Nehring a warning look. 'It must have been a long and unpleasant ride,' he said. 'Perhaps not as unpleasant as moving an army under these conditions…'

'You have been implicated in a plot against His Imperial Majesty Emperor Boris,' the cloaked man continued. The three men began to fan out across the tent. 'His Imperial Majesty offers you a choice. You can return to Altdorf, stand trial and be executed. Or you can remain here and fall on your own sword.' A cruel smile flickered on the man's face. 'If you choose execution, Commander Kreyssig asks you to remember the traitor von Schomberg.'

The cruelty in Boeckenfoerde's smile matched that of the Kaiserjaeger officer. 'I have heard about the Grand Master. A shameful business. Only an animal would take pride in such work.'

The three Kaiserjaeger reached for their swords. Instantly, Nehring had his own blade unsheathed. The Reiksmarshal remained seated, motioning for his guests and his adjutant to be calm.

'You came here to arrest me?' Boeckenfoerde asked.

The officer's voice was filled with scorn when he

answered. 'This tent is surrounded,' he hissed. 'I have twenty Kaiserjaeger outside and they only wait my word to butcher you like a pig!'

Boekenfoerde nodded, as though considering the threat posed by the Kaiserjaeger. 'Has it occurred to you where you are?' he asked. 'Have you given any thought to where this tent is? I have four thousand soldiers out there and at the slightest sound of violence coming from this tent, they will take up arms and… as you put it… butcher you like a pig.' He smiled as he watched the colour drain out of the officer's face. 'Nehring, take their swords. These gentlemen don't need them any more.'

'You won't get away with this,' the officer growled as Nehring plucked the sword from his unresisting grip. 'That is the army of his Imperial Majesty! When I tell them you are a traitor…'

The Reiksmarshal rose from his chair and stepped out from behind his table. He tapped his finger on the map pinned to the wall of his tent. 'His Imperial Majesty has just sent this army marching through the worst of winter with barely enough provisions to provide for half of them and winter gear for even less. And what enemy draws us to such reckless and heroic pursuits? Some new orc invasion or marauding Norscans? No, we march to force the Grand Duke of Talabecland to open the markets in Talabheim so Boris can get a few more crowns in tax revenue.' Boeckenfoerde's eyes were like daggers as he glared at the men from Altdorf. 'I don't think you'll find too many here with any great love for Goldgather. Loyalty to me is the only thing that has brought them this far.

'If you tell those men who you are and why you came here, they won't leave enough of you left for the crows to pick at.' The Reiksmarshal turned away from the map, retrieving his sword from where it leaned against his cot. 'I suggest you ride back to Altdorf before I tell them myself.'

The Kaiserjaeger were quick to heed the warning, nearly falling over themselves as they scrambled out of the tent. Boeckenfoerde was an excellent judge of a man's mettle, and he'd had these pegged as ambitious thugs the moment they stepped into his tent. Their kind would kill for their leaders, but they wouldn't die for them. Faced with the choice of dying to accomplish their mission, they could only turn tail and run.

Nehring watched the Kaiserjaeger mount their horses and ride off, then slipped back inside the general's tent. He was surprised to find the Reiksmarshal packing his gear. He gazed quizzically at the general.

'Call the officers,' Boeckenfoerde told him. 'They'll have to be told about this.'

'But you said the men would stand with you,' Nehring reminded.

The Reiksmarshal sighed. 'Some of them might. I hope many of them will, but a lot of those men have families back in Altdorf and in the Reikland. If the conspirators have failed to depose Boris, then those families would be imperilled if these men took up arms against the Emperor.'

'What about you?' Nehring asked. 'What will you do?'

'I'm certainly not going back to Altdorf,' the Reiksmarshal said. 'I'll take whatever men stand with me and head for someplace out of Boris's reach. Talabheim would be a good prospect.

'They might need an extra army soon.'

*Nuln*
*Ulriczeit, 1111*

THE BLAZE OF a rushlight drove back the darkness. Walther blinked against the harsh glare. For days now he had existed in perpetual blackness, the only sensations he could experience limited to the chill of his cell and the skittering of rats behind the walls. His eyes, deprived of vision for so long, burned with agony. The rat-catcher pressed his bloodied palms to his face in an effort to shield himself from the rushlight.

Fellgiebel stood in the doorway, his icy eyes studying the man sprawled on the stone floor. The cell, a little room buried beneath the Freiberg Hundertschaft's watch station, was scarcely six feet across and only a little taller. It was without furnishing or accoutrement; the straw pallet had already been stolen by an opportunistic watchman to sell as fodder and the wooden slop bucket had met a similar fate.

When he told the guard to wait outside and closed the door, Fellgiebel and his prisoner were utterly alone and without distraction. The captain nodded when he saw the look of horror that crossed Walther's features. Clearly the man appreciated the situation he was in. Officially, peasants were the property of their lords and the watch wasn't allowed to mutilate them or render them any harm which would cause permanent injury. To do so would require compensation to the lord, something a simple Dienstmann couldn't afford. Thus, by the letter of the law, there were limits to what tortures a militia like the Hundertschaft had recourse to.

Of course there were loopholes. An accident, for instance, would place the onus of compensation upon the peasant himself. It was frightening how many accidents there were in Nuln.

'I grow weary of these discussions,' Fellgiebel said, his gloved hands clasped together before him. The captain's cold gaze fixed upon Walther's bloodied face. 'You are going to talk, you know. It is just a question of time and pain.'

Walther struggled up from the floor, using the icy stone wall to prop up his battered body. With every motion, broken bones ground against each other, bringing moans of anguish from the rat-catcher. By an effort of will that seemed to tax his very soul, Walther forced himself to meet Fellgiebel's gaze and address his tormentor.

'What… what has… happened…' He closed his eyes, dredging up some last speck of courage to steel his faltering voice. 'The Black Rose, how…'

'The Black Rose is under quarantine,' Fellgiebel said, his voice like a knife. 'No one goes in, no one comes out.' A cruel sneer curled his lip. 'Plague, you know. The place is alive with it. At least for now.'

Walther sagged back against the wall, his broken body heaving as dry sobs racked his frame. 'Zena,' he groaned. In his mind he could picture her, alone and shunned in some corner of the tavern, her body covered in the black buboes of the plague.

Fellgiebel stepped out from the doorway and began pacing across the small cell. 'Ah, yes, your girl. You've mentioned her a few times now. She must be very close to you.' There was a menacing gleam in the reptilian eyes as the captain stared down at Walther. 'Perhaps I should collect her for a little discussion. Just a short one. I doubt a woman would share your stamina, Schill. Or your stubborn endurance.'

Walther shook his head. The threat had been made so many times now that it held no further horrors for him. Fellgiebel had used that particular method of persuasion too often. If he had any intention of carrying through with it, he would have done so by now. The fact that he hadn't convinced Walther that plague really had beset the Black Rose. Even Fellgiebel wasn't so arrogant in his authority as to brave the Black Plague.

'Do you want me to tell you what you want to hear?' Walther said. 'Or do you want the truth?'

Fellgiebel stopped pacing. His cheerless smile spread. 'The truth, Schill. That is all I have ever wanted. The truth about your friend Aldinger and the others. Where they are. What they know. What they are planning to do.' The captain's voice dropped to a conspiratorial whisper. 'Aldinger was a knight, you know. A refugee from the Reiksknecht. The others are probably Reiksknecht too. Our great and glorious Emperor has placed a bounty on all Reiksknecht. They are traitors and it is every man's duty to turn them over to the Emperor.' Fellgiebel tried to make his smile a bit friendlier. 'If you tell me where they are, I'll share the reward with you.'

The only answer from the prisoner was a miserable cough, the closest he could manage to a laugh. Fellgiebel ignored the gesture and resumed his pacing. 'We shall forget the Reiksknecht, then. Tell me about the rat you captured. Why were the professors so interested in it? What did they tell you about it?'

Again, Walther tried to laugh. This line of questioning had been going on for a fortnight, always made with the same note of urgency. Even more than his denial of knowing Aldinger or the Reiksknecht, his insistence that he knew nothing special about the giant rat seemed to infuriate Fellgiebel. The captain wouldn't believe Walther's story that the professors hadn't been particularly interested in the rat but more in the humiliation the existence of such a creature could deal to their reputations as scholars and their theories about the structure of life. As for any special information they had imparted to him, every one of the scholars had insisted the thing was an impossibility, later trying to justify their stance by claiming the giant Walther had caught was simply a one-time freak.

'I grow tired of asking this,' Fellgiebel said, coming to a halt and fixing Walther with his reptilian stare. 'What do you know? What plans did you make with Aldinger? Who else is involved?' The captain watched Walther closely, looking for any sign that his prisoner would speak. Walther just stared up at him with that mixture of fright and abhorrence with which the sane regard the mad.

'Very well,' Fellgiebel said. 'I did warn you this would be the last time.' The captain strode across the cell, not towards the door but to the bare wall at the end of the room. 'I had hoped to spare you this. You do not believe it now, but I have been trying to help you.' The coldness ebbed from the captain's eyes, replaced by a quivering terror. His gloved hand reached out to the corner of the wall, his fingers brushing against the stone. His entire body trembling, Fellgiebel hesitated. Swiftly he wrenched his hand away from the wall and turned upon Walther.

'Tell me, before it is too late!' the captain demanded. 'Hanging, the rack, whatever the Hundertschaft can do to you is nothing compared to what awaits if you don't speak!' Fellgiebel tugged away one of his gloves. Walther recoiled in loathing as he saw the captain's hand. It was lean and hairy, covered in bony nodules, more like the paw of some hideous beast than the hand of a man. Despite the evidence of his own eyes, it took a moment for Walther to appreciate the hideous truth. The captain of the Freiberg Hundertschaft was a mutant!

'They are not pretty, are they?' Fellgiebel asked. 'I was… contaminated helping the inquisitors of Verena cull mutants from the sewers. I couldn't tell anyone about my… condition or I would have been burned.' He cast a fearful look at the blank wall at the back of the cell. 'But someone learned just the same. The price for silence was service.' The captain's lean face became flush with desperation. 'Speak, Walther! Believe me when I tell you there are worse things than death in this world!'

The rat-catcher leaned forwards, forcing his eyes to meet those of his captor. 'Do you want the truth, or just what you want to hear?'

Fellgiebel snarled in frustration, turning away and dragging the glove back over his hand. 'On your head be it!' he cried, stalking back towards the wall. 'The gods have mercy on you,' he said as he pressed his finger against a hidden catch. The wall shuddered as it pivoted inwards, retreating into yawning blackness. A foul, noxious reek wafted into the cell, an evil animalistic smell that caused every hair on Walther's body to stand on end. Painfully, the rat-catcher started to drag himself away from the secret passage.

Fellgiebel walked away, turning his back to the tunnel. A mad giggle bubbled from his lips, only a supreme effort of will forcing it back down. When the captain was composed, he cast a final, pitying look at Walther. 'Forgive me,' he whispered.

Walther didn't hear Fellgiebel. His attention was riveted to the tunnel and what was transpiring in those black depths. Beady red eyes gleamed from the darkness, and with them came a furtive rustling and chittering that was monstrously familiar to the rat-catcher. His body trembled as eyes and sounds drew closer, as shadowy figures emerged from the tunnel. He screamed as the flickering light revealed rodent-shapes with clutching paws and glistening fangs. He was still screaming when hand-like paws seized him and dragged him into the tunnel.

Fellgiebel kept his back turned, not watching as his secret masters dragged Walther away. He felt his heart sicken, his stomach roil with disgust. If there had been another way – but his masters were impatient and he had been left without a choice. No man deserved what he had done to Walther. No man deserved to become the captive of the skaven.

The sound of the hidden door sliding shut told Fellgiebel when it was all over. Only then did he turn around, making a careful inspection of the cell to ensure that no trace of the skaven had been left behind. The disappearance of Walther Schill would barely raise an eyebrow. Many peasants who succumbed to torture vanished. Without a body, the nobles had a hard time claiming their compensations.

An insane giggle returned to Fellgiebel's lips as he started to leave the cell. It was some time before he was able to compose himself, to slip back into the emotionless personality of the cruel watch captain and subdue the terrified agent of the underfolk.

'The rats caught the rat-catcher,' Fellgiebel laughed. There was no amusement in the laughter, only the emptiness of a man who was a traitor to his own race.

*Altdorf*
*Vorhexen, 1111*

THE PALACE GUARD slid from Erich's blade, clutching at the crimson stain spreading across his golden livery. The knight pushed his dying victim aside, bounding forwards to confront a second soldier who had Mihail Kretzulescu pinned against the wall. The guard swung about in alarm as he caught the sound of Erich's approach, but before he could bring his halberd around, the knight's sword was slashing across the man's eyes. The blinded wreck collapsed to the floor, shrieking in agony.

Erich helped Kretzulescu out from the little niche the Sylvanian had hidden himself in. The palatine's shoulder was deeply gashed, his black tunic damp with blood. 'I'm afraid I'm not much use in a fight,' he apologised. 'It's a different thing fighting a man than it is hunting ghouls in the marshes.'

'At least you stood your ground,' Erich reassured him. 'That is all one man can demand of another.'

The sounds of conflict gradually faded away, replaced by the moans of the wounded and the dying. Erich looked down the marble-walled gallery, feeling a twinge of sadness when he saw the lush tapestries hanging on the walls befouled with blood. The sudden appearance of the rebels in the very heart of the Palace had caught the defenders unawares, putting the element of surprise firmly on their side. He knew they couldn't count on that advantage much longer. Already servants must be carrying word of their presence. Numbers were still on the side of the Palace Guard. If the rebels were to have any chance in achieving their purpose, they had to find Emperor Boris before an overwhelming force could be marshalled against them.

To that end, Prince Sigdan had split their force the moment they gained the Palace. One group, led by the prince, had headed upwards to search the apartments of the Emperor's private residence. Another party headed by Duke Konrad had turned to the lower floors, where the audience chambers, reception halls and more functionary chambers of the Palace were situated.

Erich had been put in charge of a group of twenty men and sent to investigate the middle levels of the Palace, the trophy rooms and show rooms, the libraries and conservatories. The indecent extravagances of

Boris Goldgather had sickened the knight at every turn. He'd discovered chambers that had been emptied so that stacks of expensive stained glass might be heaped inside, layers of dust caked about their silver frames indicating the neglect to which they had fallen. Rooms stocked with camel-skin divans and alabaster vases imported from Araby, artworks from Tilea, wondrous mechanical automata from the dwarf kingdoms, all of these had suffered similar abandonment. Erich even discovered a room filled with teakwood boxes containing little painted tiles and recalled the scandal surrounding the Emperor's extravagant purchase of a famous Estalian fresco and the king's ransom he had paid out to have the fresco painstakingly dismantled and transported across half the Old World. That had been nearly a decade ago and the Emperor had made no effort to reassemble the fresco. It seemed once the thrill of acquisition was gone, he took no further interest in the treasures he squandered the Empire's wealth upon.

After scouring an entire floor without a trace of another living soul, it was impressed upon Erich the exact magnitude of their labour. He could have a hundred men and several hours and still not make a proper job of it. As it stood, he hoped that Count van Sauckelhof's prayers to Ranald weren't being ignored.

While Erich was taking a quick count of his small force, determining that two Sylvanians had fallen in the skirmish and besides Kretzulescu there were three wounded, a loud voice began shouting triumphantly from one of the chambers leading off the gallery. Erich recognised the bellow as belonging to Baron Thornig, but what had caused his excitement the knight was at a loss to explain. Fearing the worst, he motioned the two Reiksknecht in their little group to follow him and set off at a run to find the Middenlander.

The room the shouts came from looked like an armoury, so filled was it with weapons and armour. A half-dozen corpses wearing the gold of the Palace Guard were sprawled around the doorway, showing every sign of having made a vicious effort at defence. Beyond the doorway virtually every sort of armament was on display, lying placidly upon velvet-lined tables and stands. Erich saw the thin rapiers of Estalia and the brutish axes of Kislev, the heavy lances of Bretonnia and a thorny sword-like bludgeon of inhuman origin. There seemed no pattern to the assortment of weaponry, a dwarf axe resting beside a blade of elven make, a crude orc axe beside a curved scimitar from Araby.

Then Erich noticed a gruesome horned helm of blackened iron hanging upon a silver hook, the splinters of a shadow box dangling all around it. Erich could understand why the trophy had been hidden, and why whoever had smashed the shadow box had quickly retreated. There was no mistaking that helm, not for anyone who had examined an illuminated copy of the *Deus Sigmar*. The knight felt a sense of awe as he stared at this relic from the founding of the Empire – the helm of Morkar the Despoiler.

At once the smallness and unimportance of his own life pressed down upon the knight's spirit. Who was he, captain of an outlawed order of knights, to challenge the authority and legacy of the emperors? Who was he to question a power that dated back to Sigmar himself?

Despair closed its claws about his heart as he stared up at the hoary battle trophy. Erich found his grip on his sword weakening, his sense of purpose faltering. Giving up now was the only thing that made sense any more. There was no hope of victory, no triumph waiting at the end of the ordeal. Only death and humiliation and shame.

Baron Thornig's bellow snapped Erich from the pernicious influence of the helm. The knight glared at the lifeless iron mask, sensing its malignant mockery. Now that he was aware of its influence, it seemed weaker, unable to manipulate his fear, but Erich wanted to take no chances. Cautiously, he stepped away from the relic of the ancient Chaos warlord and made his way across the room to where Thornig continued to howl and shout.

'You'll bring the whole Palace down on us!' Erich snarled at the Middenlander.

Baron Thornig just smiled and pointed his fist at the table beside him. The stand was richly carved from the lip of its recessed surface to each of the clawed dragon-feet at the ends of its legs. A casing of transparent crystal covered the display, and the surface beneath the trophy ensconced below looked to be nothing less than dragonskin.

But Erich paid scant attention to these trappings of opulence. His eyes were instantly locked upon the relic itself. Like the helm of Morkar, there was no mistaking what it was. Unlike that grim trophy, however, the relic's draw was unmistakable. Looking upon it, Erich could feel vigour surge through his veins.

'Ghal Maraz,' Erich whispered.

Baron Thornig laughed. 'I thought that would be worth seeing. But it's too damn fine to leave with a leech like Goldgather.' So saying, the Middenlander raised his own warhammer, a weapon that seemed small and crude beside the magnificent hammer which had once filled the hands of Sigmar himself.

Erich gasped in horror, lunging to restrain Baron Thornig. 'You don't mean to destroy it!' he shouted.

Baron Thornig shook him off and raised his hammer once more. 'Of course not!' he shouted, bringing the warhammer smashing down and shattering the crystal casing.

'I mean to steal it!'

## ⟢ CHAPTER XVII ⟣

*Altdorf*
*Vorhexen, 1111*

ERICH WIPED THE blood from his blade, feeling a twinge of regret as the young soldier lay bleeding at his feet. The man had fought bravely and fiercely, and despite his years he had given the knight many close moments. Experience had prevailed, however, and in the end all it had taken was one ill-timed slash to allow Erich to slip past his adversary's guard and run him through.

There were many such brave fighters lying strewn throughout the arcade overlooking the grand ballroom. Many of them wore the gold of the Palace Guard, but mixed among them were members of Baron Thornig's retinue, several of Duke Konrad's men and even a few of Erich's fellow Reiksknecht. But for the timely intervention of Erich and his force, Prince Sigdan might have been repulsed and overwhelmed by Boris's faithful defenders.

Now those defenders had been pushed back into the Harmony Salon, overlooking the ballroom. Bracing the doors with tables and chairs, the Palace Guard were making a staunch defence until Aldo Broadfellow made a suggestion. The halfling had no appetite for battle, and it took a mind such as his to conceive a better way to force entry into the salon. Instead of smashing their way into the room, the rebels piled tapestries, furnishings, paintings and anything else that looked like it might burn.

At Prince Sigdan's order, the pile of battered finery and art was doused in lamp oil and set alight. Coils of thick black smoke boiled through the arcade, spilling out into the halls and almost choking the invaders until Duke Konrad ordered the doors to the connecting chambers thrown open and the windows smashed to vent the fumes. Count van Sauckelhof took vindictive delight in ordering the obliteration of the Emperor's prized *Kaiseraugen*, hurling an iron sconce into the crystal panes as the first blow against the decadent opulence that had characterised Boris's reign.

Before the next bell tolled from the spires of the Great Cathedral, the barricaded doorway had been reduced to smouldering rubble. The rebels shouldered their way past the flaming wreckage, pressing on into the mirror-walled room beyond. Every furnishing had been pushed up against the door, leaving only the massive hydraulis still standing. Too heavy to move, the immense water organ formed the Emperor's last refuge. Sheltering behind its bulk, Boris Goldgather glared at his enemies as they stormed into the room.

'Boris Hohenbach!' Prince Sigdan shouted as he marched through the crumbling doorway, with boots scraping against the charred planks of the wood-covered floor. 'For crimes against the Empire and its people, you are called upon to abdicate your throne and relinquish the powers you have abused and of which you are unworthy!'

The Emperor's eyes narrowed with hate as he heard Prince Sigdan's demand. He cast his gaze across the rebels filing into the salon, then looked over at his own depleted forces. Coughing, half-smothered by the smoke, his Palace Guard still formed ranks around him, raising their shields and drawing their swords. The black-armoured figure of Baron Peter von Kirchof stepped out from the ranks of the defenders. The Emperor smirked as he saw the faces of his enemies go pale. In all the Empire, no man was better with a sword than von Kirchof, the Emperor's Champion.

'I do not recognise your authority,' Boris growled. 'But if you think I am guilty of some injustice, then I give you leave to prove my guilt in personal combat with my representative.'

Von Kirchof acknowledge his sovereign's words with a curt military bow. Then the champion's sword was drawn from its sheath. A gasp of outrage rose from Duke Konrad's lips.

'Beast Slayer!' the furious duke raged. 'The Runefang of Drakwald! That blade belongs to the Count of Drakwald! You have no right to bestow it upon this... this hired killer!'

Emperor Boris leaned out from behind the water organ, his eyes glittering malignantly. 'There is no Count of Drakwald,' he sneered. 'The trappings of that realm are forfeit to the Imperial Court.'

Duke Konrad started forwards, in his blind anger ready to confront even the incredible swordsmanship of Baron von Kirchof. Erich grabbed the Drakwalder by the shoulder, restraining his reckless advance.

'We have collected trinkets too,' Erich called out. He laughed as he saw Boris's look of smug victory collapse as Baron Thornig held aloft Ghal Maraz. 'What kind of emperor are you without the Hammer of Sigmar?' the knight scoffed.

Boris reeled against the side of the organ, his face growing purple with indignation. A portly man in black robes and a physician's cap dashed out from the little knot of courtiers who had taken shelter with their Emperor, fumbling about in his bags as he tried to administer a restorative to his sovereign. The stunned Emperor waved away the efforts of his personal physician.

'You dare such sacrilege?' Boris demanded, throwing his head back and fixing the conspirators with his withering gaze. 'That is the holy hammer of our lord and saviour, Sigmar Heldenhammer, first emperor of the glorious Empire of mankind!' A hint of a smile curled his lips as he saw doubt flash across the faces of some of the rebels. It seemed they hadn't thought of their little revolt in terms of blasphemy and heresy. Ready to turn against Boris Hohenbach, they weren't ready to defy Sigmar Heldenhammer. Inwardly, the Emperor sneered at their religious qualms, though outwardly he wore the mantle of pious outrage.

'You are a fine one to speak of sacrilege,' Erich challenged. 'By whose order was Arch-Lector Hartwich killed?'

At once, any doubts of purpose the rebels felt were extirpated. Prince Sigdan, drawing the Runefang of Reikland from its scabbard, stalked across the charred floor. He stopped well away from von Kirchof, looking past the champion to the tyrant hiding behind the hydraulis. 'Archers!' the Prince of Altdorf cried and at his command ten Drakwald bowmen nocked arrows and took aim.

'I will not play your games, Goldgather,' the prince declared. 'You will abdicate now, relinquish all claim upon the crown, or we will burn this room and everyone in it. Anyone who makes a move to stop us will be shot down.' He turned his head at a flash of purple cloth amongst the courtiers. 'If your pet warlock makes another move, if he even breathes wrong, he can be the first to die.' Karl-Maria Fleischauer did a perfect impression of a statue as the threat reached the warlock's ears.

Prince Sigdan smiled coldly as he saw the resignation on Boris's face, as the Emperor's shoulders slumped in defeat. 'Fetch quill and parchment!' he ordered Baron von Klauswitz. 'His Imperial Majesty has one last diktat to write down.'

WHILE THE REBELS were storming their way into the Harmony Salon, a different assault was unfolding at the gates of the Imperial Palace. The siege of the Courts of Justice having been broken, the Kaiserknecht, supported by troops from both the Schuetzenverein and the Kaiserjaeger, began a vicious attack. Bowmen loosed arrows at the rebels holding the gate while the knights brought the stout gibbet-post from the Widows' Plaza to employ as a ram against the portals themselves.

Despite the viciousness and energy of the attack, the rebels soon discovered it was nothing more than a diversion. Having guessed the strategy of the conspirators, Commander Kreyssig decided to use their own tricks against them. While the rebels were looking outwards, Kreyssig led a force through the escape tunnels – those of modern vintage and with an entrance underneath a nondescript wine shop – to effect a clandestine entry to the Palace.

Once inside, Kreyssig sent the bulk of his troops to attack the defenders at the gates from behind. When the gates were thrown open, the rebels would have no hope of holding the Palace. Indeed, there was only one thing that could still carry the day for them. Detaching twenty men from his main force, including the hulking Scharfrichter Gottwald Drechsler, Kreyssig hastened to locate Emperor Boris.

He was under no delusion that his fate was not dependent upon the safety of His Imperial Majesty. Without the protection and patronage of Boris Goldgather, Kreyssig would be a man alone, cast out to suffer the retribution of the nobility. If he would save his own skin, he had to save the Emperor's crown.

A FRANTIC HALFLING messenger from the gate rushed into the salon, bearing word that they were under attack by the Emperor's soldiers. The news sobered the jubilant conspirators. The inmates of the salon had been disarmed and herded against the wall. Emperor Boris had been coerced into signing his own abdication and affixing the Imperial Seal to it. A feeling of triumph had gripped them all, a sense that everything would soon be set right.

'Give up now, and I promise you will only suffer exile,' Boris said as he heard the report. He extended his ring-laden hand to reclaim the diktat held by Prince Sigdan.

Prince Sigdan laughed at the scheming tyrant. 'I would expect the same mercy you showed Grand Master von Schomberg,' he said. 'And I wouldn't be too excited. We anticipated this. You above all people should know how well stocked the cellars of the Palace are. I imagine we could endure a whole year under siege. And by then, your enemies – and I assure you they are many – will flock to Altdorf to ensure you abide by this proclamation.'

A snarl on his face, Boris leaned back against the water organ, sending a sickly note from the instrument

as his elbow pressed down on the keys. Aldo Broadfellow grinned at the defeated tyrant, making a great
display of his bare, hairy feet. The halfling elder turned
to Prince Sigdan.

'I have a request,' Aldo said. 'Now that he's not
emperor any more, I'd like to see him take off his shoes.'
The halfling wiggled his bare toes. 'It'll be recompense
for all the times he made me wear boots.'

The request brought a much needed laugh to the
rebels, but their laughter faded when a second messenger came racing into the salon.

'The gates have fallen!' the halfling squealed. 'Somehow Kaiserjaeger got inside the Palace and attacked our
men from behind!'

The conspirators went pale, the last flush of victory
draining out of them like blood from a corpse.

Boris Goldgather rose from beside the water organ
and held out his hand. 'Give me that parchment,' he
told Prince Sigdan. 'If you surrender before my men get
here, I promise I will still be lenient. But I suggest you
hurry. My offer will expire very shortly.

'And then, so will all of you.'

*Bylorhof*
*Ulriczeit, 1111*

A GREAT BONFIRE blazed in Bylorhof's town square.
Doors had been torn from the homes of plague victims
and broken to splinters with sledges, used as kindling
for the roaring fires. Long tables surrounded the blaze,
their surfaces littered with trenchers of mutton and
platters of steamed lamprey and boiled heron. Bowls
of almond milk and suet, mugs of spiced cider and

hot ale, great plates of blancmange – these were all arrayed in a great feast. A riotous confusion of chairs and divans, couches and benches was at the disposal of the banqueters.

The Plague had done its work too well in Bylorhof. The townsfolk had capitulated to the inevitable. Hoarded stores had emerged from their places of hiding, valuable stock had been butchered and cooked. All thought of tomorrow was forbidden, for the plague made it impossible to consider the future. The moment was all the Sylvanians could depend upon, and they seized it in a mad embrace.

Peasants danced about the flames while shepherds strummed a discordant melody upon battered mandolins. Men toasted one another with great swallows of ale, tearing at slabs of mutton with their knives and spitting the gristle into the bonfire. Tipsy revellers, assuming the duties of cupar and sluger, traipsed about the tables, filling cups and exchanging empty trenchers for full ones. Often they would pause beside a prone diner, kicking his chair to see if he was merely intoxicated or if the Black Plague had removed his presence from the feast.

There were many such chairs with pale, lifeless figures slumped against the table, the stink of their sores seeming to goad the other diners to further excess and gluttony.

At the head of the table, his chair raised slightly, sat the founder of the feast. Despairing of escaping Bylorhof and joining his master behind the stone walls of the castle, Cneaz Litovoi had orchestrated the wild abandon. Better a quick end amidst song and dance than a slow, wasting demise alone in the dark. Such had been his conviction and the glassy stare in his unseeing eyes as he slouched in his chair indicated that he had achieved his desire.

The Cneaz had surrounded himself with the most prominent of the town's denizens, the merchants and guildmasters. Among these was the sinister figure of Dr Bruno Havemann. The celebrants had insisted the plague doktor wear his costume to the feast, by turns toasting him for his endless efforts to stop the Black Plague or jeering him for the same. The physician endured the mercurial affections of his hosts, his beaked face nodding in solemn recognition of their regard. Madness ruled Bylorhof now, and he was not one to question the whims of the mad.

His boot lashed out, kicking one of the enormous rats scurrying under the table, scavenging the scraps dropped by dead hands. The vermin squeaked in protest, scampering away, its scaly tail dragging behind it. Havemann watched the rodent flee with grim satisfaction. Perhaps he couldn't stop the plague, but at least he didn't have to suffer the presence of rats at his table.

The face behind the bird-like mask contorted in a grimace as his gaze drifted past the dancers and the bonfire. At the other end of the square, a mob of people had appeared. From the distance, Havemann couldn't quite make them out, but there was no mistaking the black habit of a Morrite priest.

Frederick van Hal stalked across the square, his followers marching behind him with clumsy, uneven steps. As he advanced, the revellers fell silent. They cringed away from the dark priest and gazed with horror at the throng following behind him. Screams rippled about the square. Banqueters rose from the table and fled into the streets.

Havemann kept his seat. Even when the rotten, monstrous appearance of the priest's congregation became apparent to him, the plague doktor was unmoved.

'Have you come to collect me for your garden?'

Havemann asked the priest. The beaked face turned, regarding the dead guildmasters seated to either side of him. 'I should think there is carrion enough to sate your god.'

Frederick van Hal glared across the table at the grotesque plague doktor. 'There is always room for one more,' he said, his voice a whispered snarl. 'But first I will have justice for my nephew, who died from your fakery. Justice for my brother's wife, who was driven to suicide by your deceit. Justice for my brother, who was murdered by your hand.'

The plague doktor took each of Frederick's accusations with perfect nonchalance. 'You are too late for justice,' Havemann sneered. He reached a hand to the side of his mask, loosening the strap which bound it in place. The bird-like beak fell away, exposing a chubby, almost childlike visage. All across Havemann's face were ugly black sores, the mark of the plague.

Frederick lifted a hand to his breast, ripping at the embroidered raven stitched to his robe. The symbol of his god frayed beneath his clawing fingers. A terrible resolve burned in the necromancer's eyes.

'The gods may have cheated me of justice,' Frederick hissed. 'But there is always time for vengeance.'

At his gesture, the zombies surged forwards, knocking over the table and converging upon the diseased doktor.

Bruno Havemann was a long time dying. The necromancer's magic saw to that.

DREGATOR MIKLOS STORMED from his tent, crushing his lynx-fur hat tight about his head as he emerged into the biting cold. The lord of the Nachtsheer glared at his soldiers, offended by their disturbance of his ablutions. The dregator considered adding a few of the soldiers to the gallows, but reflected that such draconian measures might be counterproductive. It wouldn't do to let the peasants think there was disunity among Count von Drak's troops. Such a supposition might give them hope and hope might encourage foolish ideas about breaking the quarantine.

The nobleman's gloves creaked as he drew his baton of office from his belt, its jewels gleaming in the moonlight. He scowled as he marched past the Nachtsheer. These men were supposed to be the finest soldiers in Sylvania. If they couldn't handle a sickly peasant rabble…

The sentries at the fence turned and saluted as Dregator Miklos came stalking towards them, leaning their crossbows against the piled logs and timber. Other soldiers in the red and black livery of the Nachtsheer maintained a grim vigil. Even as the nobleman curtly returned the salute, he saw them loose bolts across the field separating them from the infected town.

'My lord,' one of the sentries said. 'The peasants are making an effort to withdraw from the town. We have warned them to turn back, but they keep coming.'

The scowl was still on the dregator's face. 'Try shooting into them instead of over their heads,' he snapped. 'The entire province is threatened by the plague. Now is no time for timidity!'

The scolded soldier bowed his head sheepishly. 'My lord, we have targeted them,' he objected. 'We have loosed three volleys into them and they still keep coming!'

Dregator Miklos hissed in disbelief. He stared out across the barrier, watching the peasant mob stumbling its way through the snow. He'd watched the crossbowmen shoot, but he'd heard no outcry from the peasants. Either the fools weren't aiming at them or they were all as blind as bats! His irritation mounting, the nobleman seized one of the crossbows leaning against the fence. Choosing one of the approaching peasants, he aimed and loosed, smiling cruelly as the bolt crunched into the peasant's chest.

His smile faded and the dregator dropped the weapon. It was impossible that he could have missed! He had seen the peasant's body jerk as the bolt slammed into it! Miklos reached to his neck, fingering the talismanic charms dangling at his throat. A feeling of superstitious dread ran down his spine.

'Kill them!' he snarled at the soldiers. 'Kill them all!' He glared at the soldiers around him, trying to hide his fear. His gloved hand slapped against the heraldic dragon on the sentry's livery. 'You are Nachtsheer,' he spat. 'Are you going to be frightened by a bunch of peasant scum!' He reached down and drew the soldier's sword from its scabbard, pushing the weapon into the warrior's hand. 'Get out there and cut them down!'

The Nachtsheer displayed no eagerness to carry out Dregator Miklos's command, but they were too disciplined to question his authority. In short order a dozen armoured warriors were climbing over the fence, swords in their hands and murder in their faces. Growling the name of Count Malbork von Drak as their battle cry, the Nachtsheer marched upon the peasant rabble.

The moons decided at that moment to emerge from behind the black clouds dotting the sky. Silvery light bathed the town and its surroundings, illuminating for the first time the dark, shambling figures of the peasants.

Shouts of horror rose from the ranks of the Nachtsheer as they beheld the nature of their would-be victims. They were peasants, dressed in the crude homespun wool of Sylvanian serfs. But their flesh was decayed, rotten with worms and frostbite, their faces were leering skulls and their eyes were pits devoid of thought and emotion. Clawed hands gripped crude spears, bill forks and a score other rough weapons scavenged from farm implements.

Fear overwhelmed the discipline of the mercenaries. First one, then another, broke ranks and fled back towards the barrier. Prepared to slaughter peasants, the warriors were unprepared to face unliving monsters.

As the soldiers fled, a dreadful vitality swept through the shambling ranks of the zombies. Dry moans escaped ragged mouths, loathsome hunger smouldered in lifeless eyes. Strengthened by the darkest magic, the zombies pursued their routed foe, racing forwards with speed and hideous purpose. The fleeing soldiers were dragged down by the undead, mangled and butchered by the hatchets and knives clenched in desiccated hands.

Dregator Miklos could only watch in terror as his men were slaughtered. His mind whirled with strategy and tactics, urging him to spring into action, to call back his cavalry scouts, to summon the troops at the other watchposts, to do something to oppose the monstrous horror. Terror held him in an icy grip, all the arrogant self-assurance of the tyrannical dregator unable to break its frightful hold.

A dark shape strode through the ravening mass of zombies, a figure cloaked in the black habit of a Morrite priest, his pale hands clenched about an ebony staff. Beneath the hood of the priest's habit, a mask fashioned from the face of a skull concealed the necromancer's visage. Scraps of flesh and beads of blood still dripped from the macabre ornament, staining the exposed cheeks and chin of the fiend.

The necromancer stopped a few yards from the fence,

his imperious gaze staring out from behind the sockets of his mask. He gestured at the logs, his lips moving in a whispered incantation. With a wave of his hand, a malevolent surge of energy crashed down upon the fence. Before the dregator's horrified gaze, the timbers began to splinter and rot, crumbling into dust in the space of a few heartbeats.

Waving his hand again, the necromancer scattered the dust, leaving only the white snow between himself and the Nachtsheer encampment. The barrier removed, he strode towards Dregator Miklos. The lips beneath the skull mask spread in a malignant smile.

'I am Vanhal, the fallen,' the necromancer hissed. He pointed a bony finger at the nobleman's chest. Miklos gasped as he felt his heart quiver, as the palpitations began to slow. Whatever entreaty was on his lips went unspoken as his body crashed into the snow.

'I am Vanhal,' Frederick snarled at the crumpled corpse. 'And I bring hell to Sylvania.'

*Skavenblight*
*Vorhexen, 1111*

PUSKAB FOULFUR PULLED his bloated body onto the narrow ledge, his heart pounding as some of the ancient masonry crumbled beneath his weight. He wrapped his arm about the neck of a stone gargoyle, its face worn into a featureless lump by the centuries. The effort to keep from turning his head was too great and the plague priest risked a downwards glance. The side of the Shattered Tower descended hundreds of feet before vanishing into the fog. He could pick out the jagged fissures in the wall, could see the black lines of rain gutters spiralling about the structure. Balconies, so tiny at this height that they were almost unrecognisable, jutted from the lower tiers, worm-oil lanterns glowing from their balustrades.

His arduous ascent had taken him far. It was from one such balcony that he had started his climb, scrambling up the uneven face of the tower, trying to balance safety and caution against strategy and speed. A single misstep, a moment of carelessness and Puskab would lose his grip upon the aged masonry. He would plummet to the streets of Skavenblight hidden somewhere below the fog, hurtle like a falling star into the ruined desolation of the city.

The plague priest gnashed his fangs as he contemplated all the unfair advantages that had been given to his adversary. The window from which Blight had started his climb was a good hundred feet higher than Puskab's balcony. The Wormlord had been equipped with steel climbing claws and a stout cord woven from skaven-tails. Before starting his climb, Blight had imbibed a full pot of skaven-brew, that potent mixture of blood and powdered warpstone which would excite the metabolism of any ratman and increase the swiftness of his reactions. Puskab knew his enemy had partaken of this mixture because he had smelled the discarded pot as it sailed past him on its way to the streets below, narrowly missing the plague priest's head.

Still, Puskab contented himself with the one advantage the scheming Wormlord didn't possess. That was a real and sincere faith in the Horned One. Plots and tricks were all Blight had to protect himself. Puskab had the divine power of his god to sustain him, to bring him victorious from any ordeal.

The corpulent ratman laughed as he recalled the sickly smell of Blight when the fool realised he had been manipulated. He had honestly expected a plague priest to turn against his own kind in favour of a heretic and unbeliever? The plague monks had their rivalries and hates, but these were never allowed to threaten the might of Clan Pestilens or impede the spread of the Horned One's faith. Blight had arranged everything so that Puskab could challenge Nurglitch and claim his position as one of the Lords of Decay, little imagining that it was he himself who would suffer the challenge. Puskab wondered if the fool realised now that it had indeed been the Poxmaster who had loosed the Black Plague upon Clan Verms.

The flea-breeding Verms had been marked for destruction from the start. Puskab had developed parasites to carry the plague to other ratmen almost before Clan Pestilens had started experimenting on humans. He had carried his own fleas into the Hive, fleas bloated with plague germs, fleas that had spread among his guards and assistants. He had used his magic to preserve the lives of those skaven working in close proximity to himself in order to allay suspicion, but there had been no magic to guard the hundreds of ratkin the lab-rats came into contact with. The diseased fleas had spread and brought Clan Verms to its knees.

There had been a delicious irony when Blight sent Puskab to lead the assassins against Nurglitch. It was Puskab himself who had passed warning to the Arch-Plaguelord through the buzzing voices of his fever-flies. Informed of the primitive drives which motivated the diggerfangs, the plague monks had simply built great fires within the Inner Temple, heating the thick stone walls. The spiders, faced with an even greater heat than that of the worm-oil goads, had retreated, charging straight back into the faces of their handlers! So much for the murderous machinations of the Wormlord!

Blight would suffer for his impudence, trying to turn Clan Pestilens against itself, as though the disciples of the Horned One could be used and manipulated like some common warlord clan!

The plague priest's bitter growl ended in a frightened *yelp*. A brick came sailing down out of the darkness, crashing against the side of the gargoyle and knocking chips from its folded wings. Puskab flinched, pressing a stinging paw to his mouth. He squeezed his bulk against the wall as another brick shot towards him. It glanced off the ledge, vanishing into the mists far below.

Blight had reached the top of the tower, using all of his advantages to beat the plague priest. The rules of the challenge dictated that the combatants could in no way strike out against one another until both stood within the belfry atop the Shattered Tower and heard the Broken Bell toll the midnight dirge. Neither by magic or force was either ratman allowed to attack his enemy before the bell struck the thirteenth stroke. But how could a skaven be held accountable if some unfortunate accident claimed his opponent before he could reach the belfry?

Puskab redoubled his efforts, a prayer to the Horned One wheezing through his lips as his claws dug at the broken wall. He scrambled upwards, exploiting the grip afforded by one of the jagged fissures running down the side of the Shattered Tower. His fingers and toes wedged into the crack, he scurried up towards the belfry.

A great slab of stone crashed against the side of the tower, sending a cascade of debris raining down into the fog. Puskab's paws were knocked from the fissure, his body flailing backwards as his feet struggled to maintain their purchase. A second slab hurtled past, smashing his tail as it bounced against the wall. The plague priest howled in pain, a spasm of agony rushing through his veins. By a supreme effort, he pulled himself back to the wall, ignoring the broken, bloodied mangle of his tail.

Eyes narrowed with vengeful determination, Puskab drew upon his sorcerous powers. Green flame blazed up from his eyes, ribbons of mephitic vapour rose from his nostrils. Evoking the great name of the Horned One, the plague priest's jaws opened wide, spewing forth a reeking miasma that swept upwards. He might not be able to use his magic directly against Blight, but he could use it to hinder any 'accidents'. The Wormlord would have a hard time dropping a brick onto the head of someone he couldn't see.

Like a living thing, the magical miasma crawled up the face of the Shattered Tower, engulfing the crooked belfry. Puskab was near enough to hear Blight's snarls and curses as the mist surrounded him and blinded him to what was going on below. Hastily, Puskab abandoned the fissure he had been using, scrabbling along a rain gutter until he reached the tower's sharp corner. He chittered softly as he watched another slab of stone shoot past, clearly directed against someone using the crack to make his ascent.

The belfry was just visible through the haze of sorcery, tilting at a steep angle away from the Shattered Tower, its crooked roof a shambles of cracked tiles and splintered beams. Octagonal pillars supported the steeply gabled roof at every side, forming narrow archways. Faceless gargoyles leered from the slender ledge which ran about the bases of the pillars, their toothless mouths open in silent roars.

As Puskab hurried to climb the last few yards between himself and the belfry, the entire tower began to shake. A thunderous note boomed through the heavens, its dolorous tone causing the ratman's bones to vibrate.

The quivering masonry beneath his clutching paws flaked and crumbled, forcing him to dig his claws even deeper into the stone.

A pause, a moment of silence, and then the deafening bellow was repeated, sounding across the night like the angry howl of a daemon king. The tower shook and shivered, the lone skaven clinging to its side struggled to maintain his hold against the violent clamour. Ears ringing, body trembling, Puskab clenched his fangs and waited for the din to be repeated. He understood what the thunderous scream was – the ringing of the Broken Bell. It would toll thirteen times. If he failed to reach the platform of the belfry by that time, then his life would be forfeit. Blight would be free to use any means at his disposal to kill the tardy challenger.

Hissing psalms of putrescence and decay, Puskab scurried towards the belfry, moving only in those moments of shocking silence between the tolls of the bell. Five. Six. Seven. Again and again the Broken Bell screamed out the notes of Puskab's doom. The plague priest's heart hammered in his chest, his glands expelled themselves in a burst of despair. His fat fingers fumbled at the stones, his broken tail lashed against the crumbling masonry.

Eight. Nine. Ten. The belfry seemed as far away as ever to Puskab. With each toll, the fury of the Broken Bell increased, the reverberations quivering ever more violently through the tower. A horned gargoyle snapped from its mooring, streaking past Puskab on its way to the street hundreds of feet below. A shower of cracked tiles came sliding away from the gabled roof, pelting the plague priest with stinging fragments.

Puskab clenched his fangs, averting his face against the deluge, and struggled upwards.

Blight Tenscratch was standing between two of the

pillars when the bell tolled the thirteenth note, his eyes darting from side to side, trying to pierce the veil of miasma. A heavy chunk of stone, chiselled away from one of the pillars, was clenched in the Wormlord's paws. He hissed triumphantly when he heard the final note sound.

'Fool-meat!' Blight growled. 'Think-dare to challenge me!' The Wormlord's voice dropped in a peal of vicious laughter.

'I am here,' Puskab snarled, heaving his bloated bulk over the ledge and onto the platform. His eyes lingered for an instant upon the monstrous bell suspended beneath the roof, a great black mass of corroded metal, a jagged split down its side, strange symbols engraved into its rim. There was something unholy and unnatural about the Broken Bell, about the way it seemed to drain light from its surroundings, soaking the illumination into itself like a sponge. The effect was chilling and terrifying, setting Puskab's fur on end.

Alone with the horrible bell for almost an hour, Blight had become accustomed to its malefic emanations to a degree. Enough so that he recognised Puskab's distraction and pounced upon it. The Wormlord hefted the heavy chunk of stone, hurling it at the distracted plague priest. The block cracked against Puskab's side, its momentum nearly pitching him over the side of the platform. He yelped in pain, twisting about to face the foe whose presence he had almost forgotten.

Blight chittered triumphantly as he saw the way Puskab's arm hung limp and ragged at his side. He drew a fat-bladed dagger from his belt, twisting his paw so that light played across the edge. 'I will wear-take your pelt,' he growled. 'Teach-learn all traitor-meat not to trifle with Clan Verms!'

Puskab fixed the Wormlord with a merciless sneer.

'You will suffer-rot, liar-fool,' he promised. Awkwardly, he pulled his gnarled wooden staff from where it had been bound across his back, removing it with his left paw. His right continued to dangle at his side, limp and bloody.

Blight didn't hesitate. While the Broken Bell's clapper was still swaying from the violence of its final toll, the Wormlord sprang at Puskab, lunging at the plague priest's left side. His crooked sword slashed out, ripping through his enemy's robe, blocked at the last instant by the intercepting sweep of the wooden staff. Blight used his momentum to rake the claws of his foot across his foe's knee.

The plague priest lashed out with his staff, but the heavy wood whistled through emptiness. Blight sprang away, coiling about one of the pillars with his twisted body, using it as a fulcrum to propel himself at his enemy. The notched sword flashed at Puskab's head, crunching through one of his antlers. The Wormlord's other paw shot out, latching about the priest's throat. The cloth of Blight's robe rippled as a long, creeping thing slithered out from under his sleeve. Brightly marked in splotches of red and yellow, a huge centipede reared its fanged head, poised to strike at the priest's throat.

Even as Blight's malignant laughter hissed between his fangs, the centipede faltered. Its long antennae drooped, its legs became slack. Like a strip of gaudy ribbon, the bug flopped lifelessly from the Wormlord's sleeve, its tiny organs unable to withstand the pestilential aura of the plague priest.

Before the treacherous Blight could pull away, he felt claws digging into his back, prisoning him against the plague priest's fat frame. Puskab's supposedly useless and broken arm held him in a merciless grip. The Grey

Lord struggled to bring his sword to bear, but was unable to shift past the warding length of the priest's staff.

'Now see-learn power-might of Horned One,' Puskab hissed, leaning towards Blight, savouring the stark terror filling his eyes. Drawing upon the sickly magic of his god, the plague priest opened his decayed jaws, letting a froth of bile and blood surge from his diseased guts.

Blight's fur smoked, his flesh sizzled as the stream of corruption washed over his face. The notched sword clattered to the floor, the clawed fingers dropped away from Puskab's throat. Howling in agony, the stricken Wormlord reeled away from the plague priest. Puskab lunged at his staggering enemy, leaping into the air and bringing his gnarled staff cracking down upon the crown of Blight's skull in a double-pawed effort that had every ounce of his massive weight behind it.

The Wormlord's head shattered like an egg, blood and brains splattering across the platform. Blight's body swayed drunkenly on its feet for a moment, then toppled against one of the columns. Puskab hobbled over to it, prying the lifeless claws from the aged stone. Vindictively, he pushed it over the side with the butt of his staff.

When the council saw Blight's broken body lying at the foot of the Shattered Tower, they would know that Puskab Foulfur was triumphant. They would know that the Wormlord was no more, his place as Lord of Decay forfeit to the Poxmaster of Clan Pestilens.

Puskab leaned against his staff, gazing out across the sprawl of Skavenblight. By the gleam of the moons and stars, he could see the taller buildings rising above the fog. He could see the vast morass of the swamps and marshes beyond the city, the paddies of black corn and the rickety barges collecting their sickly harvest.

He could see the distant lights of the man-warren called Miragliano and the far-off peaks of the Irrana Mountains.

The sight brought an avaricious gasp from Puskab's lips. Soon all of it would belong to Clan Pestilens, the marshes, the mountains, the man-warrens, all of it! They would bring the diseased glory of the Horned One to every corner of the earth! Nothing would oppose them this time, not the man-things, not the dwarf-things, not their own perfidious kind! The world would be crushed beneath the Black Plague, razed as it writhed in the decayed majesty of the Horned One!

The man-things of the Empire were only the beginning. Two seats upon the council now belonged to Clan Pestilens. The balance of power had shifted. The plague monks could now counterbalance the double-vote of Seerlord Skrittar all on their own. They would use that strength to draw other clans away from the heresies of the grey seers. And those who would not see the wisdom of embracing truth would suffer.

A new world was coming.

The world of the Black Plague.

# ━◄ CHAPTER XVIII ►━

*Altdorf*
*Vorhexen, 1111*

'KILL HIM!' THE oath came snarling from the lips of Duke Konrad, his hand tightening about the grip of Beast Slayer, the sword which, like all the other trappings of rule, Emperor Boris had stripped away from him.

The suggestion was taken up heartily by many of the rebels. A gang of Westerlanders raced out into the hallway, returning with the knotted cord from one of the tapestries, holding their improvised noose aloft with terrible purpose. The formerly defiant Boris Goldgather cringed against the side of the hydraulis, only Baron von Kirchof moving to stand beside him in his moment of peril. The swordless champion's bravado brought a sneer from Count van Sauckelhof, who simply ordered his men to fetch a second noose.

It was Prince Sigdan who rallied to the Emperor's defence. Stepping before the enraged rebels, he interposed himself between them and their prey. 'We can't do this!' the prince declared.

'Kreyssig will be too late to stop us,' Erich vowed. 'They'll execute all of us when they catch us. Regicide won't make us any less dead.'

Prince Sigdan gave the vengeful knight a look of reproof. 'This isn't about him, or about us,' he said. 'This is about the Empire. With the Palace in our hands, with the Emperor deposed, we could have played for time, built alliances. We've lost that opportunity now. We've lost everything.'

'We still have that pig,' Mihail Kretzulescu stated. 'Killing him might not do any good, but it'll make me feel good on my way to hell.'

Again, Prince Sigdan shook his head and moved to retard the advance of the lynch mob. 'Killing him won't do any good, but it will do great harm. The unity of the Empire hangs by a thread and this scheming churl has seen to it that *he* is that thread. Kill him and you plunge the Empire into anarchy.' The prince fixed his stern gaze upon Kretzulescu. 'Tell me, without the Emperor's promise that Sylvania will be made its own province, what will Count von Drak do?'

Kretzulescu's cadaverous face coloured as the question drove itself home. Almost embarrassedly he stared at Baron von Klauswitz. When he spoke, he addressed his words to the Stirlander. 'Without the Emperor's promise, Count von Drak would seek to seize independence through force of arms,' the palatine confessed.

'That's right!' Boris shouted. 'Without me you treacherous jackals will be at each other's throats! Like starving rats at the bottom of a barrel!'

'If he abdicated, our stewardship would have legitimacy,' Prince Sigdan said. 'The other provinces would hold to the hope that all the favours Boris has promised them will bear fruit. No one will trust regicides.' He turned and glared hatefully at Boris Goldgather. 'The varlet's own crimes make it impossible to kill him. For the good of the Empire, we have to let him live.'

The sombre, horrible statement swept through the minds of the rebels. With a roar of impotent fury, Duke Konrad turned about and drove the Runefang into one of the mirrors on the salon wall, transfixing the reflection of the reviled sovereign. One of the Drakwald archers loosed an arrow at Boris, the missile striking the water organ he was sheltered behind, quivering in the wood as the Emperor ducked against the side of the hydraulis. Before the bowman could nock another arrow, he was subdued by his own comrades. Crying, the archer was dragged from the salon.

Prince Sigdan turned on the ashen-faced Emperor. 'Your word that these men will go free,' he said. 'If anyone is to atone for this revolt, let it be me.'

Emperor Boris rose to his feet, grimacing as his shoulder brushed against the arrow that had so nearly ended his rule. 'We, Boris I, Protector of the Empire, Defier of the Dark, Emperor Himself and the Son of Emperors, Baron of Kutenholz, Duke of Scheinfeld, Chief Defender of the Faith of Holy Sigmar, do avow that all those who submit to our judgement will be treated with honour and leniency.' A cruel smile twisted its way onto the Emperor's face as his eyes bored into those of the prince. 'With one exception,' he added.

'You can't trust him!' Baron Thornig growled. 'I'd sooner hand a knife to a goblin and ask it to shave me!'

Prince Sigdan walked over to the furious Middenlander, setting his hand on the baron's shoulder. 'I don't trust him,' he said. 'That is why we must ensure his honesty.' The prince let his hand drop to the ancient metal of Ghal Maraz, feeling the slumbering power of Sigmar's hammer crackle beneath his touch. 'There is no symbol more sacred to the authority of an emperor than Sigmar's hammer. You will need to take it someplace safe, hide it until you are certain Boris has honoured his word. Take the decree of abdication along with it.' Sigdan turned back towards the Emperor. 'You understand the conditions?'

Boris Goldgather glared back at the rebel prince. 'I have said I will accept your offer of surrender,' he said. 'Especially in one particular.'

'Whatever we're going to do, we'd better decide quick!' Erich cried. From his place near the doorway the knight could hear sounds of fighting in the ballroom below. It would only be a matter of minutes before the Kaiser-jaeger reached the upper arcade and the salon.

'Captain, I rely upon you to get Baron Thornig and Ghal Maraz out of the Palace,' Prince Sigdan told Erich. He turned his attention to Count van Sauckelhof, whose Westerland sea-dogs made up the bulk of the force which had stormed the salon. 'Count, you will need to buy them as much time to get away as you can. Purchase it with blood if necessary.'

The Westerlander saluted Prince Sigdan. 'We'll give them as much time as they need,' he swore. The sea-dogs were already filing from the salon, broadswords and cudgels clenched in their fists. Count van Sauck-elhof cast his gaze across the other retainers who had accompanied their disparate group. 'I'll be thankful for any volunteers,' he said.

'I will need only ten men to help me here,' Prince Sigdan said when he saw most of the rebels moving to help the Westerland count. 'My own men and four oth-ers,' he suggested. Three of the Sylvanians and one of the Reiksknecht turned away from the doorway, leaving van Sauckelhof with a force of some forty men, among them Baron von Klauswitz.

'Archers form up along the arcade,' Duke Konrad

called. 'Pick off as many of Kreyssig's thugs as you can before they get close.' The Drakwalder bowmen saluted their lord and marched off behind the other defenders.

'We'll keep them occupied as long as we can,' Count van Sauckelhof promised Erich as he passed. 'Ranald guide your steps.'

'And Sigmar watch over you,' Erich told the nobleman, feeling his heart sink. There was no delusion about van Sauckelhof's chances against the Emperor's troops.

Caustic laughter rippled across the room as the warriors marched out to the arcade. Boris Goldgather sneered at the assembly of rebels left behind. 'You spend their lives needlessly. You have my word I will show leniency. There is no need for this subterfuge, I assure you.'

Prince Sigdan ignored the Emperor's promises. 'You'd better be going,' he told Erich and Baron Thornig. 'As soon as the Kaiserjaeger liberate this jackal, you can expect them to come looking for you.'

Baron Thornig bowed before the prince. 'For a delusional Sigmarite, you've the heart of an Ulrican,' he said. His hairy hand patted the haft of Ghal Maraz. 'Don't worry, the only way they take this trinket back is by prying it from my cold dead hands.'

'You should come with us,' Erich insisted, tears in his voice. 'That maggot will never keep his word.'

'He might,' Prince Sigdan told him, 'if you two quit gabbing and get Ghal Maraz somewhere he can't find it.' A wry smile flickered on his face and he jabbed his thumb towards the captive sovereign and his retainers. 'Besides, somebody has to stay here and play nursemaid.'

Erich's spirit was leaden as he turned and strode from the salon. For the second time, he was abandoning a brave man, a man he looked up to as leader and lord, to a cruel and merciless fate.

* * *

GRIM IN THEIR black livery, the Kaiserjaeger trooped into the Harmony Salon, immediately confiscating weapons from the rebels. They had listened to the shouts of combat ringing across the arcade. The fight was over in a hideously short time. The answer for the brevity of the battle marched into the salon beside a vengeful Adolf Kreyssig.

Baron von Klauswitz had turned against his fellow conspirators. In the heat of battle, he and his Stirlanders had turned against the others, throwing the rebel ranks into confusion. Victory for the Kaiserjaeger had swiftly followed.

The other rebels glared at the double-traitor. Von Klauswitz squirmed under their gaze, keeping close to the immense bulk of Gottwald Drechsler, as though seeking protection from the vicious executioner.

'You are unharmed, your Imperial Majesty?' Kreyssig asked as he made his way across the salon.

Emperor Boris stepped out from behind the water organ, his expression shifting from relief to undisguised malignance. 'Our dignity has been impugned, but we are unwounded,' he said. His lip curled in a sneer as he watched the Kaiserjaeger disarming his former captors. He shifted his gaze to Drechsler. 'You will be a busy man, Scharfrichter.'

The cold words brought a howl of rage from Duke Konrad. The Drakwalder hurled himself at the smirking sovereign, but before he could close with his hated foe, he was clubbed down by Baron von Kirchof. The duke's blood dripped from the gilded pommel of Beast Slayer, which the Emperor's Champion had recovered from the mirrored wall.

Emperor Boris shook his head reprovingly. 'That is a poor show, baron,' he said. 'Duke Konrad is a Hohenbach. His blood is my blood. His home is my home.' He turned his attention to the bloodied nobleman. 'I am afraid I cannot let a mere duke possess so fine a weapon as a Runefang. Therefore, in my capacity as Emperor, I hereby instate you as Count Konrad Aldrech, Grand Count of Drakwald.' He laughed as he saw the look of incredulity spread across his kinsman's features. The laughter ended with a vituperative hiss.

'Baron, return the count's sword to him,' Emperor Boris ordered.

Count Konrad's death rattle echoed from the mirrors, his body twitching as life bled out from it. Baron von Kirchof slowly cleansed the gore from Beast Slayer with a strip torn from the dead man's cloak. Sight of the callous murder brought a shriek of terror rising from Baron von Klauswitz's throat. The Stirlander prostrated himself before the Emperor.

'Mercy, your Imperial Majesty!' von Klauswitz cried. 'I have been loyal to you from the start! I only played along with these traitors to learn what that Sylvanian scum was plotting! I am loyal, your Imperial Majesty!'

'I have no use for traitors,' Boris said. 'Especially those whose loyalty shifts with each change of the wind.'

The Emperor snapped his jewelled fingers and a pair of Kaiserjaeger seized von Klauswitz and dragged him from the salon. 'The grand duke will pay a severe fine for inflicting a traitor upon my court, as will all those who are represented by this faithless rabble,' Boris declared. 'And they will pay well to keep their enemies from learning of this scandal and using it against them.'

'You have broken your word,' Prince Sigdan said, glaring daggers at the Emperor.

'An empty promise given to a rebel and a traitor,' Emperor Boris snarled, but his reply caused Kreyssig to stare anxiously at the renegade prince.

'What promise?' Kreyssig demanded, all deference

vanished from his voice. The tone so shocked Emperor Boris that it took him some time to sputter out a reply.

'He sent two of his rabble to sneak off with Ghal Maraz and a decree they forced me to sign,' Boris reported. The Emperor's voice grew more confident. 'They were to return them to me if I allowed their friends to be released unharmed.' He chuckled malignantly. 'But now they'll return them to keep me from hanging this scum.'

Hearing the Emperor's oath, Prince Sigdan whirled upon the guards flanking him. His knee caught the leftmost Kaiserjaeger in the stomach, doubling him over and knocking the sword from his grip. Even as the other guards swung around to club the nobleman senseless, Sigdan was scrambling for the sword. Before any could stop him, the prince brought the sharp edge of the blade slicing across his throat.

'There goes your bargaining chip!' Kreyssig raged, shaking his fist at the dying prince. Noting their commander's rage, the Kaiserjaeger forced the remaining rebels to their knees, ready to smash them senseless at the slightest move.

Emperor Boris walked forwards and scowled down at the dead Sigdan. 'It is of no consequence. Sooner or later the pig would have died.'

'His followers still have Ghal Maraz!' Kreyssig yelled, astonished by his sovereign's lack of concern.

'A hoary old trinket,' Boris scoffed. 'I'll have some dwarfs knock up another one. Nobody will know the difference.'

'They will if those traitors show that hammer to anyone,' Kreyssig hissed through clenched teeth.

Understanding suddenly dawned on Emperor Boris. Prince Sigdan had spoken of hiding Ghal Maraz, but if Baron Thornig decided to take it to one of the other provinces, combined with the decree of abdication, one of the elector counts would have enough justification to compel the others to depose him!

Emperor Boris grabbed Kreyssig's arm. 'You have to find them! Catch them! There were two of them! They can't have gone far! They must still be in the Palace!'

Kreyssig shook off the Emperor's grip. A crafty gleam came into his eyes. 'No, I don't think they're in the Palace any more. But I know where they did go.'

Barking orders to his men, Kreyssig detached Gottwald Drechsler and five Kaiserjaeger to accompany him.

Boris Goldgather watched the soldiers run from the room, sweat beading his brow. If Kreyssig failed to find those two traitors...

Sharp laughter broke the Emperor's gloomy thoughts. He looked aside to see Aldo Broadfellow's fat frame bouncing with humour. 'Where do you think they'll take Ghal Maraz to? Wolfenburg or Mordheim? Who would you like to see as the next emperor?'

Boris glared at the defiant halfling, noting with particular distaste the hairy naked feet. 'Get this animal some boots,' he spat. 'Iron boots,' he added, the cruel smile working itself back onto his face.

'His feet look cold.'

*Middenheim*
*Vorhexen, 1111*

GRAF GUNTHAR DIDN'T say anything, he just leaned forwards in his saddle and stared down at his son. The look in his eyes conveyed such pain and fear that Mandred felt all the pride inside him wither and die. The Graf was still silent when a tall knight with a thick blond mane of hair addressed the riders on the causeway.

'Grand Master Arno,' he called out. 'You and your men have violated the Graf's decree. By the letter of the law, your lives are forfeit.'

The Grand Master bowed his head. 'We understood that when we left the city, Grand Commander Vitholf. What we did was... necessary.'

'As is what we must do,' Vitholf said, emotion threatening to overwhelm his voice. He stiffened his posture, trying to compose himself. 'Against the Graf's orders, you have ridden into Warrenburg. You have been exposed to the plague and become a threat to Middenheim. You are hereby declared outlaw and exiled from the dominion of Graf Gunthar.'

Arno sighed as he heard the pronouncement. It was pretty much what he had expected to hear. 'Serve the Order of the White Wolf well, Grand Master Vitholf,' he said.

'I will strive to bring the Order the same honour you have bestowed upon it,' Vitholf swore.

Arno and his knights began to turn their horses about, to retrace their path back down to the shanty-town. Mandred, unable to maintain his father's pained gaze, started to follow them.

'You have not been dismissed, Prince of Middenheim,' Graf Gunthar's deep voice barked. He spurred his horse forwards, descending halfway down the causeway before drawing rein again. He pointed at his son. 'You have disobeyed my command. For that I strip you of rank and authority. Until you are old enough to act like the prince, you will not be prince!'

Mandred's jaw clenched as he heard his father's furious words. 'Is that all, your highness?' he growled.

Graf Gunthar clenched his fist, his arm pulling back

as though he would reach across the span separating them and strike his son. Instead he pointed his hand at the gate. 'Get inside!' he ordered.

'My place is with Grand Master Arno,' Mandred stated defiantly.

'Your place is where I tell you!' Graf Gunthar shouted. His enraged eyes bored into those of the prince. 'Are you enough of a man to go of your own volition, or must I have you carried in like an unruly child?'

Mandred glared at his father. For a moment, he considered calling the Graf's bluff, but he couldn't forget the pain he saw on his father's face.

Turning in his saddle, Mandred nodded apologetically to Arno and his knights. 'Come along, Franz,' he said, spurring his horse up towards the gate. It took him only a moment to realise his bodyguard wasn't following him. Wheeling his steed around, he found Franz hadn't even moved.

'I'm sorry, your grace,' the knight said. 'But I can't go with you. It's too late.' He reached a hand to his tunic, pulling it open to display the black blisters marking his throat. Mandred stared in mute horror at the sign of the plague. He knew that sometimes it could strike quickly, but it seemed impossible to him that a man could be riding down beastkin one moment and in the next find himself a victim of the Black Plague.

Franz bowed and turned his horse around before the prince could say anything. Before Mandred overcame his shock, the faithful knight was already halfway to Warrenburg.

'Goodbye, old friend,' he whispered.

Now he understood what his father meant. But that understanding was too late.

* * *

THE GRAF'S ENTOURAGE rode slowly through the streets of Middenheim. None of the riders spoke, their spirits subdued by the knowledge that they had abandoned brave men to the Black Plague, shamed by the knowledge that it was what they had to do.

Mandred rode beside his father, feeling the guilt inside him growing with every step. It had been his idea to ride to the defence of Warrenburg; he had led the way. In his mind, he had accepted the possibility it would mean all their lives, that they might fall in battle or contract the plague. But actually seeing it, watching Franz ride back into the shantytown and certain death – that had sobered him in a way nothing else could.

'You should have left me out there,' Mandred said, his voice low and subdued.

The Graf smiled at him. 'Do you think I could?' he asked. 'Is that what you think of me?'

'It's wrong,' Mandred said. 'If Franz... I was right beside him. I might be carrying the same pestilence with me.' Panic crept into the prince's voice. 'Even now I might be bringing death into our city!'

Graf Gunthar nodded his head. 'A wise leader thinks of his own people first. He puts their needs, their safety ahead of anyone. He lets nothing jeopardise that. He lets nothing come between himself and his obligation to his subjects. That is the difference between a good man and a grasping tyrant.

'One day you will be Graf. One day you will lead our people.' Graf Gunthar leaned over his saddle, drawing near his son so that Mandred couldn't mistake his whispered words. 'When that day comes, remember this day. Remember that I was weak. Remember that when the choice had to be made, I chose to save my son instead of my people.'

Bewilderment shone on Mandred's face. 'I don't understand.'

'My duty was to leave you out there,' Graf Gunthar said. 'To keep any chance of the plague from reaching my subjects. But you are my son! Ulric forgive me, but I'd see this whole city die before I abandoned you!'

Mandred shook his head, stunned by the passion in his father's voice. 'I never thought…'

'You never thought your father was so weak,' the Graf said. He sat straight in his saddle, turning his gaze from Mandred to the street ahead.

'When the time comes, son, be a stronger leader than I was.'

*Altdorf*
*Vorhexen, 1111*

THE DANK STENCH of the sewers washed over the two fugitives as they hurried down the black tunnels. The beady eyes of rats gleamed as their lantern cast its rays into the darkness. It was always with profound relief that the men watched their verminous spectators slink deeper into the shadows.

'Ranald's own luck,' Baron Thornig grunted as his foot slipped from the ledge and sloshed into the channel of effluent coursing beneath the Palace. Even a noble-man hardened to battle didn't want to think about the sort of muck now coating his boot. The hairy Midden-lander shifted the heavy bulk of Ghal Maraz where it was lashed across his shoulders and accepted Erich's hand. Straining, the knight pulled the baron back onto the ledge.

'You can thank Ranald that part of the floor in the

old escape tunnel dropped down into the sewers,' Erich said, yet even as he said it a flicker of doubt tugged at him. He still couldn't escape the impression that the floor had been dug out, not fallen in.

Baron Thornig scowled at the muck on his boot. 'I'd thank him better if he kept his gifts a bit cleaner.'

*Better than you deserve, you manipulative bastard.* Erich resisted the temptation to push the Middenlander back into the channel. He couldn't forget that this man had used his own daughter as a sordid weapon against his enemies. A weapon who had clearly failed based upon the quick deployment of the Kaiserjaeger to the Imperial Palace. The hideous sacrifice Baron Thornig had allowed Princess Erna to make had been for nothing. Even if she had eliminated Kreyssig, Emperor Boris would just appoint another monster in his place.

'Where the blazes are we?' Baron Thornig grumbled, squinting at the murky walls. 'It all looks the same to me.'

Erich turned the lantern around, shining it at the channel between the ledges. A faint current was detectable in the stream of filth. 'If we follow the direction of the flow, we'll eventually reach the ri…'

The knight bit off the last words. From ahead he could see the glow of moving lights and the murmur of whispering voices. Instantly, his mind was thrown back to the reckless escape from Lady Mirella's cellar. There were Kaiserjaeger ahead of them, searching the sewers for them! They must have discovered the old escape tunnel.

'We can't go that way,' Erich whispered to Baron Thornig.

'Where do we go?' the Middenlander asked.

Erich shook his shoulders. 'It doesn't matter, just as long as we keep Ghal Maraz out of their hands.'

Carefully, the knight backed away, leading his companion down one of the older culverts. The two fugitives raced along the ledge, hurrying to the next intersection, trying to put as irregular a path between themselves and their pursuers as they could.

So intent were they upon the Kaiserjaeger they had seen that they weren't aware of the other group of hunters until they came around a slime-covered corner and saw a squad of black-liveried thugs marching in their direction. At their head, his face like the leering visage of a forest devil, was Adolf Kreyssig.

'There you are,' Kreyssig hissed. He pointed a finger at the two rebels. 'Kill them,' he growled at the thugs behind him.

Outnumbered and outguessed, the two fugitives turned and ran back into the darkness. Erich cursed himself for being outsmarted. Finding the sewer opening, Kreyssig had sent a gang of his thugs to the river entrance while he followed the route the fugitives had taken. Underestimating the peasant was a mistake Erich swore he would never make again.

If there was an 'again.'

This section of the sewers, flowing beneath the manors and townhouses of the nobility, was a confusion of side passages and cul-de-sacs. If they could just put enough distance between themselves and their pursuers, Erich was certain they could lose them. The biggest factor against them was the glow of their lantern. The light was like a beacon, drawing the Kaiserjaeger on, yet neither of the rebels dared even consider dousing it.

Ahead, the tunnel twisted into a much narrower channel, the ledges disappearing entirely, forcing the men to slog their way through the filthy channel. They struggled to make way through the sucking mire, the sluggish current just enough to make each step a trial of balance and determination. All around them, they could see the glistening eyes of rats and hear the rodents slithering through the water.

Suddenly, something stepped out from a fissure in the tunnel wall. It was the same sort of shadowy, slouching shape Erich imagined he had seen before. Only now it stood revealed in all its loathsome horror. A twisted monstrosity, merging the verminous flesh of an enormous rat with the posture and build of a man. Grimy armour and a filthy cloak girded the obscenity's body while in its claws it held a rusty sword.

Erich cried out in disgust and horror. Baron Thornig turned and staggered away, losing his footing and plunging into the muck. It took every ounce of courage he possessed for the knight to turn his back on the rat-fiend to help the foundering Middenlander.

Kaiserjaeger or no, the men fled back the way they had come. Whatever fate they might expect from Kreyssig, at least it would take place in the clean world of man, not the abominable realm of myth and legend. Better to die in the clutches of a tyrant than to slip into the paws of the underfolk!

Neither man could keep from looking back as they retreated. Erich shuddered at every turn, fancying he could see the ratman's eyes shining in the darkness. Nor, if his impression was true, was the monster alone. The terrifying retreat from the vermin under Lady Mirella's now repeated itself, only magnified a thousandfold. Erich called out to Sigmar, to Ulric, to Taal and Shallya, to any god that might hear for deliverance from such nightmarish abominations.

Around the next corner, the fugitives again saw the glow from Kreyssig's lanterns. The triumphant shouts of the pursuing Kaiserjaeger stirred a last desperate urge for survival. With the ratmen at their back and the

Kaiserjaeger ahead, Erich darted down the side-passage to their left, the only option open to them now.

The knight could feel his heart thundering against his ribs as he squirmed and squeezed his way through the narrow opening. He gripped Baron Thornig's arm, pulling the Middenlander after him. For one terrible instant, the baron became caught. Shrieking in horror, he drew away from Erich. A moment of panicked activity, and the baron removed the impediment. Erich heard the metallic crash as Ghal Maraz was dumped unceremoniously onto the slime-coated flagstones.

'We can't leave it behind!' Erich shouted, but the terrified baron was already forcing the knight forwards. Erich fought back, refusing to abandon the most sacred symbol in all the Empire. To an Ulrican like Baron Thornig, it might be just another dwarf trinket, but to a Sigmarite, there was no more holy relic in the entire world. Redoubling his efforts, the knight forced the panicked Middenlander back. The baron wrapped his hairy arms around Erich, trying to lift the knight and carry him.

In his struggle to resist, Erich dropped the lantern, plunging them both into darkness. Terror rushed in to flood the knight's brain. Impelled by the panicked persistence of Baron Thornig, he shifted about and squirmed down the narrow crack.

The two men emerged into a rough chamber, its crumbling stone walls and piles of broken masonry making it seem like a cellar. A number of shattered stone sarcophagi made it clear they were in some sort of family crypt of incredible antiquity.

Erich had only a moment to take in his surroundings, however. The light was that being cast by the lanterns of the Kaiserjaeger. Kreyssig stood upon a sarcophagus, his arms folded across his chest, a contemptuous smirk on his face.

'You should have used the main channel,' Kreyssig said, nodding his chin at a broad opening in the southern wall of the crypt. 'It's quicker.'

Baron Thornig dropped to his knees, his eyes still wide with terror. 'Adolf, please! You must listen! There are… things… following…'

The commander of the Kaiserjaeger chuckled malevolently. 'Is that really my dear father-in-law? I would never have believed him a party to any conspiracy to depose our great and gracious Boris Goldgather.' His voice lowered into a vicious hiss. 'At least right up until the moment my wife tried to slit my throat. Tell me, father, after I execute you, how long do I have to keep her alive before I can claim the title?'

With every word, the horror in Baron Thornig's eyes faded a little more, burned away by a swelling hatred. Kreyssig saw the change, dropping down from his perch and taking a few steps back. 'Kill them and bring me the hammer,' he said, waving his thugs forwards.

Erich drew his sword, prepared to sell his life as dearly as he could. He singled out the murderous bulk of Drechsler. If he could only take one enemy with him, he vowed it would be the Scharfrichter. He glanced aside at the baron, hoping the man's senses would rally before he was butchered out of hand by the advancing Kaiserjaeger.

The Kaiserjaeger wore confident expressions as they stalked forwards, but before they reached Erich, those expressions changed. Colour drained from their complexions and they staggered back in gasping horror. Erich didn't need to turn around to know what they had seen. Lunging for a nearby sarcophagus, the knight rolled into cover and watched as a swarm of chittering monstrosities came spilling from the narrow crack in the wall.

'Forget the mutants!' Kreyssig was shouting. 'Get the rebels!' But for once fear of their commander wasn't enough to make the Kaiserjaeger obey. Ancient night-terrors, fables learned in the cradle, horror stories told about winter hearths, all of these came rushing through the minds of the soldiers. The instinctive loathing and fear of vermin of every breed and stripe gripped their brains. Crying out with the same disgust Erich had voiced, the Kaiserjaeger met the ratmen.

Erich watched as Reikland steel clashed against the rusted blades of the verminous monsters, as brawny men matched their strength against the wiry suppleness of ratkin. The speed of the monsters was unbelievable, only the spastic crudity of their swordsmanship allowing the Kaiserjaeger any chance at all.

Then Erich found his gaze wandering away from the general fray to focus upon one combatant. Gotthard Drechsler was fending off three of the ratmen at once. The executioner's legs were slashed, his torso betraying a jagged cut, but already two ratmen lay broken at his feet. While the knight watched, the Scharfrichter caught one of his enemies with his huge sword. The ratkin's body was flung across the crypt by the impact, bones cracking as it smashed against the crumbling wall. Even as the creature crumpled to the floor, Drechsler brought the flat of his blade smashing down upon the snout of another foe, shattering its muzzle and leaving the rat-man twitching at his feet.

Where Erich might have sympathised with another combatant, rallied to their shared humanity against a subhuman abomination, he could feel only hate. In his mind flashed the memory of Grand Master von Schomberg's humiliating and cruel execution, and the Scharfrichter's role in that atrocity. Revenge decided his actions. Clutching his sword, Erich sprang from cover.

Drechsler was still engaged with the last of his adversaries when Erich came at him. The knight felt no dishonour in attacking such a butcher from ambush. Any right Drechsler had to chivalry had been forfeited in the Widows' Plaza.

The knight's sword stabbed deep in the executioner's back, piercing him through the belly. Drechsler screamed in agony, spinning around and swatting Erich with the back of his hand. The knight reeled, feeling as though he'd been kicked by a horse. Through his spinning gaze he could see Drechsler lurching towards him, the tip of the sword still protruding from his body. By an incredible feat of stamina, the executioner ignored his wound and raised his massive zweihander for a murderous sweep. Erich saw death glistening in the Scharfrichter's eyes.

Then a verminous shape pounced upon the executioner's broad back, rodent fangs burying themselves in his neck. Drechsler howled in agony as blood spurted from torn veins, as his monstrous enemy worried at his flesh. The zweihander fell from his weakened fingers. He clutched feebly at the ratman on his back, but the creature squirmed away from his hands, dropping to the floor and watching with savage glee as the dying man slumped to his knees. A titter of malignant laughter rushed past the ratman's fangs as Drechsler crashed face-first to the floor.

Erich staggered back, fumbling for the dagger in his belt, sickened as he watched Drechsler's blood dripping from the ratman's muzzle. Myth or monster, he would not die in such a way!

Above the sounds of battle and the squeaks of the monsters, the voice of Adolf Kreyssig continued to ring out, desperately trying to stop the chaos. His Kaiser-jaeger, however, remained deaf to Kreyssig's cries. There was only one man who noted the commander's voice. Ignored by both ratkin and Kaiserjaeger, Baron Thornig rose to his feet. Glaring at Kreyssig, the Middenlander tightened his grip on his warhammer. With a fierce bellow of 'Erna!' the baron charged his enemy.

The war cry did not go unheard. Kreyssig noted the maddened Middenlander's rush, darting aside as Baron Thornig swung his massive hammer at him. The weapon swept past the commander, smashing against the wall of the crypt instead. Masonry rained down from the crumbling wall as a jagged crack slithered its way up to the stone ceiling.

'Relent, you fool!' Kreyssig snarled, slashing his blade across the baron's arm. Thornig ignored the cut, striking once more at the peasant. Again, the blow failed to connect with his enemy, crashing instead against the wall.

This time, the entire crypt shook. The ratkin raised their muzzles towards the ceiling, frightened squeaks rippling from their throats. In a single, chittering mob, they broke and scattered, clawing at each other in their haste to squeeze back into the fissure.

An instant later great blocks of stone came thundering down from the roof. Erich saw one of them smash into Baron Thornig, battering the enraged Middenlander to the floor. Another mass of rubble pulverised a wounded Kaiserjaeger, reducing him to a red smear on the ground.

The other Kaiserjaeger ran for the south exit. Erich could see Kreyssig start after them, then turn back towards Baron Thornig's body. Stones smashed down around the commander as he darted through the collapsing crypt. There was an exultant look of triumph on his face as he ripped the warhammer from Thornig's lifeless fingers. That expression quickly faded when he saw his prize wasn't Ghal Maraz, just a heavy chunk of Middenheim steel. He just had time to appreciate his mistake before a mass of stone came crashing down. Kreyssig screamed, raising his arms in a futile effort to shield himself.

It was the last thing Erich saw before a stone slammed into the back of his head and his world collapsed into darkness.

ERICH VON KRANZBEUHLER awoke to pain. His body felt like one enormous sore, hurting in places he didn't even know existed. The smell and the darkness told him he was still in the sewers.

He was surprised to be alive.

A furtive rustling sound snapped him from bleary contemplation of his wounds to terrified awareness. There was a lantern resting beside him. Frantically, he reached for it, never questioning its presence. Feeding more oil to the flame, he found that he wasn't in the crypt, but in an entirely different part of the sewers. Such understanding had barely registered, however, before he was pressing himself against the wall, stark terror racing through his veins.

Crouched only a few feet from him was one of the ghastly ratmen, studying him with its beady red eyes. The creature bared its fangs as the lamplight washed over it. Erich's horror only increased when the thing spoke to him in a shrill, squeaky whisper.

'Man-thing leave-go,' the ratman said, pointing a clawed finger down the tunnel. 'Scurry-hurry, quick-quick!' it added, a long scaly tail slapping against the floor behind it, either in a display of annoyance or as an emphatic gesture. The creature lowered its finger, pointing at something lying on the ledge beside Erich. 'Take-hide king-hammer,' it squeaked, its body trembling in fear.

Erich forced himself to follow the ratkin's pointing

claw. When he did, he was shocked to see Ghal Maraz resting on the ledge. Somehow, for whatever reason, the ghastly ratmen had recovered Sigmar's hammer and returned it to him.

Despite his horror and disgust, Erich tried to force words of gratitude. The monster, perhaps the same that had fought Drechsler, had no patience for such propriety. Again, it lashed its tail and pointed imperiously down the tunnel. 'Take-go, quick-quick!'

Painfully, Erich rose to his feet and gathered up the warhammer. He noticed the flow in the channel was moving in the direction the ratman pointed. If he followed the passage, he would reach the river.

Wearily, Erich turned and made his way down the tunnel. When he looked back, the ratman was gone, the lantern failing to reveal even the shine of its eyes. Why the ratmen had brought him here, why they had saved him and helped him were mysteries he couldn't fathom. Perhaps they weren't so different from men and dwarfs and halflings, despite their monstrous appearance. Perhaps they too couldn't abide tyranny and a world governed by fear.

Whatever their purpose, Erich was thankful. He would take Ghal Maraz far from Altdorf, far beyond Boris Goldgather's reach. It would be the first blow in a new struggle to end the tyrant's reign.

IN THE DARKNESS, the skaven watched their pawn creep towards the river, malicious mirth hissing past their fangs. Adolf Kreyssig had been a useful pawn, but Erich von Kranzbeuhler would be an even better one. He would take the king-hammer away to another of the man-thing warlords. Then that warlord would declare himself emperor-thing and the man-warrens would make war against each other.

Whatever the Black Plague didn't kill, the man-things would slaughter in their war, further draining their strength.

Whichever man-thing won didn't matter. The skaven would be there to vanquish the exhausted survivor.

From the ruins, the skaven would inherit all.

## ABOUT THE AUTHOR

*C. L. Werner* was a diseased servant of the Horned Rat long before his first story in *Inferno!* magazine. His Black Library credits include the Chaos Wastes books, *Mathias Thulmann: Witch Hunter*, *Runefang*, the Brunner the Bounty Hunter trilogy and the Thanquol and Boneripper series. Currently living in the American south-west, he continues to write stories of mayhem and madness set in the Warhammer World.

Visit the author's website at
*www.vermintime.com*

# THE GREAT BETRAYAL

*The War of Vengeance*

## NICK KYME

*An extract from* The Great Betrayal
*by Nick Kyme*

On sale August 2012

CACOPHONOUS THUNDER ROLLED across the slopes of Karag Vlak. Earth trembled for miles. Fire wreathed the darkling sky. It warred with the furnace at the mountain peak, glowing hot and angry through swathes of pyroclastic cloud. Shadows lurked within it, drifting against the wind on thin, membranous wings…

Thurgin Ironhand eyed the enemy racing at his throng across the hellish plain and scowled.

'They are swift,' he said, feeling the tremor of their hoof beats through his iron-wrought armour. Runes of warding fashioned into its breastplate began to ignite in a chain of forge-bright flares that painted the metal like parchment.

Never before had the dwarfs waged war against such a foe. All of the urk and grobi festering beneath the Worlds Edge could not come close in number to the glistening horde riding down upon them now.

Two hundred feet away from bloodying his axe and Thurgin gave an order, growled through the mouthpiece of his war helm and carried to every warrior of his throng through its runecraft.

'Lock shields!'

Across the slopes of Karak Vlag, ten thousand dwarfs obeyed.

That was but the first rank.

Deep into the valley, standing upon the Fist of Agrin, Thurgin knew the High King fought alone. It was said of him that he could break the stars. To witness that rune blade he bore, gripped two handed and splitting heads as effortlessly as barrels, Thurgin could believe it.

The enemy closed, coming fast and hard on hooves of silver flame.

Thurgin, thane-king, felt the solidity of his clan brothers at either shoulder and smiled.

This would be a good day for the dwarfs.

Vengeance would be won.

He bellowed, his voice louder than a hundred war horns, 'Khazuk!'

The throng answered, its many ranks adding to the fury of their reply, 'KHAZUK!'

Axes and hammers began to beat shields, rising in tempo as the riders closed.

'Khazuk!'

Thurgin slid the ornate faceplate over his eyes and nose until it clanked and the world became a slit of honed anger.

His brothers' chorus resonated through his helm, chiming with the clash of arms.

'KHAZUK!'

It meant death.

Death to the enemies of the dwarfs.

* * *

GLARONDRIL THE SILVEN spurred his riders to greater effort. The enemy was close, a thick wedge of mailed warriors clutching blades and shields.

Twenty thousand noble lords at his command, armour glittering with the falling sun, lowered their lances.

They had ridden hard and far to reach this hellish plain. Glarondril would not be found wanting on the slopes of the mountain. He would see it through to the end, even if that meant his death. Whispering words of command to his mount, he drew the riders into a spear tip of glittering silver.

'In the name of the Phoenix King,' he roared, unable to keep his battle lust sheathed any longer. A sword of blue flame slid soundlessly from his scabbard. 'For the glory of Ulthuan!'

So close… Glarondril saw their hooded eyes, shimmering like moist gemstones, and smelled the reek of their foul breath, all metal and earth.

'None shall live!'

The blue-fire sword was held aloft as a thicket of lance heads drew down upon the enemy.


THURGIN FELT HIS body tense just before the moment of impact.

'Hold them, break them!' he raged. 'No mercy. Kill them all!'

Here before them was a foe worthy of dwarfish enmity.

The shield wall dug in, backs and shoulders braced.

Over fifty thousand in this single throng; his muster from Karak Izril was large but far from the largest of the hold.

Behind them he heard the slow tread of the *gronti-duraz*, felt the resonance of their advance as the low, sober chanting of their masters compelled them. Thurgin was glad to have the stone-clad giants at his back.

Lightning cracked the sky as magical anvils were made ready.

On the far mountain flank, obscured by rolling fog, the bolt tips of ballista twinkled in the dying light like an endless celestial array.

Dwarfs did not need the stars, or the sun. They were dwellers of the earth, solid and determined. They would need those traits today as they would need all the craft of the runesmiths and the engines of the guilds.

Never before had the dwarfs faced a foe such as this. They meant to drive them from the Old World forever.

The enemy reached them.

Thurgin knew there would be no quarter given.

GLARONDRIL AND HIS knights swept into the armoured horde piercing flesh and shattering bone. Incandescent fire reaved from the jaws of their mounts in a tide that burned the foe to ash. No defence was proof against the Dragon Princes of Caledor. No foe, however determined, could resist their charge.

Hundreds died in the first seconds, their corpses left to ruin in the fell sun. What began as a contest swiftly became a slaughter.

'For the king!' shouted Glarondril above the eager roar of his mount, as he took the enemy leader's head.

'FOR THE KING!' urged Thurgin, chopping into the riders blunted on the dwarfs' wall of shields. They buckled as they hit it, mounts and riders sent sprawling only to be crushed by those that followed or butchered by dwarfish axes.

'Forward!'

The throng of Karak Izril moved slow but inexorably, like a landslide and with the same momentum. Already broken against the dwarfs' resilience, the riders were scattered. Hounded without mercy, the enemy cavalry had lost two thirds of its warriors before the charge was ended.

Seeing no gain in pursuit, Thurgin called the throng to a halt.

He looked to the sky at a vast shadow approaching him out of the sun.

'We have the east flank in our fist,' he called to it.

Glarondril landed with a grace the dwarf had not thought possible for the winged monsters he rode, and bowed in the saddle to the thane-king. So too did his beast.

'Well met, Thurgin son of Gron.' He wiped the ichor-blood from his sword before sheathing it.

'High prince,' the dwarf answered with a nod of deference, standing amidst a host of sundered daemon corpses.

'We had best make the most of our good fortune then,' remarked the elf.

'Indeed…' Thurgin turned his eye northwards.

Four behemoths, avatars of Ruin all, towered in the distance. Before them the innumerable hordes of Chaos made flesh.

And on a stool of rock, miles across, still farther away stood High King Snorri Whitebeard and the elf lord Malekith, alone and besieged by hell.